S0-BBP-036

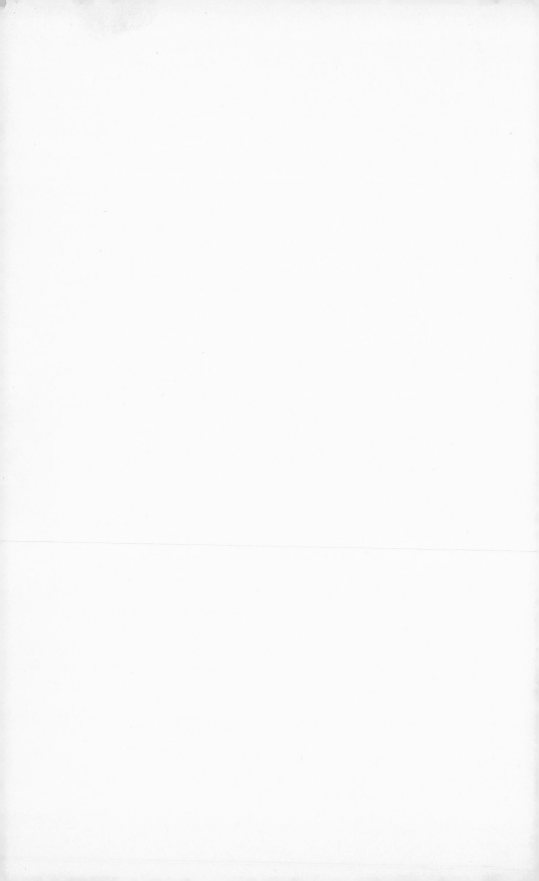

THE HUNCHBACK
OF NOTRE DAME

The
HUNCHBACK
of
NOTRE DAME

by VICTOR HUGO

Illustrated with Paintings by
Rowland Wheelwright

GRAMERCY BOOKS
New York • Avenel

Foreword copyright © 1995 by Random House Value Publishing, Inc.
All rights reserved.

This edition is published by Random House Value Publishing, Inc.,
40 Engelhard Avenue, Avenel, New Jersey 07001.

Printed and bound in the United States of America

Library of Congress Cataloging-in-Publication Data

Hugo, Victor. 1802–1885.
  [Notre-Dame de Paris. English]
  The hunchback of Notre Dame / Victor Hugo ; illustrated by Rowland
Wheelwright.
    p. cm.
  ISBN 0–517–12375–4
  1. France—History—Louis XI, 1461–1483—Fiction. 2. Paris (France)
—History—To 1515—Fiction. I. Title.
PQ2288.A31 1995
843' .7—dc20   95–19682
                                              CIP

Cover design by Bill Akunevicz, Jr.

8 7 6 5 4 3 2 1

COLOR ILLUSTRATIONS

Plates follow page 128

SHE DANCED, WHIRLED, TURNED ROUND,
ON AN OLD PERSIAN CARPET.

THE PROCESSION OF THE POPE OF FOOLS WAS NOW
ENTERING THE PLACE DE GRÈVE.

A NUMBER OF CURIOUS AND IDLE PERSONS BEGAN
TO FOLLOW THEM.

THE CAPTAIN LIFTED UP A CORNER OF THE TAPESTRY.

ALL AT ONCE ABOVE THE HEAD OF THE CAPTAIN
SHE BEHELD ANOTHER HEAD.

QUASIMODO FELLED BOTH OF THEM TO THE GROUND.

"TAKE PITY ON ME. THEY ARE COMING."

"DAMNATION!" CRIED THE PRIEST AS HE FELL.

FOREWORD

IN THE Gothic Cathedral of Notre Dame, in fifteenth-century Paris, there lived a man who was so grotesque, so deformed, that had he been made of stone, he could have taken a place among the gargoyles on the cathedral's facade. This monstrosity of a man—one-eyed, deaf, humpbacked, lame— was born in the teeming imagination of Victor-Marie Hugo, who gave him a home high in the bell tower. The Cathedral of Notre Dame was fused into the spirit of Quasimodo, the hunchback, for the poor fellow so rarely left the bell tower that "he came at last to resemble it, to be incrusted with it . . . to be molded by the cathedral."

This magnificent building, which is lovingly personified by Hugo (her stained-glass rose windows are eyes; her bells are voices), is a mysterious living presence throughout *The Hunchback of Notre Dame,* which was originally published in French in 1831 with the title *Notre Dame de Paris.* Hugo wrote with authority about the cathedral and its city. Seeking an authenticity unparalleled by other writers of his day, he had spent three years researching fifteenth-century Paris. He walked the streets of the city, studying the old buildings; he climbed every staircase of Notre Dame, explored every nook and every closet, and carefully examined every inscription. He pored over ancient documents, learning all he could about Paris in the time of Louis XI, and chose his characters' names and habits from this research. The book itself, he said, was inspired by a one-word inscription in a stone of the cathedral: *Anankè,* which in Greek means "fatality," or fate. The omnipotence of fate is a major theme in the novel.

In *The Hunchback of Notre Dame,* Victor Hugo transports us back to fifteenth-century Paris, creating a colorful tableaux of medieval society. Some modern readers may not be fascinated by his lengthy digressions crammed with history and descriptions of architecture, but no one can deny that the story is spellbinding.

The Middle Ages was one of the favorite subjects of the romantic school of literature, which was emerging—amid much controversy—in the nineteenth century. Although Hugo rejected the labels of "classicism" and "romanticism," among his literary peers he was the leader of a movement to cast off the coolness, symmetry, and rational order of neoclassical writing and instead embrace a freer, passionate style. Hugo was already acclaimed for his poetry and drama in this subjective, emotional genre. It was his *Notre Dame de Paris* that flung open the doors to romanticism in the novel. In the preface to an earlier work, his play *Cromwell,* Hugo said that romanticism should embody a struggle between two opposing forces—beautiful and ugly, comic and tragic, grotesque and sublime. Romantic literature is emotional, fanciful, spontaneous. *The Hunchback of Notre Dame,* with its focus on the common people, its melancholy Gothic setting, its evocation of mysticism and imagination, and its dramatic contrasts, epitomized the ideals of the romantic writers.

The novel was published to wide acclaim. It was described as "epic" and "colossal" and compared with Homer's *Iliad*, although a couple of reviewers criticized the "immorality" of the plot, and some readers were shocked that a clergyman played a villain. *Notre Dame de Paris* became a huge success. It was translated into many languages and read all over Europe and the Americas. Hugo's book even sparked a renaissance in medieval architecture and design in homes, offices, and public buildings. It also created an interest in architectural preservation at a time when medieval structures were changed or destroyed at whim, with no reverence for the beauty or integrity of the design.

Hugo's characters are unforgettable, and readers are hypnotically drawn into their world. We can only look on helplessly as the misshapen Quasimodo becomes a tragic hero; as La Esmeralda, the dazzlingly beautiful gypsy girl, becomes a victim of her unwitting allure; and as the archdeacon Frollo, his life turned upside down by desire, plummets uncontrollably into the depths of evil, all the while blaming sorcery and fate for his undoing.

Fate had dealt Hugo himself a challenging hand. His childhood was tumultuous and unstable, for his parents disagreed on matters both political and personal and often lived apart. His father was a Napoleonic general stationed at various times in Italy and Spain. On occasion Victor's mother and her three sons would join General Hugo abroad; at other times they stayed in France. Traveling through areas torn by fighting, young Victor, who was frail and sensitive, saw the results of war, the horrors of torture and mutilation. As a result, throughout his life he was melancholy and had a hatred of torture and capital punishment, both of which are dealt with in *The Hunchback of Notre Dame.* Hugo began writing poetry when he was fourteen, and at fifteen he submitted a poem to a competition sponsored by the French Academy. The judges did not believe this poem came from the pen of a teenager, so his mother produced his birth certificate as proof. In 1822, at the age of twenty, he married his childhood playmate, Adèle. They had five children, the first of whom died in infancy.

Hugo was only twenty-seven years old when he signed the contract with his publisher to write *Notre Dame de Paris,* but a few years passed between the conception of the novel and its completion. The deadline came and went, but Hugo—who needed money for his growing family—instead became involved with a potentially lucrative theatrical project. His publisher was furious and, in a revised contract with a new deadline, imposed a financial penalty of one thousand francs per week if the manuscript was late. According to Adèle, Hugo was under extreme pressure to produce the book. "He bought himself a bottle of ink and a thick, knitted shawl of gray wool in which he could wrap himself from head to heel, locked away his formal clothes, so as to be safe from any temptation to leave the house, and walked into his novel as though it had been a prison." The confinement worked: at the end of four and a half months, during which Hugo left his home only once, the novel was complete. *The Hunchback of Notre Dame* had been written in one tremendous burst of creative energy. On the very day Hugo wrote the last sentence, his wife said, he finished the bottle of ink, prompting him to jest that a fitting title for the book would be: "What to do with a bottle of ink."

Victor Hugo surely made the most of many bottles of ink in his lifelong literary career. The writer who began as a poet in his youth, and won early recognition in his teens, went on to produce not only volumes of lyric and epic poetry, but plays, novels, essays, and criticism as well. He enjoyed a reputation as one of the foremost writers of his day, a man whose work inspired artists and composers. The Hugos lived a life of wealth and influence, their home the gathering place for contemporary poets. But life in the Hugo home was far from perfect. Adèle was no intellectual, and she had never pretended to understand or appreciate her husband's poetry. In 1833, Hugo met a woman who did—Juliette Drouet, who became his mistress and devoted her life to him until her death half a century later. An extraordinary womanizer, Hugo also had innumerable brief and extended liaisons with other women throughout his life.

Over the years Hugo suffered staggering personal tragedies. His favorite brother was institutionalized for insanity; his beloved daughter Léopoldine and her husband died in a boating accident soon after their marriage in 1843; and several decades later his daughter Adèle succumbed to the familial strain of madness. In his middle years Hugo was increasingly drawn to politics, and in 1845, when he was forty-three, he accepted a political post, which began a stormy political career.

When Napoleon III seized total control of the country in 1851, Hugo, who had publicly denounced him, was forced to flee. He went first to Belgium, and then to the Channel Islands of Jersey and, later, Guernsey. Throughout, Hugo, a man of tremendous energy, appetites, and ego (his own motto for himself was Ego Hugo), continued his prodigious literary output. Some of his finest works, including the novel *Les Misérables*, were published from exile. More than a decade into his exile, Hugo wrote to his son Charles: "I find it a consolation that I am regarded as more than a writer of verse and story by my fellow countrymen. To them I am a national institution embodying in my one person all the best that is France." In 1870 he returned to Paris as a national hero. When he died in 1885, at the age of eighty-three, his body was laid in state under the Arc de Triumph.

Today, to the French, Victor Hugo is best known for his poetry. In the United States, his epic historical novels—*The Hunchback of Notre Dame* and *Les Misérables*—have attained a mythic status. In *The Hunchback of Notre Dame,* Hugo sought no less than to recreate fifteenth-century Paris in all its splendor and squalor, portraying every strata of society, from the nobility to the peasants, vagabonds, and thieves. The people, the customs, and the laws of old Paris all come alive in this masterful slice of medieval life.

NINA ROSENSTEIN

Westfield, New Jersey
1995

Book One

CHAPTER I

THE GREAT HALL OF THE PALACE OF JUSTICE

IT IS this day three hundred and forty-eight years six months and nineteen days since the good people of Paris were awakened by a grand peal from all the bells in the three districts of the City, the University and the Ville. The 6th of January, 1482, was, nevertheless, a day of which history has not preserved any record. There was nothing worthy of note in the event which so early set in motion the bells and the citizens of Paris. It was neither an assault of the Picards or the Burgundians, nor a procession with the shrine of some saint, nor a mutiny of the students, nor an entry of our "most redoubted lord, Monsieur the King," not even an execution of rogues of either sex, before the Palace of Justice of Paris. Neither was it an arrival of some bedizened and befeathered embassy, a sight of frequent occurrence in the fifteenth century. It was but two days since the last cavalcade of this kind, that of the Flemish embassadors commissioned to conclude a marriage between the dauphin and Margaret of Flanders, had made its entry into Paris, to the great annoyance of the Cardinal of Bourbon, who, in order to please the king, had been obliged to receive this vulgar squad of Flemish burgomasters with a good grace, and to entertain them at his Hotel de Bourbon with a goodly morality, mummery, and farce, while a deluge of rain drenched the magnificent tapestry at his door.

What set in motion all the population of Paris on the 8th of January was the double solemnity, united from time immemorial, of the Epiphany and the Festival of Fools. On that day there was to be an exhibition of fire-works in the Place de Grève, a May-tree planted at the chapel of Braque, and a mystery performed at the Palace of Justice. Proclamation had been made to this effect on the preceding day, with sound of trumpet in the public places, by the provost's officers in fair coats of purple camlet, with large white crosses on the breast.

That morning, therefore, all the houses and shops remained shut, and crowds of citizens of both sexes were to be seen wending their way toward one of the three places specified above. Be it however observed, to the honor of the taste of the cockneys of Paris, that the majority of this concourse were proceeding toward the fire-works, which were quite seasonable, or to the mystery which was to be represented in the great hall of the palace, well covered in and sheltered, and that the curious agreed to let the poor leafless May shiver all alone beneath a January sky in the cemetery of the chapel of Braque.

All the avenues to the Palace of Justice were particularly thronged, because it was known that the Flemish embassadors, who had arrived two days before, purposed to attend the representation of the mystery, and the election of the Pope of Fools, which was also to take place in the great hall.

It was no easy matter on that day to get into this great hall, though then reputed to be the largest room in the world. To the spectators at the windows, the palace yard crowded with people had the appearance of a sea, into which five or six streets, like the mouths of so many rivers, disgorged their living streams. The waves of this sea, incessantly swelled by fresh accessions, broke against the angles of the houses, projecting here and there like promontories into the irregular basin of the place. In the center of the lofty Gothic façade of the palace, the grand staircase, with its double current ascending and descending, poured incessantly into the palace like a cascade into a lake. Great were the noise and clamor produced by the cries of some, the laughter of others, and the trampling of the thousands of feet. From time to time this clamor and this noise were redoubled; the current which propelled the crowd toward the grand staircase turned back, agitated and whirling about. It was a dash made by an archer, or the horse of one of the provost's sergeants kicking and plunging to restore order—an admirable maneuver which the provosty bequeathed to the constabulary, the constabulary to the maréchaussée, and the maréchaussée to the present gendarmerie of Paris.

Doors, windows, loopholes, the roofs of the houses, swarmed with thousands of calm and honest faces gazing at the palace and at the crowd, and desiring nothing more; for most of the good people of Paris are quite content with the sight of the spectators—nay, a blank wall behind which something or other is going forward is to us an object of great curiosity.

If it could be given to us mortals living in the year 1830 to mingle in imagination with those Parisians of the fifteenth century, and to enter with them, shoved, elbowed, hustled, that immense hall of the palace so straitened for room on the 6th of January, 1482, the sight would not be destitute either of interest or of charm; and all that we should have around us would be so ancient as to appear absolutely new. If it is agreeable to the reader, we will endeavor to retrace in imagination the impressions which he would have felt with us on crossing the threshold of the great hall, amid this motley crowd, coated, gowned, or clothed in the paraphernalia of office.

In the first place, how one's ears are stunned with the noise! how one's eyes are dazzled! Overhead is a double roof of pointed arches, ceiled with carved wood, painted sky blue, and studded with *fleurs-de-lis* in gold; underfoot, a pavement of alternate squares of black and white marble. A few paces from us stands an enormous pillar, then another and another—in all seven pillars, intersecting the hall longitudinally, and supporting the return of the double-vaulted roof. Around the first four pillars are shops, glistening with glass and jewelry; and around the other three, benches worn and polished by the hose of the pleaders and the gowns of the attorneys. Along the lofty walls, between the doors, between the windows, between the pillars, is ranged the interminable series of all the kings of France ever since Pharamond: the idolent kings with pendent arms and downcast eyes; the valiant and warlike kings with heads and hands boldly raised toward heaven. The tall, pointed windows are glazed with panes of a thousand hues; at the outlets are rich doors finely carved; and the whole, ceiling, pillars, walls, wainscot, doors, statues, covered from top to bottom with a splendid coloring of blue and gold, which, already somewhat tarnished at the time we behold it, was almost entirely buried in dust and cobwebs in the year of grace 1549, when Du Dreul still admired it by tradition.

Now figure to yourself that immense oblong hall, illumined by the dim light of a January day, stormed by a motley and noisy crowd, pouring in along the walls, and circling round the pillars, and you will have a faint idea of the general outline of the picture, the curious details of which we shall endeavor to delineate more precisely.

It is certain that if Ravaillac had not assassinated Henry IV., there would have been no documents of his trial deposited in the Rolls Office of the Palace of Justice, and no accomplices interested in the destruction of those documents; consequently, no incendiaries obliged, for want of better means, to burn the Rolls Office in order to burn the documents, and to burn the Palace of Justice in order to burn the Rolls Office; of course there would have been no fire in 1618. The old palace would still be standing with its old great hall, and I might then say to the reader, "Go, look at it," and thus we should both be spared trouble—myself the trouble of writing, and him that of perusing, an indifferent description. This demonstrates the novel truth that great events have incalculable consequences.

It is, indeed, possible that the accomplices of Ravaillac had no hand in the fire of 1618. There are two other plausible ways of accounting for it: first, the great "star of fire, a foot broad, and a foot and a half high," which fell, as everybody knows, from the sky upon the palace on the 7th of March, after midnight; secondly, this stanza of Theophile:

> "Certes ce fut nu triste jeu,
> Quand à Paris dame Justice,
> Pour avoir mangé trop d'épice,
> Se mit tout le palais en feu."[1]

Whatever may be thought of this threefold explanation, political, physical, and poetical, of the burning of the Palace of Justice in 1618, the fact of the fire is unfortunately most certain. Owing to this catastrophe, and, above all, to the successive restorations which have swept away what it spared, very little is now left of this elder Palace of the Louvre, already so ancient in the time of Philip the Fair, that the traces of the magnificent buildings erected by King Robert, and described by Hegaldus, had then to be sought for. What has become of the Chancery Chamber where St. Louis consummated his marriage? the garden where he administered justice, habited in a camlet coat, a surcoat of linsey-woolsey without sleeves, and a mantle over all of black serge, reclining upon carpets with Joinville? Where is the chamber of the Emperor Sigismond?—that of Charles IV.?—that of John Lackland? Where is the flight of steps from which Charles VI. promulgated his edict of amnesty?—the slab whereon Marcel murdered, in the presence of the dauphin, Robert de Clermont and the Maréchal de Champagne?—the wicket where the bulls of the anti-pope Benedict were torn in pieces, and whence those who had brought them were taken, coped and mitered in derision, and carried in procession through all Paris?—the great hall, with its gilding, its azure, its pointed arches, its statues, its pillars, its immense vaulted roof, cut and carved all over?—and the gilded chamber?—and the stone lion at the gate, kneeling, with head couched and tail between his legs, like the lions of King Solomon's throne, in the reverential attitude which befits strength in the presence of justice?—and the beautiful doors?—and the painted windows?—and the chased iron-work which discouraged Biscornette?— and the delicate carvings of Du Hancy? What has time, what have men, done with these wonders? What has been given to us for all

1. In Paris 'twas but sorry sport
   When Justice, prey to greediness,
   Gorged upon bribes unto excess
   And set on fire her own High Court.

this ancient French history, for all this Gothic art?—the heavy elliptic arches of M. de Brosse, the clumsy architect of the porch of St. Gervais. So much for art; and as for history, we have the traditions of the great pillar which still reverberates the gossip of the Patrus. This is no great matter. Let us return to the veritable great hall of the veritable old palace.

One of the extremities of this prodigious parallelogram was occupied by the famous marble table, of a single piece so long, so broad, and so thick, that, as the ancient terriers say, in a style that might have given an appetite to Gargantua, "never was there seen in the world a slice of marble to match it;" and the other by the chapel where Louis XI. placed his own effigy kneeling before the Virgin, and to which, reckless of leaving two vacant niches in the file of royal statues, he removed those of Charlemagne and St. Louis, saints whom he conceived to possess great influence with Heaven as king of France. This chapel, still new, having been built scarcely six years, was in that charming style of delicate architecture, wonderful sculpture, and sharp, deep carving, which marks with us the conclusion of the Gothic era, and prevails till about the middle of the sixteenth century in the fairy fantasies of the revival of the art. The small rose mullion over the porch was in particular a masterpiece of lightness and delicacy; you would have taken it for a star of lace-work.

In the middle of the hall, opposite to the great door, an inclosed platform lined with gold brocade, backed against the wall, and to which there had been made a private entrance by means of a window from the passage to the gilded chamber, was erected expressly for the Flemish envoys and the other distinguished personages invited to the representation of the mystery.

On this marble table, according to established usage, the mystery was to be performed. Arrangements for this purpose had been made early in the morning. The rich marble floor, scratched all over by the heels of the clerks of the Bazoche, supported a cage of woodwork of considerable height, the upper floor of which, exposed to view from every part of the hall, was to serve for the stage, while the lower, masked by hangings of tapestry, formed a sort of dressing-room for the actors. A ladder, undisguisedly placed outside, was to be the channel of communication between the two, and its rude steps were to furnish the only medium as well for entrances as for exits. There was no movement, however abrupt and unexpected, no piece of stage-effect so sudden, but had to be executed by the intervention of this ladder. Innocent and venerable infancy of the art of machinery!

Four sergeants of the bailiff of Paris, whose duty it was to superin-
tend all the amusements of the people, as well on festivals as on
days of execution, were stationed one at each corner of the marble
table.

It was not till the great clock of the palace had struck the hour of
twelve that the performance was to begin—a late hour, to be sure,
for a theatrical representation, but it had been found necessary to
suit it to the convenience of the embassadors.

Now, the whole assembled multitude had been waiting ever since
the morning. Many of these honest, sight-loving folks had, indeed,
been shivering from daybreak before the steps of the palace; nay,
some declared that they had passed the night under the great
porch, to make sure of getting in. The crowd increased every moment, and like water that rises above its level, began to mount along
the walls, to swell about the pillars, to cover the entablatures, the
cornices, all the salient points of the architecture, all the relievos of
the sculpture. Accordingly, the weariness, the impatience, the free-
dom of a day of license, the quarrels occasioned every moment by
a sharp elbow or a hobnailed shoe, and the tediousness of long waiting, gave, long before the hour at which the embassadors were to
arrive, a sharp, sour tone to the clamor of the populace, kicked,
cuffed, jostled, squeezed, and wedged together almost to suffocation.
Nothing was to be heard but complaints and imprecations against
the Flemings, the provost of the merchants, the Cardinal of Bourbon,
the bailiff of the palace, Mme. Margaret of Austria, the sergeant-
vergers, the cold, the heat, the bad weather, the Bishop of Paris,
the Pope of Fools, the pillars, the statues, this closed door, that open
window—all to the great amusement of the groups of scholars and
serving-men distributed through the crowd, who mingled with all
this discontent their sarcasms and mischievous sallies, which, like
pins thrust into a wound, produced no small aggravation of the
general ill-humor.

There was among others a knot of these merry wights, who, after
knocking the glass out of one of the windows, had boldly seated
themselves on the entablature, and thence cast their eyes and their
jokes alternately within and without, among the crowd in the hall
and the crowd in the place. From their mimicries, their peals of
laughter, and the jeers which they exchanged from one end of the
hall to the other with their comrades, it was evident that these young
clerks felt none of the weariness and ennui which overpowered the
rest of the assembly, and that they well knew how to extract from

the scene before them sufficient amusement to enable them to wait patiently for the promised spectacle.

"Why, 'pon my soul, 'tis you, Joannes Frollo de Molendino!" cried one of them, a youth with a fair complexion, handsome face, and arch look, perched on the acanthi of a capital; "you are rightly named, Jehan du Moulin, for your arms and legs are exactly like the four sails of windmill. How long have you been here?"

"By the devil's mercy," replied Joannes Frollo, "more than four hours, and I hope they will be counted into my time of purgatory. I heard the King of Sicily's eight chanters strike up the first verse of high mass at seven o'clock in the holy chapel."

"Rare chanters, forsooth!" rejoined the other, "with voices sharper than their pointed caps! The king, before he founded a mass to Monsieur St. John, ought to have ascertained whether Monsieur St. John is fond of Latin chanted with a Provençal twang."

"And it was to employ those cursed singers of the King of Sicily that he did it!" cried an old woman among the crowd at the foot of the window. "Only think! a thousand livres Parisis for one mass, and granted out of the farm-rent of the sea-fish sold in the market of Paris, into the bargain!"

"Silence!" ejaculated a lusty, portly personage, who was holding his nose by the side of the fish-woman; "how could the king help founding a mass? Would you have him fall ill again?"

"Admirably spoken, Sire Gilles Lecornu, master-furrier of the king's robes!" shouted the little scholar clinging to the capital.

A general peal of laughter from his comrades greeted the unlucky name of the poor master-furrier of the king's robes.

"Lecornu! Gilles Lecornu!"[1] cried some of them.

"*Cornutus et hirsutus*,"[2] said another.

"Ay, no doubt," replied the little demon of the capital. "What is there to laugh at? An honorable man, Gilles Lecornu, brother of Master Jehan Lecornu, provost of the king's household, son of Master Mahiet Lecornu, first porter of the wood of Vincennes, all citizens of Paris, all married from father to son!"

A fresh explosion of mirth succeeded; all eyes were fixed on the fat master-furrier, who, without uttering a word in reply, strove to withdraw himself from the public gaze: but in vain he puffed and struggled till he was covered with perspiration; the efforts which he made served only to wedge in his bloated, apoplectic face, purple with rage and vexation, the more firmly between the shoulders of his neighbors.

1. Lecornu, "horned."

2. *Cornutus et hirsutus*, "horned and shaggy or hairy."

At length, one of these, short, pursy, and venerable as himself, had the courage to take his part.

"What abomination! Scholars dare to talk thus to a citizen! In my time they would have been scourged with rods and burned with them afterward."

The whole band burst out, "Soho! who sings that tune? What screech-owl of ill-omen is that?"

"Stay: I know him," said one: "'tis Master Andry Musnier."

"One of the four sworn booksellers to the university," said another.

"Everything goes by fours at that shop," cried a third: "the four nations, the four faculties, the four festivals, the four proctors, the four electors, the four booksellers."

"Musnier, we will burn thy books!"

"Musnier, we will beat thy serving-man!"

"Musnier, we will tear thy wife's rags off her back!"

"The good, fat Mademoiselle Oudarde."

"Who is as fresh and as buxom as though she were a widow."

"The devil fetch you all!" muttered Master Andry Musnier.

"Master Andry," rejoined Jehan, still perched on his capital, "hold thy tongue, man, or I will drop upon thy head."

Master Andry lifted his eyes, appeared to be measuring for a moment the height of the pillar, estimating the weight of the wag, mentally multiplying this weight by the square of the velocity, and he held his tongue.

Jehan, master of the field of battle, triumphantly continued, "I would do it too, though I am the brother of an archdeacon."

"Pretty gentry those belonging to our universities! not even to enforce respect for our privileges on such a day as this!"

"Down with the rector, the electors and the proctors!" cried Joannes.

"Let us make a bonfire to-night with Master Andry's books in the Champ Gaillard!" exclaimed another.

"And the desks of the scribes!" said his neighbor.

"And the wands of the bedels!"

"And the chair of the rector!"

"Down," responded little Jehan, "down with Master Andry, the bedels, and the scribes! down with the theologians, the physicians, the decretists! down with the proctors, the electors, and the rector!"

"It must surely be the end of the world!" murmured Master Andry, clapping his hands to his ears.

"The rector! there goes the rector!" cried one of those at the window.

All eyes were instantly turned toward the place.

"Is it really our venerable rector, Master Thibaut?" inquired Jehan du Moulin, who, from his position on the pillar within, could not see what was passing without.

"Yes, yes," replied the others, "'tis he! 'tis Master Thibaut, the rector!"

It was, in fact, the rector and all the dignitaries of the university, going in procession to meet the embassy, and at that moment crossing the palace yard. The scholars who had taken post at the window greeted them as they passed with sarcasms and ironical plaudits. The rector, who was at the head of his company, received the first volley, which was a sharp one.

"Good-morrow, Mr. Rector! Soho! good-morrow, then!"

"How has he managed to get hither—the old gambler? how could he leave his dice?"

"Ho, there! Mr. Rector Thibaut, how often did you throw double-six last night?"

"How he trots along on his mule! I declare the beast's ears are not so long as his master's!"

"Oh, the cadaverous face—haggard, wrinkled, and wizened, with the love of gaming and dicing!"

Presently it came to the turn of the other dignitaries.

"Down with the bedels! down with the mace-bearer!"

"Robin Poussepain, who is that yonder?"

"It is Gilbert le Suilly, chancellor of the college of Autun."

"Here, take my shoe; you are in a better place than I am; throw it at his head."

"*Saturnalitias mittimus ecce nuces.*"[1]

"Down with the six theologians in their white surplices!"

"Are they the theologians? Why, I took them for the six white geese given by St. Genevieve to the city for the fief of Roogny."

"Down with the physicians!"

"May the devil strangle the proctor of the German nation!"

"And the chaplains of the holy chapel, with their gray amices!"

"Ho, there, masters of arts! you in smart black copes and you in smarter red ones!"

"What a rare tail they make to the rector!"

"You would suppose it was a Doge of Venice going to marry the sea."

Meanwhile, Master Andry Musnier, sworn bookseller to the university, inclining his lips toward the ear of Master Gilles Lecornu, master-furrier of the king's robes, "I tell you, sir," he whispered, "it

---

1. "Lo, we send thee Saturnalian nuts."

is the end of the world. Never were known such excesses of the scholars. It is the cursed inventions of the age that ruin everything—artillery, serpentines, bombards, and above all, printing, that other pestilence from Germany. No more manuscripts! no more books! Printing is cutting up the bookselling trade. The end of the world is certainly at hand."

"I perceive so," said the master-furrier, "because velvets had become so common."

At this moment the clock struck twelve.

"Aha!" said the whole assembled multitude with one voice. The scholars were mute; and there ensued a prodigious bustle, a general movement of feet and heads, a grand detonation of coughing and handkerchiefs; each individual took his station, and set himself to rights. Profound silence succeeded; every neck was outstretched, every mouth open, every eye fixed on the marble table; but nothing was to be seen save the four sergeants of the bailiff, who still stood there, stiff and motionless as four painted statues. Every face then turned toward the platform reserved for the Flemish embassadors; the door remained shut, and the platform empty. The crowd had been waiting ever since morning for three things: noon, the Flanders embassy, and the mystery. Noon alone had been punctual to its time. This was rather too bad.

They waited one, two, three, five minutes, a quarter of an hour; nothing came. Not a creature appeared either on the platform or on the stage. Meanwhile impatience grew into irritation. Angry words were circulated, at first, it is true, in a low tone. "The mystery! the mystery!" was faintly muttered. A storm, which as yet only rumbled at a distance, began to gather over the crowd. It was Jehan du Moulin who drew from it the first spark.

"The mystery, and let the Flemings go to the devil!" shouted he with all his might, twisting like a snake about his capital. The crowd clapped their hands. "The mystery!" they repeated, "and send Flanders to all the devils!"

"Let us instantly have the mystery," resumed the scholar, "or I recommend that we should hang the bailiff of the palace by way of comedy and morality."

"Well said!" cried the people; "and let us begin with hanging the sergeants!"

Prodigious were the acclamations that followed. The four poor devils turned pale, and began to look at each other. The crowd moved toward them, and they saw the frail wooden balustrade which separated them from the people already bending and giving way to the pleasure of the multitude.

The moment was critical. "Down, down with them!" was the cry, which resounded from all sides. At this instant the tapestry of the dressing-rooms, which we have described above, was thrown open, and forth issued a personage, the mere sight of whom suddenly appeased the crowd, and changed, as if by magic, its indignation into curiosity.

"Silence! silence!" was the universal cry.

The personage in question, shaking with fear in every limb, advanced to the edge of the marble table, with a profusion of bows, which, the nearer he approached, more and more resembled genuflections. Meanwhile tranquillity was pretty well restored; nothing was to be heard but that slight noise which always rises even from a silent crowd.

"*Messieurs les bourgeois*, and *Mesdemoiselles les bourgeoises*," said he, "we are to have the honor of declaiming and performing, before his eminence Monsieur the Cardinal, a very goodly morality called 'The good Judgment of Madame the Virgin Mary.' The part of Jupiter will be enacted by myself. His eminence is at this moment attending the most honorable the embassy of Monsieur the Duke of Austria, which is detained till now to hear the speech of Monsieur the Rector of the University, at the gate of Baudets. The moment his eminence the cardinal arrives we shall begin."

It is very certain that nothing but the interposition of Jupiter saved the necks of the four unlucky sergeants of the bailiff of the palace. Had we even the honor of inventing this most true history, and were we in consequence responsible for it before the tribunal of criticism, it is not against us that the classic precept of antiquity, *Nec Deus intersit*,[1] could at this moment be adduced. For the rest, the costume of his godship was very superb, and had contributed not a little to quiet the crowd by engrossing all their attention. He was attired in a brigandine of black velvet with gilt studs; on his head he wore a helmet adorned with silver gilt buttons; and, but for the rouge and the thick beard, which divided his face between them; but for the roll of gilt pasteboard, garnished all over with stripes of tinsel, which he held in his hand, and in which the practiced eye easily recognized the thunder-bolt of Jove; but for his flesh-colored legs, and feet sandaled after the Greek fashion, he might have sustained a comparison for his stately port with a Breton archer of the corps of M. de Berry.

1. Ever let a God intervene.

CHAPTER II

PIERRE GRINGOIRE

WHILE HE WAS speaking, however, the universal satisfaction, nay, admiration, excited by his costume, was dispelled by his words; and when he arrived at that unfortunate conclusion, "The moment his eminence the cardinal arrives, we shall begin," his voice was drowned by the hootings of the multitude.

"The mystery! the mystery! Begin immediately!" shouted the people. And, amid the tempest of voices was heard that of Joannes de Molendino, which pierced through the uproar like a fife in a band of rough music: "Begin immediately!" screeched the young scholar.

"Down with Jupiter and the Cardinal de Bourbon!" vociferated Robin Poussepain and the other clerks roosted in the window.

"The morality immediately!" repeated the populace; "this instant! or the sack and the cord for the comedians and the cardinal!"

Poor Jupiter, affrighted, aghast, pale beneath his rouge, dropped his thunder-bolt, took off his helmet, and bowed trembling and stammering: "His eminence—the embassadors—Madame Margaret of Flanders—" He knew not what to say. In good sooth he was afraid of being hanged—hanged by the populace for waiting, hanged by the cardinal for not waiting; he had the same prospect on either side, that is to say, the gallows.

Luckily for him, another person came forward to extricate him from this dilemma, and to assume the responsibility.

An individual who had stationed himself within the balustrade, in the vacant space left around the marble table, and whom no one had yet perceived, so completely was his tall, slender figure screened from sight by the diameter of the pillar against which he had been leaning—this individual, tall and slender, as we have said, fair, pale, still young, though his forehead and cheeks were already wrinkled, with sparkling eyes and smiling lips, habited in black serge worn threadbare with age, approached the marble table, and made a sign to the horror-stricken actor, who was too much engrossed to notice him.

He advanced a step further. "Jupiter!" said he; "my dear Jupiter!"

Still the other heard him not. At length, the tall, pale man, losing his patience, called out almost under his very nose, "Michel Giborne!"

"Who calls me?" said Jupiter, starting like one suddenly awakened.

"I," replied the personage in black.

"Aha!" said Jupiter.

"Begin immediately," rejoined the other. "Comply with the wish of the audience. I undertake to pacify Monsieur the Bailiff, who will pacify Monsieur the Cardinal."

Jupiter breathed again.

"Gentlemen citizens," cried he with all the force of his lungs to the crowd who continued to hoot him, "we shall begin forthwith."

"*Evoe, Jupiter! Plaudite cives!*"[1] shouted the scholars.

"Huzza! huzza!" cried the populace.

A clapping of hands that was absolutely deafening ensued; and, after Jupiter had retired behind his tapestry, the hall still shook with acclamations.

Meanwhile, the unknown personage who had so magically laid the tempest had modestly withdrawn into the penumbra of his pillar, where he would no doubt have remained invisible, motionless, and mute as before, but for two young females, who, being in the front rank of the spectators, had remarked his colloquy with Michel Giborne Jupiter.

"Master!" said one of them, beckoning him to come to her.

"Hold your tongue, my dear Lienarde," said her neighbor, a buxom, fresh-colored damsel, gayly tired in her Sunday bravery; "he is not a clerk, but a layman; you must not call him master, but messire."

"Messire!" said Lienarde.

The unknown advanced to the balustrade. "What would you with me, my pretty damsels?" inquired he, eagerly.

"Oh! nothing," said Lienarde, quite confused: "it is my neighbor, Gisquette la Gencienne, who wants to speak to you."

"Not so," replied Gisquette, blushing; "it was Lienarde who called you *master*, and I told her she must say *messire*."

The two young females cast down their eyes. The other, who desired nothing better than to engage them in conversation, surveyed them with a smile.

"Then you have nothing to say to me?"

"Oh, dear, no!" answered Gisquette.

"Nothing," said Lienarde.

1. "Hurrah for Jupiter! Applaud, ye citizens!"

The tall, fair young man was just retiring, but the two inquisitive girls had no mind to let him go so easily.

"Messire," said Gisquette, with the impetuosity of a sluice that is opened, or of a woman who has taken her resolution, "you must know that soldier who is to play the part of the Virgin Mary in the mystery?"

"You mean the part of Jupiter?" rejoined the unknown.

"Ah, yes!" said Lienarde; "she is stupid, I think. You know Jupiter, then?"

"Michel Giborne?" answered the pale man. "Yes, madame."

"What a goodly beard he has!" said Lienarde.

"Will it be fine—what they are going to say up there?" timidly inquired Gisquette.

"Mighty fine, I assure you," replied the unknown, without the least hesitation.

"What will it be?" said Lienarde.

"'The good Judgment of Madame the Virgin,' a morality, an't please you, madame."

"Ah! that's a different thing," rejoined Lienarde.

A short silence ensued; it was broken by the unknown informant. "This morality is quite a new piece; it has never been performed."

"Then," said Gisquette, "it is not the same that was given two years ago, at the entry of Monsieur the Legate, in which three handsome girls enacted the parts of——"

"Of syrens," continued Lienarde, modestly casting down her eyes. Gisquette looked at her and did the same. The tall, slim man then proceeded, with a smile: "The morality which will be represented to-day was composed expressly for the Princess of Flanders."

"Will there be any love songs in it?" asked Gisquette.

"Oh, fy! in a morality!" said the unknown; "they would be inconsistent with the character of the piece. If it were a mummery, well and good."

"What a pity!" exclaimed Gisquette. "On that day there were at the conduit of Ponceau wild men and women who fought together, and put themselves into a great many attitudes, singing little songs all the while."

"What is fit for a legate," dryly replied the unknown, "may not be fit for a princess."

"And near them," resumed Lienarde, "was a band of musicians playing delightful tunes."

"And, for the refreshment of passengers," continued Gisquette, "the conduit threw out wine, milk and hypocras, at three mouths, for every one to drink that listed."

"And a little below the Ponceau," proceeded Lienarde, "at the Trinity, the 'Passion' was represented by persons, without speaking."

"If I recollect right," cried Gisquette, "it was Christ on the cross, and the two thieves on the right and left."

Here the young gossips, warming at the recollection of the entry of Monsieur the Legate, began to speak both together.

"And further on, at the Porte aux Peintres, there were other characters magnificently dressed."

"And at the conduit of St. Innocent, a hunter pursuing a doe with a great noise of dogs and horns."

"And then, at the shambles, those scaffolds representing Dieppe!"

"And when the Legate passed, you know, Gisquette, how our people attacked it, and all the English had their throats cut."

"And then the superb personages at the Pont au Change, which was covered all over with an awning."

"And as the Legate passed, more than two hundred dozen of all sorts of birds were let loose upon the bridge. What a fine sight that was, Lienarde!"

"This will be a finer to-day," remarked the interlocutor, who seemed to listen to them with impatience.

"You promise us, then, that this mystery will be a very fine one?" said Gisquette.

"Certainly," replied he, adding with a degree of emphasis, "I made it myself."

"Indeed!" exclaimed the young females in amazement.

"Indeed!" responded the poet, bridling up a little; "that is to say, there are two of us: Jehan Marchand, who sawed the planks and put together the wood-work of the theater, and I who wrote the piece. My name is Pierre Gringoire."

The author of the "Cid" could not have said with greater pride, Pierre Corneille.

Our readers may probably have perceived that some time must have elapsed between the moment when Jupiter disappeared behind the tapestry and that in which the author of the new morality revealed himself so abruptly to the simple admiration of Gisquette and Lienarde. It was an extraordinary circumstance that the crowd, a few minutes before so tumultuous, now waited most meekly on the faith of the comedian; which proves that everlasting truth, confirmed by daily experience in our theaters, that the best way to make the public wait with patience is to affirm that you are just going to begin.

At any rate, the young scholar Joannes did not fall asleep at his post.

"Soho, there!" he shouted all at once, amid the quiet expectation which had succeeded the disturbance. "Jupiter, Madame the Virgin, puppets of the devil, are ye making your game of us? The mystery! The mystery! Begin at once, or look to yourselves!"

This was quite enough to produce the desired effect. A band of instruments, high and low, in the interior of the theater, commenced playing; the tapestry was raised, and forth came four persons bepainted and bedecked with various colors, who climbed the rude stage ladder, and, on reaching the upper platform, drew up in a row before the audience, to whom they paid the usual tribute of low obeisance. The symphony ceased, and the mystery commenced.

The performers, having been liberally repaid for their obeisances with applause, began, amid solemn silence on the part of the audience, a prologue which we gladly spare the reader. On this occasion, as it often happens at the present day, the public bestowed much more attention on the dresses of the performers than on the speeches which they had to deliver; and, to confess the truth, the public were in the right. All four were habited in robes half white and half yellow, which differed in nothing but the nature of the stuff; the first being of gold and silver brocade, the second of silk, the third of woolen, and the fourth of linen. The first of these personages carried a sword in the right hand, the second two gold keys, the third a pair of scales, and the fourth a spade; and, to assist those dull perceptions which might not have been seen clearly through the transparency of these attributes, there were embroidered in large black letters at the bottom of the robe of brocade, "My name is Nobility;" at the bottom of the silken robe, "My name is Clergy;" at the bottom of the woolen robe, "My name is Trade;" and at the bottom of the linen robe, "My name is Labor." The sex of the two male characters, Clergy and Labor, was sufficiently indicated to every intelligent spectator by the shortness of their robes and the fashion of their caps, while the two females had longer garments, and hoods upon their heads.

Any person, too, must have been exceedingly perverse or impenetrably obtuse not to collect from the prologue that Labor was wedded to Trade, and Clergy to Nobility; and that the two happy couples were the joint possessors of a magnificent golden dolphin, which they intended to adjudge to the most beautiful of women.

Accordingly, they were traveling through the world in quest of this beauty: and, after successively rejecting the Queen of Golconda, the Princess of Trebizond, the daughter of the great Khan of Tartary and many others, Labor and Clergy, Nobility and Trade had come to rest themselves upon the marble table of the Palace of Justice; at the same time bestowing on the honest auditory as many maxims and apophthegms as could in those days have been picked up at the Faculty of Arts, at the examinations, disputations and acts, at which masters take their caps and their degrees.

All this was really exceedingly fine; but yet, among the whole concourse upon whom the four allegorical personages were pouring, as if in emulation of each other, torrents of metaphors, there was not a more attentive ear, a more vehemently throbbing heart, a wilder-looking eye, a more outstretched neck, than the eye, the ear, the neck and the heart of the author, of the poet, of the worthy Pierre Gringoire, who a few moments before could not deny himself the pleasure of telling his name to two handsome girls. He had retired a few paces from them, behind his pillar, and there he listened, he watched, he relished. The hearty applause which had greeted the opening of his prologue still rang in his ears; and he was completely absorbed in that kind of ecstatic contemplation with which an author sees his ideas drop one by one from the lips of the actor, amid the silence of a vast assembly.

With pain we record it, this first ecstasy was soon disturbed. Scarcely had Gringoire raised to his lips the intoxicating cup of joy and triumph, when it was dashed with bitterness.

A ragged mendicant, who could make nothing by his vocation, lost as he was among the crowd, and who had, probably, not found a sufficient indemnity in the pockets of his neighbors, conceived the idea of perching himself upon some conspicuous point, for the purpose of attracting notice and alms. During the delivery of the prologue, he had accordingly scrambled, by the aid of the pillars of the reserved platform, up to the cornice which ran round it below the balustrade, and there he seated himself silently, soliciting the notice and the pity of the multitude by his rags and a hideous sore which covered his right arm.

The prologue was proceeding without molestation, when, as ill luck would have it, Joannes Frollo, from the top of his pillar, espied the mendicant and his grimaces. An outrageous fit of laughter seized the young wag, who, caring little about interrupting the performance and disturbing the profound attention of the audience, merrily cried, "Only look at that rapscallion begging yonder!"

Reader, if you have ever thrown a stone into a pond swarming with frogs, or fired a gun at a covey of birds, you may form some conception of the effect produced by this incongruous exclamation amid the general silence and attention. Gringoire started as at an electric shock; the prologue stopped short, and every head turned tumultuously toward the mendicant, who, so far from being disconcerted, regarded this incident as a favorable opportunity for making a harvest, and began to drawl out, in a doleful tone, and with half-closed eyes, "Charity, if you please!"

"Why, upon my soul!" resumed Joannes, "'tis Clopin Trouillefou! Hoho! my fine fellow, you found the wound on your leg in the way, and so you've clapped it on your arm, have you?"

As he thus spoke, he threw, with the dexterity of a monkey, a piece of small coin into the greasy hat which the beggar held with his ailing arm. The latter pocketed, without wincing, both the money and the sarcasm, and continued, in a lamentable tone, "Charity, if you please!"

This episode considerably distracted the attention of the audience; and a number of the spectators, with Robin Poussepain and all the clerks at their head, loudly applauded this extempore duet, performed, in the middle of the prologue, by the scholar with his squeaking voice and the mendicant with his monotonous descant.

Gringoire was sorely displeased. On recovering from his first stupefaction, he bawled out lustily to the four actors on the stage, "Why the devil do ye stop? Go on! go on!" without even condescending to cast a look of disdain at the two interrupters.

At this moment he felt a twitch at the skirt of his surtout; he turned round in an ill humor, and had some difficulty to raise a smile, which, however, he could not suppress. It was the plump, handsome arm of Gisquette la Gencienne, thrust through the balustrade, which thus solicited his attention.

"Sir," said the damsel, "will they go on with the mystery?"

"Most certainly," replied Gringoire, not a little shocked at the question.

"In that case, messire," she resumed, "will you have the courtesy to explain to me——"

"What they are going to say?" asked Gringoire, interrupting her. "Well, listen."

"No," rejoined Gisquette, "but what they have been saying so far."

Gringoire started like a person with a wound which you have touched in the quick.

"A plague on the stupid wench!" muttered he between his teeth.

Gisquette had completely ruined herself in his good opinion.

The actors had, meanwhile, obeyed his injunction; and the public, seeing that they had resumed the performance, began again to listen, but not without losing a great many beauties, from the abrupt division of the piece into two parts, and the species of soldering which they had to undergo. Such, at least, was the painful reflection mentally made by Gringoire. Tranquillity, however, was gradually restored; the scholar held his tongue, the beggar counted the money in his hat, and the piece proceeded swimmingly.

It was, in truth, a masterly work; and we verily believe that managers might avail themselves of it at the present day, with some modifications. The plot was simple; and Gringoire, in the candid sanctuary of his own bosom, admired its clearness. As the reader may easily conceive, the four allegorical characters were somewhat fatigued with their tour through the three parts of the world, without finding an opportunity of disposing, agreeably to their intentions, of their golden dolphin. Thereupon followed a panegyric on the marvelous fish, with a thousand delicate allusions to the young bridegroom of Margaret of Flanders, at that moment sadly shut up at Amboise, and never dreaming that Labor and Clergy, Nobility and Trade, had been making a tour of the world on his account. The said dolphin then was young, handsome, bold, and, above all—magnificent origin of every royal virtue!—the son of the lion of France. I declare that this bold metaphor is truly admirable; and that the natural history of the theater is not at all startled, on an occasion of this kind, at a dolphin, the offspring of a lion. It is precisely these out-of-the-way and Pindaric medleys that are evidences of enthusiasm. Critical justice, nevertheless, requires the admission that the poet ought to have developed this original idea in somewhat less than the compass of two hundred verses. It is true that the mystery was to last from the hour of twelve till that of four, according to the ordinance of Monsieur the Provost, and that it was absolutely necessary to say something or other. Besides, the audience listened very patiently.

All at once, in the midst of a quarrel between Mme. Trade and Mme. Nobility, at the moment when Master Labor was delivering this emphatic line—

"More stately beast was ne'er in forest seen,"

the door of the reserved platform, which had hitherto remained so unseasonably closed, was still more unseasonably thrown open, and the sonorous voice of the usher abruptly announced, "His Eminence Monseigneur the Cardinal of Bourbon."

CHAPTER III

MONSEIGNEUR THE CARDINAL

POOR GRINGOIRE! the noise of all the big double petards at St. John's, the discharge of a hundred matchlocks, the detonation of that famous serpentine of the Tower of Billy, which at the siege of Paris, on the 29th of September, 1465, killed seven Burgundians by one shot, nay, the explosion of all the gunpowder in the magazine at the gate of the Temple, would not have so shocked his ear at that solemn and dramatic moment as these few words from the lips of an usher—"His Eminence Monseigneur, the Cardinal of Bourbon."

Not that Pierre Gringoire either feared or disdained Monsieur the Cardinal; he had neither that weakness nor that arrogance. A genuine eclectic, as we should say nowadays, Gringoire possessed one of those firm and elevated, calm and moderate minds which always know how to steer a middle course, and are full of reason and liberal philosophy, at the same time that they make much of cardinals—an admirable race, widely separated from that of the philosophers; to whom Wisdom, like another Ariadne, seems to have given a ball of thread which they keep winding up from the commencement of the world, through the labyrinth of human affairs. We find them always and everywhere the same, that is to say, ever accommodating themselves to the times. And, without reckoning our Pierre Gringoire, who might be their representative in the fifteenth century, if we were to bestow on him that illustration which he deserves, it was certainly their spirit which animated Father Du Breul when he wrote, in the sixteenth, these simply sublime words, worthy of all ages: "I am a Parisian by nation, and a Parrhisian by speech; for *Parrhisia*, in Greek, signifies liberty of speech, which I have used even unto Messeigneurs the Cardinals, uncle and brother of Monseigneur the Prince of Conty: at the same time with respect for their high dignity, and without giving offense to any one of their retinue, which, methinks, is saying a great deal."

There was, then, neither hatred of the cardinal nor disdain of his presence in the disagreeable impression which it made on Pierre Gringoire. On the contrary, our poet had too much good sense, and too threadbare a frock, not to feel particularly anxious that many an allusion in his prologue, and particularly the eulogy on the dolphin, the son of the lion of France, should find its way to the ear of a most eminent personage. But it is not interest that predominates in the noble nature of poets. Supposing the entity of the poet to be represented by the number 10, it is certain that a chemist, on analyzing it, would find it to be composed of one part interest and nine parts vanity. Now, at the moment when the door opened for the cardinal the nine parts of Gringoire's vanity, swollen and inflated by the breath of popular admiration, were in a state of such prodigious enlargement as completely to smother that imperceptible particle of interest which we just now discovered in the constitution of poets; a most valuable ingredient, nevertheless, the ballast of reality and of humanity, without which they would never descend to this lower world. Gringoire was delighted to see, to feel, in some measure, a whole assembly, of varlets, it is true—but what does that signify?— stupefied, petrified, and stricken as it were, insensible by the immeasurable speeches which succeeded each other in every part of this epithalamium. I affirm that he participated in the general happiness, and that, unlike La Fontaine, who, on the first representation of his comedy of "The Florentine," inquired, "What paltry scribbler wrote this rhapsody?" Gringoire would gladly have asked his neighbor, "Who is the author of this masterpiece?" Now imagine what must have been the effect produced upon him by the abrupt and unseasonable arrival of the cardinal.

What he had reason to apprehend was but too soon realized. The entry of his eminence upset the auditory. All heads turned mechanically toward the platform. Not another word was to be heard. "The cardinal! the cardinal!" was upon every tongue. The unlucky prologue was cut short a second time.

The cardinal paused for a moment on the threshold of the platform, with supercilious looks surveying the auditory. Meanwhile the tumult increased, each striving to raise his head above his neighbor's to obtain a better view of his eminence.

He was, in fact, a very distinguished personage, the sight of whom was well worth any other comedy. Charles, Cardinal of Bourbon, Archbishop and Count of Lyons, primate of the Gauls, was at once allied to Louis XI. through his brother Pierre, Lord of Beaujeu, who was married to the king's eldest daughter, and to Charles the Bold by his mother, Agnes of Burgundy. Now the predominant, the distinctive, trait in the character of the primate of the Gauls was a courtier spirit and devotedness to power. The reader may form some conception of the numberless embarrassments in which he had been involved by this two-fold relationship, and of the temporal rocks among which his spiritual bark had been obliged to luff, that it might not be wrecked either against Louis or against Charles, that Charybdis and Scylla which had ingulfed the Duke of Nemours and the Constable of St. Pol. Thanks to Heaven, he had contrived pretty well to escape the dangers of the voyage, and had arrived at Rome without obstruction. But, though he was in port, and precisely because he was in port, he could never call to mind without agitation the various chances of his political life, so long harassed by labors and alarms. Accordingly, he was accustomed to say that the year 1476 had been to him both black and white; thereby meaning that he had lost in that year his mother, the Duchess of Bourbonnais, and his cousin, the Duke of Burgundy, and that one mourning had consoled him for the other.

In other respects he was a good sort of man; he led a jovial life as cardinal, loved to make merry with the growth of the royal vineyard of Chaillot, did not hate the gamesome Richarde la Garmoise and Thomasse la Saillarde, bestowed alms on young damsels rather than on wrinkled hags, and for all these reasons was a great favorite with the populace of Paris. Wherever he went he was surrounded by a little court of bishops and abbots of high families, wenches and boon companions, who had no objection to join in a carouse; and more than once the pious souls of St. Germain d'Auxerre, as they passed in the evening under the illumined windows of the cardinal's residence, had been scandalized on hearing the same voices which had chanted vespers to them a few hours before lustily singing, to the clatter of glasses, the bacchanalian song of Benedict XII., that pope who added a third crown to the tiara—*Bibamus papaliter*.[1]

It was no doubt this popularity, to which he was so justly entitled, that preserved him at his entrance from any unfavorable demonstrations on the part of the crowd, which a moment before had been so dissatisfied, and by no means disposed to pay respect to a cardinal on the very day that they were going to elect a pope. But the Parisians are not apt to bear malice; and besides, by insisting on the commencement of the performance, the honest citizens had gained a victory over the cardinal, and this triumph was enough for them. Moreover, Monsieur the Cardinal of Bourbon was a comely man; he had a superb scarlet robe, which he wore very gracefully; of course he had in his favor all the women, that is to say, the better half of

1. Let us drink like a pope.

the audience. It would be decidedly unjust and in bad taste to hoot a cardinal for coming to the play a little after the time prescribed, when he is a handsome man and wears his scarlet robe in a graceful manner.

He entered, therefore, bowed to the audience with that hereditary smile which the great have for the people, and proceeded slowly toward his arm-chair covered with scarlet velvet, apparently thinking of something very different from the scene before him. His train, which we should nowadays call his staff, of abbots and bishops, followed him as he advanced to the front of the platform, to the no small increase of the tumult and curiosity of the spectators. Each was eager to point them out, to tell their names, to recognize at least one of them—Monsieur the Bishop of Marseilles, Alaudet, if I recollect rightly; or the Dean of St. Denis; or the Abbot of St. Germain des Pres, that libertine brother of one of the mistresses of Louis XI.; but, as it may be supposed, with abundance of blunders and mistakes. As for the scholars, they swore lustily. It was their day, their feast of fools, their saturnalia, the annual orgies of the Bazoche[1] and of the schools. There was no turpitude but was authorized on that day. Was it not then the least they could do to swear at their ease, and to curse a little in the name of God, on so fine a day, in the good company of churchmen and lewd women? Accordingly, they made good use of the license, and amid the general uproar, horrible was the clamor of the blasphemies and enormities proceeding from the tongues thus let loose—the tongues of clerks and scholars, restrained during the rest of the year by the fear of the red-hot iron of St. Louis. Poor St. Louis! how they set him at naught in his own Palace of Justice! Each of them had fixed upon a black, gray, white, or purple cassock for his butt among the new occupants of the platform. As for Joannes Frollo de Molendino, he, as brother of an arch-deacon, boldly attacked the scarlet; and, fixing his audacious eyes on the cardinal, he sung at the top of his voice, *"Cappa repleta mero."*[2]

All these circumstances, which we here reveal for the edification of the reader, were so smothered by the general tumult as to pass unnoticed by the reverend party on the platform: had it, indeed, been otherwise, the cardinal would not have heeded them, so deeply were the liberties of that day ingrafted on the manners of the age. He was, moreover, wholly preoccupied—and his countenance showed it—by another solicitude, which closely pursued him,

1. The company of clerks of the Parliment of Paris.

2. "A cloak stuffed with old wine!"

and, indeed, entered the platform almost at the same time with him, namely, the Flanders embassy.

Not that he was a profound politician, and was calculating the possible consequences of the marriage of his cousin Margaret of Burgundy with his cousin Charles, Dauphin of Venice; or how long the good understanding patched up between the Duke of Austria and the King of France was likely to last; or how the King of England would take the slight offered to his daughter. These matters gave him no uneasiness, and he enjoyed himself every evening over the royal growth of Chaillot, without ever dreaming that a few bottles of the same wine—first doctored a little, it is true, by Coictier the physician—cordially presented to Edward IV. by Louis XI. would one day rid Louis XI. of Edward IV. The most honorable the embassy of Monsieur the Duke of Austria brought upon the cardinal none of these cares; but it vexed him in another way. It was in truth rather hard, as we have already observed at the beginning of this book, that he, Charles of Bourbon, should be obliged to give hearty welcome and good entertainment to paltry citizens; he, a cardinal, to burgomasters; he, a Frenchman, a boon companion, to Flemings fond of beer—and that too in public. This was certainly one of the most disagreeable tasks he had ever undertaken to please the king.

He turned, therefore, toward the door, and with the best grace in the world—so well had he studied his part—when the usher, with his sonorous voice, announced Messieurs the envoys of Monsieur the Duke of Austria. It is scarcely necessary to remark that all the spectators did the same.

The forty-eight embassadors of Maximilian of Austria, headed by the reverend father in God, Jehan, Abbot of St. Bertin, Chancellor of the Golden Fleece, and Jacques de Goy, Sieur Dauby, High-bailiff of Ghent, then entered two and two, with a gravity which formed a remarkable contrast amid the volatile ecclesiastical retinue of Charles of Bourbon. Deep silence pervaded the assembly, broken only by stifled laughter at the mention of the uncouth names and all the petty titles which each of these personages repeated with imperturbable solemnity to the usher, who then flung them, names and qualities pell-mell and cruelly mangled, among the crowd. There was Master Loys Roelof, echevin of the city of Louvain; Messire Clays d'Etuelde, echevin of Brussels; Messire Paul de Baeust, Sieur de Vormizelle, President of Flanders; Master Jehan Coleghens, burgomaster of the city of Antwerp; Master George de la Moere, and Master Gheldolf van der Hage, echevins of the city of Ghent; and the Sieur de Bierbecque, Jehan Pinnock, Jehan Dymaerzelle, etc., etc., bailiffs, echevins, burgomasters; burgomasters, echevins, bailiffs; all stiff, starched, formal, tricked out in velvets and damasks, and ensconced in caps of black velvet with prodigious tassels of Cyprus gold thread; fine Flemish heads after all, with austere but goodly faces, of the same family as those which Rembrandt has brought out, so grave and so expressive, from the dark ground of his night-piece; personages who all had it written on their brows that Maximilian of Austria had good reason "to place full confidence," as his manifesto declared, "in their discretion, firmness, experience, loyalty, and rare qualities."

There was, however, one exception. This was a sharp, intelligent, crafty-looking face, a physiognomy compounded of that of the monkey and the diplomatist, toward the owner of which the cardinal advanced three steps with a low bow, and whose name, nevertheless, was plain Guillaume Rym, councilor and pensionary of the city of Ghent.

Few persons there knew who this Guillaume Rym was. He was a man of rare genius, who in times of revolution would have raised himself to distinction, but was forced in the fifteenth century to resort to the hollow ways of intrigue, and to live in the saps, as saith the Duke of St. Simon. For the rest, he was duly appreciated by the first sapper in Europe; he wrought in familiar concert with Louis XI., and frequently lent a helping hand to the king in his secret necessities—circumstances absolutely unknown to the crowd, who marveled at the respect paid by the cardinal to so insignificant a person as the Flemish bailiff.

CHAPTER IV

MASTER JACQUES COPPENOLE

WHILE THE PENSIONARY of Ghent and his eminence were exchanging a low obeisance and a few words in a still lower tone, a man of lofty stature, with jolly face and broad shoulders, stepped forward for the purpose of entering abreast with Guillaume Rym; they looked for all the world like a bull-dog beside a fox. His felt cap and leathern vest were conspicuous amid the velvets and silks which surrounded him. Presuming that he was some groom who had mistaken the way, the usher stopped him.

"No admittance here, my friend," said he.

The man in the leathern vest pushed him back.

"What means the fellow?" cried he in a voice which drew the attention of the whole hall to this strange colloquy. "Dost not see that I belong to them?"

"Your name?" asked the usher.

"Jacques Coppenole."

"Your quality?"

"Hosier; at the sign of the Three Chains in Ghent."

The usher was staggered. To have to announce bailiffs, and burgomasters, and echevins, was bad enough; but a hosier!—no—he could not make up his mind to that. The cardinal was upon thorns. The whole assembly was all eye and ear. For two days his eminence had been taking pains to lick these Flemish bears, in order to make them a little more producible in public, and his failure was galling. Meanwhile, Guillaume Rym, with his sly smile, stepped up to the usher, and said in a very low whisper: "Announce Master Jacques Coppenole, clerk to the echevins of the city of Ghent."

"Usher," said the cardinal in a loud tone, "announce Master Jacques Coppenole, clerk to the echevins of the most noble city of Ghent."

Now it is very certain that Guillaume Rym, had he been left to himself, would have shuffled off the difficulty, but Coppenole had heard the cardinal.

"No, by the rood!" cried he, with his voice of thunder, "Jacques Coppenole, hosier. Hark ye, usher, neither more nor less. By the rood! hosier—that's quite fine enough! Monsieur the Archduke has more than once sought his gloves among my hose."

A burst of laughter and applause ensued. A witticism or a pun is instantly comprehended at Paris, and consequently sure to be applauded. Coppenole, be it moreover observed, was one of the people, and the assembly by which he was surrounded belonged to the same class. The communication between them was in consequence prompt, electric, and hearty. The lofty bravado of the Flemish hosier, at the same time that it humbled the courtiers, awakened in all those plebeian minds a sense of dignity, still but vague and indistinct in the fifteenth century. This hosier, who had just held Monsieur the Cardinal at defiance, was their equal—a soothing reflection to poor devils accustomed to pay obedience and respect to

the servants of the very sergeants of the bailiff of the Abbot of St.
Genevieve, the train-bearer of the cardinal.

Coppenole bowed haughtily to the cardinal, who returned the
obeisance of the high and mighty burgher dreaded by Louis XI.
Then, while Guillaume Rym, a "cunning man and spiteful," as saith
Philip de Comines, looked after both with a smile of conscious
superiority, they proceeded to their places—the cardinal mortified
and disconcerted; Coppenole, calm and proud, thinking, no doubt,
that his title of hosier was as good as any other, and that Mary of
Burgundy, the mother of that Margaret whose marriage Coppenole
had come to negotiate, would have felt less dread of him as a
cardinal than as a hosier: for it was not a cardinal who would have
raised the people of Ghent against the favorites of the daughter of
Charles the Bold; it was not a cardinal who would have steeled the
multitude by a word against her tears and her entreaties, when the
Princess of Flanders proceeded to the very foot of the scaffold to beg
their lives of her subjects; while the hosier had but to lift his finger
and off went your heads, ye most illustrious gentlemen, Guy d'Hymbercourt, and Chancellor William Hugonet!

The poor cardinal's probation, however, was not yet over: he was
doomed to drink to the very dregs the cup of penance for being in
such company. The reader has, perhaps, not forgotten the impudent
beggar who at the commencement of the prologue perched himself
beneath the fringe at the cardinal's gallery. The arrival of the illustrious guests had not dislodged him from his roost, and while the
prelates and embassadors were packing themselves, like real
Flemish herrings, in the boxes of the gallery, he had placed himself
at his ease, and carelessly crossed his legs over the architrave. Nobody, however, had at first noticed this extraordinary piece of
insolence, the universal attention being directed to another quarter.
Neither was he, on his part, aware of what was going forward in
the hall; there he sat, rocking to and fro with the utmost unconcern,
repeating, as from a mechanical habit, the ditty of "Charity, if you
please!" To a certainty he was the only one in the whole assembly
who had not deigned to turn his head at the altercation between
Coppenole and the usher. Now, as luck would have it, the hosier of
Ghent, with whom the people already sympathized so strongly, and
on whom all eyes were fixed, took his seat in the first row in the
gallery, just above the mendicant. Great was, nevertheless, their
astonishment at seeing the Flemish embassador, after taking a survey of the fellow nestled under his nose, slap him familiarly on his
shoulder covered with tatters. The mendicant turned sharply

round: surprise, recognition, pleasure, were expressed in both faces; and then, without caring a pinch of snuff for the spectators, the hosier and the scurvy rogue shook hands and began to talk in a low tone, while the rags of Clopin Trouillefou, clapped against the cloth of gold with which the gallery was hung, produced the effect of a caterpillar upon an orange.

The novelty of this singular scene excited such a burst of merriment in the hall, that the cardinal could not help noticing it; he leaned forward, and as, from the place where he sat, he had but a very imperfect view of the squalid figure of Trouillefou, he naturally supposed that he was soliciting alms. Incensed at this audacity, he cried, "Mr. Bailiff of the Palace, throw me that varlet into the river."

"By the mass! Monseigneur the Cardinal!" exclaimed Coppenole, "that varlet is a friend of mine."

"Huzza! huzza!" shouted the crowd. From that moment, Master Coppenole had "great influence over the populace at Paris, as well as at Ghent; for," adds Philip de Comines, "men of that kidney are sure to have it, when they are so beyond measure disorderly."

The cardinal bit his lips. Turning to his neighbor, the Abbot of St. Genevieve, he said in an undertone: "Right pleasant embassadors these, sent to us by Monsieur the Archduke to announce Madame Margaret!"

"Your eminence," replied the abbot, "is throwing away your civilities upon these Flemish hogs: *Margaritas ante porcos.*" [1]

"Say rather," answered the cardinal, with a smile, "*porcosante Margaritam.*" [2]

The whole petty cassocked court was in raptures at this sally. The cardinal felt somewhat relieved; he was now quits with Coppenole; he too had gained applause for his pun.

Now, let such of our readers as are capable of generalizing an image and an idea, to adopt the phraseology of the present day, permit us to ask if they have formed a clear conception of the spectacle presented, at the moment to which we are calling their attention, by the vast parallelogram of the great hall of Paris. In the middle of the hall, backed against the western wall, a wide and magnificent gallery hung with gold brocade, into which, through a small door-way with pointed arch, advance in procession a number of grave personages, successively announced by a bawling usher. On the front seats already many venerable figures, muffled in ermine, velvet, and scarlet. On the floor of the hall, in front and on either side of the gallery, which maintains a dignified silence, a great crowd and a great uproar. A thousand vulgar eyes fixed on

1. "Pearls before swine."
2. "Swine before a pearl." (A pun on the meaning of the word Margaret—"a pearl.")

every face in the gallery; a thousand whispers at every name. The scene, forsooth, is a curious one, and well deserving the attention of the spectators. But what is that kind of scaffold yonder at the further end, on which are seen four parti-colored figures? and who is that pale-faced man in a black frock at the foot of it? Why, courteous reader, that is poor Pierre Gringoire and his prologue. We had all quite and clean forgotten him; and this was precisely what he was afraid of.

From the moment that the cardinal entered, Gringoire had not ceased to bestir himself for the salvation of his prologue. At first he enjoined the actors, who were in a state of suspense, to proceed and to raise their voices; then, perceiving that nobody listened to them, he ordered them to stop; and for the quarter of an hour that the interruption had lasted he had been incessantly bustling about, calling upon Gisquette and Lienarde to encourage their neighbors to call for the continuation of the prologue—but all in vain. Not a creature would turn away from the cardinal, the embassy, and the gallery, the sole center of that vast circle of visual rays. There is also reason to believe, and we record it with regret, that the audience was beginning to be somewhat tired of the prologue, at the moment when his eminence arrived and made such a terrible diversion. After all, the gallery exhibited precisely the same spectacle as the marble table—the conflict between Labor and Clergy, Nobility and Trade. And many people liked much better to see them without disguise, living, breathing, acting, elbowing one another, in that Flemish embassy, in that episcopal court, under the cardinal's robe, under the vest of Coppenole, than talking in verse, painted, tricked out, resembling effigies of straw stuffed into the yellow and white tunics in which Gringoire had inwrapped them.

When, however, our poet perceived that some degree of tranquillity was restored, he devised a stratagem for regaining the public attention.

"Sir," said he, turning to a jolly citizen whose face was the image of patience, "don't you think they had better go on?"

"With what?" asked the other.

"Why, with the mystery," replied Gringoire.

"Just as you please," rejoined his neighbor.

This demi-approbation was quite enough for Gringoire. Mingling as much as possible with the crowd he began to shout with all his might. "The mystery! the mystery! go on with the mystery!"

"The devil!" said Joannes de Molendino. "What is it they are singing down yonder?" [Gringoire was, in fact, making as much noise as half a dozen persons.] "I say, comrades; the mystery is over, is it not? They want to begin it again; we'll not suffer that."

"No, no," cried all the scholars. "Down with the mystery! down with it!"

This only served to redouble Gringoire's activity, and he bawled louder than ever, "Go on! go on!"

This clamor drew the attention of the cardinal.

"Mr. Bailiff of the Palace," said he to a stout man in black, stationed a few paces from him, "are those knaves in a holy-water font, that they make such an infernal racket?"

The bailiff of the palace was a sort of amphibious magistrate, a kind of bat of the judicial order, a something between the rat and the bird, the judge and the soldier.

He stepped up to his eminence, and sorely dreading his anger, he explained to him, with faltering tongue, the popular inconsistency, how that noon had arrived before his eminence, and that the comedians had been forced to begin without waiting for him.

The cardinal laughed outright. "By my faith!" he exclaimed, "the rector of the university should have done the same! What say you, Master Guillaume Rym?"

"Monseigneur," answered Master Guillaume Rym, "we ought to be glad that we have escaped half of the play. The loss is so much gained."

"May those fellows continue their farce?" asked the bailiff.

"Go on, go on," said the cardinal; "'tis the same to me."

The bailiff advanced to the front of the gallery, and enjoined silence by a motion of his hand. "Burgesses and inhabitants," he cried, "to satisfy those who wish the piece to proceed, and those who are desirous that it should finish, his eminence orders it to be continued."

The characters on the stage resumed their cue, and Gringoire hoped that at any rate the rest of his piece would be heard out. This hope, however, was destined, like his other illusions, to be very soon blasted. Silence was, indeed, in some degree restored among the audience, but Gringoire had not observed that at the moment when the cardinal ordered the mystery to be continued, the gallery was far from full, and that after the Flemish envoys had taken their seats, other persons, forming part of the train, kept coming in, and the names and qualities of these, proclaimed every now and then by the bawling voice of the usher, broke in upon his dialogue and made great havoc with it. Gringoire was the more incensed at this strange accompaniment, which rendered it difficult to follow the piece, because he felt that the interest increased as it proceeded, and that his work needed nothing but to be heard. Indeed, a more ingenious and more dramatic plot could scarcely be invented. The four characters of the prologue were bewailing their mortal embarrassment, when Venus appeared to them in person, attired in a robe embroidered with the arms of the city of Paris. She came to prefer her claim to the dolphin promised to the most beautiful female; it was supported by Jupiter, whose thunder was heard rumbling in the dressing-room, and the goddess had well-nigh carried her point—that is to say, without metaphor, established her right to the hand of Monsieur the Dauphin—when a child, in a dress of white damask, and holding a daisy—diaphanous personification of the Princess of Flanders—entered the lists against Venus. This unexpected incident produced an instant change in the state of affairs. After some controversy, Venus Margaret, and the whole party, agreed to refer the matter to the decision of the Holy Virgin. There was another striking part, that of Don Pedro, King of Mesopotamia; but owing to so many interruptions it was difficult to discover its connection with the plot of the piece.

All these beauties were unfortunately neither appreciated nor understood. The moment the cardinal entered, it was as if an invisible and magic thread had suddenly drawn all eyes from the marble table to the gallery, from the southern extremity to the west side of the hall. Nothing could break the spell thrown over the audience; every eye remained fixed on one point, and the new-comers, and their confounded names, and their faces, and their dresses, created an endless diversion. This was most mortifying. Excepting Gisquette and Lienarde, who turned about from time to time when Gringoire pulled them by the sleeve, and the pursy patient neighbor, not a creature listened, or even looked at the poor forsaken morality.

With what anguish of spirit did he see his whole edifice of glory and poesy tumbling down piecemeal! To think that the same auditory which had been on the point of rebelling against Monsieur the Bailiff from impatience to hear his work, now that they might witness its performance, cared nothing at all about it! A performance, too, which had begun amid such unanimous applause! Oh! the incessant flowing and ebbing of popular favor! How near they had been to hanging the sergeants of the bailiff! What would he not have given for the return of that delicious moment!

The brutal monologue of the usher ceased at last; all the company had arrived: Gringoire breathed once more, and the actors proceeded with spirit. All at once, what should Master Coppenole the hosier do, but rise from his seat, and Gringoire stood aghast to hear him, amid the breathless attention of the spectators, commence this abominable harangue:

"Gentlemen burgesses and yeomen of Paris, I know not, by the rood! what we are about here. Down there, on yonder stage, I see some mountebanks who seem disposed to fight. I cannot tell whether this is what you call a mystery; let it be what it will, it is not amusing; they bang one another with their tongues, and that is all. Here have I been waiting this quarter of an hour for the first blow, but nothing comes of it; they are cravens only who clapperclaw each other with abuse. You should have sent to London or Rotterdam for bruisers, and, by my faith! you would have had thumps which you would have heard all over the place; but these paillards are contemptible. They might have given us at least a morris-dance or some other mummery. To be sure, nothing was said about that; they promised me that I should see the Festival of Fools and the election of pope. We have our Pope of Fools at Ghent, too, and, by the rood! in this respect we are not behind your famous city. But the way we do is this—we collect a crowd, such as there is here; then every one that likes puts his head in turn through a hole, and grins at the others, and he who makes the ugliest face is chosen pope by acclamation—that's it. 'Tis a diverting sight, I assure you. Shall we choose your pope after the fashion of my country? 'Twill be more amusing, at any rate, than listening to those praters. If they like to come and grin through the hole, why let them. What say you, gentlemen burgesses? We have here a sufficiently grotesque specimen of both sexes to raise a hearty laugh in the Flemish fashion; and we have ugly faces enough among us to expect a capital grimace."

Gringoire would fain have replied, but horror, indignation, stupefaction, deprived him of utterance. Besides, the motion of the popular hosier was hailed with such enthusiasm by the citizens, flattered with the appellation of yeomen, that resistance would have been useless. All that he could now do was to resign himself to the stream.

CHAPTER V

QUASIMODO

IN THE TWINKLING of an eye, everything was ready for carrying into effect the idea of Coppenole. Burgesses, scholars, and lawyers' clerks had fallen to work. The little chapel opposite to the marble table was chosen for the scene of the grimaces. Having broken the glass in the little round window over the door, they agreed that the competitors should put their heads through the circle of stone that was left. To enable them to reach it, two hogsheads were brought and set one upon the other. It was determined that all candidates, whether men or women—for female were eligible—should hide their faces, and keep them covered in the chapel till the moment of exhibiting them, that the impression of the grimace might be the stronger. In a few minutes the chapel was full of competitors, and the door was shut upon them.

Coppenole from his place ordered, directed, superintended all the arrangements. During the uproar, the cardinal, not less disconcerted than Gringoire, having excused himself on the pleas of business and vespers, retired with his retinue; while the crowd, which his coming had so strongly agitated, was scarcely aware of his departure. Guillaume Rym was the only person that noticed the discomposure of his eminence. The popular attention, like the sun, pursued its revolution; setting out from one end of the hall, after pausing some time in the middle, it was now at the other extremity. The marble table, the brocaded gallery, had each had their moment; it was now the turn of Louis XI.'s chapel. The field was open to every species of fun; the Flemings and the populace alone were left.

The grimaces began. The first face that presented itself at the window, with its red eyes and widely gaping mouth, and forehead puckered up in wrinkles like hussar boots in the time of the emperor,[1] caused such convulsions of inextinguishable laughter that Homer would have taken these ruffians for immortal gods. A second and a third grimace succeeded—then another and another, following by redoubled shouts of laughter and the stampings and clatterings of

1. Napoleon.

merriment. The crowd was seized with a sort of frantic intoxication, a supernatural kind of fascination, of which it would be difficult to convey any idea to the reader of our own days. Imagine a series of visages successively presenting every geometric figure, from the triangle to the trapezium—from the cone to the polyhedron—every human expression, from love to rage; all ages, from the wrinkles of the new-born infant to those of the hag at the point of death; all the religious phantasmagorias from Faunus to Beelzebub; all the brute profiles, from the distended jaw to the beak, from the snout of hog to the muzzle of the bull. Imagine all the grotesque heads of the Pont Neuf, those nightmares petrified under the hand of Germain Pilon, suddenly starting into life, and coming one after another to stare you in the face with flaming eyes; all the masks of the carnival of Venice passing in succession before your eyeglass—in a word, a human kaleidoscope.

The orgies became more and more uproarious. Teniers could have given but an imperfect idea of the scene. Fancy Salvator Rosa's battle turned into a bacchanalian piece. There were no longer any distinctions of ranks and persons—no longer scholars, embassadors, men or women—all were lost in the general license. The great hall was one vast furnace of effrontery and jollity; where every mouth was a cry, every eye a flash, every face a contortion, every individual a posture; all was howling and roaring. The extraordinary faces which in turn presented themselves at the window acted like so many brands thrown upon a blazing fire; and from all this effervescent crowd issued, like vapor from a furnace, a sharp, shrill, hissing noise as from an immense serpent.

Meanwhile Gringoire, the first moment of dejection over, had recovered his spirits; he had braced himself against adversity. "Go on!" said he for the third time to his speaking machines, the comedians, and then paced to and fro, with long strides, before the marble table. He almost felt tempted to exhibit himself in his turn at the round window of the chapel, were it but to enjoy the pleasure of grinning at the ungrateful populace. "But no," said he mentally, "no revenge! that were unworthy of us. Let us struggle manfully to the last; the power of poesy is mighty over the populace. I will bring them back. We shall see which will conquer—the grimaces or the belles-lettres."

Alas, poor Gringoire! he was left to be the only spectator of his play; every back was turned upon him.

I am wrong; the fat patient man whom he previously consulted in a critical moment was still turned toward the theater. As for Gisquette and Lienarde they had long deserted.

Gringoire was touched to the bottom of his heart by the constancy of his only spectator. He went up and spoke to him, at the same time gently shaking his arm; for the good man was leaning upon the balustrade and napping a little.

"Sir," said Gringoire, "I am exceedingly obliged to you."

"Sir," replied the fat man, with a yawn, "for what?"

"I see," rejoined the poet, "that you are quite annoyed by all this uproar, which prevents your hearing comfortably. But, never mind; your name will be handed down to posterity, may I ask what it is?"

"Renauld Chateau, keeper of the seal of the Chatelet of Paris, at your service."

"Sir, you are the only representative of the Muses in this assembly," said Gringoire.

"You are too polite, sir," replied the keeper of the seal of the chatelet.

"You are the only one," resumed Gringoire, "who has paid any attention to the piece. What do you think of it?"

"Why, to tell the truth," answered the pursy magistrate, only half awake, "it is stupid enough."

Gringoire was forced to be content with this opinion; for thunders of applause, mingled with prodigious shouts, cut short their conversation. The Pope of Fools was elected. "Huzza! huzza! huzza!" cried the people on all sides.

It was, in truth, a countenance of miraculous ugliness which at this moment shone forth from the circular aperture. After all the faces, pentagonal, hexagonal, and heteroclite, that had followed each other at this window, without realizing the idea of the grotesque which the crowd had set up in their frantic imaginations, it required nothing short of the sublimely monstrous grimace which had just dazzled the multitude to obtain their suffrages. Master Coppenole himself applauded; and Clopin Trouillefou who had been a candidate—and God knows what intensity of ugliness his features could attain!—confessed himself conquered. We shall do the same; we shall not attempt to give the reader any idea of that tetrahedron nose, of that horse-shoe mouth, of that little left eye stubbled up with an eyebrow of carroty bristles, while the right was completely overwhelmed and buried by an enormous wen; of those irregular teeth, jagged here and there like the battlements of a fortress; of that horny lip, over which one of those teeth protruded, like the tusk of an elephant; of that forked chin; and above all of the expression, that mixture of spite, wonder, and melancholy, spread over these exquisite features. Imagine such an object, if you can.

The acclamation was unanimous; the crowd rushed to the chapel. The lucky Pope of Fools was brought out in triumph, and it was not till then that surprise and admiration were at their height; what had been mistaken for a grimace was a natural visage; indeed, it might be said that his whole person was but one grimace. His prodigious head was covered with red bristles; between his shoulders rose an enormous hump, which was counter-balanced by a protuberance in front; his thighs and legs were so strangely put together that they touched at no one point but the knees, and seen in front, resembled two sickles joined at the handles; his feet were immense, his hands monstrous; but, with all this deformity there was a formidable air of strength, agility, and courage, constituting a singular exception to the eternal rule which ordains that force, as well as beauty, shall result from harmony. He looked like a giant who had been broken in pieces and ill soldered together.

When this sort of Cyclops appeared on the threshold of the chapel, motionless, squat, almost as broad as high, "the square of his base," as a great man expresses it, the populace instantly recognized him by his coat, half red and half purple, sprinkled with silver bells, and, more especially, by the perfection of his ugliness, and cried out with one voice, "It is Quasimodo, the bell-ringer! it is Quasimodo, the hunchback of Notre Dame! Quasimodo, the one-eyed! Quasimodo, the bandy-legged! Hurrah! hurrah!" The poor fellow, it seems, had plenty of surnames to choose among.

"Let breeding women take care of themselves!" cried the scholars. The women actually covered their faces.

"Oh, the ugly ape!" cried one.

"And as mischievous as ugly," said another.

"'Tis the devil himself!" exclaimed a third.

"I am so unlucky as to live near Notre Dame, and hear him at night prowling about in the gutters."

"What! with the cats?"

"He is always on our roofs."

"The other night he came and grinned at me through my garret window. I thought it was a man. I was dreadfully frightened."

"I am sure he attends the witches' sabbaths. He once left a broom on my leads."

"Oh, the ugly hunchback!"

"Faugh!"

The men, on the contrary, were delighted. There was no end to their applause. Quasimodo, the object of all the tumult, was still standing at the door of the chapel, gloomy and grave, exhibiting himself to the popular admiration, when Robin Poussepain came up close to him and laughed him in the face. Quasimodo, without uttering a word, caught him up by the waist, and hurled him to the distance of ten paces among the crowd.

Master Coppenole, astonished at the feat, approached him. "By the rood!" he exclaimed. "Holy Father!—why thou art the finest piece of ugliness I ever beheld. Thou deservest to be Pope at Rome as well as at Paris."

As he thus spoke, he sportively clapped his hand on the monster's shoulder. Quasimodo did not stir. Coppenole continued: "My fine fellow, I should like to have a tussle with thee, were it to cost me a new douzain of twelve tournois. What sayest thou?"

Quasimodo made no reply. "What!" cried the hosier, "art thou deaf?" Quasimodo really was deaf.

Presently, beginning to feel annoyed by Coppenole's manner, he turned suddenly toward him with so formidable a grin that the Flemish giant recoiled like a bull-dog from a cat. A circle of terror and respect, having a radius of at least fifteen geometric paces, was left vacant around this strange personage.

An old woman informed Coppenole that Quasimodo was deaf.

"Deaf!" cried the hosier, with a Flemish horse-laugh. "By the rood! he is an accomplished pope."

"Ha!" said Jehan, who had at length descended from his pillar to obtain a closer view of the new pope, "'tis my brother's bell-ringer! Good-morrow, Quasimodo!"

"Confound thee, fellow!" sighed Robin Poussepain, aching all over from the effects of his fall. "He appears—he is hunchbacked. He walks—he is bandy-legged. He looks at you—he is one-eyed. You talk to him—he is deaf! And what use does this Polyphemus make of his tongue, I wonder?"

"He can talk when he likes," said the old woman. "He became deaf with ringing the bells. He is not dumb."

"He wants that qualification, then," observed Jehan.

"And he has an eye too much," added Robin Poussepain.

"Not so," rejoined Jehan, tartly; "a one-eyed man is more incomplete than one who is quite blind."

Meanwhile all the mendicants, all the lackeys, all the cut-purses, together with the scholars, went in procession to the store-room of the Bazoche to fetch the pasteboard tiara and the mock robe of the Pope of Fools. Quasimodo suffered them to be put upon him with a kind of proud docility. He was then required to sit down on a parti-colored litter. Twelve officers of the fraternity of fools hoisted it upon their shoulders; and a sort of disdainful exultation overspread the morose countenance of the Cyclops, when he saw beneath his feet all those heads of straight, handsome, well-shaped men. The roaring and ragged procession then moved off, to pass, according to custom, through the galleries in the interior of the palace, before it paraded the streets and the public places of the city.

CHAPTER VI

LA ESMERALDA

WE HAVE GREAT satisfaction in apprising the reader that during the whole of this scene, Gringoire and his play had maintained their ground. His actors, egged on by him, had continued the performance of his comedy, and he had continued to listen to them. In spite of the uproar, he was determined to go through with it, not despairing of being able to recall the attention of the public. This glimmer of hope became brighter when he saw Quasimodo, Coppenole, and the obstreperous retinue of the Pope of Fools leaving the hall. The crowd rushed out after them. "Excellent!" said he; "we shall get rid of all those troublesome knaves." Unluckily, these were the whole assembly. In the twinkling of an eye the great hall was empty.

To tell the truth, a few spectators still lingered behind, some dispersed, others in groups around the pillars, old men, women, or children, who had had enough of the uproar and tumult. Some of the scholars, too, remained, astride of the entablature of the windows, where they had a good view of the place.

"Well," thought Gringoire, "there are quite as many as I want to hear the conclusion of my mystery. Their number, indeed, is but small: but they are a select, a lettered audience."

At that moment a symphony destined to produce a striking effect at the arrival of the Holy Virgin was not forthcoming. Gringoire perceived that his musicians had been pressed into the service of the procession of the Pope of Fools. "Skip that," said he, with the composure of a stoic.

He approached a knot of citizens who seemed to be talking about his play. The fragment of their conversation which he overheard was as follows:

"Master Cheneteau, you know the Hotel de Navarre, which belonged to Monsieur de Nemours?"

"Yes; opposite to the chapel of Braque."

"Well! the exchequer has just leased it to Guillaume Alexander, the history writer, for six livres eight sols parisis per annum."

"How rents are rising!"

"Bah!" ejaculated Gringoire, with a sigh—"the others are listening, at any rate."

"Comrades," all at once shouted one of the young scapegraces in the windows, "La Esmeralda! La Esmeralda in the place!"

This intimation produced a magic effect. All who were left in the hall ran to the windows, clambering up the walls to obtain a sight, and repeating, "La Esmeralda! La Esmeralda!" Thunders of applause arose at the same moment from the place.

"What can they mean by La Esmeralda?" said Gringoire, clasping his hands in despair. "Gracious Heaven! it seems to have come to the turn of the windows now!"

Turning toward the marble table he perceived that the performance was at a stand. It was precisely the moment when Jupiter should have appeared with his thunder-bolt; but Jupiter was standing stock-still at the foot of the stage.

"Michel Giborne!" cried the incensed poet, "mind thy business! What art thou doing? Make haste up!"

"Alas!" replied Jupiter, "one of the scholars has run away with the ladder."

Gringoire looked; it was even so. The communication with the stage was completely cut off. "The varlet!" murmured he. "And why did he take the ladder?"

"To go and see La Esmeralda," answered Jupiter, in a doleful tone. "'Stay,' said he, 'here's a ladder that's of no use,' and off he scampered with it."

This was the final blow. Gringoire received it with resignation. "The devil fetch you!" said he to the performers. "If I am paid you shall be."

With downcast looks he made his retreat, but not till the very last, like a general who has been soundly beaten. "A pretty pack of asses and boobies, these Parisians!" he muttered between his teeth as he descended the winding staircase of the palace. "They come to hear a mystery, and will not listen to it. They will pay attention to everything and everybody—to Clopin Trouillefou, to the Cardinal, to Coppenole, to Quasimodo! but on the Holy Virgin they have none to bestow. Had I known, ye gaping oafs, I should have given you Virgin Marys, I warrant me! Turn your backs on such a piece! Homer, it is true, begged his bread in the Greek towns, and Naso died in exile among the Moscovites; but the fiend fly away with me if I comprehend what they mean by their La Esmeralda. And what kind of word is it, to begin with? It must surely be Egyptian!"

Book Two

CHAPTER I

FROM CHARYBDIS INTO SCYLLA

NIGHT COMES on early in the month of January. It was already dusk
when Gringoire left the palace. To him the nightfall was doubly
welcome, as he purposed seeking some obscure and sequestered
street where he might muse unmolested, and where philosophy
might apply the first dressing to the poet's wound. In fact, philosophy was his only refuge; for he knew not where he should find a
lodging. After the signal failure of his dramatic attempt, he durst
not return to that which he had occupied in the Rue Grenier-sur-
l'Eau, opposite to the Port au Foin, having made sure that Monsieur
the Provost would give him such a remuneration for his labor as
would enable him to pay Master Guillaume Doulx-Sire, farmer of
the customs on beasts with cloven hoofs, for the six months' lodging
which he owed him; that is to say, twelve sols parisis—twelve times
the value of all that he possessed in the world, including his hose,
shirt and doublet. Having considered for a moment, sheltering, *ad
interim,* under the little gateway of the prison of the treasurer of the
holy chapel, what quarters he should select for the night, having all
the pavements of Paris to choose among, he recollected having
noticed, in the preceding week, a horsing-stone at the door of a
counselor of the parliament, in the Rue de la Savaterie, and having
said to himself that this stone would be, in case of emergency, an
excellent pillow for a beggar or a poet, he thanked Providence for
having sent this seasonable idea; but, as he was preparing to cross
the palace yard, for the purpose of entering the tortuous labyrinth
of the city, with its ancient winding streets, such as those of La
Barillerie, La Vielle-Draperie, La Savaterie, La Juiverie, and others
still standing, with their houses nine stories high, he saw the procession of the Pope of Fools coming out of the palace, and advancing
across the court toward him, with loud shouts, the glare of numerous torches, and his own band of music. This sight tore open afresh
the wounds of his self-love; he took to his heels. In the keen mortification of his dramatic miscarriage, everything that reminded him
of the festival held that day touched him to the quick.

He resolved to make for the Pont St. Michel. Boys were running to and fro letting off squibs and crackers. "Curse the fire-works!" ejaculated Gringoire, and he bent his steps toward the Pont-au-Change. To the houses at the end of the bridge were attached three large pieces of canvas, with likenesses of the king, the dauphin, and Margaret of Flanders; and six smaller, on which were portrayed the Duke of Austria, and the Cardinal of Bourbon, and Monsieur de Beaujeu, and Madame Jeanne of France, and Monsieur the Bastard of Bourbon, and I know not whom besides—the whole lighted by torches. A crowd of spectators was admiring these performances.

"Happy painter, Jehan Fourbault!" said Gringoire with a deep sigh, as he turned his back on the productions of that artist. There was a street just before him; it appeared to be so dark and so deserted that he hoped there to be out of hearing as well as out of sight of all the festivities: he entered it. Presently his foot struck against some obstacle; he stumbled and fell. It was the bole of the May-tree, which the clerks of the Bazoche had placed in the morning, at the door of a president of the parliament, in honor of the day. Gringoire bore with fortitude this new misfortune; he picked himself up, and pursued his way across the river. Leaving behind him the civil and criminal court of the parliament, and pursuing his way along the high wall of the king's gardens, upon the unpaved strand, where he was ankle-deep in mud, he arrived at the western point of the city and surveyed for some time the islet of the cattle-ferry, which has since given place to the Pont Neuf with its bronze horse. The islet appeared to him, in the dark, like a black mass, beyond the white narrow strip of water which separated him from it. By the glimmer of a faint light might be indistinctly discerned the kind of cabin in the shape of a bee-hive which afforded shelter to the ferryman during the night.

"Happy ferryman!" thought Gringoire—"thou dreamest not of glory, thou writest no epithalamiums! What to thee are the marriages of kings and duchesses of Burgundy!—while I, a poet, am hooted, and shiver with cold, and owe twelve sous, and the sole of my shoe is so thin that it might serve for the horn of a lantern. Thanks to thee, ferryman; thy cabin refreshes the eye and causes me to forget Paris!"

He was awakened from his almost lyric ecstasy by the explosion of a double petard suddenly fired from the happy cabin. It was the ferryman taking his share in the rejoicings of the day. The report made Gringoire shudder.

"Accursed festival!" cried he, "wilt thou pursue me whitherso-

ever I go, even to the cabin of the ferryman?" He then looked at
the Seine flowing at his feet, and a horrible temptation came over
him. "Ah!" said he, "how gladly would I drown myself, only the
water is so cold!"

He then formed a desperate resolution. Since he found it impossible to escape the Pope of Fools, the paintings of Jehan Fourbault,
the May-trees, the squibs, and the petards, he determined to proceed to the Place de Grève, and to penetrate boldly into the very
heart of the rejoicings. "At any rate," thought he, "I shall be able to
get a warm at the bonfire, and perhaps a supper on some of the
fragments of the collation provided at the public larder of the city."

CHAPTER II

THE PLACE DE GREVE

NOTHING BUT a scarcely perceptible vestige of the Place de Grève,
as it then existed, now remains. This is the charming turret which
occupied the north angle of the place, and which, already buried
beneath the ignoble plaster that incases the fine outlines of its sculptures, will probably soon disappear, ingulfed by the inundation of
new buildings which is so rapidly swallowing up all the ancient
structures of Paris.

Those who, like ourselves, can not pass through the Place de
Grève without bestowing a look of pity and sympathy on that poor
turret, cooped up between two paltry erections of the time of Louis
XV., may easily figure to themselves the general aspect of the edifice to which it belonged, and recompose in imagination the entire
ancient Gothic place of the fifteenth century.

It was then, as at present, an irregular trapezium, bordered on
one side by the quay, and on three others by a series of lofty, narrow, and gloomy houses. By day, the spectator might admire the
variety of these edifices, covered with sculptures or carving, and exhibiting complete specimens of the various styles of domestic architecture of the Middle Ages, of the period between the fifteenth and
eleventh century; from the square window, which had already begun to supersede the pointed arch, to the semicircular Roman arch,
which had been supplanted by the pointed, and which was still ex-

tant in the ground floor of that ancient house of Roland's Tower, at the angle of the place next to the Seine, by the Rue de la Tannerie. By night, all that could be distinguished of that mass of buildings was the dark, jagged outline of the roofs stretching their chain of acute angles around the place. For one of the radical differences of the city of that time and the cities of the present day is that now the fronts face the streets and places, whereas then it was the gables. During the last two centuries the houses have turned round.

In the center of the east side of the place rose a heavy and hybrid structure in three compartments. It was called by three names which explain its history, its destination, and its architecture: the dauphin's house because Charles V., when dauphin, had resided there; La Marchandise, because it served for the Hotel de Ville; and the Pillar House, from the row of massive pillars which supported its three stories. The city there found all that is requisite for a good city like Paris; a chapel for saying prayers in; a hall for giving audience and occasionally snubbing the servants of the king; and in the lofts an arsenal well stored with artillery; for the citizens of Paris know that it is not sufficient in every conjecture to plead and to pray for the franchises of the city, and therefore they always keep in reserve a good rusty arquebuse or two in a loft in the Hotel de Ville.

The Grève wore at that time the same sinister aspect that it still retains, owing to the unpleasant ideas which it excites, and the gloomy Hotel de Ville of Dominique Bocador, which occupies the site of the Pillar House. A permanent gibbet and a pillory, or as they were called in those days, "a justice and a ladder," placed side by side in the middle of the pavement, conferred no particular attraction on this fatal spot, where so many human beings full of health and life had been suddenly cut off; where fifty years later was generated that fever of St. Vallier, that disease produced by fear of the scaffold, the most monstrous of all diseases, because it did not proceed from God, but from man.

It is consolatory, be it observed by the way, to think that the punishment of death, which three hundred years ago still encumbered the Grève, the Halles, the Place Dauphine, the Cross of Trahoir, the Swine Market, the hideous Montfauçon, the barrier of the Sergens, the Place-aux-Chats, the gate of St. Denis, Champeaux, the gate of the Baudets, and the gate of St. Jacques, with its iron wheels, its stone gibbets, and all its apparatus for executions, permanently imbedded in the pavement—to say nothing of the numberless "ladders" of the provosts, the bishop, the chapters, the abbots, the priors, possessing the power of life and death, or of the judicial drownings in the river Seine—it is consolatory, I say, to think that, at the present day, this ancient sovereign-paramount of feudal society, stripped successively of all the pieces of its armor, its luxury of pains and penalties, its penal spirit and tendency, its torture, for which it caused a new leathern bed to be made every five years at the Grand Chatelet, almost outlawed from our cities and our land, hunted from code to code, driven from place to place, should have in our immense Paris, but an ignominious corner of the Grève, but one miserable, furtive, timid, shame-faced guillotine, which always seems as if fearful of being taken in the act, so speedily does it hurry away after striking the fatal blow.

CHAPTER III

THE POET PUZZLED

WHEN PIERRE GRINGOIRE reached the Place de Grève he was quite benumbed with cold. He had gone over the Pont-aux-Meuniers, to avoid the crowd at the Pont-au-Change and the flags of Jehan Fourbault; but the wheels of all the bishop's mills had splashed him so unmercifully as he passed that his frock was drenched: it seemed, moreover, as if the failure of his play had rendered him still more chilly than ever. Accordingly, he hastened toward the bonfire which blazed magnificently in the middle of the place. A large assemblage of people formed a circle around it.

"Cursed Parisians!" said he to himself: for Gringoire, like a genuine dramatic poet, was addicted to soliloquies; "there they are, shutting me out from the fire! And yet I am in great need of a comfortable chimney-corner. My shoes leak, and all those infernal mills showering upon me into the bargain! The devil fetch the Bishop of Paris and his mills! I would fain know what a bishop has to do with a mill! Does he expect to be obliged to turn miller some day or other? If he needs nothing but my malison for that, I give it to him, and to his cathedral, and to his mills, with all my heart. Stop a moment; let's see if these boobies will sheer off presently. But what are they doing there, I want to know? Warming themselves—fine amusement. Gaping at the bonfire—pretty sight, forsooth!"

On looking more closely he perceived that the circle was much larger than it needed to have been, had the persons composing it been desirous of warming themselves at the king's fire; and that the assemblage of spectators was not drawn together solely by the beauty of the hundred blazing fagots. In an extensive space left open between the crowd and the fire, there was a young female dancing.

Whether this young female was a human being, or a fairy, or an angel, Gringoire, skeptical philosopher and satirical poet as he was, could not at the first moment decide, so completely was he fascinated by the dazzling vision. She was not tall, though she appeared to be so from the slenderness and elegance of her shape. Her complexion was dark, but it was easy to divine that by daylight her skin must have been the beautiful golden tint of the Roman and Andalusian women. Her small foot, too, was Andalusian. She danced, whirled, turned round on an old Persian carpet carelessly spread on the pavement, and every time her radiant face passed before you as she turned, her large black eyes flashed lightning.

Every eye was fixed upon her, every mouth open; and in truth, while she was thus dancing, what with the sound of the tambourine, which her two plump, exquisitely shaped arms held above her head, her bodice of gold without folds, her spotted robe which swelled with the rapidity of her motions, her bare shoulders, her finely turned legs, which her petticoat now and then discovered, her black hair, her eyes of flame, she was a supernatural creature.

"Verily," thought Gringoire, "it is a salamander, a nymph, a goddess, a bacchanal of Mount Menalæus!" At that moment one of the tresses of the salamander's hair got loose, and a piece of brass which had been fastened to it dropped to the ground. "Ha! no," said he; "'tis a gypsy!" The illusion was at an end.

She began dancing again. She picked up from the ground two swords, which she balanced on their points upon her forehead, and made them turn round one way, while she turned the other. She was, in fact, a gypsy, neither more nor less. But though the spell was dissolved, still the whole scene was not without fascination and charm for Gringoire: the bonfire threw a crude, red, trembling light on the wide circle of faces and on the tawny brow of the girl, and, at the extremity of the place, cast a faint tinge, mingled with their wavering shadows, upon the ancient, black and furrowed façade of the Maison-aux-Piliers on the one hand and upon the stone arms of the gibbet on the other.

Among the thousand faces to which this light communicated a scarlet hue, there was one which seemed to be more deeply absorbed in the contemplation of the dancer than any of the others. It was the face of a man, austere, calm and somber. This man, whose dress was concealed by the surrounding crowd, appeared to be no more than thirty-five years of age; he was, nevertheless, bald, and had merely at his temples a few tufts of thin and already gray hair. His ample and lofty brow began to be furrowed with wrinkles; but in his deep-sunk eyes there was an expression of extraordinary youth, ardent life, and profound passion. He kept them intently fixed on the Bohemian; and, while the lively girl of sixteen was delighting all the other spectators by her dancing and her capers, his reverie seemed to become more and more gloomy. At times a smile and a sigh would meet upon his lips, but the smile was by far the sadder of the two. The girl at length paused, panting with her exertions, and the people applauded with enthusiasm.

"Djali!" said the Bohemian, and up started a pretty little white goat, a nimble, lively, glossy creature, with gilt horns, gilt hoofs, and a gilt collar, which Gringoire had not yet perceived, and which had till then been lying at the corner of the carpet watching her mistress dance. "Djali," said the girl, "it is your turn now;" and seating herself, she gracefully held the tambourine before the animal. "Djali," continued she, "what month are we in?" The goat raised her fore-leg and struck one stroke upon the tambourine. It was actually the first month. The crowd applauded. "Djali," said the girl, turning the tambourine a different way, "What day of the month is this?" Djali again raised her little gilt hoof and struck six blows upon the instrument. "Djali," continued the Egyptian, again changing the position of the tambourine, "What o'clock is it?" Djali gave seven blows. At that moment the clock of the Maison-aux-Piliers struck seven. The people were astounded.

"There is sorcery at the bottom of this!" said a sinister voice in the crowd. It was that of the bald man who never took his eyes off the Bohemian. She shuddered and turned away; and thunders of applause burst forth and drowned the morose exclamation. They had the effect of effacing it so completely from her mind that she continued to question her goat.

"Djali, show me how Master Guichard Grand Remy, captain of the city pistoleers, does in the Candlemas procession." Djali raised herself on her hind legs, and began bleating and walking with such comic gravity that the whole circle of spectators roared with laughter at this parody upon the interested devotion of the captain of the pistoleers.

"Djali," resumed the girl, emboldened by the increasing applause, "show me how Master Jacques Charmolue, the king's attorney in the ecclesiastical court, preaches." The goat sat down on her rump and began bleating and shaking her fore-paws in such a strange way that, in gesture, accent, attitude, everything excepting bad French and worse Latin, it was Jacques Charmolue to the life. The crowd applauded more loudly than ever.

"Sacrilege! profanation!" ejaculated the bald man. The gypsy turned round once more. "Ah!" said she, "it is the odious man!" then lengthening her lower lip beyond the upper, she gave a pout that seemed to be habitual to her, turned upon her heel, and began to collect the donations of the multitude in her tambourine. Silver and copper coins of all sorts and sizes were showered into it. She came to Gringoire, who so readily thrust his hand into his pocket that she stopped.

"The devil!" muttered the poet, fumbling in his pocket and finding the reality, that is, nothing. The graceful girl stood before him, looking at him with her large eyes, and holding out her tambourine. Big drops of perspiration started from Gringoire's brow. If he had had Peru in his pocket, he would certainly have given it to the dancer; but Gringoire had no Peru there, and besides, America was not yet discovered. An unexpected incident luckily relieved him.

"Wilt thou begone, Egyptian grasshopper?" cried a sharp voice issuing from the darkest corner of the place. The young girl turned about in alarm. It was not the voice of the bald man; it was the voice of a female, a devout and spiteful voice. This exclamation, which frightened the gypsy, excited the merriment of a troop of boys who were strolling near the spot.

"'Tis the crazy woman in Roland's Tower," cried they, with shouts of laughter; "'tis Sacky who is scolding. Perhaps she has had no supper. Let us run to the city larder and see if we can get something for her!" And away they scampered to the Maison-aux-Piliers.

Meanwhile, Gringoire had taken advantage of the girl's agitation to sneak off. The shouts of the boys reminded him that he had not supped, either. He thought that he too might as well try his luck at the larder. But the young rogues ran too fast for him; when he arrived everything was cleared away; there was not a scrap of any kind left.

It was not pleasant to be obliged to go to bed without supper, and still less agreeable to have no bed to go to as well as no supper to eat. Such was Gringoire's predicament. He found himself closely pressed on all sides by necessity, and he thought necessity unnecessarily harsh.

He had long since discovered this truth, that Jupiter created man in a fit of misanthropy, and that, throughout the whole life of the philosopher, his destiny keeps his philosophy in a stage of siege. For his own part, he had never seen the blockade so complete; he heard his stomach beat a parley; and he declared it a scurvy trick of malicious destiny to take his philosophy by famine.

In this melancholy reverie he became more and more absorbed, when a strange kind of song, but remarkably sweet, suddenly roused him from it. It was the Egyptian girl who was singing. Her voice, like her dancing and her beauty, was indefinable, something pure, sonorous, aerial, winged, as it were. There were continued gushes of melody, unexpected cadences, then simple phrases interspersed with harsh and hissing tones; now leaps which would have confused a nightingale, but in which harmony was nevertheless preserved; and presently soft undulations of octaves, which rose and fell like the bosom of the young singer. Her fine face followed with extraordinary versatility all the caprices of her song, from the widest inspiration to the chastest dignity. You would have taken her at one time for a maniac, at another for a queen.

The words which she sung were of a language unknown to Gringoire, and apparently unknown to herself, so little did the expression thrown into the singing accord with the signification of those words. Thus these four lines were in the highest strain of mirth:

> "Un coffre de gran riqueza
> Hallaron dentro un pilar,
> Dentro del, nuevas banderas,
> Con figuras de espantar."

A moment afterward the tone which she infused into this stanza

> "Alarabes decavallo
> Sin poderse menear,
> Con espadas, y los cuellos,
> Ballestas de buen echar—"

drew tears into the eyes of Gringoire. Mirth, however, was the predominant spirit of her lays, and she seemed to sing like the bird for sheer serenity and carelessness.

The song of the gypsy had disturbed Gringoire's reverie but as the swan disturbs the water; he listened with a kind of rapture and forgetfulness of everything. It was the first respite from suffering that he had enjoyed for several hours. That respite was a short one. The same female voice which had interrupted the dancing of the gypsy was now raised to interrupt her singing. "Cease thy chirping, cricket of hell!" it cried, still issuing from the darkest corner of the place. The poor cricket stopped short. "Curse thy screeching, thou bird of foul omen!" exclaimed Gringoire, clapping his hands to his ears. The other spectators also began to murmur. "The devil take the hag!" cried more than one, and the invisible trouble-feast might have had to rue her aggressions against the Bohemian had not their attention been at that moment diverted by the procession of the Pope of Fools, which, after parading through the principal streets, was now entering the Place de Grève with all its torches and its clamor.

This procession, which set out, as the reader has seen, from the palace, was joined in its progress by all idle ragamuffins, thieves, and vagabonds in Paris; accordingly it exhibited a most respectable appearance when it reached the Grève.

Egypt marched first, headed by the duke on horseback, with his counts on foot, holding his bridle and stirrups. They were followed by the Egyptians of both sexes, pell-mell, with their young children crying at their backs; all of them, duke, counts, and commons, in rags and tatters. Next came the Kingdom of Slang, that is to say, all the rogues and thieves in France, drawn up according to their respective dignities, the lowest walking first. Thus they moved on, four by four, with the different insignia of their degrees, in this strange faculty, most of them cripples, some having lost legs, others arms. Amid the conclave of grand dignitaries it was difficult to distinguish the king of these ruffians, couched in a little car drawn by two huge dogs. After the Kingdom of Slang came the Empire of Galilee. The emperor, Guillaume Rousseau, marched majestically in his purple robe stained with wine, preceded by dancers performing military dances and scuffling together, and surrounded by his mace-bearers and subordinate officers. Lastly came the Bazoche, the company of lawyers' clerks, with their May-trees garlanded with flowers, in their black gowns, with music worthy of the Sabbath, and large candles of yellow wax. In the center of this multitude, the officers of the Fraternity of Fools bore upon their shoulders a hand-barrow, more profusely beset with tapers than the shrine of St. Genevieve in time of pestilence; and on this throne glittered, with crosier, cope, and miter, the new Pope of Fools, the bell-ringer of Notre Dame, Quasimodo the hunchback.

Each of the divisions of this grotesque procession had its particular band of music. The Egyptians played upon their African balafoes and tambourines. The men of Slang, a race by no means musical, had advanced no further than the viol, the goat's horn, and the Gothic rebec of the twelfth century. The Empire of Galilee was but little before them; the highest stretch of its music was some wretched air in the infancy of the art still imprisoned in the *re-la-mi*. It was around the Pope of Fools that all the music excellences of the age were commingled in one magnificent cacophony. It consisted only of viols, treble, alto and tenor, besides flutes and instruments of brass. Our readers may not recollect that this was poor Gringoire's orchestra.

It is impossible to convey any idea of the look of pride and self-complacency which had overspread Quasimodo's dull and hideous countenance during this triumphal procession from the palace to the Grève. It was the first gratification of self-love that he had ever experienced. Hitherto he had met with nothing but humiliation, contempt for his condition, disgust of his person. Thus, deaf as he was, he enjoyed like a real pope the acclamation of that crowd which he hated because he knew that he was hated by it. It mattered not to him that his subjects were a mob of cripples, mendicants, thieves, ruffians—still they were subjects, and he was a sovereign. He took in earnest all those ironical plaudits, all that mock reverence and respect, with which, we must however observe, there was mingled on the part of the crowd a certain degree of real fear; for the hunchback was strong, the bandy-legged dwarf was active, the deaf bell-ringer was spiteful, three qualities which tend to temper ridicule.

That the new Pope of Fools was conscious of the sentiments which he felt and of the sentiments which he inspired is more than we can undertake to assert. The mind which was lodged in that defective body had necessarily a touch of imperfection and of deafness. He had therefore but a vague, indistinct, confused perception of what he felt at that moment; enough for him that joy prevailed, pride predominated. That gloomy and unhappy visage was encircled by a halo of delight.

It was, therefore, not without surprise and alarm that at the moment when Quasimodo, in this state of half-intoxication, was borne triumphantly past the Maison-aux-Piliers, his attendants beheld a man suddenly dart from among the crowd, and with an angry gesture snatch from his hands his crosier of gilt wood, the mark of his newly-conferred dignity. This rash man was the bald-headed personage who, mingled in the group of spectators, had thrilled the poor gypsy girl by his exclamations of menace and abhorrence. He was attired in the ecclesiastical habit. At the moment when he issued from among the crowd, Gringoire, who had not before noticed him, recognized in him an old acquaintance. "Hold!" said he, with a cry of astonishment. "Sure enough it is my master in Hermes, Dom Claude Frollo, the archdeacon! What the devil would he be at with that one-eyed monster? He will eat him up."

Shrieks of terror burst from the crowd as the formidable Quasimodo leaped from the litter to the ground; and the women turned away their faces that they might not see the archdeacon torn in pieces. With one bound he was before the priest; he looked at him and dropped upon his knees. The priest pulled off his tiara, broke his crosier, and tore his cope of tinsel. Quasimodo remained kneeling, bowed his head, and clasped his hands. Then ensued between them a strange dialogue of signs and gestures, for neither of them spoke: the priest, erect, irritated, threatening, imperious—Quasimodo at his feet, humble, submissive, suppliant. And yet it is certain that Quasimodo could have crushed the priest with his thumb.

At length the archdeacon, shaking the brawny shoulder of Quasimodo, motioned him to rise and follow him. Quasimodo rose. The Fraternity of Fools, their first stupor over, were for defending their pope, who had been so unceremoniously dethroned. The Egyptians, the beggars, and the lawyers' clerks crowded yelping around the priest. Quasimodo, stepping before the priest, clinched his athletic fists; and as he eyed the assailants, he gnashed his teeth like an angry tiger. The priest resumed his sombre gravity, made a sign to Quasimodo, and withdrew in silence. Quasimodo went before, opening a passage for him through the crowd.

When they were clear of the populace, a number of curious and idle persons began to follow them. Quasimodo then fell into the rear; and, facing the enemy, walked backward after the archdeacon, square, massive, bristly, picking up his limbs, licking his tusk, growling like a wild beast, and producing immense oscillations in the crowd with a gesture or a look. They pursued their way down a dark and narrow street, into which no one durst venture to follow them, the formidable figure of Quasimodo securing an unmolested retreat.

"'Tis wonderful, by my faith!" exclaimed Gringoire. "But where shall I find a supper?"

CHAPTER IV

INCONVENIENCES OF FOLLOWING A PRETTY GIRL IN THE STREET AT NIGHT

GRINGOIRE TOOK it into his head to follow the gypsy at all hazards. He saw her with her goat turn into the Rue de Coutellerie, and to the same street he directed his course. "Why not?" said he to himself, by the way.

Gringoire, a practical philosopher of the streets of Paris, had remarked that nothing is so conducive to reverie as to follow a handsome woman without knowing whither she is going. In this voluntary resignation of free will, in this submission of one whim to another, there is a mixture of fantastic independence and blind obedience, a something intermediate between slavery and liberty, which was pleasing to Gringoire, a man of a mind essentially mixed, indecisive, and complex, incessantly suspended between all human passions and propensities, and incessantly neutralizing them one by another. He was fond of comparing himself with the tomb of Mohammed, attracted in contrary directions by two lode-stones, and eternally wavering between the ceiling and the pavement, between rising and sinking, between zenith and nadir.

Nothing tends so much to produce a disposition to follow passengers, and especially those of the fair sex, in the streets as the circumstance of having neither home nor harbor. Gringoire, therefore, walked pensively on after the girl, who quickened her pace, and made her pretty little goat trot along by her side, when she saw the shopkeepers retiring to their houses, and the tavern-keepers, who had alone kept open that day, shutting up for the night. "After all" —this was what he thought, or something very much like it—"she must lodge somewhere. The gypsies are very good-natured. Who knows——" And the suspensive points with which in his mind he cut short the sentence involved certain ideas that tickled him mightily.

Meanwhile, from time to time, as he passed the last groups of tradesmen shutting their doors, he caught some fragments of their conversation, which broke the chain of his pleasing hypotheses. Two old men, for instance, would accost each other in this manner:

"Master Thibaut Fernicle, do you know that it is very cold?"
Gringoire had known that ever since the beginning of winter.

"It is, indeed, Master Boniface Disome! Are we going to have
such another winter as we had three years ago, in '80, when wood
cost six sous the cord?"

"Pooh! that is nothing, Master Thibaut, to the winter of 1407,
when the frost lasted from Martinmas to Candlemas; ay, and the
cold was so bitter that the pen of the clerk of the parliament froze
in the great chamber every three words he wrote!"

Further on a couple of female neighbors would be chatting at
their windows, while the fog made their candles crackle again.

"Has your husband told you of the accident, Mademoiselle La
Boudraque?"

"No; but what is it, Mademoiselle Turquant?"

"You know the horse of Monsieur Gilles Godin, notary to the
Chatelets—well, he took fright at the Flemings and their procession,
and threw Master Philippot Avrillot, the invalid of the Celestins."

"Indeed!"

"As true as you are there."

The windows would then close again: but Gringoire had, nevertheless, lost the thread of his ideas. Luckily, however, he soon recovered and quickly reunited it, thanks to the gypsy girl and her
Djali, who still pursued their way before him—two elegant, delicate,
charming creatures, whose small feet, handsome shape, and graceful
manners he admired, almost confounding them in his imagination;
regarding them both as young girls for intelligence and their fondness for each other, and thinking them both goats for agility,
dexterity, and lightness of foot.

The streets, meanwhile, became every moment darker and more
deserted. The curfew had long since rung; and it was only at rare
intervals that a passenger was met on the pavement, or a light seen
at the windows. Gringoire, in following the Egyptian, had involved
himself in that inextricable labyrinth of lanes, and alleys, and cross-
ways, surrounding the ancient sepulcher of the Holy Innocents, and
which resembles a skein of thread entangled by a playful cat. "Here
are streets which have very little logic!" said Gringoire, lost in their
thousand meanders, through which, however, the girl proceeded as
along a way that was well known to her, and at a more and more
rapid pace. For his part, he should not have had the remotest
conception of where he was, had he not perceived, on turning a
corner, the octagon mass of the pillory of the Halles, the black open-

work top of which was distinctly defined against a window still lighted in the Rue Verdelet.

He had by this time begun to attract the notice of the young girl: she had more than once turned her head and looked at him with some uneasiness; nay, she had stopped short and taken advantage of a ray of light issuing from the half-open door of a bake-house to scrutinize him attentively from head to foot. Gringoire had seen her, after this, pout her lips as she had done before, and then she passed on.

This pretty grimace set Gringoire about inquiring what it might denote. It certainly conveyed an expression of disdain and dislike. He began, in consequence, to hang his head, as if to count the stones of the pavement, and to drop further behind, when, on reaching the corner of a street into which she had turned, he was startled by a piercing shriek. The street was extremely dark; a wick steeped in oil burning in an iron cage at the foot of the Blessed Virgin, at the angle of the street, nevertheless enabled Gringoire to distinguish the Bohemian struggling in the grasp of two men, who were striving to stifle her cries. The poor little goat, terrified at this attack, dropped her head, presented her horns and bleated.

"Watch! watch!" shouted Gringoire, boldly advancing. One of the men who held the girl turned upon him. It was the formidable visage of Quasimodo. Gringoire did not run away, neither did he advance another step. Quasimodo went up to him and dealt him a back-handed blow that sent him reeling three or four yards and stretched him sprawling upon the pavement; then darting back, he caught up the young girl and bore her off across one of his arms like a silken scarf. His companion followed, and the poor goat ran after the three, bleating in a most plaintive manner.

"Murder! murder!" cried the unfortunate gypsy girl.

"Halt, scoundrels, and let the wench go!" suddenly roared, in a voice of thunder, a horseman who came dashing along out of the next street. It was the captain of the archers of the king's ordnance, armed cap-a-pie, and his drawn sword in his hand. He snatched the Bohemian out of the grasp of the stupefied Quasimodo, laid her across his saddle, and, at the moment when the formidable hunch-back, recovering from his surprise, would have rushed upon him to regain his prey, fifteen or sixteen archers, who followed close at the heels of their captain, came up, armed with quarter-staves. It was part of a company of the king's ordnance, which did the duty of counter-watch, by the order of Messire Robert d'Estouteville, keeper of the provosty of Paris.

Quasimodo was surrounded, seized, and bound. He bellowed, he foamed, he kicked, he bit; and had it been daylight, no doubt his face alone, rendered doubly hideous by rage, would have sufficed to scare away the whole detachment: but night disarmed him of his most formidable weapon, his ugliness. His companion had disappeared during the struggle.

The Bohemian gracefully raised herself upon the officer's saddle. Clapping her two hands upon his shoulders, she looked at him intently for a few moments, as if charmed with his handsome face, and grateful for the seasonable succor which he had afforded her. Then, giving a sweeter tone than usual to her sweet voice, she inquired, "What is your name, sir?"

"Captain Phœbus de Chateaupers, at your service, my dear," replied the officer, drawing himself up to his full height.

"Thank you," said she; and while the captain was turning up his whiskers *a la bourguignonne*, she slid down the horse's side to the ground, and vanished with the swiftness of lightning.

CHAPTER V

SEQUEL OF INCONVENIENCES

GRINGOIRE, STUNNED by his fall, was extended on the pavement before the good Virgin at the corner of the street. By degrees he came to himself. At first he was floating for some minutes in a kind of dreamy reverie which was rather soothing, though the aerial figures of the Bohemian and her goat were coupled with the weight of the ungentle fist of Quasimodo. This state was of short duration. A painful sensation of cold in that part of his body which was in contact with the pavement, suddenly awoke him and recalled his mind to the surface. "Whence comes this cold?" he said sharply to himself. He then perceived that he was nearly in the middle of the kennel.

"Hang the hunchbacked Cyclops!" muttered he, and attempted to rise; but was so stunned and bruised that he was forced to remain where he was. His hand, however, was at liberty. He held his nose and resigned himself to his fate.

"The mud of Paris," thought he—for he had decidedly made up his mind to it that the kennel would be his bed, "the mud of Paris is particularly offensive; it must contain a great deal of volatile and nitrous salt. Besides, it is the opinion of Nicholas Flamel and of the alchemists——"

The word *alchemists* suggested to his mind the idea of the archdeacon Claude Frollo. He bethought him of the violent scene which he had just witnessed; he recollected that the Bohemian was struggling between two men, that Quasimodo had a companion; and the stately and morose figure of the archdeacon passed confusedly before his imagination. That would be extraordinary, thought he. And with this datum and upon this foundation he began to erect the fantastic edifice of hypotheses, that card-house of philosophers. Then, suddenly recalled once more to reality, "Egad!" cried he, "I am freezing!"

The place, in fact, was becoming less and less tenable. Each particle of the water in the kennel carried off a particle of radiating caloric from the loins of Gringoire; and the equilibrium between the temperature of his body and the temperature of the kennel began to be established in a way that was far from agreeable. All at once he was assailed by an annoyance of a totally different kind.

A party of boys, of those little bare-legged savages who have in all ages padded the pavement of Paris by the name of gamins, and who, when we were boys too, threw stones at us in the evening as we left school, because our trousers were not in tatters like their own; a party of these ragged urchins ran toward the spot where Gringoire lay, laughing, and whooping and hallooing, and caring very little whether they disturbed the neighborhood or not. They were dragging after them something like an enormous bag, and the mere clattering of their wooden shoes would have been enough to wake the dead. Gringoire, who was not absolutely dead, propped himself up a little to see what was the matter.

"Halloo! Hennequin Dandeche!—halloo, Jehan Pincebourde!" they bawled at the top of their voices; "old Eustache Moubon, the ironmonger at the corner, is just dead. We have got his paillasse, and are going to make a bonfire of it!"

So saying they threw down the paillasse precisely upon Gringoire, close to whom they had stopped without seeing him. At the same time one of them took a handful of straw and went to light it at the Virgin's lamp.

"'Sdeath!" grumbled Gringoire, "I am likely to be hot enough presently!"

Between fire and water he was certainly in a critical situation. He made a supernatural effort, the effort of a coiner who is going to be boiled and strives to escape. He raised himself upon his feet, threw back the paillasse upon the urchins, and hobbled away as fast as he was able.

"Holy Virgin!" cried the boys, "'tis the ironmonger's ghost!" and off they scrambled in their turn.

The paillasse was left in possession of the field of battle. Belleforet, Father Le Juge, and Corrozet relate that on the following day it was picked up with great pomp by the clergy of the quarter, and carried to the treasure-house of the Church of St. Opportune, where the sacristan, down to the year 1789, made a very handsome income with the grand miracle performed by the statue of the Virgin at the corner of the Rue Mauconseil, which had, by its mere presence, in the memorable night between the 6th and the 7th of January, 1482, exorcised the spirit of Jehan Moubon, which, to play the devil a trick, had when he died maliciously hid itself in his paillasse.

CHAPTER VI

THE BROKEN JUG

AFTER RUNNING for some time as fast as his legs would carry him, without knowing whither, knocking his head against many a corner of a street, plunging into many a kennel, dashing through many a lane, turning into many a blind alley, seeking a passage through all the meanders of the old pavement of the Halles, exploring, in his panic, what is termed in the exquisite Latin of the charters *tota via, cheminum, et viaria,*[1] our poet stopped short, in the first place for want of breath, and in the next collared, as it were, by a dilemma which just occurred to his mind. "It seemeth to me, Master Pierre Gringoire," said he to himself, clapping his finger to the side of his nose, "that you are running about like a blockhead. The young rogues were not a whit less afraid of you than you of them. It seemeth to me, I tell you, that you heard their wooden shoes clattering off to the south, while you are scudding away to the north. Now, either they have run away, and then the paillasse, which they have no doubt left behind in their fright, is precisely the hospital bed for which you have been running about ever since morning, and which the Virgin, blessed be her name! miraculously sends to

1. Every way, highway and byway.

reward you for having composed in honor of her a morality accompanied by triumphs and mummeries, or the boys have not run
away; in that case they have set fire to the paillasse; and a good fire
is the very thing you want to warm, to dry, and to cheer you. In
either case, a good fire or a good bed, the paillasse is a gift of
Heaven. It was perhaps for this very reason that the Virgin at the
corner of the Rue Mauconseil caused the death of Jehan Moubon;
and it is stupid of you to run your legs off in this manner, like a
Picard from a Frenchman, leaving behind what you are seeking before you. You are a fool for your pains."

He turned, and, with eyes and ears on the alert, strove to steer his
way back to the lucky paillasse, but in vain. His course was incessantly checked by intersections of houses, blind alleys, spots where
several streets terminated, and where he was forced to pause in
doubt and hesitation, more perplexed and more entangled in the
intricacies of those dark, narrow lanes and courts than he would
have been in the maze of the Hotel de Tournelles itself. At length,
losing all patience, he solemnly ejaculated: "Curse these branching
streets! the devil must have made them in the image of his fork."

This exclamation relieved him a little, and a kind of reddish light
which he perceived at the extremity of a long, narrow lane helped
cheer his spirits. "God be praised!" said he, "yonder it is. Yonder is
my paillasse burning!" And comparing himself with the mariner
who is wrecked in the night, "Salve," he piously ejaculated, "Salve
maris stella!" [1]

Whether this fragment of the seaman's hymn was addressed to
the Blessed Virgin or to the paillasse is more than we can take it
upon us to decide.

Before he had proceeded many steps down the long lane, which
was sloping and unpaved, and which became more and more muddy
the further he went, he perceived something that had a most extraordinary appearance. Here and there, all the way along it,
crawled a number of indistinct and shapeless masses, proceeding
toward the light at the bottom of the lane.

Nothing makes a man so adventurous as an empty pocket. Gringoire continued to advance, and soon came up with the hindmost
of these strange figures, which was leisurely wriggling itself along
after the others. On a near approach, he perceived that it was only
a wretched cripple in a bowl, who was hopping along upon both
hands. At the moment when he was passing this species of spider
with human face it accosted him in a lamentable tone: "La buona
mancia! la buona mancia!" [2]

1. "Hail, star of the sea!"
2. "Charity, sir, charity!"

"The devil fetch thee," said Gringoire, "and me along with thee, if I know what thou meanest!" And he walked on.

He overtook another of these moving masses. This was a cripple too—a man who had suffered such mutilation in legs and arms that the complicated system of crutches and wooden legs by which he was supported gave him the appearance of a walking scaffold. Gringoire, who was fond of lofty and classic comparisons, likened him in imagination to the living tripod of Vulcan.

This living tripod took off its hat to him as he passed, but held it up under Gringoire's chin, like a barber's basin, at the same time bawling in his ear, "*Señor caballero, para comprar un pedaso de pan!*" [1]

"This fellow," said Gringoire, "seems to be talking too; but 'tis an odd language, and he must be cleverer than I am if he understands it."

He would have quickened his pace, but, for the third time, something obstructed the way. This something, or rather somebody, was a little blind man with Jewish face and long beard, who, rowing on in the space around him with a stick, and towed by a great dog, sung out with nasal twang and Hungarian accent, "*Facitote caritatem.*" [2]

"Come," said Pierre Gringoire, "here is one at last who speaks a Christian language. I must have a most benevolent look for people to ask charity of me, in this manner, in the present meager state of my purse. My friend," continued he, turning toward the blind man, "it is not a week since I sold my last shirt, or as you understand no language but Cicero's, *Vendidi hebdomade nuper transita meam ultimam chemisam.*"

This said, he turned his back on the blind man and pursued his way. At the same time, however, the blind man quickened his pace, and in a trice up came the two cripples, in great haste, with a tremendous clatter of bowl and crutches upon the pavement. All three, jostling each other at the heels of poor Gringoire, opened upon him at once.

"*Caritatem!*"[3] sung the blind man.

"*La buona mancia!*"[4] sung the man of the bowl.

The other cripple joined in the concert with "*Un pedaso de pan!*"[5]

Gringoire stopped his ears. "Oh, Tower of Babel!" exclaimed he.

He began to run for it. The blind man ran. The man of the bowl ran. The man with wooden legs ran. Presently he was surrounded by halt, and lame, and blind, by one-armed and one-eyed, and lepers

1. "Sir Cavalier, something with which to buy a piece of bread!"
2. "Give alms." 3. "Charity!" 4. "Spare a trifle!" 5. "A morsel of bread!"

with their hideous sores, some issuing from houses, others from the adjoining courts, and others from cellars, howling, bellowing, yelping, hobbling, rushing toward the light, and bedraggled with mire, like snails after a shower.

Gringoire, still followed by his three persecutors, and not knowing what to think of the matter, walked on in some alarm amid the others, turning aside, and passing the cripples on crutches, stepping over the heads of those in bowls, and entangled in this crowd of limping, shuffling wretches, like the English captain who found himself suddenly surrounded by a prodigious host of land-crabs.

The idea occurred to him to try to return. But it was too late. The whole legion had closed behind him, and his three mendicants stuck to him like bird-lime. He proceeded, therefore, propelled at once by this irresistible tide, by fear, and by a dizziness which made the whole scene appear to him like a horrible dream.

At length he reached the extremity of the lane. It opened into a spacious place, where a thousand scattered lights flickered in the confused haze of night. Gringoire pursued his way into it, hoping by the lightness of his heels to escape from the three infirm specters who stuck so closely to him.

"*Onde vas hombre?*"[1] cried the cripple upon crutches, throwing them down, and running after him on two as goodly legs as ever stepped upon the pavement of Paris. At the same moment the other cripple, standing bolt upright upon his feet, clapped his heavy bowl cased with iron upon Gringoire's head, by way of cap, and the blind man stared him in the face with a pair of flaming eyes.

"Where am I?" cried the affrighted poet.

"In the Cour des Miracles," replied a fourth specter, who had joined them.

"Miracles, upon my soul!" rejoined Gringoire; "for here are blind who see and lame who run."

A sinister laugh was their only answer.

The poor poet cast his eyes around him. He was actually in that dreaded Cour des Miracles, into which no honest man had ever penetrated at such an hour, a magic circle, in which the officers of the Chatelet and the sergeants of the provost who ventured within it were disposed of in a trice; the haunt of thieves; a hideous wen on the face of Paris; a sewer disgorging every morning and receiving every night that fetid torrent of vice, mendicity, and roguery which always overflows the streets of great capitals; a monstrous hive to which all the drones of the social order retired at night with their booty; the hospital of imposture where the gypsy, the unfrocked

---

1. "Where is the man off to?"

monk, the ruined scholar, the blackguards of all nations, Spaniards, Italians, Germans; of all religions, Jews, Christians, Mohammedans, idolators; covered with painted wounds, beggars by day transmogrified themselves into banditti at night; immense robing-room, in short, whither all the actors of that eternal comedy which theft, prostitution, and murder are performing in the streets of Paris, resorted at that period to dress and undress.

It was a spacious area, irregular and ill-paved, like all the open places of Paris in those days. Fires, around which swarmed strange-looking groups, were blazing here and there. All was bustle, confusion, uproar. Coarse laughter, the crying of children, the voices of women, were intermingled. The hands and heads of this multitude, black upon a luminous ground, were making a thousand antic gestures. A dog which looked like a man, or a man who looked like a dog, might be seen from time to time passing over the place on which trembled the reflection of the fires, interspersed with broad, ill-defined shadows. The limits between races and species seemed to be done away with in this city, as in a pandemonium. Men, women, brutes, age, sex, health, disease, all seemed to be in common among these people. They were jumbled, huddled together, laid upon one another; each there partook of everything.

The faint and flickering light of the fires enabled Gringoire to distinguish, in spite of his agitation, all round the immense place a hideous circumference of old houses, the decayed, worm-eaten, ruinous fronts of which, each perforated by one or two small, lighted windows, appeared to him in the dark like enormous heads of old hags ranged in a circle, watching the witches' sabbath rites and winking their eyes. It was like a new world, unknown, unheard of, deformed, creeping, crawling, fantastic.

Gringoire, more and more terrified, held by the three mendicants as by three vises, deafened by a crowd of other faces bleating and barking around him—the unlucky Gringoire strove to rally his presence of mind, and to recollect whether it was Saturday or not. But his efforts were vain; the thread of his memory and of his thoughts was broken; and, doubting everything, floating between what he saw and what he felt, he asked himself this puzzling question: "If I am, can this be? if this is, can I be?"

At this moment a distinct shout arose from amid the buzzing crowd by which he was surrounded: "Lead him to the king! lead him to the king!"

"Holy Virgin!" muttered Gringoire—"the king of this place—why, he can be nothing but a goat."

"To the king! to the king!" repeated every voice.

He was hurried away. The rabble rushed to lay hands on him, but the three mendicants held him fast in their grip, tearing him away from the others and bawling, "He is ours!" The poet's doublet, previously in wretched plight, was utterly ruined in this struggle.

While crossing the horrible place, the vertigo which had confused his senses was dispelled. He had taken but a few steps before a conviction of the reality flashed upon him. He began to become used to the atmosphere of the place. At the first moment there had risen from his poetic brain, and perhaps, to speak quite simply and prosaically, from his empty stomach, a fume, a vapor, which, spreading itself between objects and him, and permitted him to catch a glimpse of them only in the distorting haze of the nightmare, in that darkness of dreams which shows all outlines as shaking, all forms as grinning, all objects as heaped together in preposterous groups, dilating things into chimeras and men into phantoms. By degrees this hallucination gave place to views less wild and less exaggerating. Reality burst upon him, paining his eyes, treading upon his toes, and demolishing piecemeal the whole frightful poesy by which he had at first fancied himself to be surrounded. He could not help perceiving that he was not walking in the Styx, but in the mud; that he was not elbowed by demons, but by robbers; that his soul was not in danger, but merely his life, because he lacked that excellent mediator between the ruffian and the honest man—the purse. In short, upon examining the scene more closely and more coolly, he fell from the witches' sabbath down to the tavern. The Cour des Miracles was in fact nothing but a tavern, but a tavern for ruffians, quite as much stained with blood as with wine.

The sight which presented itself when his ragged escort had at length brought him to the place of his destination was not calculated to carry him back to poetry, were it even the poetry of hell. It was more than ever the prosaic and brutal reality of the tavern. If our history did not pertain to the fifteenth century, we should say that Gringoire had descended from Michael Angelo to Callot.

Around a great fire, which burned upon a large circular hearth, and the flames of which rose among the red-hot bars of a trevet, unoccupied at the moment, sundry crazy tables were placed here and there at random; for the waiter had not deigned to study geometrical symmetry in their arrangement, or to take care at least that they should not intersect each other at too unusual angles. On these tables shone pots flowing with wine and beer, and round these pots were grouped a great many jolly faces, empurpled by the fire and by drink. Here a man, with huge paunch and jovial phiz, was whistling the while he took off the bandages from a false wound, and removed the wrappers from a sound and vigorous knee, which had been swathed ever since morning in a dozen ligatures. At the back of him was a shriveled wretch preparing with suet and bullock's blood his black pudding for the ensuing day. Two tables off, a sharper in the complete dress of a pilgrim was twanging a stave of a religious hymn. In another place a young rogue was taking a lesson in epilepsy from an old cadger, who was also teaching him the art of foaming at the mouth by chewing a bit of soap. By the side of these a dropsical man was ridding himself of his protuberance, while four or five canters of the other sex were quarreling about a child they had stolen in the course of the evening. Circumstances these which, two centuries later, "appeared so ridiculous to the court," as Sauval tells us, "that they furnished pastime for the king, and were introduced into a royal ballet called 'Night,' divided into four parts, and performed upon the stage of the Petit Bourbon." "Never," adds a spectator of this performance, "were the sudden metamorphoses of the Cour des Miracles more successfully represented."

From every quarter burst forth the coarse laugh and the obscene song. Each did just as he pleased, swearing and descanting without listening to his neighbor. The pots jingled, quarrels arose, and broken mugs occasioned a destruction of rags.

A large dog was seated on his haunches looking at the fire. Young children were present at these orgies. The stolen boy was crying bitterly. Another, a stout fellow about four years old, was sitting on a high bench, dangling his legs at the table, which reached up to his chin, and saying not a word. A third was gravely spreading with his finger the melted tallow which ran from a candle upon the table. The last, a little urchin crouching in the dirt, was almost lost in a kettle which he was scraping with a tile, and from which he was extracting sounds that would have thrown Stradivarius into a swoon.

Near the fire stood a hogshead, and upon this hogshead was seated a mendicant. This was the king upon his throne. The three vagabonds who held Gringoire led him before the hogshead, and for a moment the whole motley assemblage was silent, excepting the kettle inhabited by the boy. Gringoire durst not breathe or raise his eyes.

"*Hombre, quita tu sombrero,*"[1] said one of the three fellows in whose clutches he was, and before he knew what was meant, one

1. "Take off your hat, man!"

of the others took off his hat—a shabby covering, it is true, but still useful either against sun or rain. Gringoire sighed.

"What varlet have we here?" asked the king. Gringoire shuddered. This voice, though it now had a tone of menace, reminded him of another which had that very morning given the first blow to his mystery by drawling out amid the audience, "Charity, if you please!" He raised his eyes. It was Clopin Trouillefou himself.

Clopin Trouillefou, invested with the insignia of royalty, had not a rag more or a rag less than usual. The sore on his arm had disappeared. He held in his hand one of the whips composed of thongs of white leather which were used by the vergers in those days to keep back the crowd. On his head he wore a cap of such peculiar form that it was difficult to tell whether it was a child's biggin or a king's crown—so much are the two things alike. Gringoire, however, had regained some hope, though without knowing why, on recognizing in the King of the Cour des Miracles the provoking beggar of the great hall.

"Master," he stammered forth, "my lord—sire—what ought I to call you?" he at length asked, having arrived at the culminating point of his crescendo, and not knowing how to get higher or to descend again.

"Call me your majesty, or comrade, or what you will. But make haste. What hast thou to say in thy defense?"

"In thy defense!" thought Gringoire; "I don't half like that——It was I—I—I—" he resumed, with the same hesitation as before, "who this morning——"

"By the devil's hoofs!" cried Clopin, interrupting him, "thy name, knave, and nothing more. Mark me. Thou art in the presence of three mighty sovereigns, myself, Clopin Trouillefou, King of Thunes, and supreme ruler of the realm of Slang; Mathias Hunyadi Spicali, Duke of Egypt and Bohemia, that sallow old crone whom thou seest yonder, with a clout round his head; and Guillaume Rousseau, Emperor of Galilee, the porpoise who is too busy with his neighbor to attend to us. We are thy judges. Thou hast entered our territories without being one of our subjects; thou hast violated the privileges of our city. Thou must be punished, unless thou art a prig, a cadger, or a stroller—or, to use the gibberish of those who call themselves honest people, a thief, a beggar, or a vagrant. Art thou any of these? Justify thyself: state thy qualities."

"Alas!" sighed Gringoire, "I have not that honor. I am the author—"

"Enough!" exclaimed Trouillefou, without suffering him to proceed. "Thou shalt be hanged. And quite right too, messieurs honest citizens! As you deal by our people among you, so we will deal by yours among us. The law which you make for the Vagabonds, the Vagabonds will enforce with you. 'Tis your fault if it is a harsh one. It is but proper that an honest man should now and then be seen grinning through a hempen collar—that makes the thing honorable. Come, my friend, divide thy rags with a good grace among these wenches. I will have thee hanged to amuse the Vagabonds, and thou shalt give them thy purse to drink. If thou hast any mummery to make, go down into the cellar; there is a capital crucifix in stone which we picked up at St. Pierre-aux-Bœufs. Thou hast four minutes to settle the affairs of thy soul."

This was an alarming announcement.

"Well said, upon my life! Clopin Trouillefou preaches like his holiness the pope," cried the Emperor of Galilee, breaking his pot to prop up his table.

"Most puissant emperors and kings," said Gringoire, quite coolly —I never could make out how he recovered sufficient firmness to talk so resolutely—"you cannot mean what you say. My name is Pierre Gringoire; I am the poet whose morality was presented in the great hall of the palace."

"Oho! master!" said Clopin. "I was there too. But, comrade, because we were annoyed by thee in the morning, is that any reason why thou shouldst not be hung to-night?"

"I shall be puzzled to get myself out of this scrape," thought Gringoire. He made, nevertheless, another effort.

"I do not see," said he, "why poets should not be classed among vagabonds. Æsop was a vagabond, Homer a beggar, Mercury a thief."

Clopin interrupted him: "I verily believe thou thinkest to bamboozle us with thy palaver. 'Sdeath! as thou must be hanged, make no more ado."

"Pardon me, most illustrious King of Thunes," replied Gringoire, disputing the ground inch by inch: "is it worth while—only one moment—you will not condemn me unheard——"

His voice was absolutely drowned by the uproar which prevailed around him. The little urchin continued to scrape his kettle with greater energy than ever; and, to mend the matter, an old woman had just placed on the red-hot trevet a frying-pan full of fat, which yelped and crackled over the fire, like a dog that has been pipetailed by a troop of mischievous boys.

Clopin Trouillefou appeared to be conferring for a moment with the Duke of Egypt, and the Emperor of Galilee, who was quite drunk. He then cried out sharply, "Silence, there!" and, as the kettle and the frying-pan paid no attention to him, but continued their duet, he leaped from his hogshead, gave one kick to the kettle, which rolled away with the boy to the distance of ten paces, and another to the frying-pan, which upset all the fat into the fire. He then gravely reascended his throne, caring no more for the smothered crying of the child than for the grumbling of the hag whose supper had gone off in a blaze.

Trouillefou made a sign, and the duke, the emperor, and the high dignitaries of the Kingdom of Cant, ranged themselves around him in a semicircle, the center of which was occupied by Gringoire, who was still held fast by his captors. It was a semicircle of rags and tatters and tinsel, of forks and hatchets, of bare brawny arms and legs, of squalid, bloated, stupid-looking faces. In the middle of this round-table of ragamuffins, Clopin Trouillefou, like the doge of this senate, like the chief of this clan, like the pope of this conclave, overawed, in the first place by the whole height of his hogshead, and in the next by a certain haughty, ferocious, and formidable look, which made his eyes sparkle, and corrected the bestial type of the vagabond race in his savage profile. You would have taken him for a wild boar among domestic swine.

"Fellow," said he to Gringoire, stroking his deformed chin with his horny hand, "I see no reason why thou shouldst not be hanged. Thou seemest, indeed, to have a dislike to it, but that is natural enough; you citizens are not used to it. You have too frightful an idea of the thing. After all, we mean thee no harm. There is one way to get out of the scrape for the moment. Wilt thou be one of us?"

The reader may conceive what effect this proposition must have produced upon Gringoire, who saw that he had no chance of saving his life, and began to make up his mind to the worst. He caught eagerly at the proposed alternative.

"Certainly; most assuredly I will," said he.

"Thou consentest," rejoined Clopin, "to enroll thyself among the men of Slang?"

"The men of Slang, decidedly so," answered Gringoire.

"Thou acknowledgest thyself one of the crew?" proceeded the King of Thunes.

"One of the crew."

"A subject of the Kingdom of Cant?"

"Of the Kingdom of Cant."

"A Vagabond?"

"A Vagabond."

"With all thy soul?"

"With all my soul."

"Take notice," said the king: "thou shalt nevertheless be hanged."

"The devil!" ejaculated the poet.

"Only," continued Clopin, with imperturbable gravity, "thou shalt not be hanged quite so soon, but with more ceremony, at the cost of the good city of Paris, on a fair stone gibbet, and by the hands of honest men. That is some consolation."

"As you say," replied Gringoire.

"There are some other advantages which thou wilt enjoy. As one of the crew, thou wilt not have to pay rates, either for lamp, scavenger, or poor, to which the honest burgesses of Paris are liable."

"Be it so," said the poet. "I am a Vagabond, a subject of the Kingdom of Cant, one of the crew, a man of Slang, anything you please; nay, I was all these before, august King of Thunes, for I am a philosopher; *et omnia in philosophia, omnes in philosopho continentur,*[1] you know."

The august King of Thunes knit his brow. "What do you take me for, my friend? What Hungary Jew gibberish are you talking now? I know nothing of Hebrew. One may be a ruffian without being a Jew."

Gringoire strove to slip in an excuse between these brief sentences cut short by anger. "I beg your majesty's pardon; it is not Hebrew, but Latin."

"I tell thee," rejoined Clopin, furiously, "I am not a Jew, and I will have thee hanged, varlet; ay, and that little Jew peddler beside thee, whom I hope some day to see nailed to a counter, like a piece of base coin as he is."

As he thus spoke he pointed to the little bearded Hungarian Jew, who, acquainted with no other language but that in which he had accosted Gringoire, was surprised at the ill-humor which the King of Thunes appeared to be venting upon him. At length King Clopin became somewhat more calm. "Knave," said he to our poet, "thou hast a mind, then, to be a Vagabond?"

"Undoubtedly," replied Gringoire.

"'Tis not enough to have a mind," said his surly majesty; "good-will puts not one more onion into the soup. To be admitted into our brotherhood thou must prove that thou art fit for something. Show us thy skill at picking a pocket."

"Anything you please," said the poet.

Clopin made a sign. Several of the Vagabonds left the circle and

1. "All things are included in philosophy, all men in the philosopher."

presently returned. They brought two poles, each having a flat horizontal piece of wood fastened at the lower extremity, upon which it stood upright on the ground. Into the upper ends of these two poles the bearers fitted a cross-bar, and the whole then formed a very handy portable gibbet, which Gringoire had the satisfaction to see set up before his face in a trice. Nothing was wanting, not even the cord, which dangled gracefully from the cross-bar.

"What are they about now?" said Gringoire to himself, while his heart sunk within him. A tinkling of small bells put an end to his anxiety. It was the figure of a man, a kind of scarecrow in a red dress, so profusely bestudded with little bells that they would have sufficed for the caparison of thirty Castilian mules, which the Vagabonds were suspending by the neck from the rope. The chatter of these thousand bells, occasioned by the swinging of the rope, gradually subsided, and at length ceased entirely with the motion of the effigy.

Clopin pointed to a crazy stool placed under the figure.

"Get upon that," said he to Gringoire.

"'Sdeath!" rejoined the poet, "I shall break my neck.. Your stool halts like a distich of Martial's; it has one hexameter and one pentameter foot."

"Get up, knave!" repeated Clopin.

Gringoire mounted the stool, and, after some oscillations of head and arms, recovered his center of gravity.

"Now," continued the King of Thunes, "cross thy right leg over thy left and stand on tiptoe."

"*Morbleu!*" cried Gringoire, "then you absolutely insist on it that I shall break some of my limbs?"

Clopin shook his head. "Hark ye, my friend, thou talkest too much for me. In two words this is what thou hast to do. Thou must stand on tiptoe as I tell thee, so as to reach the pocket of the figure. Thou must take out a purse that is in it, and if thou canst do this without making any of the bells speak, 'tis well; thou shalt be a Vagabond. We shall then have nothing to do but to baste thee soundly for a week or so."

"*Ventre Dieu!*" exclaimed Gringoire. "And if the bells should give mouth in spite of me?"

"Why, then thou shalt be hanged. Dost thou comprehend me?"

"Not at all," answered Gringoire.

"Well, then, I tell thee once more: Thou must pick the pocket of that figure of a purse, and if a single bell stirs while thou art about it thou shalt be hanged. Dost thou understand that?"

"I do," said Gringoire. "And then?"

"If thou art clever enough to prig the purse without setting the bells a-chattering, thou art a Canter, and shalt be soundly thrashed every now and then for a week. Thou understandest that, no doubt?"

"But what better shall I be? Hanged in one case, beaten in the other?"

"And a Canter!" rejoined Clopin, "a Canter! Is that nothing? It is for thy own benefit that we shall beat thee, to inure thee to blows."

"Many thanks to you!" replied the poet.

"Come, bear a hand!" said the king, stamping upon his hogshead, which sounded like a big drum. "To thy task, knave! And recollect, if I hear but a single bell thou shalt change places with that figure."

The crew applauded Clopin's words, and ranged themselves in a circle round the gallows, with so pitiless a laugh that Gringoire saw he amused them too much not to have to fear the worst from them. The only hope he had left was the most precarious chance of succeeding in the ticklish task imposed upon him. Before he set about it he addressed a fervent prayer to the effigy which he was going to rob, and which he would have softened as easily as the Vagabonds. The myriad of bells, with their little copper tongues, seemed to him so many gaping jaws of serpents, ready to bite and to hiss.

"Oh!" said he, aside, "is it possible that my life depends on the slightest vibration of the smallest of these bells?" He tried the effect of a last effort on Trouillefou: "And if there should come a gust of wind?"

"Thou shalt be hanged," replied the King of Thunes without hesitation.

Finding that there was neither respite, nor reprieve, nor any possible evasion for him, he went resolutely to work. Crossing his right leg over the left, and raising himself on tiptoe, he stretched out his arm; but at the moment when he touched the effigy, he found himself tottering upon the stool, which had but three legs; he lost his balance, mechanically caught at the figure, and fell plump on the ground, stunned by the fatal jingle of the thousand bells of the figure, which, yielding to the impulsion of his hand, at first turned round upon itself, and then swung majestically between the two poles.

"*Sacré!*" cried he as he fell, and he lay like one dead, with his face toward the ground. He heard, however, the horrid chime above his head, the diabolical laugh of the Canters, and the voice of Trou-illefou, who said, "Pick up the varlet and hang him out of hand."

He rose. They had already taken down the effigy to make room for him. The Vagabonds made him once more mount the stool. Clopin stepped up to him, put the rope about his neck, and patting him on the shoulder, "Farewell, my friend!" said he. "Thou canst not escape now, even with the devil's luck and thine own."

The word "mercy!" died away on the lips of Gringoire. He glanced around him, but there was no hope; they were all laughing.

"Bellevigne de l'Etoile," said the King of Thunes to a porpoise of a fellow who stepped forth from the ranks, "scramble up to that cross-bar." The monster mounted with an agility for which no one would have given him credit, and Gringoire, raising his eyes, be-held him with terror crouching on the cross-beam over his head.

"Now," resumed Clopin, "the moment I clap my hands, thou, Andry the Red, kick away the stool; thou, François Chanteprune, pull the varlet's legs; and thou, Bellevigne, spring upon his shoulders —all three at once, d'ye hear?"

Gringoire shuddered.

"Are ye there?" said Clopin Trouillefou to the three ruffians ready to rush upon the unfortunate poet. The wretched man passed a moment of horrid suspense, while Clopin carelessly kicked into the fire a few twigs which the flame had not consumed. "Are ye there?" he repeated, opening his hands for the decisive clap.

He stopped short, as if a sudden thought had occurred to him, "Wait a moment!" said he; "I forgot. . . . It is customary with us not to hang a blade till the women have been asked whether any of them will have him. Comrade, this is thy last chance."

Gringoire breathed once more. It was the second time that he had come to life within the last half hour. He durst not, therefore, place much reliance upon this reprieve.

Clopin again mounted his hogshead. "This way, gentlewomen!" cried he. "Is there any among you who will have this knave? Come forward and see! A husband for nothing! Who wants one?"

Gringoire, in his wretched plight, looked far from tempting. The female mumpers showed no eagerness to accept the offer. The un-happy man heard them answer, one after another: "No, no; hang him, and that will be a pleasure for us all."

Three of them, however, stepped forward from among the crowd to take a look at him. The first was a strapping, broad-faced wench. She closely examined the deplorable doublet and the threadbare frock of the philosopher. She shrugged her shoulders. "Queer toggery!" grumbled she. Then turning to Gringoire: "Where is thy cloak?"

"I have lost it," answered he.

"Thy hat?"

"They have taken it from me."

"Thy shoes?"

"They are nearly worn out."

"Thy purse?"

"Alas!" stammered Gringoire, "I have not a dénier left."

"Hang, then, and be thankful!" replied the wench, turning on her heel and striding away.

The second, an old wrinkled hag, dark and hideously ugly, walked round Gringoire. He almost trembled lest she should take a fancy to him. At length she muttered to herself, "He is as lean as a carrion," and away she went.

The third was young, fresh-looking, and not ill-favored. "Save me!" said the poor poet to her in a low tone. She surveyed him for a moment with a look of pity, cast down her eyes, twitched her petticoat, and stood for a moment undecided. He narrowly watched all her motions. It was the last glimmer of hope. "No," said she at last, "no; Guillaume Longjoue would beat me," and she rejoined the crowd.

"Comrade," said Clopin, "thou art unlucky." Then, standing up on his hogshead, "Will nobody bid?" cried he, imitating the manner of an auctioneer, to the high diversion of the crew. "Will nobody bid? once, twice, three times!" then turning to the gallows, with a nod of the head, "Gone!"

Bellevigne de l'Etoile, Andry the Red, and François Chanteprune again surrounded the gibbet. At that moment cries of "La Esmeralda! La Esmeralda!" arose among the Vagabonds. Gringoire shuddered, and turned the way from which the clamor proceeded. The crowd opened and made way for a bright and dazzling figure. It was the gypsy girl.

"La Esmeralda!" ejaculated Gringoire, struck, amid his agitation at the sudden manner in which that magic name connected his scattered recollections of the events of the day. This extraordinary creature appeared by her fascination and beauty to exercise sovereign sway over the Cour des Miracles itself. Its inmates of both sexes respectfully drew back for her to pass, and at sight of her their brutal faces assumed a softer expression. With light step she approached the sufferer. Gringoire was more dead than alive. She eyed him for a moment in silence.

"Are you going to hang this man?" said she gravely to Clopin.

"Yes, sister," replied the King of Thunes, "unless thou wilt take him for thy husband."

Her lower lip was protruded into the pretty pout already described.

"I will take him," said she.

Gringoire was now thoroughly convinced that he had been in a dream ever since morning, and that this was but a continuation of it. The shock, though agreeable, was violent. The noose was removed, the poet was dismounted from the stool, on which he was obliged to sit down, so vehement was his agitation.

The Duke of Egypt, without uttering a word, brought an earthenware jug. The gypsy girl handed it to Gringoire. "Drop it on the ground," said she to him. The jug broke into four pieces.

"Brother," said the Duke of Egypt, placing a hand upon the head of each, "she is thy wife. Sister, he is thy husband. For four years. Go."

CHAPTER VII

A WEDDING NIGHT

IN A FEW moments our poet found himself in a small room with covered ceiling, very snug and very warm, seated at a table which appeared to desire nothing better than to draw a few loans from a cupboard suspended close by, having a prospect of a good bed and a *tête-à-tête* with a handsome girl. The adventure was like absolute enchantment. He began seriously to take himself for the hero of some fairy tale; and looked round from time to time to see whether the chariot of fire drawn by griffins, which could alone have conveyed him with such rapidity from Tartarus to Paradise, was still there. Now and then, too, he would fix his eyes on the holes in his doublet, as if to satisfy himself of his identity. His reason, tossed to and fro in imaginary space, had only this thread to hold by.

The girl appeared to take no notice of him; she moved backward and forward, setting things to rights, talking to her goat, and now and then pouting her lip. At length she sat down near the table, and Gringoire had a good opportunity to scrutinize her.

You have been a child, reader, and may perhaps have the good fortune to be so still. I dare say you have often (I know I have for whole days together—ay, and some of the best-spent days of my life) followed from bush to bush, on the bank of a stream, on a fine sunshiny day, some beautiful green-and-blue dragon-fly, darting off every moment at acute angles, and brushing the ends of all the branches. You remember with what amorous curiosity your attention and your eyes were fixed on those fluttering wings of purple and azure, amid which floated a form rendered indistinct by the very rapidity of its motion. The aerial creature, confusedly perceived through this flickering of wings, appeared to you chimerical, imaginary, a thing neither to be touched nor seen. But when at length it settled on the point of a rush, and, holding your breath the while, you could examine those delicate wings of gauze, that long robe of enamel, those two globes of crystal, what astonishment did you not feel, and what fear lest this beautiful figure should again vanish into an airy, undefinable phantom. Recollect these impressions, and you will easily conceive what Gringoire felt on contemplating, in a visible and palpable form, that Esmeralda of whom he had till then had but a glimpse amid the whirling dance and a crowd of spectators.

He became more and more absorbed in his reverie. "This then," thought he, while his eye vaguely followed her motions, "is La Esmeralda! a celestial creature! a street-dancer! So much and so little. It was she who gave the finishing stroke to my mystery this afternoon, and it is she who saves my life to-night. My evil genius! my good angel! A sweet girl, upon my word! and who must love me to distraction, to have taken me in this manner. For," said he, rising all at once with that candor which formed the ground-work of his character and of his philosophy, "I know not exactly how it has come to pass, but I am her husband."

With this idea in his head and in his eyes, he approached the girl with such ardent impetuosity that she drew back. "What do you want with me?" inquired she.

"Can you ask such a question, adorable Esmeralda?" rejoined Gringoire in so impassioned a tone that he was astonished at it himself.

The Egyptian opened her large eyes. "I know not what you mean," said she.

"What!" replied Gringoire, warming more and more, and thinking that, after all, it was but a virtue of the Cour des Miracles that he had to do with, "am I not thine, my sweet friend? art thou not mine?" With these words he fondly threw his arm round her waist.

The drapery of the Bohemian glided through his hands like the skin of an eel. Bounding from one end of the cell to the other, she stooped and raised herself again, with a little dagger in her hand, before Gringoire could see whence it came, with swollen lip, distended nostril, cheeks as red as an apricot, and eyes flashing lightning. At the same moment the little white goat placed itself before her in the attitude of attack, presenting to Gringoire two very pretty but very sharp gilt horns. All this was done in a twinkling.

Our philosopher stood petrified, alternately eying the goat and her mistress. "Holy Virgin!" he at length ejaculated, when surprise allowed him to speak, "what a couple of vixens!"

"And you," said the Bohemian, breaking silence on her part, "must be a very impudent fellow."

"Pardon me," replied Gringoire, smiling. "But why did you take me for your husband?"

"Ought I to have let you be hanged?"

"Then," rejoined the poet, somewhat disappointed in his amorous hopes, "you had no other intention in marrying me but to save me from the gallows?"

"And what other intention do you suppose I could have had?"

Gringoire bit his lips. "Go to," said he to himself; "I am not so triumphant in love affairs as I imagined. But, then, of what use was it to break the poor jug?"

Meanwhile Esmeralda's dagger and the horns of her goat were still upon the defensive.

"Mademoiselle Esmeralda," said the poet, "let us capitulate. I am not a clerk to the Chatelet, and shall not provoke you thus to carry a dagger in Paris, in the teeth of the provost's ordinances and prohibitions. You must, nevertheless, be aware that Noel Lescrivain was sentenced a week ago to pay a fine of ten sous parisis for having carried a short sword. But that is no business of mine; so to return to the point—I swear to you by my hopes of Paradise not to approach you without your permission and consent; but, for Heaven's sake, give me some supper!"

In reality Gringoire, like Despreaux, was not of a very amorous temperament. He belonged not to that chivalric and military class who take young damsels by assault. In love, as in all other affairs, he was for temporizing and pursuing middle courses; and to him a good supper, with an agreeable companion, appeared, especially when he was hungry, an excellent interlude between the prologue and the winding-up of a love adventure.

The Egyptian made no reply. She gave her disdainful pout, erected her head like a bird, and burst into a loud laugh; the pretty little dagger vanished as it had come, so that Gringoire could not discover where the bee concealed its sting.

In a moment a loaf of rye bread, a slice of bacon, some wrinkled apples and a jug of beer were set upon the table. Gringoire fell to with such avidity as if all his love had been changed into appetite. His hostess, seated before him, looked on in silence, visibly engaged with some other thought, at which she smiled from time to time, while her soft hand stroked the head of the intelligent goat, closely pressed between her knees. A candle of yellow wax lighted this scene of voracity and reverie.

The first cravings of his stomach being appeased, Gringoire felt a degree of false shame on perceiving that there was only one apple left. "Do you not eat something, Mademoiselle Esmeralda?" said he. She replied in the negative by a shake of the head, and her pensive looks were fixed on the vaulted ceiling of the cell.

"What the devil can she be thinking of?" said Gringoire to himself, turning his eyes in the same direction as hers. "It is impossible that yon ugly head carved on the groining can thus engross her attention. Surely I may stand a comparison with that."

"Mademoiselle," said he, raising his voice. She appeared not to hear him. "Mademoiselle Esmeralda!" he again began in a still louder tone, to just as little purpose. The spirit of the damsel was elsewhere, and the voice of Gringoire had not the power to recall it. Luckily for him, the goat interfered, and began to pull her mistress gently by the sleeve.

"What do you want, Djali?" said the Egyptian, sharply, starting like one awakened out of a sound sleep.

"She is hungry," said Gringoire, delighted at the opportunity of opening the conversation.

La Esmeralda began crumbling some bread, which Djali gracefully ate out of the hollow of her hand. Gringoire, without giving her time to resume her reverie, ventured upon a delicate question. "Then you will not have me for your husband?" said he.

The damsel looked at him intently for a moment, and replied, "No."

"For your lover?" asked Gringoire.

She pouted her lip and again replied, "No."

"For your friend?" continued Gringoire.

She again fixed her eyes steadfastly upon him. "Perhaps," said she, after a moment's reflection.

This "perhaps," so dear to philosophers, emboldened Gringoire. "Do you know what friendship is?" he inquired.

"Yes," replied the Egyptian; "it is to be as brother and sister, two souls which touch each other without uniting, like two fingers of the same hand."

"And love?" proceeded Gringoire.

"Oh, love!" said she, and her voice trembled and her eye sparkled. "It is to be two and yet but one—it is a man and a woman blending into an angel!—it is heaven itself."

The street-dancer, as she uttered these words, appeared invested with a beauty which powerfully struck Gringoire, and seemed in perfect unison with the almost Oriental exaggeration of her language. A faint smile played upon her pure and rosy lips: her bright and serene brow was now and then clouded for a moment, according to the turn of her thoughts, as a mirror is by the breath; and from her long, dark, downcast eyelashes emanated a sort of ineffable light, which imparted to her profile that ideal suavity which Raphael subsequently found at the mystic point of intersection of virginity, maternity and divinity.

Gringoire nevertheless proceeded. "And what should one be," said he, "to please you?"

"A man."

"What am I, then?"

"A man has a helmet on his head, a sword in his fist, and gold spurs at his heels."

"So, then," rejoined Gringoire, "without a horse one cannot be a man. Do you love any one?"

She remained pensive for a moment, and then said with a peculiar kind of expression, "I shall soon know that."

"Why not me?" replied the poet, tenderly.

She eyed him with a serious look. "Never can I love any man but one who is able to protect me."

Gringoire blushed and made sure that this stroke was aimed at him. It was evident that the girl was alluding to the little assistance he had afforded her in the critical situation in which she had found herself two hours before. At the recollection of the circumstance, which his own subsequent adventures had banished from his mind, he struck his forehead.

"Indeed," said he, "I ought to have begun with that subject. Forgive the confusion of my ideas. How did you contrive to escape from Quasimodo's clutches?"

This question made the gypsy girl shudder. "Oh, the horrid hunchback!" she exclaimed, covering her face with her hands, and she shivered as from the effect of intense cold.

"Horrid, indeed!" said Gringoire, without relinquishing his ideas; "but how did you get away from him?"

La Esmeralda smiled, sighed, and made no reply.

"Do you know why he followed you?" resumed Gringoire, seeking to return to his question by a roundabout way.

"I do not," said the girl. "But," added she, sharply, "you followed me too. Why did you follow me?"

"In good sooth," replied Gringoire, "I do not know either."

Both were then silent. Gringoire took up his knife and began to cut the table. The damsel smiled and seemed to be looking at something through the wall. All at once she commenced singing in a voice scarcely articulate:

> "Quando las pintadas aves
> Mudos estan, y la tierra." [1]

She then abruptly broke off and began to caress her Djali.

"That is a pretty creature of yours," observed Gringoire.

" 'Tis my sister," replied she.

"Why are you called La Esmeralda?" inquired the poet.

"I can't tell."

"No, sure!"

She drew from her bosom a small oblong bag, attached to a necklace of small red beads, and emitting a very strong scent of camphor. The outside was of green silk, and in the middle of it there was a large bead of green glass in imitation of emerald.

"Perhaps it is on account of this," said she.

Gringoire extended his hand to lay hold of the bag, but she started back. "Don't touch it," said she; " 'tis an amulet. You might do injury to the charm, or the charm to you."

The curiosity of the poet was more and more excited. "Who gave you that?" he asked.

She laid her finger upon her lips, and replaced the amulet in her bosom. He ventured upon further questions, but could scarcely obtain an answer to them.

"What is the meaning of La Esmeralda?"

"I know not," said she.

"To what language does the word belong?"

1. When the speckled birds are moulting, and the cock also.

"It is Egyptian, I believe."

"I thought so," said Gringoire. "You are not a native of France?"

"I don't know."

"Are your parents living?"

She began singing to the tone of an old song:

> "My father's a bird,
> And my mother's his mate;
> I pass the broad waters
> Without boat or bait."

"How old were you when you came to France?"

"I was quite a child."

"And to Paris?"

"Last year. At the moment we were entering the Papal Gate, I saw the yellow banners flying in a line over our heads. It was then the end of August, and I said: 'We shall have a sharp winter.'"

"And so we have," said Gringoire, delighted with this commencement of conversation; "I have done nothing but blow my fingers since it set in. Why, then, you possess the gift of prophecy?"

"No," replied she, relapsing into her laconic manner.

"The man whom you call the Duke of Egypt is the chief of your tribe, I presume?"

"Yes."

"And yet it was he who married us," timidly observed the poet.

Her lip exhibited the accustomed pout. "I don't even know your name," said she.

"My name, if you wish to know it, is Pierre Gringoire."

"I know a much finer," said she.

"How unkind," replied the poet. "Never mind; you shall not make me angry. You will, perhaps, love me when you are better acquainted with me; and you have related your history to me with such candor that I cannot withhold mine from you.

"You must know, then, that my name is Pierre Gringoire, and that my father held the situation of notary at Gonesse. He was hanged by the Burgundians, and my mother was murdered by the Picards at the siege of Paris, twenty years ago; so, at six years old I was left an orphan with no other sole to my foot but the pavement of Paris. I know not how I passed the interval between six and sixteen. Here, a fruit-woman gave me an apple or a plum; there, a baker tossed me a crust of bread; at night I threw myself in the way of the watch, who picked me up and put me in prison, where I found at least a bundle of straw. In spite of this kind of life I grew tall and slim, as you see. In winter I warmed myself in the sunshine, under the porch of the hotel of Sens, and I thought it very absurd that the bonfires of St. John should be deferred nearly to the dog-days. At sixteen I began to think of adopting a profession, and successively tried my hand at everything. I turned soldier, but was not brave enough; I became a monk, but was not devout enough, and, besides, I could not drink hard enough. In despair, I apprenticed myself to a carpenter, but was not strong enough. I had a much greater fancy to be a school-master. True, I had not learned to read; but what of that? After some time I discovered that, owing to some deficiency or other, I was fit for nothing, and therefore set up for a poet. This is a profession to which a man who is a vagabond may always betake himself, and it is better than to thieve, as some rogues of my acquaintance advised me to do. One day, as good luck would have it, I met with Dom Claude Frollo, the Reverend Archdeacon of Notre Dame, who took a liking to me, and to him I owe it that I am this day a learned man, not unpracticed either in scholastics, poetics, or rhythmics, nor even in hermetics, that sophia of all sophias. I am the author of the mystery that was performed to-day before a prodigious concourse of people, with immense applause, in the great hall of the Palace of Justice. I have also written a book of six hundred pages on the prodigious comet of 1465, which turned a man's brain, and have distinguished myself in other ways. Being somewhat of an artillery carpenter, I assisted in making that great bombard which you know burst at the bridge of Charenton, on the day it was tried, and killed twenty-four of the spectators. So, you see, I am no bad match. I know a great many curious tricks, which I will teach your goat, for instance, to mimic the Bishop of Paris, that cursed Pharisee whose mills splash the passengers all along the Pont aux Meuniers. And then my mystery will bring me in a good deal of hard cash, if I can get paid for it. In short, I am wholly at your service, damsel. My science and my learning shall be devoted to you. I am ready to live with you in any way you please; as husband and wife, if you think proper, as brother and sister, if you like it better."

Gringoire paused, waiting the effect of his address on his hearer. Her eyes were fixed on the ground.

"Phœbus," said she, in an under-tone, and then turning to the poet—"Phœbus, what does that mean?"

Gringoire, though unable to discover what connection there could be between the subject of his speech and this question, was not displeased to have an opportunity of displaying his erudition. "It is a Latin word," said he, "and means the sun."

"The sun!" she exclaimed.

"It is the name of a certain handsome archer who was a god," added Gringoire.

"A god!" repeated the Egyptian, and there was in her tone something pensive and impassioned.

At this moment one of her bracelets, having accidentally become loose, fell to the ground. Gringoire instantly stooped to pick it up; when he raised himself the damsel and the goat were gone. He had heard the sound of a bolt upon the door, communicating no doubt with an adjoining cell, which fastened on the inside.

"No matter, so she has left me a bed!" said our philosopher. He explored the cell. It contained not any piece of furniture fit to lie down upon, excepting a long coffer, and the lid of this was carved in such a manner as to communicate to Gringoire, when he stretched himself upon it, a sensation similar to that experienced by Micromegas when he lay at his full length upon the Alps.

"Well," said he, accommodating himself to this uncomfortable couch as well as he could, "'tis of no use to grumble. But at any rate this is a strange wedding night!"

Book Three

CHAPTER I

NOTRE DAME

THE CHURCH of Notre Dame at Paris is no doubt still a sublime and majestic edifice. But, notwithstanding the beauty which it has retained even in its old age, one cannot help feeling grief and indignation at the numberless injuries and mutilations which time and man have inflicted on the venerable structure, regardless of Charlemagne, who laid the first stone of it, and of Philip Augustus, who laid the last.

On the face of this aged queen of our cathedrals we always find a scar beside a wrinkle. *Tempus edax, homo edacior*[1]—which I should translate thus: Time is blind, man stupid.

If we had leisure to examine with the reader, one by one, the different traces of destruction left upon the ancient church, we should find that time had had much less hand in them than men, and especially professional men.

In the first place, to adduce only some capital examples, there are assuredly few more beautiful specimens of architecture than that façade, where the three porches with their pointed arches; the plinth, embroidered and fretted with twenty-eight royal niches; the immense central mullioned window, flanked by its two lateral windows, like the priest by the deacon and the sub-deacon; the lofty and light gallery of open-work arcades supporting a heavy platform upon its slender pillars; lastly, the two dark and massive towers with their slated pent-houses—harmonious parts of a magnificent whole, placed one above another in five gigantic stages—present themselves to the eye in a crowd yet without confusion, with their innumerable details of statuary, sculpture, and carving, powerfully contributing to the tranquil grandeur of the whole—a vast symphony of stone, if we may be allowed the expression; the colossal product of the combination of all the force of the age, in which the fancy of the workman, chastened by the genius of the artist, is seen starting forth in a hundred forms upon every stone: in short a sort of human creation, mighty and fertile like the divine creation, from which it

1. Time is voracious, and man even more so.

seems to have borrowed the twofold character of variety and eternity.

What we here said of the façade must be said of the whole church; and what we say of the cathedral of Paris must be said of all the churches of Christendom in the Middle Ages. But to return to the façade of Notre Dame, such as it appears to us at present, when we piously repair thither to admire the solemn and gorgeous cathedral, which, to use the language of the chroniclers, "by its vastness struck terror into the spectator."

That façade, as we now see it, has lost three important accessories: in the first place, the flight of eleven steps, which raised it above the level of the ground; in the next, the lower range of statues which filled the niches of the three porches, and the upper range of twenty-eight more ancient sovereigns of France which adorned the gallery of the first story, commencing with Childebert and ending with Philip Augustus, holding in his hand "the imperial globe."

Time, raising by a slow and irresistible progress the level of the city, occasioned the removal of the steps; but if this rising tide of the pavement of Paris has swallowed up, one after another, those eleven steps which added to the majestic height of the edifice, time has given to the church more perhaps than it has taken away: for it is time that has imparted to the façade that somber hue of antiquity which makes the old age of buildings the period of their greatest beauty.

But who has thrown down the two ranges of statues?—who has left the niches empty?—who has inserted that new and bastard-pointed arch in the middle of the beautiful central porch?—who has dared to set up that tasteless and heavy door of wood, carved in the style of Louis XV., beside the arabesques of Biscornette? The men, the architects, the artists of our days.

And if we step within the edifice, who has thrown down that colossal St. Christopher, proverbial among statues for the same reason as the great hall of the palace among halls, and the steeple of Strasburg among steeples?—who has brutally swept away those myriads of statues which peopled all the intercolumniations of the nave and the choir, kneeling, standing, on horseback, men, women, children, kings, bishops, soldiers, of stone, marble, gold, silver, copper, and even wax? Not time, most assuredly.

And who has substituted to the old Gothic altar, splendidly encumbered with shrines and reliquaries, that heavy sarcophagus of marble with its cherubs and its clouds, looking for all the world like a stray specimen of the Val de Grace or the Invalides?—who has stupidly inserted that clumsy anachronism of stone in the Carlovingian pavement of Hercandus? Is it not Louis XIV. fulfilling the vow of Louis XIII.?

And who has put cold white glass instead of those deeply colored panes which caused the astonished eyes of our ancestors to pause between the rose of the great porch and the pointed arches of the chancel? What would a subchorister of the sixteenth century say on beholding the yellow plaster with which our Vandal archbishops have bedaubed their cathedral? He would recollect that this was the color with which the executioner washed over the houses of criminals; he would recollect the hotel of the Petit Bourbon, thus beplastered with yellow on account of the treason of the constable, "and a yellow of so good quality," saith Sauval, "and so well laid on, that more than a century hath not yet faded its color;" he would imagine that the sacred fane has become infamous, and flee from it as fast as he could.

And if we go up into the cathedral without pausing over the thousand barbarisms of all kinds, what has been done with that charming little belfry which stood over the point of intersection of the transept, and which, neither less light nor less bold than its neighbor, the steeple of the Holy Chapel (likewise destroyed), rose, light, elegant, and sonorous, into the air, overtopping the towers? It was amputated (1787) by an architect of taste, who deemed it sufficient to cover the wound with that large plaster of lead, which looks, for all the world, like the lid of a saucepan.

It is thus that the wonderful art of the Middle Ages has been treated in almost every country, especially in France. In its ruins we may distinguish three kinds of injuries, which have affected it in different degrees: in the first place Time, which has here and there chapped and everywhere worn its surface; in the next, revolutions, political and religious, which, blind and furious by nature, have rushed tumultuously upon it, stripped it of its rich garb of sculptures and carvings, broken its open-work and its chains of arabesques and fanciful figures, torn down its statues, sometimes on account of their miters, at others on account of their crowns; lastly, the fashions, more and more silly and grotesque, which since the splendid deviations of the regeneration have succeeded each other in the necessary decline of architecture. The fashions have in fact done more mischief than revolutions. They have cut into the quick; they have attacked the osseous system of the art; they have hacked, hewn, mangled, murdered, the building, in the form as well as in the symbol, in its logic not less than in its beauty. And then they have renewed—a presumption from which at least time and revolutions have been exempt. In the name of good taste, forsooth, they have impudently clapped upon the wounds of Gothic architecture their paltry gewgaws of a day, their ribbons of marble, their pompons of metal, a downright leprosy of eggs, volutes, spirals, draperies, garlands, fringes, flames of stone, clouds of bronze, plethoric cupids, chubby cherubs, which begins to eat into the face of art in the oratory of Catherine de Medicis, and puts it to death two centuries later, writhing and grinning in the boudoir of the Dubarry.

Thus, to sum up the points to which we have directed attention, three kinds of ravages nowadays disfigure Gothic architecture: wrinkles and warts on the epidermis—these are the work of time; wounds, contusions, fractures, from brutal violence—these are the work of revolutions from Luther to Mirabeau; mutilations, amputations, dislocations of members, restorations—this is the barbarous Greek and Roman work of professors, according to Vitruvius and Vignole. That magnificent art which the Vandals produced academies have murdered. With Time and revolution, whose ravages are at any rate marked by impartiality and grandeur, has been associated a host of architects, duly bred, duly patented, and duly sworn, despoiling with the discernment of bad taste, substituting the chicories of Louis XV. to the Gothic lace-work, for the greater glory of the Parthenon. This is truly the ass's kick to the expiring lion; the old oak throwing out its leafy crown, to be bitten, gnawed, and torn by caterpillars.

How widely different this from the period when Robert Cenalis, comparing Notre Dame at Paris with the famous temple of Diana at Ephesus, "so highly extolled by the ancient heathen," pronounced the Gallican cathedral "more excellent in length, breadth, height, and structure."

Notre Dame, however, is not what may be called a complete building, nor does it belong to any definite class. It is not a Roman church, neither is it a Gothic church. Notre Dame has not, the Abbey of Tournus, the heavy, massive squareness, the cold nakedness, the majestic simplicity of edifices which have the circular arch for their generative principle. It is not, like the Cathedral of Bourges, the magnificent, light, multiform, efflorescent, highly-decorated production of the pointed arch. It cannot be classed among that ancient family of churches, gloomy, mysterious, low, and crushed as it were by the circular arch; quite hieroglyphic, sacerdotal, symbolical; exhibiting in their decorations more lozenges and zigzags than flowers, more flowers than animals, more animals than human figures; the work not so much of the architect as of the bishop; the first transformation of the art, impressed all over with theocratic and military discipline, commencing in the Lower Empire and terminating with William the Conqueror. Neither can our cathedral be placed in that other family of churches, light, lofty, rich in painted glass and sculptures; sharp in form, bold in attitude; free, capricious, unruly, as works of art; the second transformation of architecture, no longer hieroglyphic, unchangeable, and sacerdotal, but artistical, progressive, and popular, beginning with the return from the Crusades and ending with Louis XI. Notre Dame is not of pure Roman extraction, like the former, neither is it of pure Arab extraction, like the latter.

It is a transition edifice. The Saxon architect had set up the first pillars of the nave, when the pointed style, brought back from the Crusades, seated itself like a conqueror upon those broad Roman capitals designed to support circular arches only. The pointed style, henceforward mistress, constructed the rest of the church; but, unpracticed and timid at its outset, it displays a breadth, a flatness, and dares not yet shoot up into steeples and pinnacles, as it has since done in so many wonderful cathedrals. You would say that it is affected by the vicinity of the heavy Roman pillars.

For the rest, those edifices of the transition from the Roman to the Gothic style are not less valuable as studies than the pure types of either. They express a shade of the art which would be lost but for them—the ingrafting of the pointed upon the circular style.

Notre Dame at Paris is a particularly curious specimen of this variety. Every face, every stone of the venerable structure is a page not only of the history of the country, but also of the history of art and science. Thus, to glance merely at the principal details, while the little Porte Rouge attains almost to the limits of the Gothic delicacy of the fifteenth century, the pillars of the nave, by their bulk and heaviness, carry you back to the date of the Carlovingian Abbey of St. Germain des Pres. You would imagine that there were six centuries between that doorway and those pillars. There are none, down to the alchemists themselves, but find in the symbols of the grand porch a satisfactory compendium of their science, of which the Church of St. Jacques de la Boucherie was so complete a hieroglyphic. Thus the Roman abbey and the philosophical church, Gothic art and Saxon art, the heavy round pillar, which reminds you of Gregory VII., papal unity and schism, St. Germain des Pres, and St. Jacques de la Boucherie—are all blended, combined, amalgamated in Notre Dame. This central mother-church is a sort of chimera among the ancient churches of Paris; it has the head of one, the limbs of another, the trunk of a third, and something of them all.

These hybrid structures, as we have observed, are not the less interesting to the artist, the antiquary, and the historian. They show how far architecture is a primitive art, inasmuch as they demonstrate (what is also demonstrated by the Cyclopean remains, the pyramids of Egypt, the gigantic Hindoo pagodas) that the grandest productions of architecture are not so much individual as social works, rather the offspring of nations in labor than the inventions of genius; the deposit left by a people; the accumulations formed by ages; the residuum of the successive evaporations of human society—in short, a species of formations. Every wave of time superinduces its alluvion, every generation deposits its stratum upon the structure, every individual brings his stone. Such is the process of the beavers, such that of the bees, such that of men. The great emblem of architecture, Babel, is a bee-hive.

Great edifices, like great mountains, are the work of ages. It is frequently the case that art changes while they are still in progress. The new art takes the structure as it finds it, incrusts upon it, assimilates itself to it, proceeds with it according to its own fancy, and completes it if it can. The thing is accomplished without disturbance, without effort, without reaction, agreeably to a natural and quiet law. Certes, there is matter for very thick books, and often for the universal history of mankind, in those successive inoculations of various styles at various heights upon the same structure. The man, the artist, the individual, are lost in these vast masses without any author's name, while human skill is condensed and concentrated in them. Time is the architect, the nation is the mason.

To confine our view here to Christian European architecture, that younger sister of the grand style of the East, it appears to us like an immense formation divided into three totally distinct zones laid upon another: the Roman[1] zone, the Gothic zone, and the zone of the revival, which we would fain call the Greco-Roman. The Roman stratum, which is the most ancient and the lowest, is occupied by the circular arch, which again appears, supported by the Greek column, in the modern and uppermost stratum of the revival. The

1. This is the same that is likewise called, according to countries, climates, and species, Lombard, Saxon, and Byzantine. These four are parallel and kindred varieties, each having its peculiar character, but all derived from the same principle—the circular arch.

pointed style is between both. The edifices belonging exclusively to one of these three strata are absolutely distinct, one, and complete. Such are the Abbey of Jumieges, the Cathedral of Rheims, the Holy Cross at Orleans. But the three zones blend and amalgamate at their borders, like the colors of the solar spectrum. Hence the complex structures, the transition edifices. The one is Roman at the foot, Gothic in the middle, Greco-Roman at the top. The reason is that it was six centuries in building. This variety is rare; the Castle of Etampes is a specimen of it. But the edifices composed of two formations are frequent. Such as Notre Dame at Paris, a building in the pointed style, the first pillars of which belong to the Roman zone, like the porch of St. Denis, and the nave of St. Germain des Pres. Such too is the charming semi-Gothic capitular hall of Bocherville, exhibiting the Roman stratum up to half its height. Such is the Cathedral of Rouen, which would be entirely Gothic were it not for the extremity of its central steeple, which penetrates into the zone of the revival.[1]

For the rest, all these shades, all these differences affect only the surface of edifices; it is but art which has changed its skin. The constitution itself of the Christian Church is not affected by them. There is always the same internal arrangement, the same logical disposition of parts. Be the sculptured and embroidered outside of a cathedral what it may, we invariably find underneath at least the germ and rudiment of the Roman basilica. It uniformly expands itself upon the ground according to the same law. There are without deviation two naves, intersecting each other in the form of a cross, the upper extremity of which, rounded into an apsis, forms the chancel; and two aisles for processions and for chapels, a sort of lateral walking-places into which the principal nave disgorges itself by the intercolumniations. These points being settled, the number of chapels, porches, towers, pinnacles is varied to infinity, according to the caprice of the age, the nation, and the art. Accommodation for the exercises of religion once provided and secured, architecture does just what it pleases. As for statues, painted windows, mullions, arabesques, open-work, capitals, basso-relievos —it combines all these devices agreeably to the system which best suits itself. Hence the prodigious external variety of those edifices within which reside such order and unity. The trunk of the tree is unchangeable, the foliage capricious.

1. It was precisely this part of the steeple, which was of wood, that was destroyed by the fire of heaven in 1823.

CHAPTER II

BIRD'S-EYE VIEW OF PARIS

WE HAVE just attempted to repair for the reader the admirable Church of Notre Dame at Paris. We have briefly touched upon most of the beauties which it had in the fifteenth century, and which it no longer possesses; but we have omitted the principal, namely, the view of Paris then enjoyed from the top of the towers.

It was in fact when, after groping your way up the dark spiral staircase with which the thick wall of the towers is perpendicularly perforated, and landing abruptly on one of the two lofty platforms deluged with light and air, that a delightful spectacle bursts at once upon the view—a spectacle *sui generis*, of which some conception may easily be formed by such of our readers as have had the good fortune to see one of the few Gothic towns still left entire, complete, homogeneous, such as Nuremberg in Bavaria, Vittoria in Spain, or even smaller specimens, provided they are in good preservation, as Vitre in Bretagne, and Nordhausen in Prussia.

The Paris of three hundred and fifty years ago, the Paris of the fifteenth century, was already a gigantic city. We modern Parisians in general are much mistaken in regard to the ground which we imagine it has gained. Since the time of Louis XI. Paris has not increased above one third; and certes it has lost much more in beauty than it has acquired in magnitude.

The infant Paris was born, as everybody knows, in that ancient island in the shape of a cradle, which is now called the City. The banks of that island were its first inclosure; the Seine was its first ditch. For several centuries Paris was confined to the island, having two bridges, the one on the north, the other on the south, the two *têtes-de-ponts*, which were at once its gates and its fortresses—the Grand Chatelet on the right bank and the Petit Chatelet on the left. In process of time, under the kings of the first dynasty, finding herself straitened in her island and unable to turn herself about, she crossed the water. A first inclosure of walls and towers then began to encroach upon either bank of the Seine beyond the two Chatelets. Of this ancient inclosure some vestiges were still remaining in the past century; nothing is now left of it but the memory and here and there a tradition. By degrees the flood of houses, always propelled from the heart to the extremities, wore away and overflowed this inclosure. Philip Augustus surrounded Paris with new ramparts. He imprisoned the city within a circular chain of large, lofty, and massive towers. For more than a century the houses, crowding closer and closer, raised their level in this basin, like water in a reservoir. They began to grow higher; story was piled upon story; they shot up like any compressed liquid, and each tried to lift its head above its neighbors in order to obtain a little fresh air. The streets became deeper and deeper, and narrower and narrower; every vacant place was covered and disappeared. The houses at length overleaped the wall of Philip Augustus, and merrily scattered themselves at random over the plain, like prisoners who had made their escape. There they sat themselves down at their ease and carved themselves gardens out of the fields. So early as 1367 the suburbs of the city had spread so far as to need a fresh inclosure, especially on the right bank; this was built for it by Charles V. But a place like Paris is perpetually increasing. It is such cities alone that become capitals of countries. They are reservoirs into which all the geographical, political, moral, and intellectual channels of a country, all the natural inclined planes of its population, discharge themselves; wells of civilization, if we may be allowed the expression, and drains also, where all that constitutes the sap, the life, the soul of the nation, is incessantly collecting and filtering, drop by drop, age by age. The inclosure of Charles V. consequently shared the same fate as that of Philip Augustus. So early as the conclusion of the fifteenth century it was overtaken, passed, and the suburbs kept traveling onward. In the sixteenth, it seemed very visibly receding more and more into the ancient city, so rapidly did the new town thicken on the other side of it. Thus, so far back as the fifteenth century, to come down no further, Paris had already worn out the three concentric circles of walls which, from the time of Julian the Apostate, lay in embryo, if I may be allowed the expression, in the Grand and Petit Chatelets. The mighty city had successively burst its four mural belts, like a growing boy bursting the garments made for him a year ago. Under Louis XI. there were still to be seen ruined towers of the ancient inclosures, rising at intervals above the sea of houses, like the tops of hills from amid an inundation, like the archipelagos of old Paris submerged beneath the new.

Since that time Paris has, unluckily for us, undergone further transformation, but it has overleaped only one more inclosure, that of Louis XV., a miserable wall of mud and dirt, worthy of the king who constructed it and the poet by whom it was celebrated:

"Le mur murant Paris rend Paris murmurant."

In the fifteenth century Paris was still divided into three totally distinct and separate cities, each having its own physiognomy, individuality, manners, customs, privileges, and history:—the City, the University, and the Ville. The City, which occupied the island, was the mother of the two others, and cooped up between them, like— reader, forgive the comparison—like a little old woman between two handsome strapping daughters. The University covered the left bank of the Seine from the Tournelle to the Tower of Nesle, points corresponding the one with the Halle aux Vins, and the other with the Mint of modern Paris. Its inclosure encroached considerably upon the plain where Julian had built his baths. It included the Hill of St. Genevieve. The highest point of this curve of walls was the Papal Gate, which stood nearly upon the site of the present Pantheon. The Ville, the most extensive of the three divisions, stretched along the right bank. Its quay ran with several interruptions along the Seine, from the Tower of Billy to the Tower du Bois, that is to say, from the spot where the Grenier d'Abondance now stands to that occupied by the Tuileries. These four points, at which the Seine intersected the inclosure of the capital, the Tournelle and the Tower of Nesle on the left, and the Tower of Billy and the Tower du Bois on the right, were called by way of eminence "the four towers of Paris." The Ville penetrated still further into the fields than the University. The culminating point of the inclosure of the Ville was at the gates of St. Denis and St. Martin, the sites of which remain unchanged to this day.

Each of these great divisions of Paris was, as we have observed, a city, but a city too special to be complete, a city which could not do without the two others. Thus they had three totally different aspects. The City, properly so called, abounded in churches; the Ville contained the palaces; and the University, the colleges. Setting aside secondary jurisdictions, we may assume generally that the island was under the bishop, the right bank under the provost of the merchants, the left under the rector of the University, and the whole under the Provost of Paris, a royal and not a municipal officer. The City had the Cathedral of Notre Dame, the Ville the Louvre and the Hotel de Ville, and the University the Sorbonne. The Ville contained the Halles, the City the Hotel Dieu, and the University the Pre aux Clercs. For offenses committed by the stu-

dents on the left bank, in their Pre aux Clercs, they were tried at
the Palace of Justice in the island, and punished on the right bank
at Montfaucon, unless the rector, finding the University strong and
the king weak, chose to interfere; for it was a privilege of the scholars to be hung in their own quarter.

Most of these privileges, be it remarked by the way, and some of
them were more valuable than that just mentioned, had been ex-
torted from different sovereigns by riots and insurrections. This is
the invariable course—the king never grants any boon but what is
wrung from him by the people.

In the fifteenth century that part of the Seine comprehended
within the inclosure of Paris contained five islands: the Ile Louviers,
then covered with trees and now with timber, the Ile aux Vaches,
and the Isle Notre Dame, both uninhabited and belonging to the
bishop [in the seventeenth century these two islands were converted into one, which has been built upon and is now called the
Isle of St. Louis]; lastly the City, and at its point the islet of the
Passeur aux Vaches, since buried under the platform of the Pont
Neuf. The City had at that time five bridges: three on the right;
the bridge of Notre Dame and the Pont au Change of stone, and the
Pont aux Meuniers of wood; two on the left, the Petit Pont of stone,
and the Pont St. Michel of wood; all of them covered with houses.
The University had six gates, built by Philip Augustus; these were,
setting out from the Tournelle, the Gate of St. Victor, the Gate of
Bordelle, the Papal Gate, and the gates of St. Jacques, St. Michel,
and St. Germain. The Ville had six gates, built by Charles V., that
is to say, beginning from the Tower of Billy, the gates of St. Antoine,
the Temple, St. Martin, St. Denis, Montmartre, and St. Honore. All
these gates were strong, and handsome, too, a circumstance which
does not detract from strength. A wide, deep ditch, supplied by the
Seine with water, which was swollen by the floods of winter to a running stream, encircled the foot of the wall all round Paris. At night
the gates were closed, the river was barred at the two extremities of
the city by stout iron chains, and Paris slept in quiet.

A bird's-eye view of these three towns, the City, the University,
and the Ville, exhibited to the eye an inextricable knot of streets
strangely jumbled together. It was apparent, however, at first sight
that these three fragments of a city formed but a single body. The
spectator perceived immediately two long parallel streets, without
break or interruption, crossing the three cities, nearly in a right line,
from one end to the other, from south to north, perpendicularly to
the Seine, incessantly pouring the people of the one into the other,

connecting, blending them together and converting the three into one. The first of these streets ran from the Gate of St. Jacques to the Gate of St. Martin; it was called in the University the street of St. Jacques, in the City Rue de la Juiverie, and in the Ville, the street of St. Martin; it crossed the river twice by the name of Petit Pont and Pont Notre Dame. The second, named Rue de la Harpe on the left bank, Rue de la Barillerie in the island, Rue St. Denis on the right bank, Pont St. Michel over one arm of the Seine, and Pont au Change over the other, ran from the Gate of St. Michel in the University to the Gate of St. Denis in the Ville. Still, though they bore so many different names, they formed in reality only two streets, but the two mother-streets, the two great arteries of Paris. All the other veins of the triple city were fed by or discharged themselves into these.

Besides these two principal diametrical streets crossing Paris breadthwise, and common to the entire capital, the Ville and the University had each its chief street running longitudinally parallel with the Seine, and its course intersecting the two arterial streets at right angles. Thus in the Ville you might go in a direct line from the Gate of St. Antoine to the Gate of St. Honore; and in the University from the Gate of St. Victor to the Gate of St. Germain. These two great thoroughfares, crossed by the former, constituted the frame upon which rested the mazy web of the streets of Paris, knotted and jumbled together in every possible way. In the unintelligible plan of this labyrinth might moreover be distinguished on closer examination, two clusters of wide streets, which ran, expanding like sheaves of corn, from the bridges to the gates. Somewhat of this geometrical plan subsists to this day.

What, then, was the aspect of this whole, viewed from the summit of the towers of Notre Dame in 1482? That is what we shall now attempt to describe. The spectator, on arriving breathless at that elevation, was dazzled by the chaos of roofs, chimneys, streets, bridges, belfries, towers, and steeples. All burst at once upon the eye—the carved gable, the sharp roof, the turret perched upon the angles of the walls, the stone pyramids of the eleventh century, the slated obelisk of the fifteenth, the round and naked keep of the castle, the square and embroidered tower of the church, the great and the small, the massive and the light. The eye was long bewildered amid this labyrinth of heights and depths in which there was nothing but had its originality, its reason, its genius, its beauty, nothing but issued from the hand of art, from the humblest dwelling with its painted and carved wooden front, elliptical doorway, and overhanging stories, to the royal Louvre, which then had a colonnade of towers. But when the eye began to reduce this tumult of edifices to some kind of order, the principal masses that stood out from among them were these:

To begin with the City, "The island of the City," says Sauval, who, amid his frivolous gossip, has occasionally some good ideas, "the island of the City is shaped like a great ship which hath taken the ground and is stuck fast in the mud, nearly in the middle of the channel of the Seine." We have already stated that in the fifteenth century this ship was moored to the two banks of the river by five bridges. This resemblance to a vessel had struck the heralds of those times; for it is to this circumstance, and not to the siege of the Normans, that, according to Favyn and Pasquier, the ship blazoned in the ancient arms of Paris owes its origin. To those who can decipher its heraldry is an algebra, a language. The entire history of the second half of the Middle Ages is written in heraldry, as the history of the first half in the imagery of the Roman churches: 'tis but the hieroglyphics of the feudal system succeeding those of theocracy.

The City, then, claimed the first notice, with its stern to the east and its head to the west. Turning toward the latter, you had before you a countless multitude of old roofs, above which rose the widely swelling, lead-covered cupola of the Holy Chapel, like the back of an elephant supporting its tower. In this case, indeed, the place of the tower was occupied by the lightest, the boldest, the most elegant steeple that ever allowed the sky to be seen through its cone of lacework. Just in front of Notre Dame, three streets disgorged themselves into the Parvis, a handsome square of old houses. On the south side of this square was the Hotel Dieu, with its grim, wrinkled, overhanging front, and its roof which seemed to be covered with warts and pimples. Then to the right and to the left, to the east and to the west, within the narrow compass of the City, rose the steeples of its twenty-one churches of all dates, of all forms, of all dimensions, from the low and crazy Roman campanile of St. Denis du Pas to the slender spires of St. Pierre aux Bœufs and St. Landry. Behind Notre Dame, to the north, the cloisters unfolded themselves with their Gothic galleries; to the south the semi-Roman palace of the bishop; to the east the open area called the Terrain. Amid this mass of buildings the eye might still distinguish, by the lofty miters of stone which crowned the topmost windows, then placed in the roofs even of palaces themselves, the hotel given by the city in the time of Charles VI. to Juvenal des Ursins; a little further on, the tarred sheds of the market of Palus; beyond that the new choir of St. Germain le Vieux, lengthened in 1458 at the expense of one end of the Rue aux Feves; and then, at intervals, an open space thronged with people; a pillory erected at the corner of a street; a fine piece of the pavement of Philip Augustus, composed of magnificent slabs, channeled for the sake of the horses and laid in the middle of the way; a vacant back court with one of those transparent staircase turrets which were constructed in the fifteenth century, and a specimen of which may still be seen in the Rue de Bourdonnais. Lastly, on the right of the Holy Chapel toward the west, the Palace of Justice was seated, with its group of towers, on the bank of the river. The plantations of the king's gardens, which covered the western point of the City, intercepted the view of the islet of the Passeur. As for the water, it was scarcely to be seen at either end of the City from the towers of Notre Dame; the Seine being concealed by the bridges, the bridges by the houses.

When the eye passed these bridges, whose roofs were green with moss, the effect not so much of age as of damp from the water, if it turned to the left, toward the University, the first building which struck it was a clump of towers, the Petit Chatelet, the yawning gateway of which swallowed up the end of the Petit Pont; then, if it followed the bank of the river from east to west, from the Tournelle to the Tower of Nesle, it perceived a long line of houses with carved beams projecting, story beyond story, over the pavement, an interminable zigzag of tradesmen's houses, frequently broken by the end of a street, and from time to time also by the front or perhaps the angle of some spacious stone mansion, seated at its ease, with its courts and gardens, amid this populace of narrow, closely-crowded dwellings, like a man of consequence among his dependents. There were five or six of these mansions on the quay, from the logis de Lorraine, which divided with the Bernardines the extensive inclosure contiguous to the Tournelle, to the Hotel de Nesle, whose principal tower was the boundary of Paris, and whose pointed roofs for three months of the year eclipsed with their black triangles corresponding portions of the scarlet disk of the setting sun.

On this side of the Seine there was much less traffic than on the other; the students made more noise and bustle there than the artisans, and there was no quay, properly speaking, except from the Bridge of St. Michel to the Tower of Nesle. The rest of the bank of the Seine was in some places a naked strand, as beyond the Bernardines; in others a mass of houses standing on the brink of the water, as between the two bridges.

Great was the din here kept up by the washer-women; they gabbled, shouted, sung, from morning till night, along the bank, and soundly beat their linen, much the same as they do at present. Among the sights of Paris this is by no means the dullest.

The University brought the eye to a full stop. From one end to the other it was a homogeneous, compact whole. Those thousand roofs, close, angular, adhering together, almost all composed of the same geometrical element, seen from above, presented the appearance of a crystallization of one and the same substance. The capricious ravines of the streets did not cut this pie of houses into too disproportionate slices. The forty-two colleges were distributed among them in a sufficiently equal manner. The curious and varied summits of these beautiful buildings were the production of the same art as the simple roofs which they overtopped; in fact, they were but a multiplication by the square or the cube of the same geometrical figure. They diversified the whole, therefore, without confusing it; they completed without overloading it. Geometry is a harmony. Some superb mansions too made here and there magnificent inroads among the picturesque garrets of the left bank; the logis de Nevers, the logis de Rome, the logis de Reims, which have been swept away: the Hotel de Cluny, which still subsists for the consolation of the artist, and the tower of which was so stupidly uncrowned some years ago. That Roman palace with beautiful circular arches, near Cluny, was the baths of Julian. There were likewise many abbeys, of a more severe beauty than the hotels, but neither less handsome nor less spacious. Those which first struck the eye were the Bernardines with their three steeples; St. Genevieve, the square tower of which, still extant, excites such regret for the loss of the rest; the Sorbonne, half college, half monastery, an admirable nave of which still survives; the beautiful quadrangular cloister of the Mathurins; its neighbor, the cloister of St. Benedict; the Cordeliers, with their three enormous gables, side by side, and the Augustines, the graceful steeple of which made the second indentation (the Tower of Nesle being the first) on this side of Paris, setting out from the west. The colleges, which are in fact the intermediate link between the cloister and the world, formed the mean, in the series of buildings, between the mansions and the abbeys, with an austerity full of elegance, a sculpture less gaudy than that of the palaces, an architecture less serious than that of the convents. Unfortunately, scarcely any vestiges are left of these edifices, in which Gothic art steered with such precision a middle course between luxury and economy. The churches—and they were both numerous and splendid in the University, and of every age of architecture, from the circular arches of St. Julian to the pointed ones of St. Severin—the churches overtopped all; and like an additional harmony in this mass of harmonies, they shot up every instant above the slashed gables, the open-work pinnacles and belfries, and the airy spires, the line of which also was but a magnificent exaggeration of the acute angle of the roofs.

The site of the University was hilly. To the southeast the Hill of St. Genevieve formed an enormous wen; and it was a curious sight to see from the top of Notre Dame that multitude of narrow, winding streets, now called *Le Pays Latin*, those clusters of houses which, scattered in all directions from the summit of that eminence, confusedly covered its sides down to the water's edge, seeming some of them to be falling, others to be climbing up again, and all to be holding fast by one another. An incessant stream of thousands of black specks crossing each other on the pavement caused everything to appear in motion to the eye; these were the people diminished by distance and the elevated station of the spectator.

Lastly, in the intervals between those roofs, those spires, and those numberless peculiarities of buildings, which waved, notched, twisted the outline of the University in so whimsical a manner, were to be seen, here and there, the mossy fragment of a massive wall, a solid round tower, an embattled gateway, belonging to the inclosure of Philip Augustus. Beyond these were the green fields and high roads, along which were a few straggling houses, which became thinner and thinner in the distance. Some of these suburban hamlets were already places of consequence. Setting out from La Tournelle, there was first the bourg St. Victor, with its bridge of one arch over the Bievre, its abbey, where was to be seen the epitaph of Louis le Gros, and its church with an octagon steeple flanked by four belfries of the eleventh century; then the bourg St. Marceau which had already three churches and a convent; then leaving the mill of the Gobelins and its four white walls on the left, there was the faubourg St. Jacques du Haut Pas, a charming pointed Gothic structure; St. Magloire, a beautiful nave of the fourteenth century, converted by Napoleon into a magazine for hay; Notre Dame des Champs, containing Byzantine mosaics. Lastly, after leaving in the open country the Carthusian convent, a rich structure contemporary with the Palace of Justice, and the ruins of Vauvert, the haunt of dangerous persons, the eye fell, to the west, upon the three Roman pinnacles of St. Germain des Pres. The village of St. Germain, already a large parish, was composed of fifteen or twenty streets in the rear; the sharp spire of St. Sulpice marked one of the

corners of the bourg. Close to it might be distinguished the quadrangular inclosure of the Fair of St. Germain, the site of the present
market; next, the pillory of the abbey, a pretty little circular tower
well covered with a cone of lead; the tile-kiln was further off, so
were the Rue du Four, which led to the manorial oven, the mill, and
the hospital for lepers, a small detached building but indistinctly
seen. But what particularly attracted attention and fixed it for some
time on this point, was the abbey itself. It is certain that this monastery, which had an air of importance both as a church and as a
lordly residence, this abbatial palace, where the bishops of Paris
deemed themselves fortunate to be entertained for a night, that
refectory to which the architect had given the air, the beauty, and
the splendid window of a cathedral, that elegant chapel of the Virgin, that noble dormitory, those spacious gardens, that portcullis,
that draw-bridge, that girdle of battlements cut out to the eye upon
the greensward of the surrounding fields, those courts where men-
at-arms glistened among copes of gold—the whole collected and
grouped around three lofty spires with circular arches, firmly seated
upon a Gothic choir, formed a magnificent object against the
horizon.

When, at length, after attentively surveying the University, you
turn to the right bank, to the Ville, the character of the scene suddenly changes. The Ville, in fact, much more extensive than the
University, was also less compact. At the first sight you perceived
that it was composed of several masses remarkably distinct. In the
first place, to the east, in that part of the town which is still named
after the marsh into which Cæsar was enticed by Camulogenes,
there was a series of palaces. Four nearly contiguous mansions, the
hotels of Jouy, Sens, Barbeau, and the Queen's House, mirrored
their slated roofs, diversified with slender turrets, in the waters of
the Seine. Those four buildings filled the space between the Rue des
Nonaindières, and the Abbey of the Celestins, the spire of which
gracefully relieved their line of gables and battlements. Some
greenish walls upon the water's edge, in front of these buildings,
did not prevent the eye from catching the beautiful angles of their
fronts, their large quadrangular windows with stone frames and
transoms, the pointed arches of their porches, surcharged with statues, and all those charming freaks of architecture which give to
the Gothic art the air of resorting to fresh combinations in every
building. In the rear of these palaces ran, in all directions, sometimes palisaded and embattled like a castle, sometimes embowered
in great trees like a Carthusian convent, the immense and multiform

inclosure of that marvelous hotel of St. Pol, where the King of France had superb accommodation for twenty-two princes equal in rank to the dauphin and the Duke of Burgundy, with their attendants and retinues, without reckoning distinguished nobles, or the emperor, when he visited Paris, or the lions which had their hotel apart from the royal habitation. Be it here remarked that the apartments of a prince in those days consisted of not fewer than eleven rooms, from the hall of parade to the oratory, exclusive of galleries, and baths, and stoves, and other "superfluous places" attached to each set of apartments; to say nothing of the private gardens of each of the king's guests; of the kitchens, the cellars, the servants' rooms, the general refectories of the household; of the offices, where there were twenty-two general laboratories, from the bake-house to the wine-cellar; of places appropriated to games of every sort, the mall, tennis, the ring; of aviaries, fish-ponds, menageries, stables, libraries, arsenals, foundries. Such was then the palace of a king, a Louvre, a hotel St. Pol. It was a city within a city.

From the tower where we have taken our station, the hotel of St. Pol, though almost half concealed by the four great buildings above mentioned, was still a right goodly sight. The three hotels which Charles V. had incorporated with his palace, though skillfully united to the principal building by long galleries with windows and small pillars, might be perfectly distinguished. These were the hotel of the Petit Muce, with the light balustrade which gracefully bordered its roof; the hotel of the Abbot of St. Maur, having the appearance of a castle, a strong tower, portcullises, loop-holes, bastions, and over the large Saxon doorway the escutcheon of the abbot; the hotel of the Count d'Etampes, the keep of which, in ruin at the top, appeared jagged to the eye, like the comb of a cock; clumps of old oaks here and there forming tufts like enormous cauliflowers; swans disporting in the clear waters of the fish-ponds, all streaked with light and shade; the dwelling of the lions with its low pointed arches supported by short Saxon pillars, its iron grating, and its perpetual bellowing; beyond all these the scaly spire of the Ave Maria; on the left the residence of the Provost of Paris, flanked by four turrets of delicate workmanship; at the bottom, in the center, the hotel of St. Pol, properly so called, with its numerous façades, its successive embellishments from the time of Charles V., the hybrid excrescences with which the whims of architects had loaded it in the course of two centuries, with all the apsides of its chapels, all the gables of its galleries, a thousand weather-cocks marking the four winds, and its two lofty contiguous towers, whose conical roofs, surrounded at their base with battlements, looked like sharp-pointed hats, with the brims turned up.

Continuing to ascend that amphitheater of palaces spread out far over the ground, after crossing a deep ravine parting the roofs of the Ville, the eye arrived at the Logis d'Angouleme, a vast pile erected at various periods, parts of which were quite new and white, and harmonized no better with the whole than a red patch upon a blue doublet. At the same time the remarkably sharp and elevated roof of the modern palace, covered with lead, upon which glistened incrustations of gilt copper, rolled themselves in a thousand fantastic arabesques, that roof so curiously damasked, gracefully lifted itself from amid the imbrowned ruins of an ancient building, whose old clumsy towers, bellying like casks, and cracked from top to bottom, were ready to tumble to pieces with age. In the rear rose the forest of spires of the palace of the Tournelles. There was not a view in the world, not excepting Chambord or the Alhambra, more aerial, more impressive, more magical, than this wood of pinnacles, belfries, chimneys, weather-cocks, spirals, screws, lanterns, perforated as if they had been struck by a nipping-tool, pavilions and turrets, all differing in form, height, and altitude. You would have taken it for an immense chess-board of stone.

To the right of the Tournelles that cluster of enormous towers, black as ink, running one into another, and bound together, as it were, by a circular ditch; that keep containing many more loopholes than windows; that draw-bridge always up, that portcullis always down—that is the Bastile. Those black muzzles protruding between the battlements, and which you take at a distance for gutters, are cannon.

At the foot of the formidable edifice, just under its guns, is the Gate of St. Antoine, hidden between its two towers.

Beyond the Tournelles, as far as the wall of Charles V. were spread out the royal parks, diversified with rich patches of verdure and flowers, amid which might be recognized by its labyrinth of trees and alleys the famous garden which Louis XI. gave to Coictier. The doctor's observatory rose above the maze in the form of a detached massive column, having a small room for its capital. In this laboratory were concocted terrible astrological predictions. The site of it is now occupied by the Place Royale.

As we have already observed, the quarter of the palace of which we have endeavored to give the reader some idea, filled the angle which the wall of Charles V. formed with the Seine to the east. The center of the Ville was occupied by a heap of houses of the inferior class. Here in fact the three bridges of the City disgorged themselves on the right bank, and bridges make houses before palaces. This accumulation of dwellings of tradesmen and artisans, jammed together like cells in a hive, had its beauty. There is something grand in the houses of a capital as in the waves of the sea. In the first place, the streets, crossing and intwining, formed a hundred amusing figures; the environs of the Halles looked like a star with a thousand rays. The streets of St. Denis and St. Martin, with their numberless ramifications, ran up one beside the other, like two thick trees intermingling their branches; and then the streets of la Platerie, la Verrerie, and la Tixeranderie, wound over the whole. There were some handsome buildings that overtopped the petrified undulation of this sea of roofs. At the head of the Pont aux Changeurs, behind which the Seine was seen foaming under the wheels of the Pont aux Meuniers, there was the Chatelet, no longer a Roman castle, as in the time of Julian the Apostate, but a feudal castle of the thirteenth century, and of stone so hard that in three hours the pick-ax could not chip off a piece larger than your fist. There too was the rich square tower of St. Jacques de la Boucherie, with its angles all blunted by sculptures, and already an object of admiration, though it was not finished till the fifteenth century. It had not then those four monsters which, perched to this day at the corners of the roof, look like four sphinxes, giving to modern Paris the enigma of the ancient to unravel. They were not erected till the year 1526 by Rault, the sculptor, who had twenty francs for his labor. There was the Maison aux Piliers, of which we have conveyed some idea to the reader; there was St. Gervais, since spoiled by a porch in a good taste; there was St. Mery, whose old pointed arches were little less than circular; there was St. Jean, the magnificent spire of which was proverbial; there were twenty other buildings which did not disdain to bury their marvels in this chaos of deep, black, narrow streets. Add to these the sculptured stone crosses, more numerous even than the gibbets, the burying-ground of the Innocents, the architectural inclosure of which was to be seen at a distance above the roofs; the pillory of the Halles, the top of which was perceptible between two chimneys of the Rue de la Cossenerie; the ladder of the Croix du Trahoir, in its crossing always black with people; the circular walls of the Halle au Blé; the remains of the ancient inclosure of Philip Augustus, to be distinguished here and there, drowned by the houses, towers overgrown with ivy, gates in ruins, crumbling and shapeless fragments of wall; the quay, with its thou-

sand shops and its bloody slaughter-houses; the Seine covered with
craft, from the Port au Foin to the Port l'Evêque, and you will have
a faint image of the central trapezium of the Ville as it was in 1482.

Besides these two quarters, the one of palaces, the other of
houses, the Ville presents a third feature—a long zone of abbeys,
which bordered almost its whole circumference from east to west,
and formed a second inclosure of convents and chapels within that
of the fortifications which encompassed Paris. Thus, immediately adjoining to the park of Tournelles, between the street St. Antoine
and the old street of the Temple, there was St. Catherine's with its
immense extent of gardens and cultivated grounds, which were
bordered only by the wall of Paris. Between the old and the new
street of the Temple there was the Temple, a grim, tall cluster of
gloomy towers, standing in the center of a vast embattled inclosure.
Between the new street of the Temple and the street St. Martin was
the abbey St. Martin, amid its gardens—a superb fortified church,
whose girdle of towers and tiara of steeples were surpassed in
strength and splendor by St. Germain des Pres alone. Between the
streets of St. Martin and St. Denis was the inclosure of the Trinity;
and lastly, between the streets of St. Denis and Montorgueil, the
Filles Dieu. Besides the latter were to be seen the tumbling roofs
and the unpaved area of the Cour des Miracles. It was the only
profane link that intruded itself into this chain of convents.

The fourth and last compartment, which was sufficiently obvious
of itself in the agglomeration of buildings on the right bank which
occupied the western angle of the inclosure and covered the margin
of the river, was a new knot of palaces and mansions that had
sprung up at the foot of the Louvre. The old Louvre of Philip Augustus, that immense building, whose great tower rallied around it
twenty-three other towers, without reckoning turrets, appeared at a
distance to be incased in the Gothic summits of the hotel of Alençon
and of the Petit Bourbon. That hydra of towers, the giant guardian
of Paris, with its twenty-four heads ever erect, with its monstrous
ridges, cased in lead or scaled with slate, and glistening all over
with the reflection of metals, terminated in a striking manner the
configuration of the Ville to the west.

Thus, an immense island, as the Romans termed it, of common
houses, flanked on the right and left by clusters of palaces, crowned,
the one by the Louvre, the other by the Tournelles, begirt on the
north by a long belt of abbeys and cultivated inclosures, the whole
blended and amalgamated to the eye; above these thousands of
buildings whose tiled and slated roofs formed so many strange

chains, the tattooed, figured, carved steeples and spires of the forty-four churches of the right bank; myriads of streets running in all directions, bounded on one hand by a high wall with square towers (the wall of the University had circular towers); on the other side by the Seine, intersected by bridges and studded with craft—such was the Ville in the fifteenth century.

Beyond the walls there were suburbs crowding about the gates, but the houses composing them were less numerous and more scattered than in those belonging to the University. In the rear of the Bastile there were a score of huts grouped about the Cross of Faubin, with its curious sculptures, and the Abbey of St. Antoine des Champs, with its flying buttresses; then Popincourt, lost in the corn-fields; then la Courtille, a jovial hamlet of pot-houses; the bourg St. Laurent, with its church, whose steeple seemed at a distance to belong to the Gate of St. Martin, with its pointed towers; the faubourg St. Denis, with the vast inclosure of St. Ladre; beyond the Gate of Montmartre, la Grange Bateliere, belted with white walls; behind it, with its chalky declivities, Montmartre, which had then almost as many churches as windmills, but has retained the mills only; for the material bread is nowadays in more request than the spiritual. Lastly, beyond the Louvre were seen the faubourg of St. Honore, already a very considerable place, stretching away into the fields, la Petit Bretagne embosomed in wood, and the Marche aux Porceaux, in the center of which stood the horrible caldron for boiling the coiners of counterfeit money. Between la Courtille and St. Laurent your eye has already remarked, on the summit of a height squatted upon the desert plains, a kind of building resembling at a distance a colonnade in ruins. This was neither a Parthenon nor a temple of the Olympian Jupiter—it was Montfauçon.

Now, if the enumeration of so many edifices, concise as we have purposely made it, has not effaced in the mind of the reader the general image of old Paris as fast as we constructed it, we will compress our description into a few words. In the center, the island of the City resembling in figure an enormous tortoise; its bridges scaly, with slates protruding like feet from beneath the gray shell of roofs. On the left the dense, compact, bristling trapezium of the University; on the right the vast semicircle of the Ville, in which gardens and buildings were much more intermingled. The three divisions, City, University, and Ville, marbled by streets without number: the Seine, the "flourishing Seine," as Father Du Breul calls it, studded with boats and islands and intersected by bridges, running across the whole. All around an immense plain checkered by handsome villages and cultivated lands bearing all sorts of crops; on the left Issy, Vanvres, Vaugirard, Montrouge, Gentilly, with its round tower and its square tower; on the right twenty others, from Conflans to Ville l'Evêque. At the horizon, a border of hills arranged in a circle, like the rim of the basin. Lastly, in the distance to the east, Vincennes and its seven quadrangular towers; to the south, Bicetre and its pointed turrets; to the north, St. Denis and its spire; to the west, St. Cloud and its keep. Such was the Paris seen from the top of the towers of Notre Dame by the ravens living in the year 1482.

The Paris of that time was not merely a handsome city; it was a homogeneous city, an architectural and historical production of the Middle Ages, a chronicle of stone. It was a city formed of two strata only, the bastard Roman and the Gothic, for the pure Roman had long before disappeared, excepting at the baths of Julian, where it still peered above the thick crust of the Middle Ages. As for the Celtic stratum, no specimens of that were now to be found even in digging wells.

Fifty years later, when the regeneration came to blend with this unity so severe and yet so diversified the dazzling luxury of its fantasies and its systems, its extravagancies of Roman arches, Greek columns and Gothic ellipses, its sculpture so delicate and so ideal, its particular style of arabesques and acanthi, its architectural paganism contemporaneous with Luther, Paris was perhaps still more beautiful, though less harmonious to the eye and to the mind. But this splendid moment was of short duration; the regeneration was most impartial; it was not content with building up, it wanted to throw down; it is true enough that it needed room. Thus Gothic Paris was complete but for a minute. Scarcely was St. Jacques de la Boucherie finished when the demolition of the old Louvre was begun.

Since that time the great city has been daily increasing in deformity. The Gothic Paris, which swept away the bastard Roman, has been in its turn swept away; but can any one tell what Paris has succeeded it?

There is the Paris of Catherine de Medicis at the Tuileries; the Paris of Henry II. at the Hotel de Ville—two edifices still in a grand style; the Paris of Henry IV. at the Place Royale—fronts of brick with stone quoins, slated roofs and tri-colored houses; the Paris of Louis XIII. at Val de Grace—a squat, clumsy style, something paunch-bellied in the column and hunchbacked in the dome; the Paris of Louis XIV. at the Invalides—grand, rich, gilded, cold; the

Paris of Louis XV. at St. Sulpice—volutes, knots of ribbons, clouds, vermicellies, chicories, and the Lord knows what, all in stone; the Paris of Louis XVI. at the Pantheon—a wretched copy of St. Peter's at Rome; the Paris of the Republic at the School of Medicine—a poor Greek and Roman style, resembling the Coliseum or the Parthenon as the constitution of the year 3 does the laws of Minos—it is called in architecture the Messidor style; the Paris of Napoleon at the Place Vendôme—this is sublime—a column of bronze made of cannon; the Paris of the Restoration at the Exchange—a very white colonnade supporting a very smooth frieze; the whole is square and cost twenty millions.

With each of these characteristic structures a certain number of houses scattered over the different quarters range themselves by a similarity of style, fashion and attitude; these are easily distinguished by the eye of the connoisseur. Possessing this tact, you discover the spirit of an age and the physiognomy of a king even in the knocker of a door.

The Paris of the present day has no general physiognomy. It is a collection of specimens of various ages, the finest of which have disappeared. The capital increases only in houses, and what houses! At the rate that Paris is now going on, it will be renewed every fifty years. Thus the historical signification of its architecture is daily becoming obliterated. The monuments of past times are becoming more and more rare, and you fancy you see them ingulfed one after another in the deluge of houses. Our fathers had a Paris of stone; our children will have a Paris of plaster.

As for the modern structures of new Paris we would rather abstain from any mention of them. Not but that we admire them quite as much as is fitting. M. Soufflot's St. Genevieve is certainly the most beautiful Savoy cake that ever was made in stone. The Palace of the Legion of Honor is also a most remarkable piece of pastry. The dome of the Halle au Blé is an English jockey-cap on a large scale. The towers of St. Sulpice are two big clarionets, and that is a shape as well as any other; the telegraph, writhing and grinning, forms a charming accession upon their roof. St. Roch has a porch comparable for magnificence to that of St. Thomas Aquinas alone. It has also a Calvary in alto-relievo in a cellar, and a sun of gilt wood. These are absolutely wonderful things. The lantern in the labyrinth of the Jardin des Plantes is also a most ingenious work. As for the Exchange, which is Greek in its colonnade, Roman in the circular arches of its doors and windows, and belongs to the regenerated style in its great elliptic vault—it is indubitably a most pure and classic structure; in proof of which it is crowned by an attic such as was never seen at Athens—a beautiful straight line, gracefully broken here and there by stove-pipes. Add to this that if it is a rule that the architecture of an edifice should be adapted to its destination in such a manner that this destination may be obvious on a mere inspection of the building, we cannot too highly admire a structure which is equally suitable for a king's palace, a house of commons, a town hall, a college, a riding-house, an academy, a warehouse, a court of justice, a museum, a barrack, a sepulcher, a temple, a theater. And after all it is an exchange. A building ought moreover to be adapted to the climate. This is evidently designed expressly for our cold and rainy atmosphere. It has a roof nearly flat, as in the East, so that in winter, after snow, it is necessary to sweep the roof, and it is most certain that a roof is intended to be swept. As for that destination to which we just adverted, it fulfills it marvelously well; in France it is an exchange, in Greece it would have been a temple.

These are no doubt most splendid structures. Add to them a great many handsome streets, amusing and diversified as the Rue de Rivoli, and I despair not that Paris, viewed from a balloon, may some day present to the eye that richness of lines, that luxury of details, that diversity of aspects, a certain combination of the grand with the simple, of the beautiful with the unexpected, which characterizes a draught-board.

Admirable, however, as the Paris of the present day appears to you, build up and put together again in imagination the Paris of the fifteenth century; look at the light through that surprising host of steeples, towers, and belfries; pour forth amid the immense city, break against the points of its islands, compress within the arches of the bridges the current of the Seine, with its large patches of green and yellow, more changeable than a serpent's skin; define clearly the Gothic profile of this old Paris upon a horizon of azure, make its contour float in a wintery fog which clings to its innumerable chimneys; drown it in deep night, and observe the extraordinary play of darkness and light in this somber labyrinth of buildings; throw into it a ray of moonlight, which shall show its faint outline and cause the huge heads of the towers to stand forth from amid the mist; or revert to that dark picture, touch up with shade the thousand acute angles of the spires and gables, and make them stand out, more jagged than a shark's jaw, upon the copper-colored sky of evening. Now compare the two.

And if you would receive from the ancient city an impression which the modern cannot produce, ascend on the morning of some high festival, at sunrise on Easter or Whitsunday, to some elevated point from which you may overlook the whole capital, and listen to the awaking of the bells. Behold at a signal proceeding from heaven, for 'tis the Sun himself that gives it, those thousand churches trembling all at once. At first solitary tinkles pass from church to church, as when musicians give notice that they are going to begin. Then see —for at certain times the ear too seems to be indued with sight—see how, all of a sudden, at the same moment, there rises from each steeple, as it were, a column of sound, a cloud of harmony. At first the vibration of each bell rises straight, pure, and in a manner separate from that of the others, into the splendid morning sky; then, swelling by degrees, they blend, melt, amalgamate into a magnificent concert. It is now but one mass of sonorous vibrations, issuing incessantly from the innumerable steeples, which floats, undulates, bounds, whirls over the city, and expands far beyond the horizon the deafening circle of its oscillations. That sea of harmony, however, is not a chaos. Vast and deep as it is, it has not lost its transparency; you see in it each group of notes that has flown from the belfries, winding along apart; you may follow the dialogue, by turns low and shrill; you may see the octaves skipping from steeple to steeple; you watch them springing light, winged, sonorous from the silver bell; dropping dull, faint, and feeble from the wooden; you admire the rich gamut incessantly running up and down the seven bells of St. Eustache; you see clear and rapid notes dart about in all directions, make three or four luminous zigzags, and vanish like lightning. Down yonder, the Abbey of St. Martin sends forth its harsh, sharp tones; here the Bastile raises its sinister and husky voice; at the other extremity is the great tower of the Louvre, with its counter-tenor. The royal chimes of the palace throw out incessantly on all sides resplendent trills, upon which falls, at measured intervals, the heavy toll from the belfry of Notre Dame, which makes them sparkle like the anvil under the hammer. From time to time you see tones of all shapes, proceeding from the triple peal of St. Germain des Pres, passing before you. Then again, at intervals, this mass of sublime sounds opens and makes way for the *strette* of the Ave Maria, which glistens like an aigrette of stars. Beneath, in the deepest part of the concert, you distinguish confusedly the singing within the churches, which transpires through the vibrating pores of their vaults. Verily this is an opera which is well worth listening to. In an ordinary way, the noise issuing from Paris in the daytime is the talking of the city; at night it is the breathing of the city; in this case it is the singing of the city. Lend your ears then to this *tutti* of steeples; diffuse over the whole the buzz of a million human beings, the eternal murmur of the river, the infinite piping of the wind, the grave and distant quartet of the four forests placed like immense organs on the four hills of the horizon; soften down, as with a demi-tint, all that is too shrill and too harsh in the central mass of sound, and say if you know anything in the world more rich, more gladdening, more dazzling than that tumult of bells; than that furnace of music; than those ten thousand brazen tones breathed all at once from flutes of stone three hundred feet high; than that city which is but one orchestra; than the symphony rushing and roaring like a tempest.

Book Four

CHAPTER I

THE FOUNDLING

SIXTEEN YEARS before the period of the events recorded in this history, one fine morning—it happened to be Quasimodo Sunday—a living creature was laid after mass in the Church of Notre Dame in the wooden bed walled into the porch on the left hand, opposite to that great image of St. Christopher which faced the kneeling figure sculptured in stone of Antoine des Essarts, knight, till 1413, when both saint and sinner were thrown down. On this wooden bed it was customary to expose foundlings to the public charity. Any one took them who felt so disposed. Before the wooden bed was a copper basin to receive the alms of the charitable.

The living creature which lay upon this hard couch on the morning of Quasimodo Sunday, in the year of our Lord 1467, appeared to excite a high degree of curiosity in the considerable concourse of persons who had collected around it. They consisted chiefly of the fair sex, being almost all of them old women.

In the front row, nearest to the bed, were four whom from their gray cassocks you would judge to belong to some religious sisterhood. I see no reason why history should not transmit to posterity the names of these four discreet and venerable matrons. They were Agnes la Herme, Jehanne de la Tarme, Henriette la Gaultiere and Gauchere la Violette, all four widows, and sisters of the Chapter of Etienne Haudry, who had left their homes with the permission of their superior, and agreeably to the statutes of Pierre d'Ailly, for the purpose of attending divine service.

If, however, these good creatures were observing the statutes of Pierre d'Ailly, they were certainly violating at the moment those of Michael de Brache and the Cardinal of Pisa, which most inhumanly imposed upon them the law of silence.

"What is that, sister?" said Agnes to Gauchere, looking intently at the little creature yelping and writhing on the wooden couch, and terrified at the number of strange faces.

"What will the world come to," said Jehanne, "if that is the way they make children nowadays?"

"I don't pretend to know much about children," said Agnes, "but it must be a sin to look at that thing."

"'Tis not a child, Agnes—'tis a misshapen ape," observed Gauchere.

"'Tis a miracle!" ejaculated La Gaultiere.

"Then," remarked Agnes, "this is the third since Lætare Sunday, for it is not a week since we had the miracle of the scoffer of the pilgrims punished by our Lady of Aubervilliers, and that was the second miracle of the month."

"This foundling, as they call it, is a real monster of abomination," resumed Jehanne.

"He bellows loud enough to deafen a chanter," continued Gauchere.

"And to pretend that Monsieur de Reims could send this fright to Monsieur de Paris!" added La Gaultiere, clasping her hands.

"I cannot help thinking," said Agnes la Herme, "that it is some brute, something between a Jew and a beast—something, in short, that is not Christian, and ought to be drowned or burned."

"I do hope," resumed La Gaultiere, "that nobody will apply for it."

"Good God!" exclaimed Agnes, "how I pity the poor nurses at the foundling hospital in the lane yonder going down to the river, close by the archbishop's, if this little monster should be carried to them to be suckled! Why, I declare, I would rather suckle a vampire!"

"Poor La Herme! what a simpleton she is!" rejoined Jehanne. "Don't you see, sister, that this little monster is at least four years old, and that he would like a lump of meat a deal better than your breast?"

In fact, "this little monster,"—we should be puzzled ourselves to call it anything else—was not a new-born infant. It was a little, shapeless, moving mass, tied up in a hempen bag, marked with the initials of Guillaume Chartier, the then Bishop of Paris, and leaving the head alone exposed; and that head was so deformed as to be absolutely hideous: nothing was to be seen upon it but a forest of red hair, one eye, a mouth and teeth. The eye wept, the mouth cried, and the teeth seemed sadly in want of something to bite. The whole was struggling in the sack, to the no small wonderment of the crowd incessantly coming and going and increasing around it.

Dame Aloise de Gondelaurier, a noble and wealthy lady, who held by the hand a sweet little girl about six years old, and had a long veil hanging from the gold peak of her bonnet, stopped before the bed, and for a moment surveyed the unfortunate creature, while her charming little daughter Fleur-de-lys, dressed entirely in silk and velvet, pointing with her delicate finger to each letter of the permanent inscription attached to the wooden bed, spelled the words ENFANTS TROUVES [FOUNDLINGS].

"I really thought," said the lady, turning away with disgust, "that children only were exposed here."

As she turned her back she threw into the basin a silver florin, which rang among the liards, and made the poor sisters of the Chapel of Etienne Haudry lift their eyes in astonishment.

A moment afterward the grave and learned Robert Mistricolle, the king's prothonotary, passed with an enormous missal under his arm, and his wife, Damoiselle Guillemette la Mairesse, under the other, thus having at his side two regulators, the one spiritual, the other temporal.

"A foundling!" he exclaimed, after intently examining the object —"found apparently on the bank of the Phlegethon."

"He seems to have but one eye," observed Damoiselle Guillemette; "and there is a great wart over the other."

"'Tis no wart," replied Master Robert Mistricolle, "but an egg which contains another demon exactly like this, with another little egg containing a third devil, and so on."

"La! how know you that?" asked Guillemette.

"I know it pertinently," replied the prothonotary.

"Mr. Prothonotary," inquired Gauchere, "what prophesy you from this kind of foundling?"

"The greatest calamities," replied Mistricolle.

"Gracious Heaven!" exclaimed an old woman who stood by, "no wonder we had such a pestilence last year, and that the English, it is said, are going to land in force at Harfleur!"

"Perhaps that may not prevent the queen from coming to Paris in September," rejoined another; "trade is very flat already."

"I am of opinion," cried Jehanne de la Tarme, "that it would be better for the people of Paris if that little sorcerer were lying upon a fagot than upon a plank."

"Ay—a bonny blazing one!" added the old dame.

"That might be more prudent," observed Mistricolle.

For some moments a young priest had been listening to the comments of the women and the prothonotary. He was a man of an austere countenance, with an ample brow and piercing eye. Pushing aside the crowd without speaking, he examined "the little sorcerer," and extended his hand over him. It was high time, for all the pious by-standers were agog for the "bonny blazing fagot."

"I adopt this child," said the priest.

He wrapped him in his cassock and carried him away. The by-standers looked after him with horror till he had passed the Porte Rouge which then led from the church to the cloisters, and was out of sight.

When they had recovered from their first astonishment Jehanne de la Tarme, stooping till her lips were near the ear of La Gaultiere, "Sister," whispered she, "did I not tell you that yon young clerk, Monsieur Claude Frollo, is a sorcerer?"

CHAPTER II

CLAUDE FROLLO

CLAUDE FROLLO WAS, in fact, no ordinary personage. He belonged to one of those families who, in the impertinent language of the last century, were called indiscriminately *haute bourgeoisie* or *petite noblesse*. This family had inherited from the Paclets the fief of Tirechappe, which was held under the Bishop of Paris, and the twenty-one houses of which had been in the thirteenth century the subject of so many pleadings before the officials. Claude Frollo, as possessor of this fief, was one of the one hundred and forty-one seigneurs who claimed manorial rights in Paris and its suburbs; and as such his name was long to be seen registered between the Hotel de Tancarville, belonging to Master François de Rez, and the College de Tours, in the cartulary preserved in the Church of St. Martin-des-Champs.

Claude Frollo had from his childhood been destined by his parents for the church. He was taught to read Latin, to cast down his eyes, and to speak low. While quite a boy his father had placed him in the College of Torchi in the University, and there he had grown up on the missal and the lexicon.

For the rest he was a dull, grave, serious boy who studied assiduously, and learned quickly. He made but little noise in his recreations, had mingled but little in the bacchanals of the Rue du Fouarre, and had not cut a figure in that mutiny of the year 1463, which the chroniclers have gravely recorded under the title of "Sixth Disturbance of the University." He had scarcely ever been known to rally the poor scholars of Montaigue for the little hoods, after which they were nicknamed (Capettes), or the bursars of the College of Dormans for their shaven crowns and their tri-colored frocks of gray, blue, and purple cloth—*azurini coloris et bruni,* as saith the charter of the Cardinal des Quatres-Couronnes.

On the other hand he was assiduous in his attendance on the upper and lower schools of the Rue St. Jean de Beauvais. The first scholar whom the Abbé of St. Pierre de Val, at the moment of commencing his lecture on the canon law, perceived invariably stationed opposite to his chair by a pillar of the school of St. Vendregesile, was Claude Frollo, provided with his ink-horn, chewing his pen, scribbling upon his knee, and in winter blowing his fingers. The first auditor whom Messire Miles d'Isliers, Doctor in Divinity, saw entering every Monday morning, quite out of breath, on the opening of the door of the school of Chef St. Denis, was Claude Frollo. Accordingly, at the age of sixteen the young clerk might have posed a father of the church in mystic theology, a father of the council in canonical theology, and a doctor of the Sorbonne in scholastic theology.

Having passed through theology, he had fallen upon the capitularies of Charlemagne, and, with his keen appetite for knowledge, had devoured decretals after decretals, those of Theodore, Bishop of Hispala, of Bouchard, Bishop of Worms, of Yves, Bishop of Chartres; then the decree of Gratian, which succeeded the capitularies of Charlemagne; then the collection of Gregory IX.; then Honorius the Third's epistle, "Super Specula;"[1] till he made himself familiar with that long and tumultuous period, in which the canon law and the civil law were straggling and laboring amid the chaos of the Middle Ages—a period opening with Theodore in 618, and closing with Pope Gregory in 1227.

Having dispatched the decretals, he proceeded to medicine and the liberal arts. He studied the science of herbs and the science of unguents; he became skillful in the cure of fevers and of contusions, of wounds and of imposthumes. He was qualified alike to practice in medicine and in surgery. He passed through all the degrees of licentiate, master, and doctor of arts. He studied the learned languages, Latin, Greek, Hebrew, the triple sanctuary at that time but little frequented. He had a real fever for acquiring and hoarding up knowledge; and it seemed to the young man as if life had but one object, namely, to learn.

1. *Upon the Mirror.*

It was about this time that the intense heat of the summer of 1466 generated that destructive pestilence which swept away more than forty thousand human beings in the viscounty of Paris, and among others, saith Jean de Troyes, "Master Arnoul, the king's astrologer, a right honest, wise, and agreeable man." A rumor reached the University that the Rue Tirechappe in particular was afflicted with this malady. There, in the midst of their fief, dwelt the parents of Claude. The young scholar hastened in great alarm to the paternal residence. On reaching it he learned that his father and mother had died the preceding night. An infant brother was still alive, and crying, abandoned in his cradle. This babe was the only member of Claude's family that was left to him; he took the child in his arms and quitted the house, absorbed in thought. Hitherto he had lived only in learning and science; he now began to live in life.

This catastrophe was a crisis in the existence of Claude. An orphan and head of a family at nineteen, he felt himself rudely roused from the reveries of the schools to the realities of the world. Moved with pity, he conceived a passionate fondness for his helpless infant brother—a strange and delightful thing, this human affection, to him who heretofore had loved nothing but books.

This affection developed itself to an extraordinary degree: in a soul so new to the feeling it was like a first love. Separated from childhood from his parents, whom he had scarcely known, cloistered, and, as it were, spell-bound by his books, eager above all things to study and to learn, exclusively attentive till then to his understanding, which expanded itself in science, to his imagination, which grew up in letters, the young scholar had not yet had time to find out where his heart lay. The little brother, without father or mother, that infant which dropped all at once from the sky into his arms, made a new man of him. He perceived that there was something in the world besides the speculations of the Sorbonne and the verses of Homer; that human beings have need of affections; that life without love is but a dry wheel, creaking and grating as it revolves. He fancied, it is true, for he was at an age when one illusion only gives place to another, that the family affections, the ties of blood, were alone needful for him, and that the love of his little brother was sufficient to fill his heart for his whole life.

He gave himself up therefore to the love of his little Jehan with the passion of a character already ardent, energetic, and concentrated. This poor, fair, delicate creature, this orphan without any protector but an orphan, moved him to the bottom of his soul; and, grave thinker as he was, he began to muse upon Jehan with feelings of infinite compassion. He bestowed on him all possible care and attention, just as if he had been something exceedingly fragile and exceedingly valuable. He was more than a brother to the infant: he became a mother to him.

Little Jehan was still at the breast when he lost his mother: Claude put him out to nurse. Besides the fief of Tirechappe he had inherited from his father a mill situated on a hill near the Castle of Winchester, since corrupted to Bicetre. The miller's wife was just suckling a fine boy; it was not far from the University, and Claude carried little Jehan to her himself.

Thenceforward the thought of his little brother became not only a recreation but even the object of his studies. He resolved to devote himself entirely to the care of him, and never to have any other wife or any other child, but the happiness and prosperity of his brother. He attached himself therefore more strongly than ever to his clerical vocation. His merit, his learning, his condition of immediate vassal of the Bishop of Paris, threw the doors of the church wide open to him. At the age of twenty, by a special dispensation of the Holy See, he was a priest, and as the youngest of the chaplains of Notre Dame he performed the service of the altar called, on account of the lateness of the mass said there, *altare pigorum*.[1]

There, more than ever absorbed by his beloved books, which he never quitted but to run for an hour to the mill, this mixture of learning and austerity, so uncommon at this age, quickly gained him the admiration and respect of the convent. From the cloister his reputation for learning spread among the people, and among some of them it even procured him the character of a sorcerer—a frequent circumstance in that superstitious age.

It was at the moment when he was returning, on Quasimodo Sunday, from saying mass at "the altar of the lazy," which stood by the door of the choir on the right, near the image of the Blessed Virgin, that his attention was attracted by the group of old women cackling around the bed of the foundling. He approached the unfortunate little creature so hated and so threatened. Its distress, its deformity, its destitution, the thought of his young brother, the idea which suddenly flashed across his mind, that if he were to die his poor little Jehan too might perhaps be mercilessly thrown upon the same spot, assailed his heart all at once: it melted with pity, and he carried away the boy.

When he had taken the child out of the sack he found him to be, in fact, a monster of deformity. The poor little wretch had a prodigious wart over his left eye, his head was close to his shoulders,

1. The sluggards' altar.

SHE DANCED, WHIRLED, TURNED ROUND, ON AN OLD PERSIAN CARPET.
Page 57

THE PROCESSION OF THE POPE OF FOOLS WAS NOW ENTERING THE
PLACE DE GRÈVE.

Page 61

A NUMBER OF CURIOUS AND IDLE PERSONS BEGAN TO FOLLOW THEM.

Page 63

THE CAPTAIN LIFTED UP A CORNER OF THE TAPESTRY.
Page 182

ALL AT ONCE ABOVE THE HEAD OF THE CAPTAIN SHE BEHELD
ANOTHER HEAD.

Page 231

QUASIMODO FELLED BOTH OF THEM TO THE GROUND.
Page 275

"TAKE PITY ON ME. THEY ARE COMING."

Page 385

"DAMNATION!" CRIED THE PRIEST AS HE FELL.
Page 402

his back arched, his breast-bone protruded, and his legs were twisted; but he appeared lively, and though it was impossible to tell what language he attempted to speak, his cry indicated a tolerable degree of strength and health. This extreme ugliness only served to increase the compassion of Claude; and he vowed in his heart to bring up this boy for the love of his brother, that, whatever might be in the time to come the faults of little Jehan, he might have the benefit of this charity done in his behalf. It was a humane act, placed, as it were, to the account of his brother, one of the little stock of good works which he determined to lay up for him beforehand, in case the young rogue should some day run short of that kind of coin, the only one taken at the toll-gate of Paradise.

He baptized his adopted child and named him Quasimodo, either to commemorate the day on which he had found him, or to express the incomplete and scarcely finished state of the poor little creature. In truth, Quasimodo, with one eye, hunchback, and crooked legs, was but an apology for a human being.

CHAPTER III

THE BELL-RINGER OF NOTRE DAME

NOW, BY THE YEAR 1482, Quasimodo had grown up. He had been for several years bell-ringer to the Cathedral of Notre Dame, thanks to his foster-father, Claude Frollo, who had become Archdeacon of Josas, thanks to his diocesan, Messire Louis de Beaumont, who had been appointed Bishop of Paris in 1472, thanks to his patron, Olivier le Daim, barber to Louis XI., by the grace of God, king, etc., etc., etc.

In process of time, the strongest attachment took place between the bell-ringer and the church. Cut off forever from society by the double fatality of his unknown parentage and his misshapen nature, imprisoned from childhood within these impassable boundaries, the unhappy wretch was accustomed to see no object in the world beyond the religious walls which had taken him under their protection. Notre Dame had been successively, to him, as he grew up and expanded, his egg, his nest, his home, his country, the universe.

A sort of mysterious and pre-existent harmony had grown up between this creature and the edifice. While still quite a child, he crawled about, twisting and hopping, in the shade of its arches, he appeared, with his human face and his limbs scarcely human, the native reptile of the dark, damp pavement, among the grotesque shadows thrown down upon it by the capitals of the Roman pillars.

As he grew up, the first time that he mechanically grasped the rope in the tower, and, hanging to it, set the bell in motion, the effect upon his foster-father was like that produced upon a parent by the first articulate sounds uttered by his child.

Thus, by little and little, his spirit expanded in harmony with the cathedral; there he lived, there he slept; scarcely ever leaving it, and, being perpetually subject to its mysterious influence, he came at last to resemble it, to be incrusted with it, to form, as it were, an integral part of it. His salient angles dove-tailed, if we may be allowed the expression, into the receding angles of the building, so that he seemed to be not merely its inhabitant, but to have taken its form and pressure. Between the ancient church and him there were an instinctive sympathy so profound, so many magnetic affinities, that he stuck to it in some measure as the tortoise to its shell.

It is scarcely necessary to say how familiar he had made himself with the whole cathedral in so long and so intimate a cohabitation. There was no depth that Quasimodo had not fathomed, no height that he had not scaled. Many a time had he climbed up the façade composed of several elevations, assisted only by the asperities of the sculpture. Often might he have been seen crawling up the outside of the towers, like a lizard up a perpendicular wall: those twin giants, so tall, so threatening, so formidable, produced in him neither vertigo-fright, nor sudden giddiness. So gentle did they appear under his hand, and so easy to climb, that you would have said he had tamed them. By dint of leaping, scrambling, struggling among the precipices of the venerable cathedral, he had become something between a monkey and a mountain goat, just as the boy of Calabria swims before he can walk, and disports in the sea as if it were his native element.

Not only did the person but also the mind of Quasimodo appear to be molded by the cathedral. It would be difficult to determine the state of that soul, what folds it had contracted, what form it had assumed under its knotty covering, during this wild and savage life. Quasimodo was born one-eyed, humpbacked, lame. It was not without great difficulty and great patience that Claude Frollo had taught him to speak; but there was a fatality attached to the unhappy foundling. Having become a ringer of the bells of Notre

Dame at the age of fourteen, a fresh infirmity had come upon him: the volume of sound had broken the drum of his ear, and deafness was the consequence. Thus the only gate which nature had left wide open between him and the world was suddenly closed, and forever. In closing, it shut out the only ray of light and joy that still reached his soul, which was now wrapped in profound darkness. The melancholy of the poor fellow became incurable and complete as his deformity. His deafness rendered him in some measure dumb also: for, the moment he lost his hearing he resolved to avoid the ridicule of others by a silence which he never broke but when he was alone. He voluntarily tied up that tongue which Claude Frollo had taken such pains to loosen: hence, when necessity forced him to speak, his tongue was benumbed, awkward, and like a door the hinges of which have grown rusty.

If then we were to attempt to penetrate through this thick and obdurate bark to the soul of Quasimodo; if we could sound the depths of this bungling piece of organization; if we were enabled to hold a torch behind these untransparent organs, to explode the gloomy interior of this opaque being, to illumine its obscure corners and its unmeaning *cul-de-sacs*, and to throw all at once a brilliant light upon the spirit enchained at the bottom of this den, we should doubtless find the wretch in some miserable attitude, stunted and rickety, like the prisoners under the leads of Venice, who grow old doubled up in a box of stone too low to stand up and too short to lie down in.

It is certain that the spirit pines in a misshapen form. Quasimodo scarcely felt within him the blind movements of a soul made in his own image. The impressions of objects underwent a considerable refraction before they reached the seat of thought. His brain was a peculiar medium; the ideas which entered it came out quite twisted. The reflection resulting from the refraction was necessarily divergent and devious. Hence a thousand optical illusions, a thousand aberrations of judgment, a thousand by-ways into which his sometimes silly, sometimes crazy imagination would wander.

The first effect of this vicious organization was to confuse the view which he took of things. He received scarcely a single direct perception. The exterior world appeared to him at a greater distance than it does to us. The second result of his misfortune was that it rendered him mischievous. He was, in truth, mischievous because he was savage, he was savage because he was ugly. There was logic in his nature, as there is in ours. His strength, developed in a most extraordinary manner, was another cause of his propensity to mischief. *Malus puer robustus,*[1] says Hobbes. We must nevertheless do him justice: malice was probably not innate in him. From his earliest intercourse with men he had felt, and afterward he had seen, himself despised, rejected, cast off. Human speech had never been to him aught but a jeer or a curse. As he grew up he had found nothing but hatred about him. He had adopted it. He had acquired the general malignity. He had picked up the weapon with which he had been wounded.

After all, he turned toward mankind with reluctance: his cathedral was enough for him. It was peopled with figures of marble, with kings, saints, bishops who at least did not laugh in his face, and looked upon him only with an air of tranquillity and benevolence. The other statues, those of monsters and demons, bore no malice against him. They were too like him for that. Their raillery was rather directed against other men. The saints were his friends and blessed him; the monsters were his friends and guarded him; he would therefore pass whole hours crouched before one of the statues, holding solitary converse with it. If any one came by he would run off like a lover surprised in a serenade.

The cathedral was not only his society but his world—in short, all nature to him. He thought of no other trees than the painted windows, which were always in blossom; of no other shades than the foliage of stone adorned with birds in the Saxon capitals; of no other mountains than the colossal towers of the church; of no other ocean than Paris which roared at their feet.

But that which he loved most of all in the maternal edifice, that which awakened his soul and caused it to spread its poor wings, that otherwise remained so miserably folded up in its prison, that which even conferred at times a feeling of happiness, was the bells. He loved them, he caressed them, he talked to them, he understood them—from the chimes in the steeple of the transept to the great bell above the porch. The belfry of the transept and the two towers were like immense cages, in which the birds that he had reared rang for him alone. It was these same birds, however, which had deafened him: mothers are often fondest of the child which has caused them the greatest pain. It is true that theirs were the only voices he could still hear. On this account the great bell was his best beloved. He preferred her before all the other sisters of this noisy family who fluttered about him on festival days. This great bell he called Mary. She was placed in the southern tower, along with her sister Jacqueline, a bell of inferior size, inclosed in a cage of less magnitude by the side of her own. This Jacqueline was thus named

1. A sturdy boy is a naughty boy.

after the wife of Jehan Montaigu, who gave her to the church; a gift which, however, did not prevent his figuring without his head at Montfauçon. In the second tower were six other bells; and, lastly, the six smallest dwelt in the steeple of the transept, with the wooden bell, which was only rung between noon on Holy Thursday and the morning of Easter eve. Thus Quasimodo had fifteen bells in his seraglio, but big Mary was his favorite.

It is impossible to form a conception of his joy on the days of the great peals. The instant the archdeacon let him off, and said "Go," he ran up the winding staircase of the belfry quicker than another could have gone down. He hurried, out of breath, into the aerial chamber of the great bell, looked at her attentively and lovingly for a moment, then began to talk kindly to her, and patted her with his hand, as you would do a good horse which you are going to put to his mettle. He would pity her for the labor she was about to undergo. After these first caresses, he shouted to his assistants in a lower story of the tower to begin. They seized the ropes, the windlass creaked, and slowly and heavily the enormous cone of metal was set in motion. Quasimodo, with heaving bosom, watched the movement. The first shock of the clapper against the wall of brass shook the wood-work upon which it was hung. Quasimodo vibrated with the bell. "Vah!" he would cry, with a burst of idiot laughter. Meanwhile the motion of the bell was accelerated, and as the angle which it described became more and more obtuse, the eye of Quasimodo glistened and shone out with more phosphoric light. At length the grand peal began: the whole tower trembled; rafters, leads, stones, all groaned together, from the piles of the foundation to the trefoils of the parapet. Quasimodo then boiled over with delight; he foamed at the mouth; he ran backward and forward; he trembled with the tower from head to foot. The great bell, let loose, and, as it were, furious with rage, turned first to one side and then to the other side of the tower its enormous brazen throat, whence issued a roar that might be heard to the distance of four leagues around. Quasimodo placed himself before this open mouth; he crouched down and rose up, as the bell swung to and fro, inhaled its boisterous breath, and looked by turns at the abyss two hundred feet deep below him, and at the enormous tongue of brass which came ever and anon to bellow in his ear. This was the only speech that he could hear, the only sound that broke the universal silence to which he was doomed. He would spread himself out in it like a bird in the sun. All at once the frenzy of the bell would seize him; his look became wild; he would watch the rocking engine, as a spider watches a fly, and suddenly leap upon it. Then, suspended over the abyss, carried to and fro in the formidable oscillation of the bell, he seized the brazen monster by the earlets, strained it with his knees, spurred it with his heels, and with the whole weight and force of his body increased the fury of the peal. While the tower began to quake he would shout and grind his teeth, his red hair bristled up, his breast heaved and puffed like the bellows of a forge, his eye flashed fire, and the monstrous bell neighed breathless under him. It was then no longer the bell of Notre Dame and Quasimodo: it was a dream, a whirlwind, a tempest, vertigo astride of uproar; a spirit clinging to a winged monster; a strange centaur, half man, half bell; a species of horrible Astolpho, carried off by a prodigious hippogriff of living brass.

The presence of this extraordinary being seemed to infuse the breath of life into the whole cathedral. A sort of mysterious emanation seemed—at least so the superstitious multitude imagined—to issue from him, to animate the stones of Notre Dame, and to make the very entrails of the old church heave and palpitate. When it was known that he was there, it was easy to fancy that the thousand statues in the galleries and over the porches moved and were instinct with life. In fact, the cathedral seemed to be a docile and obedient creature in his hands; waiting only his will to raise her mighty voice; being possessed and filled with Quasimodo as with a familiar genius. He might be said to make the immense building breathe. He was in fact everywhere; he multiplied himself at all the points of the edifice. At one time the spectator would be seized with affright on beholding at the top of one of the towers an odd-looking dwarf, climbing, twining, crawling on all fours, descending externally into the abyss, leaping from one projecting point to another, and fumbling in the body of some sculptured Gorgon—it was Quasimodo unnesting the daws. At another, the visitor stumbled in some dark corner of the church upon a crouching, grim-faced creature, a sort of living chimera—it was Quasimodo musing. At another time might be seen under a belfry an enormous head and a bundle of ill-adjusted limbs furiously swinging at the end of a rope—it was Quasimodo ringing the vespers or the Angelus. Frequently, at night, a hideous figure might be seen wandering on the delicate open-work balustrade which crowns the towers and runs round the apsis—it was still the Hunchback of Notre Dame. At such times, according to the reports of the gossips of the neighborhood, the whole church assumed a fantastic, supernatural, frightful aspect; eyes and mouths opened here and there; the dogs and the dragons and the griffins

of stone which keep watch day and night, with outstretched neck
and opened jaws, around the monstrous cathedral, were heard to
bark and howl. At Christmas, while the great bell, which seemed
to rattle in the throat, summoned the pious to the midnight mass,
the gloomy façade of the cathedral wore such a strange and sinister
air that the grand porch seemed to swallow the multitude, while the
rose-window above it looked on. All this proceeded from Quasimodo.
Egypt would have taken him for the god of the temple; the Middle
Ages believed him to be its demon; he was the soul of it. To such a
point was he so, that to those who knew that Quasimodo once existed Notre Dame now appears deserted, inanimate, dead. You feel
that there is something wanting. This immense body is void; it is a
skeleton; the spirit has departed; you see its place, and that is all.
It is like a skull; the sockets of the eyes are still there, but the eyes
themselves are gone.

CHAPTER IV

THE DOG AND HIS MASTER

THERE WAS, however, one human being whom Quasimodo excepted
from his antipathy, and to whom he was as much, nay, perhaps more
strongly attached than to his cathedral—that being was Claude
Frollo.

The thing was perfectly natural. Claude Frollo had taken pity on
him, adopted him, supported him, brought him up. It was between
Claude Frollo's legs that, when quite small, he had been accustomed
to seek refuge when teased by boys or barked at by dogs. Claude
Frollo had taught him to speak, to read, to write. To crown all,
Claude Frollo had made him bell-ringer.

The gratitude of Quasimodo was in consequence profound,
impassioned, unbounded; and though the countenance of his foster-
father was frequently gloomy and morose, though his way of speaking was habitually short, harsh, and imperious, never had this
gratitude ceased for a moment to sway him. The archdeacon had in
Quasimodo the most submissive of slaves, the most docile of attendants, the most vigilant of warders. After the poor bell-ringer had lost
his hearing, Claude Frollo and he conversed in language of signs,

mysterious and understood by themselves alone. Thus the archdeacon was the only human creature with whom Quasimodo had kept up communication. There were but two things in the world with which he still had intercourse—Notre Dame and Claude Frollo.

Nothing on earth can be compared with the empire of the archdeacon over the bell-ringer, and the attachment of the bell-ringer to the archdeacon. A sign from Claude, and the idea of giving him pleasure would have sufficed to make Quasimodo throw himself from the top of the towers of Notre Dame. It was truly extraordinary to see all that physical strength which had attained such a surprising development in Quasimodo placed implicitly by him at the disposal of another. It bespoke undoubtedly filial submission, domestic attachment; but it proceeded also from the fascination which mind exercises upon mind. It was an imperfect, distorted, defective organization, with head abased and supplicating eyes, before a superior, a lofty, a commanding intelligence; but, above all, it was gratitude—but gratitude so carried to its extreme limit that we know not what to compare it with. This virtue is not one of those of which the most striking examples are to be sought among men. We shall therefore say that Quasimodo loved the archdeacon as never dog, never horse, never elephant, loved his master.

In 1482 Quasimodo was about twenty, Claude Frollo about thirty-six. The one had grown up, the other began to grow old.

Claude Frollo was no longer the simple student of the College of Torchi, the tender protector of an orphan child, the young and thoughtful philosopher, so learned and yet so ignorant. He was an austere, grave, morose churchman, second chaplain to the bishop, Archdeacon of Josas, having under him the two deaneries of Montlhery and Chateaufort, and one hundred and seventy-four parish priests. He was a somber and awe-inspiring personage, before whom trembled the singing boys in albs and long coats, the preceptors, the Brothers of St. Augustin, the clerk who officiated in the morning services at Notre Dame, as he stalked slowly along beneath the lofty arches of the choir, majestic, pensive, with arms folded and head so bowed upon his bosom that no part of his face was to be seen but his bald and ample forehead.

Dom Claude Frollo, however, had not meanwhile abandoned either the sciences or the education of his young brother, those two occupations of his life; but time had dashed those fond pursuits with the bitterness of disappointment. Little Jehan Frollo, surnamed Du Moulin, from the place where he had been nursed, had not as he grew up taken that bent which Claude was solicitous to give him.

His brother had reckoned upon a pious, docile, and virtuous pupil; but the youth, like those young trees which, in spite of all the gardener's efforts, obstinately turn toward the quarter from which they receive air and sun, grew and flourished and threw out luxuriant branches toward idleness, ignorance, and debauchery alone. Reckless of all restraint, he was a downright devil who often made Dom Claude knit his brow, but full of shrewdness and drollery which as often made him laugh. Claude had placed him in the same College of Torchi where he had passed his early years in study and retirement; and it was mortifying to him that this sanctuary, formerly edified by the name of Frollo, should now be scandalized by it. On this subject he frequently read Jehan very severe and very long lectures, to which the latter listened with exemplary composure. After all, the young scapegrace had a good heart; when the lecture was over he nevertheless returned quietly to his profligate courses. At one time it was a new-comer whom he worried into the payment of his footing—a precious tradition which has been carefully handed down to the present day; at another he had instigated a party of the students to make a classic attack upon some tavern, where, after beating the keeper with bludgeons, they merrily gutted the house, staving even the wine-pipes in the cellar. Then again there would be a long report in Latin, which the sub-monitor of Torchi carried in woful wise to Dom Claude with this painful marginal annotation: *Rixa; prima causa vinum optimum potatum.*[1] Lastly it was asserted—oh, horror of horrors in a lad of sixteen!—that his excesses ofttimes carried him to the gaming-houses themselves.

Grieved and thwarted by these circumstances in his human affections, Claude had thrown himself with so much the more ardor into the arms of Science, who at least does not laugh you in the face, and always repays you, though sometimes in rather hollow coin, for the attentions which you have bestowed on her. Thus he became more and more learned, and at the same time, by a natural consequence, more and more rigid as a priest, more and more gloomy as a man.

As Claude Frollo had from his youth traveled through almost the entire circle of human knowledge, positive, external, and lawful, he was forced, unless he could make up his mind to stop where he was, to seek further food for the insatiable cravings of his understanding. The antique symbol of the serpent biting its tail is peculiarly appropriate to science; and it appears that Claude Frollo knew this from experience. Several grave persons affirmed that after exhausting the *fas*[2] of human knowledge he had dared to penetrate into the *nefas*.[3] He had, it was said, tasted successively all the apples of the tree of

1. A brawl; first cause, wine–bibbing.
2. Lawful.
3. Unlawful.

knowledge, and had at last bitten at the forbidden fruit. He had taken his place by turns, as our readers have seen, at the conferences of the theologians in the Sorbonne, at the meetings of the philosophers at the image of St. Hilaire, at the disputes of the decretists at the image of St. Martin, at the congregations of the physicians at the holy-water font of Notre Dame. All the allowable and approved dishes which these four great kitchens, called the four faculties, could elaborate and set before the understanding he had feasted upon, and satiety had supervened before his hunger was appeased. He had then dug further and deeper, beneath all that finite, material, limited science; he had perhaps risked his soul, and had seated himself in the cavern at that mysterious table of the alchemists and astrologers, one end of which is occupied in the Middle Ages by Averroes, William of Paris, and Nicolas Flamel, while the other, lighted by the chandelier with seven branches, runs on to Solomon, Pythagoras, and Zoroaster. So, at least, it was conjectured, whether right or wrong.

It is certain that the archdeacon frequently visited the churchyard of the Innocents, where, to be sure, his parents lay buried with the other victims of the pestilence of 1466; but then he appeared to take much less notice of the cross at the head of their grave than the tomb erected close by it for Nicolas Flamel and Claude Pernelle.

It is certain that he had often been seen walking along the street of the Lombards and stealthily entering a small house which formed the corner of the Rue des Ecrivains and the Rue Mariavaux. It was the house built by Nicolas Flamel, in which he died about the year 1417, and which, having been ever since uninhabited, was beginning to fall to ruin, so worn were the walls by the alchemists and the professors of the occult science from all countries, who resorted hither and scratched their names upon them. Some of the neighbors even affirmed that they had once seen through a hole the archdeacon digging and turning over the mold in the two cellars, the jambs of which had been covered with verses and hieroglyphics by Flamel himself. It was supposed that Master Nicolas had buried the philosopher's stone in one of these cellars; and for two centuries the alchemists, from Magistri to Father Pacifique, never ceased delving and rummaging till the house, weakened and undermined by their researches, at last tumbled about their ears.

It is certain, moreover, that the archdeacon was smitten with a strange passion for the emblematic porch of Notre Dame, that page of conjuration written in stone by Bishop William of Paris, who has no doubt repented for having prefixed so infernal a frontispiece to the sacred poem everlastingly chanted by the rest of the edifice. It was also believed that the archdeacon had discovered the hidden meaning of the colossal St. Christopher, and of the other tall enigmatical statue which then stood at the entrance of the Parvis, and which the people called in derision Monsieur Legris. But a circumstance which everybody might have remarked was his sitting hours without number on the parapet of the Parvis, contemplating the sculptures of the porch, sometimes examining the foolish virgins with their lamps reversed, sometimes the wise virgins with their lamps upright; at others calculating the angle of the vision of the raven on the left-hand side of the porch, looking at some mysterious spot in the church, where the philosopher's stone is certainly concealed, if it is not in Nicolas Flamel's cellar. It was, be it observed by the way, a singular destiny for the Church of Notre Dame at that period to be thus loved in different degrees and with such ardor by two beings so dissimilar as Claude and Quasimodo—loved by the one, scarcely more than half man, for its beauty, its majesty, the harmonies resulting from its grand whole; loved by the other, with a mind cultivated to the utmost and a glowing imagination for its mystic signification, for its hidden meaning, for the symbol concealed beneath the sculptures of its façade, like the first text under the second of a palimpsest—in short, for the riddle which it incessantly proposes to the understanding.

Lastly, it is certain that the archdeacon had fitted up for himself in the tower nearest to the Grève, close to the belfry, a small and secret cell, which none, it was said, but the bishop durst enter without his permission. This cell had been made of old almost at the top of the tower, among the ravens' nests, by Bishop Hugo of Besançon, who had there practiced the black art in his time. None knew what that cell contained; but from the Terrain there had often been seen at night, through a small window at the back of the tower, a strange, red, intermitting light, appearing, disappearing, and reappearing at short and equal intervals, apparently governed by the blast of bellows, and proceeding rather from the flame of a fire than from that of a lamp or candle. In the dark this had a singular effect at that height, and the good wives would say: "There's the archdeacon puffing away again; hell is cracking up yonder!"

Those, after all, were no very strong proofs of sorcery; still there was sufficient smoke to authorize the conclusion that there must be some fire; at any rate, the archdeacon had that formidable reputation. It is nevertheless but just to state that the sciences of Egypt, necromancy, magic, even the whitest and most innocent, had not a more inveterate enemy, a more pitiless accuser before the officials of Notre Dame. Whether his horror was sincere or merely the game played by the rogue who is the first to cry "Stop thief!" it did not prevent his being considered by the learned heads of the chapter as a soul lost in the mazes of the Cabala, groping in the darkness of the occult sciences, and already in the vestibule of hell. The people had much the same opinion; all who possessed any sagacity regarded Quasimodo as the demon and Claude Frollo as the conjurer. It was evident that the bell-ringer had engaged to serve the archdeacon for a specific time, at the expiration of which he would be sure to carry off his soul by way of payment. Accordingly the archdeacon, in spite of the extreme austerity of his life, was in bad odor with all good Christians, and there was not a devout nose among them but could smell the magician.

And if, as he grew older, chasms were found in his science, neither had his heart remained free from them; at least there was good reason to believe so on surveying that face in which the workings of his spirit were discernible only through a dark cloud. Whence was that broad, bald brow, that head always bent down, that bosom forever heaved by sighs? What secret thought caused his lips to smile with such a bitter expression, at the very moment when his knitted brows approached each other like two bulls preparing for the fight? Why was the remnant of his hair already gray? What inward fire was it that at times burst from his eyes, so as to make them look like holes perforated in the wall of a furnace?

The symptoms of a violent moral preoccupation had acquired an unusual degree of intensity at the period of the occurrences related in this history. More than one of the singing boys had fled affrighted on meeting him alone in the church, so strange and alarming were his looks. More than once, during the service in the choir, the priest in the next stall to his had heard him mingle unintelligible parentheses with the responses. More than once the laundress of the Terrain, employed to wash for the chapter, had observed, not without horror, marks, as if scratches by claws or finger-nails, upon the surplice of Monsieur the Archdeacon of Josas.

In other respects his austerity was redoubled, and never had he led a more exemplary life. From disposition as well as profession he had always kept aloof from women: he seemed now to dislike them more than ever. At the mere rustling of a silk petticoat his hood was over his eyes. On this point he was so strict that when the king's daughter, the Lady of Beaujeu, came in the month of Decem-

ber, 1481, to see the cloisters of Notre Dame, he seriously opposed
her admission, reminding the bishop of the statute of the black book,
dated on the vigil of St. Bartholomew, 1334, which forbids access to
the cloister to every woman "whatsoever, whether old or young, mistress or servant." Whereupon the bishop was forced to appeal to the
ordinance of Otho the Legate, which excepts "certain ladies of quality, who cannot be refused without scandal," *aliquæ magnates muli-
eres quæ sina scandalo evitari non possunt*. Still the archdeacon pro-
tested, alleging that the ordinance of the legate, which dated from
1207, was anterior by one hundred and twenty-seven years to the
black book, and consequently annulled in point of fact by the latter;
and he actually refused to appear before the princess.

It was, moreover, remarked that his horror of the Egyptians and
Zingari seemed to have become more vehement for some time past.
He had solicited from the bishop an edict expressly prohibiting the
Bohemians to come and dance and play in the area of the Parvis; and
he had recently taken the pains to search through the musty archives
of the official for cases of wizards and witches sentenced to the
flames or the gallows for practicing the black art in association with
cats, swine or goats.

Book Five

CHAPTER I

ANCIENT ADMINISTRATION OF JUSTICE

A VERY lucky wight was, in the year of grace 1482, that doughty personage Robert d'Estouteville, Knight, Sieur of Beyne, Baron of Ivry and St. Andry in La Marche, Councilor and Chamberlain of the King, and the Keeper of the Provosty of Paris. It was then nearly seventeen years agone that the king had, on the 7th of November, 1465, the year of the great comet,* conferred on him the important appointment of Provost of Paris, which was considered rather as a dignity than an office. It was a marvelous thing that in '82 there should still be a gentleman holding a commission under the king whose appointment dated from the time of the marriage of the natural daughter of Louis XI. with the Bastard of Bourbon. On the same day that Robert d'Estouteville had succeeded Jacques de Villiers in the provostship of Paris, Master Jean Dauvet superseded Messire Helye de Thorrettes as first president of the Court of Parliament, Jean Jouvenal des Ursins supplanted Pierre de Morvilliers in the office of Chancellor of France, and Regnault des Dormans turned Pierre Puy out of the post of master of requests in ordinary to the king's household. And how many presidents, chancellors and masters had Robert d'Estouteville seen since he had held the provostship of Paris! It was "given to him to keep," said the letters-patent, and well had he kept it forsooth. So closely had he clung to it, so completely had he incorporated, identified himself with it, that he had escaped that mania for changing his servants which possessed Louis XI., a jealous, niggardly and toiling sovereign, who thought to keep up the elasticity of his power by frequent removals and appointments. Nay more, the gallant knight had obtained the reversion of his place for his son, and for two years past the name of the noble Jacques d'Estouteville, Esquire, figures besides his own at the head of the register of the ordinary of the provosty of Paris. Rare, indeed, and signal favor! It is true that Robert d'Estouteville was a good soldier, that he had loyally raised the banner against the

* This comet, against which Pope Calixtus ordered public prayers, is the same that was again visible in 1835.

league of the public welfare, and that he had presented the queen with a most wonderful stag made of sweetmeats, on the day of her entry into Paris. He was, moreover, on terms of friendship with Messire Tristan the Hermit, provost of the marshals of the king's household. The situation of Messire Robert was, of course, rather enviable. In the first place, he enjoyed a handsome salary, to which hung, like supernumerary bunches of grapes to his vine, the revenues of the civil and criminal registries of the provostship, and also the civil and criminal revenues of the court of the Chatelet, to say nothing of the tolls collected at the bridge of Mante and Corbeil, and other minor perquisites. Add to this the pleasure of riding in the city cavalcades and processions, and showing off among the half-scarlet, half-tawny robes of the city officers his fine military armor, which you may still admire sculptured on his tomb in the Abbey of Valmont in Normandy, and his morion embossed all over at Mont-lhery. And, then, was it nothing to have the entire supremacy over the keeper, the warden, the jailer, and the two auditors of the Chatelet, the sixteen commissaries of the sixteen quarters, the hundred and twenty horse-patrols, the hundred and twenty vergers, and the whole of the watch of the city? Was it nothing to administer justice, civil and criminal—to have a right to burn, to hang, to draw, besides the inferior jurisdiction "in the first instance," as the chapters express it, in that viscounty of Paris and the seven noble baili-wicks thereto appertaining? Can you conceive anything more grati-fying than to issue orders and pass sentence, as Messire Robert d'Estouteville daily did in the Grand Chatelet beneath the wide elliptic arches of Philip Augustus? or to go, as he was accustomed, every evening to that charming house situated in the Rue Galilee, in the purlieus of the Palais Royal, which he held in right of his wife, Mme. Ambroise de Lore, to rest from the fatigue of having sent some poor devil to pass the night in "that little lodge in the Rue de l'Escorcherie, which the provosts and echevins were wont to make their prison; the same being eleven feet long, seven feet four inches in width, and eleven feet high."

Not only had Messire Robert d'Estouteville his particular court as Provost and Viscount of Paris, but he had also a finger in the inflic-tion of the sentences decreed by the king himself. There was not a head of any distinction but passed through his hands before it was delivered up to the executioner. It was he who fetched the Duke de Nemours from the Bastile St. Antoine to convey him to the Halles, and M. de St. Pol, who, on his way to the Grève, exclaimed loudly and bitterly against his fate, to the great delight of the provost, who was no friend to the constable.

Here certes were reasons more than sufficient to make a man satisfied with his life, and yet on the morning of January 7th, 1482, Messire Robert d'Estouteville awoke in a dogged ill-humor. And the cause of this ill-humor he would have been puzzled to tell himself. Was it because the sky was gloomy? Did his old belt of Montlhery constrict with too military a pressure his provostship's goodly corporation? Had he seen a troop of ragamuffins in doublets without shirts, in hats without crowns, with wallet and flask at their side, passing along the street under his window, and setting him at defiance? Was it that vague presentiment of the three hundred and seventy livres, sixteen sols, eight deniers, of which the future king, Charles VIII., in the following year docked the revenues of the provostship? The reader has his choice; for our own part we are inclined to believe that he was in an ill-humor merely because he was in an ill-humor.

Besides, it was the morrow of a public festivity, a day of annoyance to everybody, and more especially to the magistrate, whose duty it was to clear away all the filth, material and figurative, made by a fête at Paris. And then, too, he had to sit for the trial of offenders at the Grand Chatelet. Now we have remarked that judges in general arrange matters so that the days on which they have to perform their judicial functions are their days of ill-humor, that they may be sure to have somebody on whom they can conveniently vent it in the name of the king, of the law, and of justice.

Meanwhile, the proceedings had commenced without him. His deputies did the business for him, according to custom; and ever since the hour of eight in the morning some scores of citizens of both sexes crowded into a dark corner of the court of the Chatelet, between a strong oaken barrier and the wall, gazed with great edification at the spectacle of civil and criminal justice administered somewhat pell-mell and quite at random by Master Florian Barbedienne, auditor to the Chatelet and lieutenant of Monsieur the Provost.

It was a small, low hall, with coved ceiling; at the further end stood a table studded with *fleurs-de-lis*, a large empty arm-chair of carved oak, reserved for the provost, and on the left a stool for the auditor, Master Florian. Below was the clerk busily writing. In front were the people, and before the door and the table a posse of the provost's men in frocks of purple camlet with white crosses. Two sergeants of the Parloir aux Bourgeois, in their kersey jackets, half scarlet and half blue, stood sentry before a low closed door, which was seen behind the table. A single pointed window, of scanty dimensions, incased in the thick wall, threw the faint light of a January morning on two grotesque figures—the fantastic demon of stone sculptured by way of ornament to the groining of the ceiling, and the judge seated at the extremity of the hall.

Figure to yourself, seated at the provost's table, lolling upon his elbows between two piles of papers, his feet upon the skirt of his plain brown cloth robe, furred with white lambskin, which encircled his jolly, rubicund visage and double chin, Master Florian Barbedienne, auditor to the Chatelet.

Now, the said auditor was deaf. A trifling defect this in an auditor. Master Florian, nevertheless, gave judgment without appeal, and very consistently too. It is most certain that it is quite sufficient for a judge to appear to listen; and this condition, the only essential one for strict justice, the venerable auditor fulfilled the more exactly inasmuch as no noise could divert his attention.

For the rest, he had among the auditory a merciless controller of his sayings and doings in the person of our young friend, Jehan Frollo du Moulin, who was sure to be seen everywhere in Paris except before the professors' chairs.

"Look you," said he in a low tone to his companion, Robin Poussepain, who was grinning beside him while he commented on the scenes that were passing before them—"there is the pretty Jehanneton du Buisson of the Marche Neuf! Upon my soul, he condemns her too, the old brute! He must have no more eyes than ears. Fifteen sous four deniers parisis for having worn two strings of beads! 'Tis paying rather dear, though. Soho! two gentlemen among these varlets! Aiglet de Soins and Hutin de Mailly—two esquires, *corpus Christi*. Ha! they have been dicing. When shall we see our rector here? To pay a fine of one hundred livres to the king! Bravo, Barbedienne! May I be my brother the archdeacon, if this shall prevent me from gaming—gaming by day, gaming by night, gaming while I live, gaming till I die, and staking my soul after my shirt! By'r Lady, what damsels! one after another, pretty lambs! Ambroise Lecuyere, Isabeau la Paynette, Berarde Gironin, I know them all, by my fay! Fiend, fiend, fiend! That will teach you to wear gilt belts! Ten sous parisis, coquettes! Oh! the old deaf imbecile! Oh! Florian, the blockhead! Oh! Barbedienne, the booby! There he is at his feast! Fines, costs, charges, damages, stocks, pillory, imprisonment, are to him Christmas cakes and St. John's march-pane! Look at him, the hog! Get on! What! another woman! Thibaud la Thibaude, I declare! For being seen out of the Rue Glatigny! Who is that young fellow? Gieffroy Mabonne, one of the bowmen of the guard—for swearing an oath, forsooth! A fine for you, La Thibaude! a fine for you, Gieffroy; but ten to one the old stupid will confound the two charges and make the woman pay for the oath and the soldier for incontinence. Look, look, Robin! what are they bringing in now? By Jupiter, there are all the hounds in a pack! That must be a fine head of game! A wild boar surely! And so it is, Robin, so it is! And a rare one too, God wot! Grammercy! 'tis our prince, our Pope of Fools, our bell-ringer, our one-eyed, hunchbacked, bandy-legged Quasimodo!"

Sure enough it was Quasimodo, bound, corded, pinioned. The party of the provost's men who surrounded him were accompanied by the captain of the watch in person, having the arms of France embroidered on the breast of his coat and those of the city on the back. At the same time there was nothing about Quasimodo, save and except his deformity, which could justify this display of halberts and arquebuses: he was silent, sullen, and quiet. His only eye merely gave from time to time an angry glance at the bonds which confined him. Meanwhile Master Florian was intently perusing the indorsement of a paper containing the charges alleged against Quasimodo, which had been handed to him by the clerk. By means of this precaution, which he was accustomed to take before he proceeded to an examination, he acquainted himself beforehand with the name, condition, and offense of the prisoner; was enabled to have in readiness replies to expected answers; and succeeded in extricating himself from all the sinuosities of the interrogatory without too grossly exposing his infirmity. To him, therefore, the indorsement was like the dog to the blind man. If, however, his infirmity chanced to betray itself now and then by some incoherent apostrophe or some unintelligible question, with the many it passed for profoundness, with some few for imbecility. In either case the honor of the magistracy remained unimpeached; for it is better that a judge should be reputed profound or imbecile than deaf. Accordingly, he took great pains to conceal his deafness from observation, and in general he was so successful as at last to deceive himself on this point. This is more easily done than it may be imagined. Every hunchback holds his head erect, every stammerer is fond of making speeches, every deaf person talks in a low tone. For his part he believed that he was somewhat hard of hearing; and this was the only concession that he made on this point to public opinion in moments of perfect frankness and self-examination.

After ruminating awhile on Quasimodo's affair, he threw back his head and half closed his eyes, to give himself a look of the more majesty and impartiality, so that at that moment he was both deaf and blind—a twofold condition without which there is no perfect judge. In this magisterial attitude he commenced his examination.

"Your name?"

Now, here was a case which the law had not provided for—the deaf interrogating the deaf.

Quasimodo, unaware of the question addressed to him, continued to look steadfastly at the judge without answering. The deaf judge, equally unaware of the deafness of the accused, conceiving that he had answered, as persons in his situation generally do, went on, agreeably to his mechanical routine: "Very well; your age?"

Quasimodo maintained the same silence as before. The judge again supposing that he had answered his question, continued: "Now your business?"

Still Quasimodo was silent. The people who witnessed this curious scene began to whisper and to look at one another.

"That will do," rejoined the imperturbable auditor, when he presumed that the accused had finished his third answer.

"You are accused before us, in the first place, of making a nocturnal disturbance; secondly, of an assault upon the person of a lewd woman; thirdly, of disloyalty, sedition, and resistance to the archers of the guard of our lord the king. What have you to say for yourself on these points? Clerk, have you taken down the prisoner's answers thus far?"

At this unlucky question, a roar of laughter burst from both clerk and audience, so vehement, so loud, so contagious, so universal, that neither of the deaf men could help noticing it. Quasimodo merely turned about and shrugged his hump with disdain; while Master Florian, equally astonished, and supposing that the mirth of the spectators had been provoked by some disrespectful reply of the prisoner's, rendered visible to him by the rising of his shoulders, indignantly exclaimed:

"For that answer, fellow, you deserve a halter. Know you to whom you speak?"

This sally was not likely to check the explosion of the general mirth. So odd and so ridiculous did it appear to all, that the fit of laughter spread to the very sergeants of the Parloir aux Bourgeois, a sort of knaves of spades proverbial for stupidity. Quasimodo alone preserved his gravity for this very sufficient reason that he had not the least notion of what was passing around him. The judge, more and more exasperated, thought fit to proceed in the same strain, hoping thereby to strike the prisoner with a terror that should react upon the audience.

"How dare you thus insult the auditor of the Chatelet, the deputy superintendent of the police of Paris, appointed to inquire into crimes, offenses, and misdemeanors; to control all trades; to prevent forestalling and regrating; to cleanse the city of filth and the air of contagious diseases; to repair the pavements; in short, to pay continual attention to the public welfare, and that too without wages or hope of salary! Do you know that I am Florian Barbedienne, own lieutenant of Monsieur the Provost, and moreover commissary, controller, examiner——"

The Lord knows when Master Florian would have finished this flight of eloquence had not the low door behind him suddenly opened and afforded passage to the provost himself. Master Florian did not stop short at his entrance, but turning half round upon his heel, and abruptly directing to the provost the harangue which a moment before he was launching forth against Quasimodo—"Monseigneur," said he, "I demand such punishment as it shall please you to pronounce upon the prisoner here present for audacious and heinous contempt of justice."

Out of breath with the exertion, he sat down and began to wipe off the perspiration which trickled from his forehead and fell in big drops upon the parchments spread out before him. Messire Robert d'Estouteville knit his brows and commanded attention with a gesture so imperious and expressive that Quasimodo had some inkling of what was meant.

"What hast thou done to be brought hither, varlet?" said the provost, sternly.

The prisoner, supposing that the provost was inquiring his name, broke his habitual silence, and in a harsh and guttural voice replied, "Quasimodo."

The answer was so incongruous with the question as once more to excite the risibility of the by-standers, when Messire Robert, flushed with rage, exclaimed, "Art thou making thy game of me too, thou arrant knave?"

"Bell-ringer at Notre Dame," replied Quasimodo, conceiving that the judge had inquired his profession.

"Bell-ringer!" roared the provost, who had got up that morning, as we have observed, in such an ill-humor as not to need the further provocation of these cross-grained answers—"bell-ringer! I'll have

such a peal rung on thy back as shall make thee rue thy impertinence. Dost thou hear, varlet?"

"If you want to know my age," said Quasimodo, "I believe I shall
be twenty next Martinmas."

This was too provoking—the provost lost all patience. "What,
wretch! dost thou defy the provost? Here vergers, take this fellow
to the pillory of the Grève; let him be flogged and then turn him
for an hour. 'Sdeath, he shall pay for his insolence, and my pleasure
is that this sentence be proclaimed by four trumpeters in the seven
castellanies of the viscounty of Paris."

The clerk instantly fell to work to record the sentence.

"*Ventre Dieu!* but that's a just sentence!" cried Jehan Frollo du
Moulin, from his corner.

The provost turned about, and again fixing his flashing eyes on
Quasimodo, "I verily believe," said he, "that the knave has dared to
swear in our presence. Clerk, add a fine of twelve deniers parisis for
the oath, and let half of it be given to the church of St. Eustache."

In a few minutes the sentence was drawn up. The language was
simple and concise. The practice of the provosty and viscounty of
Paris had not then been laid down by the president Thibaut Baillet,
and Roger Bammo, king's advocate; it was not then obstructed by
that forest of quirks, cavils, and quibbles which these two lawyers
planted before it at the commencement of the sixteenth century.
Everything about it was clear, explicit, expeditious. It was all
straightforward work, and you perceived at once, at the end of every path, uninterrupted by bushes or roundabout ways, the pillory,
the gibbet, and the wheel. You knew at least what you had to expect.

The clerk handed the sentence to the provost, who affixed his
seal, and left the hall to continue the round of the courts, in a mood
which was likely to increase the population of the jails of Paris.
Jehan Frollo and Robin Poussepain laughed in their sleeve, while
Quasimodo looked on with an air of calm indifference.

While Master Florian Barbedienne was in his turn reading the
sentence, previously to his signing it, the clerk, feeling compassion
for the wretched victim, and hoping to obtain some mitigation of
his punishment, approached as near as he could to the ear of the
auditor and said, pointing at the same time to Quasimodo, "The
poor fellow is deaf."

He conceived that this community of infirmity might awaken
Master Florian's lenity in behalf of the culprit. But in the first place,
as we have already mentioned, Master Florian was by no means
anxious to have it known that he was deaf; and in the next, he was

so hard of hearing as not to catch a single syllable of what the clerk said to him. Pretending, nevertheless, to hear, he replied, "Aha! that is a different thing; I did not know that. In this case let him have another hour in the pillory;" and he signed the sentence with this alteration.

"That's right!" cried Robin Poussepain, who owed Quasimodo a grudge; "this will teach him to handle people roughly."

CHAPTER II

THE *TROU AUX RATS*

WITH THE READER's permission we shall conduct him back to the Place de Grève, which we yesterday quitted with Gringoire to follow La Esmeralda.

It is the hour of ten in the morning. The appearance of the place indicates the morrow of a festival. The pavement is strewed with wrecks—rags, ribbons, feathers, drops of wax from the torches, fragments of the public banquet. A good many citizens are lounging about, kicking the half-consumed cases of the fire-works, admiring the Maison aux Pilliers, extolling the beautiful hangings of the preceding day, and looking at the nails which had held them. The venders of cider and beer are trundling their barrels among the groups. A few pedestrians, urged by business, bustle along at a quick rate. The shopkeepers are calling to one another from their doors and conversing together. The fête, the embassadors, Coppenole, the Pope of Fools, were in every mouth; each striving to crack the best jokes and to laugh the loudest. And yet four sergeants on horseback, who have just posted themselves at the four sides of the pillory, have already gathered around them a considerable portion of the populace, who were kicking their heels about the place in the hopes of enjoying the amusement of an execution.

Now if the reader, after surveying this lively and noisy scene which is performing all over the place, turns his eye toward the ancient half Gothic, half Roman building called Roland's Tower, which forms the corner of the quay to the west, he may perceive at the angle of the façade a large public breviary, richly illuminated, sheltered from the rain by a small pent-house, and secured from thieves by an iron grating, which, nevertheless, does not prevent your turning over the leaves. Beside this breviary is a narrow, pointed, unglazed window looking out upon the place, and defended by two cross-bars of iron—the only aperture for the admission of air and light to a small cell without door, formed in the basement of the wall of the old building, and full of a quiet the more profound, a silence the more melancholy, from its very contiguity to a public place, and that the most populous and the most noisy in Paris.

This cell had been noted in Paris for three centuries, ever since Mme. Roland, of Roland's Tower, from affection for her father, who had fallen in the Crusades, caused it to be cut out of the wall of her own house, for the purpose of shutting herself up in it forever, keeping no part of her mansion but this hole, the door of which was walled up and the window open winter and summer, and giving all the rest to the poor and to God. In this anticipated tomb the disconsolate lady had awaited death for twenty years, praying night and day for the soul of her father, lying upon ashes, without so much as a stone for a pillow, habited in black sackcloth, and subsisting solely upon the bread and water which the pity of the passengers induced them to deposit on her window-sill, thus living upon charity after giving away her all. At her death, at the moment of quitting this for her last sepulcher, she bequeathed it forever to afflicted females, maids, wives, or widows, who should have occasion to pray much for themselves or others, and who should wish to bury themselves alive on account of some heavy calamity or some extraordinary penance. The tears and blessings of the poor embalmed her memory, but to their great disappointment their pious benefactress could not be canonized for want of patronage sufficiently powerful. Such of them as were not most religiously disposed had hoped that the thing would be more easily accomplished in Paradise than at Rome, and had therefore at once prayed to God instead of the pope in behalf of the deceased. Most of them had been content to hold her memory sacred and to make relics of her rags. The city, seconding the intentions of the lady, had founded a public breviary, which was attached to the wall near the window of the cell, that passengers might stop from time to time, were it only that they might be induced to recite a prayer, that the prayer might make them think of alms, and that the poor recluses, the successive inmates of Mme. Roland's cell, might not absolutely perish of hunger and neglect.

In the cities of the Middle Ages tombs of this sort were not rare. In the most frequented street, in the most crowded and noisy market, in the midst of the highways, almost under the horses' feet and cart-wheels, you frequently met with a cellar, a cave, a well, a walled and grated cabin, in which a human being, self-devoted to some everlasting sorrow, to some signal expiation, spent night and day in prayer. And none of those reflections which would be awakened in us at the present time by this strange sight, this horrid cell, a sort of intermediate link between a house and a grave, between the cemetery and the city; that being cut off from all community with mankind, and henceforth numbered among the dead; that lamp consuming its last drop of oil in obscurity; that spark of life glimmering in a grave; that voice of incessant prayer in a cage of stone; that face forever turned toward the next world; that eye always lighted by another sun; that ear pressed against the side of the tomb; that soul a prisoner in this body; this body a prisoner in this dungeon, and the moaning of that afflicted soul within this two-fold envelope of flesh and granite—none of these ideas presented themselves to the multitude in those days. The unreasoning and far from subtle Piety of that period could not see so many facets in a religious act. She took the thing in the lump; and honored, venerated, upon occasion sanctified, the sacrifice, but without analyzing the sufferings, or bestowing on them only a moderate degree of pity. She carried from time to time a pittance to the wretched penitent, peeping through the hole to see if he was still alive; but she knew not his name; she scarcely knew how many years it was since he had begun to die; and to the inquiries of the stranger respecting the living skeleton who was rotting in such a cabin, cave, or cellar, the neighbors merely replied, "It is the recluse."

Thus at that day people saw everything with the naked eye, without magnifying glass, without exaggeration, without metaphysics. The microscope had not yet been invented either for material or for spiritual things.

Instances of this kind of seclusion in the heart of cities, though they raised but little wonder, were yet frequent, as we have just observed. In Paris there was a considerable number of these cells for praying to God and doing penance, and almost all of them were occupied. The clergy, it is true, disliked to see them empty, as that implied lukewarmness in their flocks; the lepers were placed in them when no penitents offered themselves. Besides the cell of the Grève, there was one at Montfaucon, another at the charnel-house of the Innocents; a third I do not exactly remember where, at the logis Clichon, I believe; and others at various places, where you still find traces of them in traditions, though the buildings have been swept away. On the Hill of St. Genevieve a kind of Job of the Middle Ages sung for thirty years the seven penitential psalms, upon a dunghill at the bottom of a cistern, beginning afresh as soon as he had finished, and raising his voice highest at night; and to this day the antiquary imagines that he hears his voice as he enters the street called *Puits qui parle.*[1]

But to return to the cell of Roland's Tower. It is right to mention that ever since the death of Mme. Roland it had seldom been for any length of time without a tenant. Many a woman had come thither to mourn, some their indiscretions and others the loss of their parents or lovers. Parisian scandal, which interferes in everything, even in such things as least concern it, pretended that very few widows had been seen among the number.

According to the fashion of the age, a Latin legend inscribed upon the wall indicated to the lettered passenger the pious destination of this cell. Down to the middle of the sixteenth century it was customary to explain the object of a building by a short motto placed over the door. Thus in France there may still be read over the postern of the seignorial house of Tourville, SILETO ET SPERA;[2] in Ireland, beneath the coat of arms over the grand entrance to Fortescue castle, FORTE SCUTUM SALUS DUCUM;[3] in England, over the principal door of the hospitable mansion of Earl Cowper, TUUM EST.[4] In those days every building was a thought.

As there was no door to the cell of Roland's Tower, there had been engraven in Roman capitals, underneath the window, these two words:

TU ORA.[5]

Hence the people, whose plain common sense never looks for profound meanings in things, and who scruple not to attach to Ludovico Magno the signification of Porte St. Denis, gave to this dark, damp, loathsome hole the name of Trou aux Rats,[6] an interpretation less sublime perhaps than the other, but certainly more picturesque.

1. The Street of the Talking Well.
2. Be silent and hope.
3. A strong shield is the safety of the leaders.
4. It is thine.
5. Pray, thou.
6. The rat–hole.

CHAPTER III

SISTER GUDULE

AT THE PERIOD of which we are treating, the cell of Roland's Tower was occupied. If the reader is desirous of knowing by whom, he has only to listen to the conversation of three honest gossips, who, at the moment at which we have directed his attention to the Trou aux Rats, were going to the very spot, proceeding from the Chatelet along the river-side toward the Grève.

Two of them were dressed like wives of respectable citizens of Paris. Their fine white neckerchiefs; their linsey-woolsey petticoats, striped red and blue; their white worsted stockings, with colored clocks, pulled up tight upon the leg; their square-toed shoes of tawny leather with black soles; and above all their head-dress a sort of high cap of tinsel loaded with ribbons and lace, still worn by the women of Champagne, and also by the grenadiers of the Russian imperial guard—indicated that they belonged to that class of wealthy tradesfolk which comes between what lackeys call a woman and what they style a lady. They wore neither gold rings nor gold crosses, evidently not on account of poverty, but simply for fear of fine. Their companion was attired nearly in the same fashion, but in her dress and manner there was something which betrayed the country woman. The height of her belt above the hips told that she had not been long in Paris. Add to this a plaited neckerchief, bows of ribbons at her shoes, the stripes of her petticoat running breadthwise instead of lengthwise, and various other enormities equally abhorrent to good taste. The first two walked with the step peculiar to the women of Paris who are showing the lions to their provincial friends. The third held a big boy by one hand while he carried a large cake in the other. The boy did not care to keep up with her but suffered himself to be dragged along, and stumbled every moment, to the no small alarm of his mother. It is true that he paid much greater attention to the cake than the pavement. Some weighty reason no doubt prevented his taking a bite, for he did no more than look wistfully at it. 'Twas cruel to make a Tantalus of the jolt-headed cub.

Meanwhile, the three demoiselles—for the term dames was then reserved for noble females—were talking all at once.

"Let us make haste, Demoiselle Mahiette," said the youngest, who was also the lustiest of the three, to her country friend. "I am afraid we shall be too late. We were told at the Chatelet that he was to be put in the pillory forthwith."

"Pooh! pooh! What are you talking of, Damoiselle Oudarde Musnier?" replied the other Parisian. "He is to stay two hours in the pillory. We shall have plenty of time. Have you ever seen any one in the pillory, my dear Mahiette?"

"Yes," answered Mahiette, "at Reims."

"Your pillory at Reims! why, 'tis not worth mentioning. A wretched cage where they turn nothing but clodpoles!"

"Clodpoles, forsooth!" rejoined Mahiette, "in the Cloth Market at Reims! We have had some noted criminals there, however—people who had murdered both father and mother. Clodpoles, indeed! what do you take us for, Gervaise?"

It is certain that the provincial lady felt somewhat nettled at the attack on the honor of her pillory. Luckily the discreet Damoiselle Oudarde gave a seasonable turn to the conversation.

"What say you, Mahiette," she asked, "to our Flemish embassadors? Have you ever had any like them at Reims?"

"I confess," replied Mahiette, "that Paris is the only place for seeing Flemings such as they."

"And their horses, what beautiful animals, dressed out as they are in the fashion of their country!"

"Ah, my dear!" exclaimed Mahiette, assuming in her turn an air of superiority, "what would you say had you been at Reims at the coronation in the year '61, and seen the horses of the princes and of the king's retinue! There were housings and trappings of all sorts; some of damask cloth and fine cloth of gold garnished with sable; others of velvet furred with ermine; others all covered with jewelry, and gold and silver bells. Think of the money that all this must have cost! And then the beautiful pages that were upon them."

"Heydey!" cried Oudarde, "what is there to do yonder? See what a crowd is collected at the foot of the bridge! There seems to be something in the midst of them that they are looking at."

"Surely I hear the sound of a tambourine," said Gervaise. "I dare say it is young Esmeralda playing her antics with her goat. Quick, Mahiette, and pull your boy along. You are come to see the curiosities of Paris. Yesterday you saw the Flemings; to-day you must see the Egyptian."

"The Egyptian!" exclaimed Mahiette, starting back, and forcibly grasping the arm of her son. "God forbid! she might steal my boy. Come, Eustache!"

With these words she began to run along the quay toward the Grève, till she had left the bridge at a considerable distance behind her. Presently the boy, whom she drew after her, tripped and fell upon his knees: she stopped to recover breath, and Oudarde and Gervaise overtook her.

"That Egyptian steal your boy!" said Gervaise. "Beshrew me, if this be not a strange fancy!"

Mahiette shook her head with a pensive look.

"And what is still more strange," observed Oudarde, "Sister Gudule has the same notion of the Egyptians."

"Who is Sister Gudule?" inquired Mahiette.

"You must be vastly ignorant at your Reims not to know that," replied Oudarde. "Why, the recluse of the Trou aux Rats."

"What! the poor woman to whom we are carrying the cake?"

Oudarde nodded affirmatively. "Just so. You will see her presently at her window on the Grève. She holds just the same opinion of those Egyptian vagabonds who go about drumming on tambourines and telling fortunes. Nobody knows why she has such a horror of the Zingari and the Egyptians. But you, Mahiette, wherefore should you take to your heels thus at the mere sight of them?"

"Oh!" said Mahiette, clasping her boy's head in both her hands, "I would not for the world that the same thing should happen to me as befell Paquette la Chantefleurie."

"Ah! you must tell us that story, good Mahiette," said Gervaise, taking her by the arm.

"I will," answered Mahiette; "but how ignorant you must be in your Paris not to know that! But we need not stop while I tell you the story. You must know, then, that Paquette la Chantefleurie was a handsome girl of eighteen just when I was so myself, that is, eighteen years ago, and it is her own fault that she is not this day, like me, a hearty, comely mother of six-and-thirty, with a husband and a boy. She was the daughter of Guybertaut, minstrel of Reims, the same that played before King Charles VII. at his coronation, when he went down our river Vesle from Sillery to Muison, and the Maid of Orleans was in the barge with him. Paquette's father died while she was quite an infant; so she had only her mother, who was the sister of Monsieur Matthieu Pradon, master-brazier here at Paris, in the Rue Parin-Garlin, who died only last year. You see she came of a good family. The mother was, unluckily, a kind, easy woman, and taught Paquette nothing but to do a little needle-work and make herself finery, which helped to keep them very poor. They lived at Reims, in the Rue Folle Peine. In '61, the year of the coronation of our King Louis XI., whom God preserve! Paquette was so lively and so handsome that everybody called her La Chantefleurie. Poor girl! what beautiful teeth she had! and how she would laugh that she might show them! Now a girl that laughs a great deal is in the way to cry; fine teeth spoil fine eyes. Chantefleurie and her mother had great difficulty to earn a livelihood; since the death of the old minstrel their circumstances had been getting worse and worse; their needle-work produced them no more than six deniers a week. How different from the time when old Guybertaut received twelve sols parisis for a single song, as he did at the coronation! One winter —it was that of the same year, '61—when the poor creatures had neither cordwood nor fagots, the weather was very cold, which gave Chantefleurie such a beautiful color that she was admired by all the men, and this led to her ruin.—Eustache, don't meddle with the cake! We all knew what had happened as soon as we saw her come to church one Sunday with a gold cross at her breast. And, look you, she was not fifteen at the time. Her first lover was the young Viscount de Cormontreuil, whose castle is about three quarters of a mile from Reims; and when she was deserted by him, she took up first with one and then with another till at last all men became alike to her. Poor Chantefleurie!" sighed Mahiette, brushing away a tear that started from her eye.

"There is nothing very extraordinary in this history," said Gervaise; "nor, as far as I can see, has it anything to do with Egyptians or children."

"Have patience," replied Mahiette; "you will soon see that it has. In '66, it will be sixteen years this very month on St. Paula's day, Paquette was brought to bed of a little girl. How delighted she was, poor thing! She had long been wishing for a child. Her mother, good soul, who had always winked at her faults, was now dead; so that Paquette had nothing in the world to love, and none to love her. For five years, ever since her fall, she had been a miserable creature, poor Chantefleurie! She was alone, alone in this life, pointed at and hooted in the streets, cuffed by the beadles, teased by little ragged urchins. By this time she was twenty—an age at which, it is said, such women begin to be old. Her way of life scarcely brought her in more than her needle-work had formerly done; the winter had set in sharp, and wood was again rare on her hearth and bread in her cupboard. She was, of course, very sorrowful, very miserable, and

her tears wore deep channels in her cheeks. But in her degraded
and forlorn condition it seemed to her that she should be less degraded and less forlorn if she had anything or any one in the world
that she could love, and that could love her. She felt that this must
needs be a child, because nothing but a child could be innocent
enough for that. Women of her class must have either a lover or a
child to engage their affections, or they are very unhappy. Now as
Paquette could not find a lover, she set her whole heart upon a
child, and prayed to God night and day for one. And He took compassion on her and gave her a little girl. Her joy is not to be described. How she did hug and fondle her infant! it was quite a tempest of tears and kisses. She suckled it herself, made it clothes out of
her own, and thenceforward felt neither cold nor hunger. Her
beauty returned. An old maid makes a young mother. In a short
time she again betook herself to her former courses, and she laid out
all the money that she received on frocks and caps and lace and little
satin bonnets, and all sorts of finery for her child.—Monsieur Eustache, haven't I told you not to meddle with that cake?—It is certain
that little Agnes—that was the name given to the child at her christening—was more bedizened with ribbons and embroidery than a
princess. Among other things she had a pair of little shoes, such as
I'll be bound Louis XI. never had. Her mother had made and embroidered them herself with the utmost art and skill of her needle.
A prettier pair of little rose-colored shoes were never seen. They
were not longer than my thumb, and you must have seen the child's
tiny feet come out or you would never believe they could go into
them. But then those feet were so small, so rosy—more so than the
satin of the shoes. When you have children, Oudarde, you will
know that nothing is so pretty as those delicate little feet and
hands."

"I desire nothing better," said Oudarde, with a sigh, "but I must
wait till it is the good pleasure of Monsieur Andry Musnier."

"Paquette's baby," resumed Mahiette, "had not merely handsome
feet. I saw it when but four months old. Oh, it was a love! Her eyes
were larger than her mouth, and she had the most beautiful dark
hair, which already began to curl. What a superb brunette she
would have made at sixteen! Her mother became every day more
and more dotingly fond of her. She hugged her, she kissed her, she
tickled her, she washed her, she pranked her up—she was ready to
eat her. In the wildness of her joy she thanked God for the gift.
But it was her tiny rosy feet above all that she was never tired of
admiring. She would pass whole hours in putting on them the little

shoes, taking them off again, gazing at them, and pressing them to her lips."

"The story is well enough," said Gervaise, in an undertone; "but where are the Egyptians?"

"Why, here," replied Mahiette. "One day a party of very strange-looking people on horseback arrived at Reims. They were beggars and vagabonds who roved about the country headed by their duke and their counts. Their visage was tawny; they had curly hair and wore silver rings in their ears. The women were uglier than the men. Their complexion was darker. They went bareheaded; a shabby mantle covered the body, an old piece of sackcloth was tied about the shoulders, and their hair was like a horse's tail. The children, who were tumbling about upon their laps, were enough to frighten an ape. These hideous people had come—so it was said—straightway from Egypt to Reims through Poland. The pope had confessed them, and ordered them by way of penance to wander for seven years together through the world without lying in a bed; and they claim ten livres tournois of all archbishops, bishops and crosiered and mitered abbots, by virtue of a bull of the pope. They came to Reims to tell fortunes in the name of the King of Algiers and the Emperor of Germany. This was quite enough, as you may suppose, to cause them to be forbidden to enter the city. The whole band then encamped without more ado on the mill hill, by the old chalk-pits, and all Reims went to see them. They looked at your palm and foretold wonderful things. At the same time there were various reports about their stealing children, cutting purses, and eating human flesh. Prudent persons said to the simple, 'Go not near them,' and yet went themselves in secret. It was quite the rage. The fact is, they told things which would have astonished a cardinal. Mothers were not a little proud of their children after the Egyptians had read all sorts of marvels written in their hands in pagan gibberish. One had an emperor, another a pope, a third a great captain. Poor Chantefleurie was seized with curiosity; she was anxious to know her luck, and whether little Agnes should one day be Empress of Armenia or something of that sort. She carried her to the encampment of the Egyptians; the women admired the infant, they fondled her, they kissed her with their dark lips, they were astonished at her tiny hand, to the no small delight of the poor mother. But above all they extolled her delicate feet and her pretty little shoes. The child was not quite a year old. She had begun to lisp a word or two, laughed at her mother like a little madcap, and was plump and fat and played a thousand engaging antics. But she was frightened at the Egyptians and fell a-crying. Her mother kissed and cuddled her, and away she went overjoyed at the good luck which the fortune-tellers had promised her Agnes. She was to be a beauty, a virtue, a queen. She returned to her garret in the Rue Folle Peine quite proud of her burden. Next day she softly slipped out for a moment while the infant lay asleep on the bed, leaving the door ajar, and ran to tell an acquaintance in the Rue Sechesserie how that there would come a time when her dear little Agnes would have the King of England and the Archduke of Ethiopia to wait upon her at table, and a hundred other marvelous things. On her return, not hearing the child cry, as she went upstairs, she said to herself, 'That's lucky! baby is asleep yet.' She found the door wider open than she had left it; she went in hastily and ran to the bed. Poor mother! the infant was gone, and nothing belonging to it was left except one of its pretty little shoes. She rushed out of the room, darted downstairs, screaming, 'My child! my child! who has taken my child?' The house stood by itself, and the street was a lonely one; nobody could give her any clew. She went through the town, searching every street; she ran to and fro the whole day, distracted, maddened, glaring in at the doors and windows like a wild beast that has lost her young. Her dress was in disorder, her hair hung loose down her back, she was fearful to look at, and there was a fire in her eyes that dried up her tears. She stopped the passengers crying, 'My child! my child! my dear little child! Tell me where to find my child, and I will be your slave, and you shall do with me what you please.' It was quite cutting, Oudarde, and I assure you I saw a very hard-hearted man, Master Ponce Lucabre the attorney, shed tears at it. Poor, poor mother! In the evening she went home. While she was away a neighbor had seen two Egyptian women slip slyly up her stairs with a large bundle, and presently come down again, shut the door, and hurry off. After they were gone, cries as if of a child had been heard proceeding from Paquette's lodging. The mother laughed with joy, flew upstairs, dashed open the door, and went in. Only think, Oudarde, instead of her lovely baby, so smiling and so plump and so ruddy, there she found a sort of little monster, a hideous, deformed, one-eyed, limping thing, squalling and creeping about the floor. She covered her eyes in horror. 'Oh,' said she, 'can it be that the witches have changed my Agnes into this frightful animal?' Her neighbors took the little imp away forthwith; he would have driven her mad. He was the misshapen child of some Egyptian or other who had given herself up to the devil. He appeared to be about four years old, and talked a language which was not a human language

—such words were never before heard in this world. Chantefleurie snatched up the tiny shoe, all that was left her of all she had loved. She lay so long without moving, without speaking, apparently without breathing, that everybody thought she was dead. All at once she trembled in every limb; she covered the precious relic with passionate kisses, and burst into a fit of sobs, as if her heart was going to break. I assure you we all wept along with her. 'Oh, my baby!' said she, 'my dear little baby! where art thou?' It made one's heart bleed. I can't help crying still at the thought of it. Our children, you see, are as the very marrow of our bones. Oh, my Eustache, my poor Eustache, if I were to lose thee, what would become of me! At length Chantefleurie suddenly sprung up and ran through the streets of Reims, shouting: 'To the camp of the Egyptians! Let the witches be burned!' The Egyptians were gone. It was dark night; nobody could tell which way they had gone. Next day, which was Sunday, there were found on a heath between Gueux and Tilley, about two leagues from Reims, the remains of a large fire, bits of ribbons which had belonged to the dress of Paquette's child, and several drops of blood. There could be no further doubt that the Egyptians had the night before held their sabbath on the heath, and feasted upon the child in company with their master, Beelzebub. When Chantefleurie heard these horrid particulars she did not weep; she moved her lips as if to speak, but could not. The day after her hair was quite gray, and on the next she had disappeared."

"A frightful story, indeed," exclaimed Oudarde, "and enough to draw tears from a Burgundian!"

"I am no longer surprised," said Gervaise, "that you are so dreadfully afraid of the Egyptians."

"You are quite right," replied Oudarde, "to get out of their way with Eustache, especially as these are Egyptians from Poland."

"Not so," said Gervaise; "it is said that they come from Spain and Catalonia."

"At any rate," answered Oudarde, "it is certain that they are Egyptians."

"And not less certain," continued Gervaise, "that their teeth are long enough to eat little children. And I should not be surprised if Esmeralda were to pick a bit now and then, though she had such a small, pretty mouth. Her white goat plays so many marvelous tricks that there must be something wrong at bottom."

Mahiette walked on in silence. She was absorbed in that reverie which is a sort of prolongation of a doleful story, and which continues till it has communicated its vibration to the inmost fibers of the heart. "And did you never know what became of Chantefleurie?" asked Gervaise. Mahiette made no reply. Gervaise repeated the question, gently shaking her arms and calling her by her name.

"What became of Chantefleurie?" said she, mechanically repeating the words whose impression was still fresh upon her ear. Then making an effort to recall her attention to the sense of those words: "Ah!" said she, sharply, "it was never known what became of her."

After a pause she added: "Some say they saw her leave Reims in the dusk of the evening by the Porte Flechembault; and others at daybreak by the old Porte Basée. Her gold cross was found hanging on the stone cross in the field where the fair is held. It was this trinket that occasioned her fall in '61. It was a present from the handsome Viscount de Cormontreuil, her first admirer. Paquette never would part with it, distressed as she had often been. She clung to it as to life. Of course, when we heard how and where it was found, we all concluded that she was dead. Yet there were persons who declared they had seen her on the road to Paris walking barefoot upon the flints. But, in this case, she must have gone out at the Gate of Vesle, and all these accounts cannot be true. My own opinion is that she did actually go by the Gate of Vesle, not only out of the town but out of the world."

"I don't understand you," said Gervaise.

"The Vesle," replied Mahiette, with a melancholy smile, "is our river."

"Poor Chantefleurie!" exclaimed Oudarde, shuddering. "Drowned!"

"Drowned!" replied Mahiette. "Ah! how it would have spoiled good Father Guybertaut's singing, while floating in his bark beneath the bridge of Tinqueux, had he been told that his dear little Paquette would some day pass under that same bridge, but without song and without bark!"

"And the little shoe?" said Gervaise.

"Disappeared with the mother," replied Mahiette.

Oudarde, a comely, tender-hearted woman, would have been satisfied to sigh in company with Mahiette; but Gervaise, who was of a more inquisitive disposition, had not got to the end of her questions.

"And the monster?" said she all at once, resuming the inquiries.

"What monster?" asked Mahiette.

"The little Egyptian monster left by the witches at Chantefleurie's in exchange for her child. What was done with it? I hope you drowned that too."

"Oh, no," replied Mahiette.

"Burned then, I suppose? The best thing too that could be done with a witch's child."

"Nor that either, Gervaise. The archbishop had compassion on the Egyptian boy; he carefully took the devil out of him, blessed him, and sent him to Paris to be exposed in the cradle at Notre Dame as a foundling."

"Those bishops," said Gervaise, grumbling, "because they are learned men, never do anything like other people. Only think, Oudarde, to pop the devil into the place of the foundling! for it is quite certain that this little monster could be nothing else. Well, Mahiette, and what became of him at Paris? No charitable person would look at him, I reckon."

"I don't know," replied her country friend. "Just at that time my husband bought the place of notary at Beru, about two leagues from Reims, and, being fully engaged with our own business, we lost sight of the matter."

Amid such conversation the worthy trio reached the Place de Grève. Engrossed by the subject of their discourse, they had passed Roland's Tower without being aware of it, and turned mechanically toward the pillory, around which the concourse of people was every moment increasing. It is probable that the scene which at this moment met their view would have made them completely forget the Trou aux Rats and their intention of calling there, had not Eustache, whom Mahiette still led by the hand, as if apprised by some instinct that they had passed the place of destination, cried: "Mother, now may I eat the cake?"

Had the boy been less hasty, that is to say, less greedy, he would have waited till the party had returned to the house of Master Andry Musnier, Rue Madame la Valence in the University, when there would have been the two branches of the Seine and the five bridges of the city between the cake and the Trou aux Rats, before he had ventured the timid question: "Mother, now may I eat the cake?"

That very question, an imprudent one at the moment when it was put by Eustache, roused Mahiette's attention.

"Upon my word," said she, "we are forgetting the recluse. Show me your Trou aux Rats, that I may carry her the cake."

"Let's go at once," said Oudarde, "'tis a charity."

This was far from agreeable to Eustache. "She sha'n't have my cake," said he, dashing his head against his two shoulders by turns, which in a case of this kind is a signal token of displeasure.

The three women turned back, and having arrived at Roland's

Tower, Oudarde said to the other two: "We must not all look in at the hole at once, lest we should frighten Sister Gudule. Do you pretend to be reading the 'Dominus' in the breviary, while I peep in at the window—she knows something of me. I will tell you when to come."

She went up by herself to the window. The moment she looked in, profound pity took possession of every feature, and her open, good-humored face changed color and expression as suddenly as if it had passed out of the sunshine into the moonlight; a tear trembled in her eye and her mouth was contracted as when a person is going to weep. A moment afterward she put her finger upon her lips and made a sign for Mahiette to come and look.

Mahiette went in silence and on tiptoe, as though approaching the bed of a dying person. It was in truth a melancholy sight that presented itself to the two women, while they looked in without stirring or breathing at the barred window of the Trou aux Rats.

The cell was small, wider than deep, with coved ceiling, and seen from within resembled the hollow of a large episcopal miter. Upon the stone floor, in one angle, a female was seated, or rather crouched. Her chin rested upon her knees, while her arms and clasped hands encircled her legs. Doubled up in this manner, wrapped in brown sackcloth, her long, lank gray hair falling over her face down to her feet, she presented at first sight a strange figure standing out from the dark ground of the cell, a sort of dun triangle which the ray entering at the window showed like one of those specters seen in dreams, half shadow and half light, pale, motionless, gloomy, cowering upon a grave or before the grating of a dungeon. It was neither a woman nor man nor living creature; it had no definite form; it was a shapeless figure, a sort of vision in which the real and the fantastic were contrasted like light and shade. Scarcely could there be distinguished under her streaming hair the forbidding profile of an attenuated face; scarcely did the ample robe of sackcloth which infolded her permit the extremity of a bare foot to be seen peeping from beneath it and curling up on the hard, cold pavement. The faint likeness of the human form discernible under this garb of mourning made one shudder.

This figure, which you would have supposed to be imbedded in the stone floor, appeared to have neither motion nor breath nor thought. Without other clothing save the sackcloth, in the month of January, barefoot upon a pavement of granite, without fire, in the gloom of a dungeon, the oblique aperture of which admitted only the chill blast, but not the cheering sun, she seemed not to suffer, not even to feel. You would have thought that she had turned herself to stone with the dungeon, to ice with the season. Her hands were clasped, her eyes fixed. At the first glance you would have taken her for a specter, at the second for a statue.

At intervals, however, her livid lips opened for the purpose of breathing, and quivered; but they looked as dead and as will-less as leaves driven by the blast. Meanwhile, those haggard eyes cast a look, an ineffable look, a profound, melancholy, imperturbable look, steadfastly fixed on a corner of the cell which could not be seen from without; a look which seemed to connect all the gloomy thoughts of that afflicted spirit with some mysterious object.

Such was the creature to whom was given, from her garb, the familiar name of Sacky, and from her dwelling that of the Recluse.

The three women—for by this time Gervaise had rejoined Oudarde and Mahiette—peeped in at the window. Their heads intercepted the faint light that entered the dungeon, but yet the wretched being whom they deprived of it appeared not to notice them. "Let us not disturb her," said Oudarde, softly; "she is praying."

Mahiette scrutinized all this time that wan, withered, death-like face, under its veil of hair, with an anxiety that increased every moment, and her eyes filled with tears. "It would indeed be most extraordinary!" muttered she. Putting her head between the bars of the aperture, she was enabled to see the corner upon which the eye of the unhappy recluse was still riveted. When she drew back her head from the window her cheeks were bathed with tears.

"What do you call this woman?" said she to Oudarde, who replied:

"We call her Sister Gudule."

"For my part," rejoined Mahiette, "I call her Paquette la Chantefleurie."

Then laying her finger upon her lips, she made a sign to the astonished Oudarde to put her head through the aperture and look. Oudarde did so, and beheld in the corner upon which the eye of the recluse was fixed in gloomy ecstasy a tiny shoe of pink satin, embroidered all over with gold and silver. Gervaise looked in after Oudarde, and the three women fell a-weeping at the sight of the unfortunate mother. Neither their looks, however, nor their tears were noticed by the recluse. Her hands remained clasped, her lips mute, her eyes fixed, and that look thus bent on the little shoe was enough to cut any one who knew her story to the heart.

The three women gazed without uttering a word; they durst not speak even in a whisper. This profound silence, this intense sorrow, this utter forgetfulness of all but one object, produced upon them the effect of a high altar at Easter or Christmas. It awed them too into silence, into devotion; they were ready to fall on their knees.

At length Gervaise, the most inquisitive, and of course the least tender-hearted of the three, called to the recluse, in hopes of making her speak, "Sister! Sister Gudule!" Thrice did she repeat the call, raising her voice every time. The recluse stirred not; it drew from her neither word, nor look, nor sigh, nor sign of life.

"Sister! Sister Gudule!" said Oudarde, in her turn, in a kinder and more soothing tone. The recluse was silent and motionless as before.

"A strange woman!" exclaimed Gervaise. "I verily believe that a bombard would not waken her."

"Perhaps she is deaf!" said Oudarde, sighing.

"Perhaps blind," added Gervaise.

"Perhaps dead," ejaculated Mahiette.

It is certain that if the spirit had not yet quitted that inert, lethargic, and apparently inanimate frame it had at least retired to and shut itself up in recesses which the perceptions of the external organs could not reach.

"What shall we do to rouse her?" said Oudarde. "If we leave the cake in the window, some boy will run away with it."

Eustache, whose attention had till this moment been taken up by a little cart drawn by a great dog, which had just passed along, all at once perceived that his mother and her friends were looking through the window at something; and, curious to learn what it was, he clambered up on a post, and thrusting his red, chubby face in at the aperture, he cried: "Only look, mother! Who is that?"

At the sound of the child's clear, fresh, sonorous voice the recluse started. She instantly turned her head; her long, attenuated fingers drew back the hair from her brow, and she fixed her sad, astonished, distracted eyes upon the boy. That look was transient as lightning. "Oh, my God!" she instantly exclaimed, burying her face in her lap, and it seemed as if her harsh voice rent itself a passage from her chest; "at least keep those of others out of my sight!"

This shock, however, had, as it were, awakened the recluse. A long shudder thrilled her whole frame; her teeth chattered; she half raised her head, and, taking hold of her feet with her hands, as if to warm them, she ejaculated, "Oh! how cold it is!"

"Poor creature," said Oudarde, with deep compassion, "would you like a little fire?"

She shook her head in token of refusal.

"Well, then," rejoined Oudarde, offering her a bottle, "here is some hippocras which will warm you."

Again she shook her head, looked steadfastly at Oudarde, and said: "Water!"

Oudarde remonstrated. "No, sister," said she, "that is not fit to drink for January. Take some of this hippocras and a bit of the cake we have brought you."

She pushed aside the cake, which Mahiette held out to her. "Some brown bread," was the reply.

"Here," said Gervaise, catching the charitable spirit of her companions, and taking off her cloak; "here is something to keep you warm. Put it over your shoulders."

She refused the cloak as she had done the bottle and the cake, with the single word, "Sackcloth."

"But surely," resumed the kind-hearted Oudarde, "you must have perceived that yesterday was a day of public rejoicing."

"Ah! yes, I did," replied the recluse; "for the last two days I have had no water in my pitcher." After a pause she added: "Why should the world think of me who do not think of it? When the fire is out the ashes get cold."

As if fatigued with the effort of speaking, she dropped her head upon her knees. The simple Oudarde conceived that in the concluding words she was again complaining of cold. "Do have a fire, then," said she.

"Fire!" exclaimed the recluse, in a strange tone; "and would you make one for the poor baby who has been under ground these fifteen years?"

Her limbs shook, her voice trembled, her eyes flashed; she raised herself on her knees; all at once she extended her white, skinny hand toward the boy. "Take away that child," cried she. "The Egyptian will presently pass."

She then sunk upon her face, and her forehead struck the floor with a sound like that of a stone falling upon it. The three women concluded that she was dead. Presently, however, she began to stir, and they saw her crawl upon hands and knees to the corner where the little shoe was. She was then out of their sight, and they durst not look after her; but they heard a thousand kisses and a thousand sighs, mingled with piercing shrieks, and dull, heavy thumps, as if from a head striking against a wall. At last, after one of these blows, so violent as to make all three start, they heard nothing more.

"She must have killed herself!" said Gervaise, venturing to put her head in at the aperture. "Sister! Sister Gudule!"

"Sister Gudule!" repeated Oudarde.

"Good God!" exclaimed Gervaise—"she does not stir. She must be dead!—Gudule! Gudule!"

Mahiette, shocked to such degree that she could scarcely speak, made an effort. "Wait a moment," said she. Then, going close to the window, "Paquette!" she cried. "Paquette la Chantefleurie!"

A boy who thoughtlessly blows a lighted cracker which hangs fire, and makes it explode in his eyes, is not more frightened than was Mahiette at the effect of this name thus abruptly pronounced.

The recluse shook all over, sprung upon her feet, and bounded to the window, her eyes at the same time flashing fire, with such vehemence that the three women retreated to the parapet of the quay. The haggard face of the recluse appeared pressed against the bars of the window. "Aha!" she cried, with a laugh, "'tis the Egyptian that calls me."

The scene which was just then passing at the pillory caught her eye. Her brow wrinkled with horror, she stretched both her skeleton arms out of her cell, and cried with a voice unlike that of a human being: "So, it is thou, spawn of Egypt, it is thou, child-stealer, that callest me. Cursed be thou for thy pains! cursed!—cursed!—cursed!"

CHAPTER IV

THE PILLORY

THESE WORDS WERE, if we may so express it, the point of junction of two scenes which had thus far been acting contemporaneously, each on its particular stage; the one, that which has just been detailed, at the Trou aux Rats; the other, which we are about to describe, at the pillory. The first had been witnessed only by the three females with whom the reader has just made acquaintance; the spectators of the other consisted of the crowd which we some time since saw collecting in the Place de Grève around the pillory and the gallows.

This crowd, to whom the appearance of the four sergeants posted at the four corners of the pillory ever since nine in the morning intimated that some poor wretch was about to suffer, if not capital punishment, yet flogging, the loss of ears, or some other infliction —this crowd had increased so rapidly that the sergeants had been

obliged more than once to keep it back by means of their horses'
heels and the free use of their whips.

The mob, accustomed to wait whole hours for public executions,
did not manifest any vehement impatience. They amused themselves with gazing at the pillory, a very simple contrivance, con-
sisting of a cube of masonry some ten feet high, hollow within. A
rude flight of steps of rough stone led to the upper platform, upon
which was seen a horizontal wheel of oak. Upon this wheel the
culprit was bound upon his knees, and with his hands tied behind
him. An axle of timber, moved by a capstan concealed from sight
within the little building, caused the wheel to revolve in the horizontal plane, and thus exhibited the culprit's face to every point of
the place in succession. This was called turning a criminal.

Thus, you see, the pillory of the Grève was by no means so interesting an object as the pillory of Halles. There was nothing
architectural, nothing monumental about it: it had no roof with
iron cross, no octagon lanterns, no slender pillars spreading at the
margin of the roof into capitals of acanthi and flowers, no fantastic
and monstrous water-spouts, no carved wood-work, no delicate
sculpture deeply cut in stone.

Here the eye was forced to be content with four flat walls and
two buttresses of unhewn stone, and a plain bare gibbet, likewise
of stone, standing beside it. The treat would have been a sorry one
for the lovers of Gothic architecture. It is true, however, that no
people ever held works of art in less estimation than the Parisian
populace in the Middle Ages, and that they cared not a pin about
the beauty of a pillory.

The culprit, tied to the tail of a cart, was at length brought forward; and when he had been hoisted upon the platform, where he
could be seen from all points of the place, bound with cords and
thongs upon the wheel of the pillory, a prodigious hooting, mingled
with laughter and acclamations, burst from the mob. They had recognized Quasimodo.

It was a strange reverse for the poor fellow to be pilloried on the
same spot where the preceding day he had been hailed and proclaimed Pope and Prince of Fools, escorted by the Duke of Egypt,
the King of Thunes, and the Emperor of Galilee. So much is certain,
that there was not a creature in that concourse, not even himself,
alternately the object of triumph and of punishment, who could
clearly make out the connection between the two situations. Gringoire and his philosophy were lacking to the spectacle.

Presently Michel Noiret, sworn trumpeter of our lord the king, commanded silence, and proclaimed the sentence agreeably to the ordinance of the provost. He then fell back behind the cart with his men in their official liveries.

Quasimodo never stirred; he did not so much as frown. All resistance, indeed, on his part was rendered impossible by what was then called, in the language of criminal jurisprudence, "the vehemence and the firmness of the bonds," which means that the chains and the thongs probably cut into the flesh. He had suffered himself to be led, and pushed, and carried, and lifted, and bound again and again. His face betrayed no other emotion than the astonishment of a savage or an idiot. He was known to be deaf; you would have supposed him to be blind also.

He was placed on his knees upon the circular floor. His doublet and shirt were taken off, and he allowed himself to be stripped to the waist without opposition. He was immeshed in a fresh series of thongs: he suffered himself to be bound and buckled: only from time to time he breathed hard, like a calf whose head hangs dangling over the tail of a butcher's cart.

"The stupid oaf!" exclaimed Jehan Frollo du Moulin to his friend Robin Poussepain (for the two students had followed the culprits as a matter of course), "he has no more idea of what they are going to do than a lady-bird shut up in a box."

A loud laugh burst from the mob when they beheld Quasimodo's naked hump, his camel breast, and his scaly and hairy shoulders. Amid all this mirth, a man of short stature and robust frame, clad in the livery of the city, ascended the platform and placed himself by the side of the culprit. His name was quickly circulated among the crowd. It was Master Pierrat Torterue, sworn tormentor of the Chatelet.

The first thing he did was to set down upon one corner of the pillory an hour-glass, the upper division of which was full of red sand that dropped into the lower half. He then threw back his cloak, and over his left arm was seen hanging a whip composed of long, white, glistening thongs, knotted, twisted, and armed with sharp bits of metal. With his left hand he carelessly turned up the right sleeve of his shirt as high as the elbow. At length he stamped with his foot. The wheel began to turn. Quasimodo shook in his bonds. The amazement suddenly expressed in his hideous face drew fresh shouts of laughter from the spectators.

All at once, at a moment when the wheel in its revolution presented the mountain shoulders of Quasimodo to Master Pierrat, he raised his arm; the thin lashes hissed sharply in the air like so many vipers, and descended with fury upon the back of the unlucky wight.

Quasimodo started like one awakened from a dream. He began to comprehend the meaning of the scene, he writhed in his bonds; a violent contraction of surprise and pain distorted the muscles of his face, but he heaved not a single sigh. He merely turned his head one way and the other, balancing it like a bull stung by a gadfly.

A second stroke succeeded the first, then came another and another. The wheel continued to turn and the blows to fall. The blood began to trickle in a hundred little streams down the swart shoulders of the hunchback, and the slender thongs, whistling in the air in their rotation, sprinkled it in drops over the gaping crowd.

Quasimodo had relapsed, in appearance at least, into his former apathy. He had endeavored, at first quietly and without great external effort, to burst his bonds. His eye was seen to flash, his muscles to swell, his limbs to gather themselves up, and the thongs, cords, and chains to stretch. The effort was mighty, prodigious, desperate; but the old shackles of the provost seemed too tough. They cracked and that was all. Quasimodo sunk down exhausted. Stupor gave place in his countenance to an expression of deep despondency. He closed his only eye, dropped his head upon his breast and counterfeited death.

Thenceforward he stirred not. Nothing could make him flinch—neither the blood which oozed from his lacerated back, nor the lashes which fell with redoubled force, nor the fury of the executioner, roused and heated by the exercise, nor the hissing and whizzing of the horrible thongs. At length an usher of the Chatelet, habited in black and mounted upon a black horse, who had taken his station by the steps at the commencement of the flogging, extended his ebony wand toward the hour-glass. The executioner held his hand; the wheel stopped; Quasimodo's eye slowly opened.

Two attendants of the sworn tormentor washed the bleeding back of the sufferer, rubbed it with a sort of ointment which in an incredibly short time closed all the wounds, and threw over him a kind of yellow frock shaped like a priest's cope; while Pierrat Torterue drew through his fingers the thongs saturated with blood, which he shook off upon the pavement.

Quasimodo's punishment was not yet over. He had still to remain in the pillory that hour which Master Florian Barbedienne had so judiciously added to the sentence of Messire Robert d'Estouteville, to the great glory of the old physiological and psychological pun: *Surdus absurdus.*[1] The hour-glass was therefore turned and the

1. A deaf man is absurd.

hunchback left bound as before, that justice might be fully satisfied.

The populace, especially in a half-civilized era, are in society what the boy is in a family. So long as they continue in this state of primitive ignorance, of moral and intellectual minority, so long you may say of them as of the mischievous urchin—"That age is without pity." We have already shown that Quasimodo was generally hated, for more than one good reason, it is true. There was scarcely a spectator among the crowd but either had or imagined he had ground to complain of the malicious hunchback of Notre Dame. His appearance in the pillory had excited universal joy; and the severe punishment which he had undergone, and the pitiful condition in which it had left him, so far from softening the populace, had but rendered their hatred more malignant by arming it with the sting of mirth.

Thus, when the "public vengeance" was once satisfied—according to the jargon still used by gownsmen—it was the turn of private revenge to seek gratification. Here, as in the great hall, the women were most vehement. All bore him some grudge—some for his mischievous disposition, and others for his ugliness; the latter were the most furious. A shower of abuse was poured upon him, accompanied by hootings and imprecations and laughter, and here and there by stones.

Quasimodo was deaf, but he was sharp-sighted, and the fury of the populace was expressed not less energetically in their countenances than in their words. Besides, the pelting of the stones explained the meaning of the bursts of laughter. This annoyance passed for awhile unheeded; but by degrees that patience, which had braced itself up under the lash of the executioner, gave way under all these stings of petty insects. The bull of the Asturias, which scarcely deigns to notice the attacks of the picador, is exasperated by the dogs and the banderillos.

At first he slowly rolled around a look of menace at the crowd; but, shackled as he was, this look could not drive away the flies which galled his wounds. He then struggled in his bonds, and his furious contortions made the old wheel of the pillory creak upon its axis. This served only to increase the jeers and the derisions of the populace.

The wretched sufferer finding, like a chained beast, that he could not break his collar, again became quiet, though at times a sigh of rage heaved all the cavities of his chest. Not a blush, not a trace of shame, was to be discerned in his face. He was too far from the social state and too near the state of nature to know what shame is.

Besides, is it possible that disgrace can be felt by one cast in a mold of extreme deformity? But rage, hatred, despair slowly spread over that hideous face a cloud which gradually became more and more black, more and more charged with an electricity that darted in a thousand flashes from the eye of the Cyclops.

This cloud, however, cleared off for a moment at the appearance of a mule bearing a priest. The instant he caught a glimpse of this mule and this priest in the distance, the face of the poor sufferer assumed a look of gentleness. The rage which had contracted it was succeeded by a strange smile, full of ineffable meekness, kindness, tenderness. As the priest approached, this smile became more expressive, more distinct, more radiant. The prisoner seemed to be anticipating the arrival of a deliverer; but the moment the mule was near enough to the pillory for its rider to recognize the sufferer, the priest cast down his eyes, wheeled about, clapped spurs to this beast, as if in a hurry to escape a humiliating appeal, and by no means desirous of being known or addressed by a poor devil in such a situation. This priest was the Archdeacon Claude Frollo.

Quasimodo's brow was overcast by a darker cloud than ever. For some time a smile mingled with the gloom, but it was a smile of bitterness, disappointment, and deep despondency. Time passed. For an hour at least he had been exposed to incessant ill-usage—lacerated, jeered, and almost stoned. All at once he again struggled in his chains with a redoubled effort of despair that made the whole machine shake; and, breaking the silence which he had hitherto kept, he cried in a hoarse and furious voice, more like the roaring of a wild beast than the articulate tones of a human tongue: "Water!"

This cry of distress, heard above the shouts and laughter of the crowd, so far from exciting compassion, served only to heighten the mirth of the good people of Paris who surrounded the pillory, and who, to confess the truth, were in those days not much less cruel or less brutalized than the disgusting crew of Vagabonds whom we have already introduced to the reader; these merely formed, in fact, the lowest stratum of the populace. Not a voice was raised around the unhappy sufferer but in scorn and derision of his distress. It is certain that at this moment he was still more grotesque and repulsive than pitiable; his face empurpled, and trickling with perspiration, his eye glaring wildly, his mouth foaming with rage and agony, and his tongue lolling out of it. It must also be confessed that had any charitable soul of either sex been tempted to carry a draught of water to the wretched sufferer, so strongly was the notion of infamy and disgrace attached to the ignominious steps of the pillory, that it would have effectually deterred the good Samaritan.

For a few minutes Quasimodo surveyed the crowd with anxious eye, and repeated in a voice more rugged than before: "Water!" He was answered with peals of laughter.

"There is water for thee, deaf varlet," cried Robin Poussepain, throwing in his face a sponge soaked in the kennel. "I am in thy debt."

A woman hurled a stone at his head. "That will teach thee to waken us at night," said she, "with thy cursed bells."

"Take that to drink thy liquor out of!" shouted a fellow, throwing at him a broken jug, which hit him upon the chest. "It was the sight of thy frightful figure that made my wife have a child with two heads."

"Water!" roared the panting Quasimodo for the third time.

At that moment he saw the populace make way. A young female in a strange garb approached the pillory. She was followed by a little white goat with gilt horns, and carried a tambourine in her hand. Quasimodo's eye sparkled. It was the Bohemian whom he had attempted to carry off the preceding night, and he had a confused notion that for this prank he was suffering his present punishment, though in fact it was because he had the misfortune to be deaf and to be tried by a deaf judge. He thought that she was coming to take revenge also, and to give him her blow as well as the rest.

He watched her with nimble foot ascend the steps. He was choked with rage and vexation. Had the lightning of his eye possessed the power, it would have blasted the Egyptian before she reached the platform. Without uttering a word she approached the sufferer, who vainly writhed to avoid her; and loosing a gourd from her girdle, she gently lifted it to the parched lips of the exhausted wretch. A big tear was seen to start from his dry and bloodshot eye, and to trickle slowly down his deformed face so long contracted by despair. It was perhaps the first that he had shed since he arrived at manhood.

Meanwhile he forgot to drink. The Egyptian pouted her pretty lip with impatience, and then put the neck of the gourd between Quasimodo's jagged teeth. He drank greedily, for his thirst was extreme.

When he had finished, the hunchback protruded his dark lips, no doubt to kiss the kind hand which had brought so welcome a relief; but the damsel, perhaps recollecting the violent assault of the foregoing night, quickly drew back her hand with the same start of terror that a child does from a dog which he fears will bite him. The poor fellow then fixed on her a look full of reproach and unutterable woe.

Under any circumstances it would have been a touching sight to see this girl, so fresh, so pure, so lovely, and at the same time so weak, humanely hastening to so much distress, deformity, and malice. On the pillory, this sight was sublime. The populace themselves were moved by it, and began clapping their hands and shouting, "Huzza! huzza!"

It was precisely at this moment that the recluse perceived from the window of her den the Egyptian on the pillory, and pronounced upon her that bitter imprecation—"Cursed be thou, spawn of Egypt! cursed! cursed! cursed!"

La Esmeralda turned pale, and with faltering step descended from the pillory. The voice of the recluse still pursued her: "Get thee down! get thee down, Egyptian child-stealer! thou wilt have to go up again one of these days!"

"Sacky is in her vagaries to-day," said the people, grumbling: and that was all they did. Women of her class were then deemed holy and reverenced accordingly. Nobody liked to attack persons who were praying night and day.

The time of Quasimodo's punishment having expired, he was released, and the mob dispersed.

Mahiette and her two companions had reached the foot of the Grand Pont on their return, when she suddenly stopped short. "Bless me!" she exclaimed, "what has become of the cake, Eustache?"

"Mother," said the boy, "while you were talking with the woman in that dark hole, a big dog came and bit a great piece out of it, so I eat some too."

"What, sir," she asked, "have you eaten it all?"

"It was the dog, mother. I told him to let it alone, but he didn't mind me—so I just took a bite too."

"'Tis a sad, greedy boy!" said his mother, smiling and scolding at once. "Look you, Oudarde, not a cherry or an apple in our garden is safe from him, so his grandfather says he will make a rare captain. I'll trim you well, Master Eustache! Go along, you greedy glutton!"

Book Six

CHAPTER I

THE DANGER OF TRUSTING A GOAT WITH A SECRET

SEVERAL WEEKS had elapsed. It was now the beginning of March. The sun, which Dubartas, that classic ancestor of periphrasis, had not yet styled "the grand duke of candles," shone forth brightly and cheerily. It was one of those spring days which are so mild and so beautiful that all Paris, pouring into the public places and promenades, keep them as holidays. On days so brilliant, so warm, and so serene, there is a particular hour at which the spectator should go to admire the porch at Notre Dame. It is the moment when the sun, already sinking in the west, looks the cathedral almost full in the face. His rays, becoming more and more horizontal, slowly withdraw from the pavement of the place, and mount along the pinnacled façade, causing its thousands of figures in relief to stand out from their shadows, while the great central rose-window glares like the eye of a Cyclops tinged by the reflections of the forge. It was now just that hour.

Opposite the lofty cathedral glowing in the sunset, upon a stone balcony over the porch of a rich Gothic building which formed the angle of the place and the street of Parvis, some young and handsome females were chatting, laughing, and disporting themselves. By the length of their veils, which fell from the top of their pointed caps, encircled with pearls, to their heels; by the fineness of their embroidered neckerchiefs which covered their shoulders, but without wholly concealing the delicate contours of their virgin bosoms; by the richness of their petticoats, which surpassed that of their upper garments; by the gauze, the silk, the velvet with which their dress was trimmed; and above all by the whiteness of their hands, which showed them to be unused to labor, it was easy to guess that they belonged to noble and wealthy families. It was, in fact, Damoiselle Fleur-de-lys de Gondelaurier and her companions, Diane de Christeuil, Amelotte de Montmichel, Colombe de Gaillefontaine, and little De Champchevrier, who were staying at the house of the Dame de Gondelaurier, a widow lady, on account of the expected visit of Monseigneur de Beaujeu and his consort, who were to come to Paris in April for the purpose of selecting ladies of honor for the Dauphiness Marguerite. Now all the gentry for a hundred miles round were anxious to obtain this favor for their daughters; and with this view numbers had already brought or sent them to Paris. Those mentioned above had been placed by their parents under the care of the discreet and venerable Dame Aloise de Gondelaurier, widow of an officer of the king's cross-bowmen, who resided with her only daughter in her own house in the Place du Parvis.

The balcony adjoined an apartment hung with rich fawn-colored Flanders leather, stamped with gold borders. The parallel beams which crossed the ceiling amused the eye by a thousand grotesque carvings, painted and gilded. On richly carved coffers were here and there blazoned splendid coats of arms, while a boar's head in Delft ware crowned a magnificent buffet, indicating that the mistress of the house was the wife or widow of a knight-banneret. At the further end, by a high fireplace, surrounded with escutcheons and armorial insignia, sat, in a rich arm-chair of crimson velvet, the Dame de Gondelaurier, whose age of fifty-five years was as legibly inscribed upon her dress as upon her face. By her side stood a young man of a bold but somewhat vain and swaggering look—one of those handsome fellows to whom all the women take a liking, though the grave man and the physiognomist shrug their shoulders at them. This young cavalier wore the brilliant uniform of captain of the archers of the king's ordnance which so closely resembles the costume of Jupiter described at the outset of this history that we need not tire the reader with a second description of it.

The damsels were seated partly in the room, partly in the balcony, some on cushions of Utrecht velvet, others on oaken stools carved with flowers and figures. Each of them held on her lap a portion of a large piece of tapestry, on which they were working together, while the other part lay upon matting that covered the floor.

They were chatting together in that low tone and with those titters so common in a party of young females when there is a young man among them. He whose presence was sufficient to set at work the self-love of all this youthful company appeared himself to care very little about it; and, while these beautiful girls were each striving to engage his attention, he seemed to be busily engaged himself in polishing the buckle of his belt with his leathern glove.

Now and then the old lady spoke to him in a very low tone, and he answered as well as he could with a sort of awkward and forced politeness. From her smiles, from various other little significant tokens, and from the nods and winks Dame Aloise directed toward her daughter Fleur-de-lys while softly speaking to the captain, it was easy to see that he was an accepted lover, and that a match was on foot and would no doubt be speedily concluded between the young officer and Fleur-de-lys. It was too easy to see from his coldness and embarrassment that, on his side at least, it was anything but a love-match. The good lady, who, fond mother as she was, doted upon her daughter, did not perceive the indifference of the captain, and strove by her words and gestures to make him notice the grace with which Fleur-de-lys plied her needle or her distaff.

"Look, nephew," said she, plucking him by the sleeve in order to whisper in his ear—"look at her now as she stoops."

"Yes, indeed," replied the young man, relapsing into his former cold and irksome silence.

A moment afterward she was required to stoop again. "Did you ever," said Dame Aloise, "behold a comelier or genteeler girl than your intended? Is it possible to be fairer? Are not her hands and arms perfect models? And her neck, has it not all the elegance of a swan's?"

"No doubt," he replied, thinking of something else all the while.

"Why don't you go and talk to her, then?" retorted the lady, pushing him toward Fleur-de-lys. "Go and say something to her. You are grown mighty shy all at once."

Now we can assure the reader that neither shyness nor modesty were to be numbered among the captain's defects. He attempted, however, to do as he was desired.

"Fair cousin," said he, stepping up to Fleur-de-lys, "what is the subject of this tapestry which you are working?"

"Fair cousin," answered Fleur-de-lys in a peevish tone, "I have told you three times already that it is the grotto of Neptune."

It was evident that the captain's cold and absent manner had not escaped the keen observation of Fleur-de-lys, though it was not perceived by her mother. He felt the necessity of making an attempt at conversation.

"And what is it intended for?" he inquired.

"For the Abbey of St. Antoine des Champs," replied Fleur-de-lys, without raising her eyes.

The captain lifted up a corner of the tapestry. "And pray, my fair cousin," said he, "who is this big fellow in the disguise of a fish, blowing the trumpet with puffed-out cheeks?"

"That is Triton," answered she.

In the tone of Fleur-de-lys's brief replies there was still something that betokened displeasure. The captain was more and more at a loss what to say. He stooped down over the tapestry. "A charming piece of work, by my fay!" cried he.

At this exclamation, Colombe de Gaillefontaine, another beautiful girl, of a delicately fair complexion, in a dress of blue damask, timidly ventured to address a question to Fleur-de-lys, in the hope that the handsome captain would answer it. "My dear Gondelaurier," said she, "have you seen the tapestries in the Hotel of La Roche-Guyon?"

"Is not that the building next to the garden of the Louvre?" asked Diane de Christeuil, with a laugh. This young lady, be it observed, had remarkably handsome teeth, and consequently never spoke without laughing.

"And near that great old tower of the ancient wall of Paris?" inquired Amelotte de Montmichel, a charming brunette with ruddy cheek and dark curling hair, who had a habit of sighing as the other of laughing, without knowing why.

At this moment Berangere de Champchevrier, a little sylph of seven years, looking down upon the place through the rails of the balcony, cried: "Oh! look, Godmother Fleur-de-lys! look at that pretty dancer dancing on the pavement and playing on the tambourine, among the people down yonder!"

"Some Egyptian, I dare say," replied Fleur-de-lys, carelessly turning her head toward the place.

"Let's see! let's see!" cried her lively companions, running to the front of the balcony, while Fleur-de-lys, thinking of the coldness of her lover, slowly followed, and the captain, released by this incident, which cut short a conversation that embarrassed him not a little, returned to the further end of the apartment with the satisfaction of a soldier relieved from duty. The service of the gentle Fleur-de-lys was, nevertheless, easy and delightful; and so it had formerly appeared to him; but now the prospect of a speedy marriage became every day more and more disagreeable. The fact is, he was of a rather inconstant disposition, and if the truth must be told, rather vulgar in his tastes. Though of high birth, he had contracted more than one of the habits of the common soldier. He was fond of the tavern, and felt comfortable only among coarse language, military gallantries, easy beauties, and easy conquests. He had, nevertheless, received from his family some education and polish; but he had been thrown into the army too young, too young placed in garrison, and the varnish of the gentleman was daily wearing off by the hard friction of his guardsman's sword-belt. Though he still paid occasional visits to his relatives, from a slight feeling of human respect that was still left him, he found himself doubly embarrassed when he called upon Fleur-de-lys; in the first place, because he distributed his love so promiscuously that he reserved a very small portion of it for her; and in the second, because in the company of so many handsome, well-bred, and modest females he was under constant apprehension lest his tongue, habituated to oaths and imprecations, should all at once get the better of the rein and launch out into the language of the tavern. Highly did he pique himself withal upon elegance in dress and appointments and comeliness of person. The reader must reconcile these things as well as he can: I am but the historian.

The captain, then, had stood for some moments, lost in thought, or not thinking at all, leaning in silence on the carved mantel-piece, when Fleur-de-lys, suddenly turning round, addressed him. After all, it went sorely against the grain with the poor girl to pout at him.

"Did you not tell us, cousin, of a little Bohemian whom you rescued one night, about two months ago, from the hands of a dozen robbers?"

"I think I did, cousin," replied the captain.

"I should not wonder," she resumed, "if it was the Bohemian dancing yonder in the Parvis. Come and see whether you know her, Cousin Phœbus."

In this gentle invitation to come to her, and the tone in which it was uttered, he detected a secret desire of reconciliation. Captain Phœbus de Chateaupers—for this is the personage whom the reader has had before him since the commencement of this chapter—advanced with slow steps toward the balcony. "Look," said Fleur-de-lys, softly grasping the captain's arm—"look at yon girl dancing in that circle. Is she your Bohemian?"

Phœbus looked. "Yes," said he; "I know her by her goat."

"Oh! what a pretty little goat!" exclaimed Amelotte, clapping her hands in admiration.

"Are its horns of real gold?" asked Berangere.

"Godmother," she began again, having all at once raised her bright eyes, which were in constant motion, to the top of the towers of Notre Dame—"who is that man in black up yonder?"

All the young ladies looked up. A man was indeed lolling upon his elbows on the topmost balustrades of the northern tower, overlooking the Grève. It was a priest, as might be known by his dress, which was clearly distinguishable, and his head was supported by both his hands. He was motionless as a statue. His eye was fixed on the place as intently as that of a hawk on a starling's nest which it has discovered.

" 'Tis the Archdeacon of Josas," said Fleur-de-lys.

"You must have good eyes to know him at this distance," observed Gaillefontaine.

"How he looks at the dancing-girl!" exclaimed Diane de Christeuil.

"Let the Egyptian take care of herself!" said Fleur-de-lys. "The archdeacon is not fond of Egypt."

" 'Tis a pity that man looks at her so," added Amelotte de Montmichel; "for she dances delightfully."

"Good Cousin Phœbus," abruptly cried Fleur-de-lys, "since you know this Bohemian, just call her up. It will amuse us."

"Yes, do!" exclaimed all the young ladies, clapping their hands.

"Where is the use of it?" rejoined Phœbus. "She has no doubt forgotten me, and I know not even her name. However, as you wish it, ladies, I will try." Leaning over the balustrade of the balcony he called out: "My girl!"

The dancer had paused for a moment. She turned her head in the direction from which the voice proceeded; her sparkling eye fell upon Phœbus, and she stood motionless.

"My girl!" repeated the captain, beckoning her to come to him.

The girl still looked steadfastly at him; she then blushed deeply, as if every drop of her blood had rushed to her cheeks, and, taking her tambourine under her arm, she made her way through the circle of astonished spectators, toward the house to which she was summoned, with slow, faltering step, and with the agitated look of a bird unable to withstand the fascination of a serpent.

A moment afterward the tapestry hung before the door was raised, and the Bohemian appeared at the threshold of the apartment, out of breath, flushed, flurried, with her large eyes fixed on the floor: she durst not advance a step further. Berangere clapped her hands.

Meanwhile, the dancer stood motionless at the door of the room. Her appearance had produced a singular effect upon the party of young ladies. It is certain that all of them were more or less influenced by a certain vague and indistinct desire of pleasing the handsome officer; that the splendid uniform was the point at which all their coquetries were aimed; and that ever since his entrance there had been a sort of secret rivalry among them, of which they were themselves scarcely conscious, but which nevertheless betrayed itself every moment in all they said and did. As, however, they all possessed nearly the same degree of beauty, they fought with equal weapons, and each might cherish a hope of victory. The coming of the Bohemian suddenly destroyed this equilibrium. Her beauty was so surpassing, that at the moment when she appeared at the entrance of the room she seemed to shed over it a sort of light peculiar to herself. In this close apartment, overshadowed by hangings and carvings, she appeared incomparably more beautiful and radiant than in the public place—like a torch which is carried out of the broad daylight into the dark. In spite of themselves, the young ladies were dazzled. Each felt wounded, as it were, in her beauty. Their battle-front—reader, excuse the term—was changed accordingly, though not a single word passed between them. The instincts of women apprehend and answer one another much more readily than the understandings of men. An enemy had come upon them: of this they were all sensible, and therefore they all rallied. One drop of wine is sufficient to redden a whole glass of water; to tinge a whole company of handsome women with a certain degree of ill-humor merely introduce a female of superior beauty, especially when there is but one man in the party.

The reception of the Bohemian was of course marvelously cold. They surveyed her from head to foot, then looked at each other with an expression which told their meaning as plainly as words could have done. Meanwhile the stranger, daunted to such a degree that she durst not raise her eyes, stood waiting to be spoken to.

The captain was the first to break silence. "A charming creature, by my fay!" cried he, in his straightforward, blundering manner. "What think you of her, my pretty cousin?"

This ejaculation, which a more delicate admirer would at least have uttered in a less audible tone, was not likely to disperse the feminine jealousies arrayed against the Bohemian.

"Not amiss," replied Fleur-de-lys to the captain's question, with affected disdain. The others whispered together.

At length Mme. Aloise, who felt not the less jealousy because she was jealous on behalf of her daughter, accosted the dancer. "Come hither, my girl," said she. The Egyptian advanced to the lady.

"My pretty girl," said Phœbus, taking a few steps toward her, "I know not whether you recollect me——"

"Oh, yes!" said she, interrupting him, with a smile and a look of inexpressible kindness.

"She has a good memory," observed Fleur-de-lys.

"How was it," resumed Phœbus, "that you slipped away in such a hurry the other night? Did I frighten you?"

"Oh, no!" said the Bohemian.

In the accent with which this "Oh, no!" was uttered immediately after the "Oh, yes!" there was an indefinable something which wounded Fleur-de-lys to the quick.

"In your stead," continued the captain, whose tongue ran glibly enough in talking to one whom from her occupation he took to be a girl of loose manners, "you left me a grimfaced, one-eyed, hunchbacked fellow—the bishop's bell-ringer, I think they say. Some will have it that the archdeacon, and others that the devil, is his father. He has a comical name—I have quite forgotten what—taken from some festival or other. What the devil did the owl of a fellow want with you, hey?"

"I don't know," answered she.

"Curse his impudence!—a rascally bell-ringer run away with a girl like a viscount! A common fellow poach on the game of gentlemen! Who ever heard of such a thing! But he paid dearly for it. Master Pierrat Torterue is the roughest groom that ever trimmed a varlet; and I assure you, if that can do you any good, he curried the bell-ringer's hide most soundly."

"Poor fellow!" said the Bohemian, who at the captain's words could not help calling to mind the scene at the pillory.

"Zounds!" cried the captain, laughing outright, "that pity is as well bestowed as a feather on a pig's tail. May I be—" He stopped short. "I beg pardon, ladies; I had like to have forgotten myself."

"Fy, sir!" said Gaillefontaine.

"He is only talking to that creature in her own language," said Fleur-de-lys, in an under-tone, her vexation increasing every moment. Nor was it diminished when she saw the captain, enchanted with the Bohemian and still more with himself, make a pirouette, repeating with blunt, soldier-like gallantry: "A fine girl, upon my soul!"

"But very uncouthly dressed," said Diane de Christeuil, grinning and showing her beautiful teeth.

This remark was a new light to her companions. It showed them the assailable side of the Egyptian. As they could not carp at her beauty, they fell foul of her dress.

"How comes it, my girl," said Montmichel, "that you run about the streets in this manner, without neckerchief or stomacher?"

"And then, what a short petticoat!" exclaimed Gaillefontaine. "Quite shocking, I declare!"

"My dear," said Fleur-de-lys, in a tone of anything but kindness, "the officers of the Chatelet will take you up for wearing that gilt belt."

"My girl," resumed Christeuil, with a bitter smile, "if you were to cover your arms decently with sleeves, they would not be so sunburned."

It was in truth a sight worthy of a more intelligent spectator than Phœbus to see how these fair damsels, with their keen and envenomed tongues, twisted, glided, and writhed around the dancing-girl; they were at once cruel and graceful; they spitefully fell foul of her poor but whimsical toilet of tinsel and spangles. There was no end to their laughs, and jeers, and sarcasms. You would have taken them for some of those young Roman ladies who amused themselves with thrusting gold pins into the breasts of a beautiful slave, or they might be likened to elegant greyhounds, turning, with distended nostrils and glaring eyes, round a poor fawn which the look of their master forbids them to devour.

What after all was a poor street-dancer to these scions of distinguished families! They seemed to take no account of her presence, and talked of her before her face, and even to herself, as of an object at once very disgusting, very mean and very pretty.

The Bohemian was not insensible to their stinging remarks. From time to time the glow of shame or the flash of anger flushed her cheek or lighted up her eye; a disdainful word seemed to hover upon her lips; her contempt expressed itself in that pout with which the reader is already acquainted; but she stood motionless, fixing upon Phœbus a look of resignation, sadness, and good-nature. In that look there was also an expression of tenderness and anxiety. You would have said that she restrained her feelings for fear of being turned out.

Meanwhile, Phœbus laughed and began to take the part of the Bohemian, with a mixture of impertinence and pity.

"Let them talk as they like, my dear," said he, clanking his gold spurs; "your dress is certainly somewhat whimsical and out of the way, but, for such a charming creature as you are, what does that signify?"

"Dear me!" exclaimed the fair Gaillefontaine, bridling up, with sarcastic smile, "how soon the gentlemen archers of the king's ordnance take fire at bright Egyptian eyes!"

"Why not?" said Phœbus.

At this reply, carelessly uttered by the captain, Colombe laughed, so did Diane, so did Amelotte, so did Fleur-de-lys, though it is true that a tear started at the same time into the eye of the latter. The Bohemian, who had hung down her head at the remark of Colombe de Gaillefontaine, raised her eyes glistening with joy and pride, and again fixed them on Phœbus. She was passing beautiful at that moment.

The old lady, who had watched this scene, felt offended, though she knew not why. "Holy Virgin!" cried she all at once, "what have I got about me? Ah! the nasty beast!"

It was the goat, which, in springing toward her mistress, had entangled her horns in the load of drapery which fell upon the feet of the noble lady when she was seated. This was a diversion. The Bohemian, without saying a word, disengaged the animal.

"Oh! here is the pretty little goat with golden feet!" cried Berangere, leaping for joy.

The Bohemian crouched upon her knees and pressed her cheek against the head of the fondling goat, while Diane, stooping to the ear of Colombe, whispered: "How very stupid of me not to think of it sooner! Why, it is the Egyptian with the goat. It is reported that she is a witch, and that her goat performs tricks absolutely miraculous."

"Well," said Colombe, "the goat must perform one of its miracles and amuse us in its turn."

Diane and Colombe eagerly addressed the Egyptian. "My girl," said they, "make your goat perform a miracle for us."

"I know not what you mean," replied the dancer.

"A miracle, a piece of magic, or witchcraft, in short."

"I don't understand you," she rejoined, and again began fondling the pretty creature, repeating, "Djali! Djali!"

At this moment Fleur-de-lys remarked a small embroidered leathern bag hung around the neck of the goat. "What is that?" she asked the Egyptian.

The girl raised her large eyes toward her and gravely answered: "That is my secret."

"I should like to know what your secret is," thought Fleur-de-lys.

The good lady had meanwhile risen. "Girl," said she, sharply, "if neither you nor your goat have any dance to show us, why do you stay here?"

The Bohemian, without making any reply, drew leisurely toward the door. The nearer she approached it, the more slowly she moved. An invincible lode-stone seemed to detain her. All at once she turned her eyes glistening with tears, toward Phœbus, and stood still.

"By my fay!" cried the captain, "you sha'n't get off thus. Come back and give us a dance. By the bye, what is your name, my pretty dear?"

"La Esmeralda," said the dancing-girl, whose eyes were still fixed upon him.

At this strange name the young ladies burst into a loud laugh.

"A terrible name that for a damoiselle!" said Diane.

"You see plainly enough," observed Amelotte, "that she is a witch."

"My girl," said Dame Aloise, in a solemn tone, "your parents never found that name for you in the font."

While this scene was passing, Berangere had enticed the goat into a corner of the room with a march-pane. They were at once the best friends in the world. The inquisitive girl loosed the little bag from the neck of the animal, opened it, and emptied its contents upon the mat: they consisted of an alphabet, each letter being separately inscribed upon a small piece of box-wood. No sooner were these playthings spread out upon a mat than, to the astonishment of the child, the goat—one of whose miracles this no doubt was—sorted out certain letters with her golden foot, arranged them and shuffled them gently together, in a particular order, so as to make a word, which the animal formed with such readiness that she seemed to have had a good deal of practice in putting it together. Berangere, clapping her hands in admiration, suddenly exclaimed: "Godmother Fleur-de-lys, come and see what the goat has done!"

Fleur-de-lys ran to her and shuddered. The letters which the goat had arranged upon the floor formed the name

PHŒBUS.

"Was it the goat that did this?" she asked, in a tremulous voice.

"Yes, indeed it was, godmother," replied Berangere. It was impossible to doubt the fact.

"The secret is out," thought Fleur-de-lys.

At the outcry of the child, all who were present, the mother, and the young ladies, and the Bohemian, and the officer hastened to the spot. The dancing-girl saw at once what a slippery trick the goat had played her. She changed color and began to tremble, like one who had committed some crime, before the captain, who eyed her with a smile of astonishment and gratification.

For a moment the young ladies were struck dumb. "Phœbus!"

they at length whispered to one another, "why, that is the name of the captain!"

"You have a wonderful memory," said Fleur-de-lys to the petrified Bohemian. Then, bursting into sobs, "Oh!" she stammered in a tone of anguish, covering her face with both her fair hands, "she is a sorceress!" the while a voice, in still more thrilling accents, cried in the recesses of her heart, "She is a rival!" She sunk fainting on the floor.

"My daughter! my daughter!" shrieked the affrighted mother. "Get thee gone, child of perdition!" said she to the Bohemian.

La Esmeralda picked up the unlucky letters in the twinkling of an eye, made a sign to her Djali, and retired at one door, while Fleur-de-lys was borne away by another.

Captain Phœbus, being left by himself, wavered for a moment between the two doors, and then followed the gypsy girl.

CHAPTER II

A PRIEST AND A PHILOSOPHER ARE TWO DIFFERENT PERSONS

THE PRIEST whom the young ladies had observed on the top of the north tower stooping over the place, and intently watching the motions of the Bohemian, was, in fact, the Archdeacon Claude Frollo.

Our readers have not forgotten the mysterious cell which the archdeacon had reserved for himself in that tower. I know not, be it remarked by the way, whether this is not the same cell, the interior of which may still be seen through a small square aperture on the east side, at about the height of a man, on the platform from which the towers rise. It is a small room, naked, empty, dilapidated, the ill-plastered walls of which are at the present day adorned with yellow engravings representing the fronts of cathedrals. This hole is, I presume, inhabited conjointly by bats and spiders, and consequently a double war of extermination is carried on there against the unfortunate flies.

Every day, an hour before sunset, the archdeacon ascended the staircase of the tower and shut himself up in this cell, where he fre-

quently passed whole nights. On this day, just as he had reached
the low door of his retreat, and put into the lock the little complicated key which he always carried with him in the pouch hanging
at his side, the sounds of a tambourine and castanets struck his ear.

These sounds came from the Place du Parvis. The cell, as we have
already stated, had but one window, looking upon the roof of the
church. Claude Frollo hastily withdrew the key, and the next moment he was on the top of the tower, in the attitude of profound
reverie in which the young ladies had perceived him.

There he was, grave, motionless, absorbed—all eye, all ear, all
thought. All Paris was at his feet, with the thousand spires of its
buildings and its circular horizon of gentle hills, with its river winding beneath its bridges and its population pouring through its streets,
with its clouds of smoke and its mountain-chain of roofs, crowding
close upon Notre Dame, with its double slopes of mail; but in this
whole city the archdeacon's eye sought but one point of the pavement, the Place du Parvis, and among the whole multitude but one
figure, the Bohemian.

It would have been difficult to decide what was the nature of that
look, and of the fire that flashed from it. It was a fixed look, but full
of tumult and perturbation. And yet, from the profound quiescence
of his whole body, scarcely shaken now and then by a mechanical
shudder, as a tree by the wind; from the stiffness of his arms, more
marble-like than the balustrade upon which they leaned; from the
petrified smile which contracted his face, you would have said that
Claude Frollo had nothing alive about him but his eyes.

The Bohemian was dancing; she made her tambourine spin round
on the tip of her finger, and threw it up in the air while she danced
Provençal sarabands—light, agile, joyous, and not aware of the
weight of that formidable look which fell plump upon her head.

The crowd thronged around her: from time to time a man habited
in a yellow and red loose coat went round the circle of spectators to
keep them back; he then seated himself in a chair, at the distance
of a few paces from the dancer, taking the head of the goat upon
his knees. This man seemed to be the companion of the Bohemian;
but Claude Frollo could not from his elevated station distinguish
his features.

From the moment that the archdeacon perceived this stranger,
his attention seemed to be divided between the dancer and him,
and the gloom which overspread his countenance became deeper
and deeper. All at once he started up, and a thrill shook his whole

frame. "Who can that man be?" he muttered—"till now I have always seen her alone!"

He then darted beneath the winding vault of the spiral staircase and descended. In passing the door of the belfry, which was ajar, he beheld an object which struck him; it was Quasimodo, leaning out at one of the apertures of those slated pent-houses which resemble enormous blinds, and intently looking down at the place. So entirely was he engrossed by the scene that he was not aware of the passing of his foster-father. "Strange!" murmured Claude. "Can it be the Egyptian that he is watching so earnestly?" He continued to descend. In a few minutes the archdeacon, full of care, sallied forth into the place by the door at the foot of the tower.

"What is become of the Bohemian?" he inquired, mingling with a group of spectators whom the tambourine had collected.

"I know not," replied one of them; "I have but just missed her. I rather think she is gone to give them a dance in yon house opposite, from which some one called to her."

Instead of the Egyptian, upon the same carpet on which but a moment before she had been cutting her capricious capers, the archdeacon now found only the man in the red-and-yellow surtout, who, to earn in his turn a few pieces of small coin, moved round the circle with his elbows against his hips, his head thrown back, his face flushed, his neck stretched, and a chair between his teeth. On this chair was tied a cat, which a neighbor had lent for the purpose, and which, being frightened, was swearing lustily.

"By Our Lady!" exclaimed the archdeacon, at the moment when the mountebank passed him with his pyramid of chair and cat; "what is Pierre Gringoire about here?"

The stern voice of the archdeacon threw the poor fellow into such a commotion that he lost the balance of his edifice, and chair and cat tumbled pell-mell upon the heads of the persons nearest to him, amid the inextinguishable laughter of the rest.

In all probability Master Pierre Gringoire—for sure enough it was he—would have had an ugly account to settle with the mistress of the cat and the owners of all the bruised and scratched faces around him, had he not availed himself of the confusion to slip away to the church after the archdeacon, who had motioned him to follow.

The cathedral was already dark and deserted, and the lamps in the chapels began to twinkle like stars amid the gloom. The great rose-window of the front alone, whose thousand colors were lighted up by a ray of the horizontal sun, glistened in the dark like a cluster of diamonds, and threw its dazzling reflection on the further extremity of the nave.

After they had advanced a few steps from the entrance, Dom Claude, stopping short with his back against a pillar, looked steadfastly at Gringoire. In this look there was nothing to excite dread in Gringoire, deeply as he was ashamed of having been caught by a grave and learned personage in that merry-andrew garb. The look of the priest had in it nothing sarcastic or ironical; it was serious, calm and piercing. The archdeacon first broke silence.

"Come hither, Master Pierre. There are many things which I want you to explain. In the first place, how happens it that I have not seen you for these two months, and that I find you in the public streets, in goodly garb forsooth, half red and half yellow, like a Caudebec apple?"

"Messire," dolefully replied Gringoire, "it is indeed a strange accoutrement, and one in which I feel about as comfortable as a cat in a cocoanut-shell cap. 'Tis a sad thing, I admit, to let the gentlemen of the watch run the risk of belaboring under this sorry disguise the shoulders of a Pythagorean philosopher. But how can I help it, my reverend master? The blame rests with my old coat, which basely forsook me in the depth of winter, upon pretext that it was dropping to tatters. What could I do? Civilization is not yet so far advanced that one may go stark naked, as Diogenes of old wished to do. Besides, a very keen wind was blowing at the time, and the month of January is not a likely season to attempt to introduce this new fashion with any hope of success. This wrapper offered itself; I took it, and gave up my old black frock, which, for an hermetic philosopher like me, was far from being hermetically close. So here I am in mountebank's garb, like St. Genest. 'Tis an eclipse, to be sure. But Apollo, you know, tended swine for Admetus."

"A respectable profession, truly, this that you have taken up!" replied the archdeacon.

"I allow, master, that it is better to philosophize or poetize, to blow up the flame in the furnace or to receive it from heaven, than to carry cats about the streets. Accordingly, when I heard your exclamation, I was struck as comical as an ass before a spit. But what would you have, messire? A poor devil must live one day as well as another; and the finest Alexandrines that ever were penned cannot stay the hungry stomach so well as a crust of bread. You know, for example, that famous epithalamium which I composed for Madame Margaret of Flanders, and the city refuses to pay me for it on the ground that it was not good enough; as if one could furnish tragedies like those of Sophocles at four crowns apiece. Of course, I was ready to perish with hunger. Luckily, I knew that I was pretty strong in the jaw, so says I to this jaw: Try feats of strength and balancing; work, and keep thyself. A band of beggars, who are my very good friends, have taught me twenty different herculean feats, and now I give to my teeth every night the bread which they have helped to earn in the day. After all, I grant that it is a sorry employment of my intellectual faculties, and that man was not made to play the tambourine, and to carry chairs between his teeth. But, my reverend master, in order to live, one must get a livelihood."

Dom Claude listened in silence. All at once his hollow eyes assumed an expression so searching and so piercing that Gringoire felt that look penetrate to the inmost recesses of his soul.

"Well, Master Pierre, but how happens it that you are now in the company of that Egyptian dancing-girl?"

"Grammercy!" replied Gringoire, "it is because she is my wife and I am her husband."

The gloomy eye of the priest glared like fire. "Wretch! is this really so?" cried he, furiously grasping Gringoire's arm. "Hast thou so completely forsaken thy God as to become the husband of that creature?"

"By my hope of paradise, monseigneur," answered Gringoire, trembling in every joint, "I swear that she allows me no more familiarity than if I were an utter stranger."

"What are you talking, then, about husband and wife?" rejoined the priest.

Gringoire lost no time in relating to him as concisely as possible the circumstances with which the reader is already acquainted, his adventure in the Cour des Miracles, his marriage with the broken jug, and the course of life which he had since followed. From his account it appeared that the Bohemian had never showed him more kindness than she had done on the first night. "'Tis a provoking thing, though," said he, as he finished his story; "but it is owing to a strange notion which those Egyptians have put into her head."

"What mean you?" asked the archdeacon, whose agitation had gradually subsided during this narrative.

"It is rather difficult to explain my meaning," replied the poet. "'Tis a superstition. My wife, as I am informed by an old fellow whom we call among ourselves the Duke of Egypt, is a child that has been either lost or found, which is the same thing. She has a charm hung round her neck which, they say, will some day cause her to find her parents, but which would lose its virtue if the girl were to lose hers."

"So then," rejoined Claude, whose face brightened up more and more, "you really believe, Master Pierre, that this creature is yet virtuous?"

"What chance, Dom Claude, can a man have against a superstition? This, I tell you, is what she has got into her head. I consider this nun-like chastity which keeps itself intact among those Bohemian females, who are not remarkable for that quality, as a very rare circumstance indeed. But she has three things to protect her: the Duke of Egypt, who has taken her under his safeguard; her whole tribe, who hold her in extraordinary veneration, like another Notre Dame; and a certain little dagger, which the hussy always carries about her somewhere or other, notwithstanding the orders of the provost, and which is sure to be in her hands if you but clasp her waist. She is a saucy wasp, I can tell you."

The archdeacon pursued his cross-examination of Gringoire. In the estimation of the latter, La Esmeralda was a handsome, fascinating, inoffensive creature, with the exception of the pout peculiar to her; a simple, warm-hearted girl, exceedingly ignorant and exceedingly enthusiastic; fond above all things of dancing, of noise, of the open air; a sort of human bee, having invisible wing at her feet, and living in perpetual whirl. She owed this disposition to the wandering life which she had always led. Gringoire had contrived to learn so much as this, that she had traveled over Spain and Catalonia, and as far as Sicily; nay, he believed that she had been carried by the caravan of Zingari to which she belonged into the kingdom of Algiers. The Bohemians, so Gringoire said, were vassals of the King of Algiers, as chief of the nation of the white Moors. So much was certain, that La Esmeralda had come to France while very young, by way of Hungary. From all these countries the girl had brought scraps of odd jargons, snatches of old songs, and foreign ideas, which made her language as curious a piece of patch-work as her dress, half Parisian and half African. For the rest, she was a favorite with the people of those quarters of the city which she frequented, for her sprightliness, her gracefulness, her personal attractions, her dancing, and her singing.

She had a notion that in the whole city there were but two persons who hated her, and of whom she often spoke with terror—the wretched recluse of Roland's Tower, who, for some reason or other, bore an implacable enmity to the Egyptians, and cursed the poor dancing-girl whenever she passed her cell, and a priest, whom she never met without being frightened by his looks and language. This last intimation disturbed the archdeacon not a little, though Gringoire scarcely noticed his agitation, so completely had the lapse of two months effaced from the memory of the thoughtless poet the singular circumstances of that night when he first met with the Egyptian, and the presence of the archdeacon on that occasion. There was nothing else that the young dancer had reason to be afraid of; she never told fortunes, so that she was safe from prosecutions for witchcraft, so frequently instituted against the gypsy women. And then Gringoire was a brother to her, if not a husband. After all, the philosopher bore this kind of Platonic marriage with great resignation. At any rate, he was sure of lodging and bread. Every morning he sallied forth from the head-quarters of the Vagabonds, mostly in company with the Egyptian; he assisted her in collecting her harvest of small coin in the streets; at night he returned with her to the same room, allowed her to lock herself up in her own cell, and slept the sleep of the righteous—"a very easy life," said he, "considering all things, and very favorable to reverie." And then, in his soul and conscience, the philosopher was not sure that he was not over head and ears in love with the Bohemian. He loved her goat almost as dearly. It was a charming, gentle, clever, intelligent creature—in short, a learned goat. There was nothing more common in the Middle Ages than those learned animals, which excited general wonder, and frequently brought their instructors to the stake. The sorceries of the golden-hoofed goat, however, were but very innocent tricks. These Gringoire explained to the archdeacon, who appeared to be deeply interested by those particulars. It was sufficient, he said, in most cases to hold the tambourine to the animal in such a way, to make it do what you wished. It had been trained to these performances by the girl, who was so extremely clever at the business that she had taken only two months to teach the goat to put together with movable letters the word PHŒBUS.

"Phœbus!" exclaimed the priest; "why Phœbus?"

"God knows," replied Gringoire. "Possibly she may imagine that this word possesses some magic virtue. She frequently repeats it in an under-tone when she thinks she is alone."

"Are you sure," inquired Claude, with his piercing look, "that it is only a word, and not a name?"

"Name! whose name?" said the poet.

"How should I know?" rejoined the priest.

"I'll just tell you, messire, what I am thinking. These Bohemians are a sort of Guebres, and worship the sun—Dan Phœbus."

"That is not so clear to me as to you, Master Pierre."

"At any rate, 'tis a point which I care very little about. Let her mutter her Phœbus as much as she pleases. So much is certain, that Djali is almost as fond of me as of her mistress."

"What is Djali?"

"Why, that is the goat."

The archdeacon rested his chin upon the points of his fingers, and for a moment appeared to be lost in thought. Then, suddenly turning toward Gringoire—"Thou wilt swear," said he, "that thou hast never touched her?"

"What! the goat?" asked Gringoire.

"No, the girl."

"Oh! my wife! I swear I never did."

"And thou art often alone with her?"

"Every evening for a full hour."

Dom Claude knitted his brow. "Oh! oh! *Solus cum solo non cogitabantur orare Pater noster.*"[1]

"Upon my life I might say the 'Pater,' and the 'Ave Maria,' and the 'Credo in Deum Patrem omnipotentem,' and she would take no more notice of me than a pig of a church."

"Swear to me, by the soul of thy mother," cried the archdeacon, with vehemence, "that thou hast not touched this creature with the tip of thy finger."

"I am ready to swear it by the body of my father also. But, my reverend master, allow me to ask you a question in my turn."

"Speak."

"How can this concern you?"

The pale face of the archdeacon crimsoned like the cheek of a bashful girl. He paused for a moment before he replied, with visible embarrassment, "Listen, Master Pierre Gringoire. You are not yet eternally lost, as far as I know. I take an interest in your welfare. Let me tell you, then, that the moment you but lay a hand on that Egyptian, that child of the devil, you become the vassal of Satan. 'Tis the body, you know, that always plunges the soul into perdition. Woe betide you if you approach this creature! That is all. Now get thee gone!" cried the priest with a terrible look; and, pushing the astonished Gringoire from him by the shoulders, he retreated with hasty step beneath the gloomy arcades of the cathedral.

1. "A man and a maid alone together don't think about paternosters."

CHAPTER III

THE BELLS

EVER SINCE the morning that Quasimodo underwent the punishment of the pillory, the good people who dwelt in the neighborhood of Notre Dame fancied that they perceived a great abatement in his ardor for bell-ringing. Before that event, the bells were going on all occasions; there were long tollings which lasted from prime to compline, chimes for high mass, merry peals for a wedding or a christening, mingling in the air like an embroidery of all sorts of charming sounds. The old church, all quaking and all sonorous, seemed to keep up a perpetual rejoicing. You felt incessantly the presence of a spirit of noise and caprice, speaking by all these brazen mouths. This spirit seemed now to have forsaken its abode: the cathedral appeared sullen and silent; holidays, funerals, and the like, were attended merely by the tolling which the ritual required, and no more: of the double sound which pervades a church, that of the organ within and of the bells without, the former alone was left. You would have said that there was no longer any musician in the belfries. Quasimodo, nevertheless, was still there. But what ailed him? Were rage and vexation on account of what he had suffered still rankling in his heart? Did he still feel in imagination the lash of the executioner, and had the despondency occasioned by such treatment extinguished even his fondness for the bells?—or was it possible that big Mary had a rival in the heart of the bell-ringer of Notre Dame, and that she and her fourteen sisters were neglected for a more beautiful and a more lovely object?

It so happened that in the year of grace, 1482, the Annunciation fell upon Tuesday, the 25th of March. On that day the air was so light and serene that Quasimodo felt some reviving affection for his bells. He went up, therefore, into the north tower, while below the bedel threw wide open the doors of the church, which were at that time formed of enormous slabs of oak, covered with hide, bordered with nails of iron gilt, and adorned with carvings, "most cunningly wrought."

Having reached the high loft of the belfry, Quasimodo gazed for some time at the six bells with a sad shake of the head, as if lamenting that some other object had intruded itself into his heart between them and him. But when he had set them in motion, when he felt this bunch of bells swinging in his hand; when he saw, for he could not hear, the palpitating octave running up and down that sonorous scale, like a bird hopping from twig to twig; when the demon of music, that demon which shakes a glittering quiver of stretti, trills, and arpeggios, had taken possession of the poor deaf bell-ringer, he was once more happy, he forgot all his troubles, his heart expanded, and his face brightened up.

He paced to and fro, he clapped his hands, he ran from rope to rope, he encouraged the six chimers with voice and gesture, as the leader of an orchestra spurs on intelligent performers.

"Go on, Gabrielle, go on," said he; "pour thy flood of sound into the place, for 'tis a holiday. Don't lag, Thibault; no idling! Move, move. Art thou rusty, lazybones? Well done! quick, quick! peal it lustily: make them all deaf like me! That's right; bravely done, Thibault! Guillaume, Guillaume, thou art the biggest, and Pasquier the least, and yet Pasquier beats thee hollow. Those who can hear, I'll engage, hear more of him than of thee. Well done! well done, my Gabrielle; harder and harder still! Soho! you two Sparrows up there! I do not hear you give out the least chirp. Of what use is it to have those brazen mouths, if ye but yawn when ye ought to sing? There, work away! 'Tis the Annunciation. The cheery sunshine requires a merry peal. Poor Guillaume! thou art quite out of breath, my big fellow!"

He was thus engaged in egging on his bells, which all six bounded and shook their shining haunches, like a noisy team of Spanish mules, urged first this way, then that by the apostrophes of the driver. All at once, casting down his eye between the large slates which like scales cover the perpendicular wall of the belfry to a certain height, he descried in the place a young female oddly accoutered, who stopped and spread upon the ground a carpet on which a little goat came and posted itself. A circle of spectators was soon formed around them. This sight suddenly changed the current of his ideas, and congealed his musical enthusiasm as a breath of air congeals melted resin. He paused, turned his back to his bells, and, leaning forward from beneath the slated pent-house, eyed the dancing-girl with that pensive, kind, nay, tender look which had once before astonished the archdeacon. Meanwhile the bells, left to themselves, abruptly ceased all at once, to the great disappointment of the lovers of this kind of music, who were listening with delight to the peal from the Pont au Change, and went away as sulky as a dog to which you have held a piece of meat and given a stone.

CHAPTER IV

CLAUDE FROLLO'S CELL

ONE FINE MORNING in the same month of March, I believe it was Saturday, the 29th, the festival of St. Eustache, it so happened that our young friend Jehan Frollo du Moulin perceived, while dressing himself, that his breeches, containing his purse, gave out no metallic sound. "Poor purse!" said he, drawing it forth from his pocket; "not one little parisis! How cruelly thou hast been gutted by dice, Venus, and the tavern! There thou art, empty, wrinkled, flaccid. Thou art like the bosom of a fury. I would just ask you, Messer Cicero and Messer Seneca, whose dog's-eared works lie scattered on the floor, of what use is it to me to know, better than a master of the mint or a Jew of that Pont aux Changeurs, that a gold crown is worth thirty-five unzains, at twenty-five sous eight deniers parisis each, if I have not a single miserable black liard to risk on the double six! Oh, Consul Cicero! this is not a calamity from which one may extricate one's self with periphrases, with *quemadmodums* and *verumenimveros.*" [1]

. He began to put on his clothes in silent sadness. While lacing his buskins, a thought occurred to him, but he gave it up immediately. Again it presented itself, and he put on his vest the wrong side out, an evident sign of some violent inward struggle. At length, dashing his cap upon the ground, he exclaimed—"Yes, I will go to my brother. I shall get a lecture, but then I shall get a crown."

Then, hastily throwing on his surcoat trimmed with fur, and picking up his cap, he rushed out of the room. He went down the Rue de la Harpe toward the city. As he passed the Rue de la Huchette his olfactories were gratified by the smell of the joints incessantly roasting there, and he cast a sheep's eye at the gigantic apparatus which one day drew from Calatagirone, the Franciscan, this pathetic exclamation—*Veramente, queste rotisserie sono cosa stupenda!* [2] But Jehan had not wherewithal to get a breakfast, and with a deep sigh

1. "How's" and "verily's."

2. In sooth, these cook-shops are prodigious!

he pursued his course under the gateway of the Petit Chatelet, that enormous cluster of massive towers which guarded the entrance to the city.

He did not even take the time to throw a stone in passing, as it was then customary, at the mutilated statue of that Perinet Leclerc, who had surrendered the Paris of Charles VI. to the English—a crime for which his effigy, defaced by stones and covered with mud, did penance for three centuries, at the corner of the streets of La Harpe and Bussy, as in a perpetual pillory.

Having crossed the Petit Pont, Jehan at length found himself before Notre Dame. Again he wavered in his purpose, and he walked for a few moments round the statue of M. Legris, repeating to himself, "I am sure of the lecture, but shall I get the crown?"

He stopped a verger who was coming from the cloisters. "Where is the Archdeacon of Josas?" he inquired.

"I believe he is in his closet in the tower," replied the verger; "and I would not advise you to disturb him there, unless you have a message from some such person as the pope or Monsieur the King."

Jehan clapped his hands. "By Jupiter!" he exclaimed—"a fine opportunity for seeing that famous den of sorcery!"

Determined by this reflection, he resolutely entered at the little back door, and began to ascend the winding stairs leading to the upper stories of the tower. "We shall see," said he to himself by the way. "By Our Lady! It must be a curious place, that cell which my reverend brother keeps so carefully to himself. They say that he has a roaring fire there sometimes to cook the philosopher's stone at. By my fay! I care no more about the philosopher's stone than any cobble-stone, and I would rather find a savory omelet on his furnace than the biggest philosopher's stone in the world!"

Having reached the pillar gallery, he stood puffing for a moment, and then swore at the endless stairs by I know not how many million cart-loads of devils. Having somewhat vented his spleen, he recommenced his ascent by the little door of the north tower, which is now shut against the public. Just after he had passed the bell-room, he came to a lateral recess in which there was a low pointed door. "Humph!" said the scholar; "this must be the place, I suppose."

The key was in the lock, and the door not fastened; he gently pushed it open far enough to look in.

The reader has no doubt turned over the admirable works of Rembrandt, that Shakespeare of painting. Among so many wonderful engravings there is one, in particular, representing Dr. Faustus, as it is conjectured, which you cannot look at without being dazzled.

The scene is a dark cell, in the middle of which is a table covered with hideous objects—skulls, globes, alembics, compasses, parchments with hieroglyphics. Before this table is the doctor dressed in a coarse, loose great-coat, and with his fur cap pulled down to his very eyebrows. The lower part of his person is not to be seen. Half risen from his immense arm-chair, he leans with his clinched fists upon the table, and is looking with curiosity and terror at a large luminous circle composed of magic letters, which glares upon the opposite wall like the solar spectrum in a dark room. This cabalistic sun seems to tremble to the eye, and fills the gloomy cell with its mysterious radiance. It is terrible and it is beautiful.

A scene not unlike the cell of Dr. Faustus presented itself to the view of Jehan when he ventured to look in at the half open door. This, too, was a gloomy hole into which the light was very sparingly admitted. It contained, too, a great arm-chair and a large table, compasses, alembics, skeletons of animals hanging from the ceiling, a globe lying upon the floor pell-mell with glass jars filled with liquids of various colors, skulls placed on parchments scrawled over the figures with letters, thick manuscripts wide open and heaped one upon another—in short, all the rubbish of science—and the whole covered with dust and cobwebs; but there was no circle of luminous letters, no doctor in ecstasy contemplating the flaming vision as the eagle gazes at the sun.

The cell, however, was not unoccupied. A man seated in the arm-chair was stooping over the table. His back was turned to Jehan, who could see no more than his shoulders and the hind part of his head; but he had no difficulty to recognize that bald crown, on which nature had made an everlasting tonsure, as if to mark by this outward symbol the irresistible clerical vocation of the archdeacon.

The door had opened so softly that Dom Claude was not aware of the presence of his brother. The young scapegrace took advantage of this circumstance to explore the cell for a few moments. To the left of the arm-chair and beneath the small window was a large furnace, which he had not remarked at the first glance. The ray of light which entered at the aperture passed through a circular cobweb, in the center of which the motionless insect architect looked like the nave of this wheel of lace. On the furnace lay in disorder all sorts of vessels, glass vials, retorts, and mattresses. There was no fire in the furnace, nor did it appear to have been lighted for a considerable time. A glass mask, which Jehan observed among the implements of alchemy, and which no doubt served to protect the

archdeacon's face when he was at work upon any dangerous substance, lay in one corner, covered with dust, and, as it were, forgotten. By its side was a pair of bellows equally dusty, the upper
surface of which bore this legend inlaid in letters of copper: SPIRA,
SPERA.

Other mottoes in great number were inscribed, according to the
custom of the hermetic philosophers, upon the walls, some written
with ink, and others cut as if with a graver. Gothic, Hebrew, Greek,
and Roman letters were all mixed together; the inscriptions ran into
one another, the more recent effacing the older, and all dove-tailing like the boughs of a clump of trees, or pikes in a battle. They
composed, in fact, a confused medley of all human philosophies,
reveries, and knowledge. There was one here and there which was
conspicuous above the rest, like a pennon among the heads of lances.
Most of them were short Latin or Greek mottoes, such as the Middle
Age was so clever at devising. *Unde? inde?—Homo homini mon-
strum.—Astra, castra: nomen, numen.—Μέγα βιβλίον, μέγα κακον.
Saper aude. Fiat ubi vult,*[1] etc. Sometimes there occurred a word
without any apparent signification, as 'Αναγχοφαγία which might
possibly disguise some bitter allusion to the monastic system; sometimes a simple maxim of clerical discipline in the form of a regular
hexameter. There were also, by the way, Hebrew scrawls, which
Jehan, who knew very little of Greek, could not decipher, and the
whole was crossed in all directions by stars, figures of men and
beasts, and triangles, which intersected one another, and contributed not a little to make the wall of the cell resemble a sheet of
paper upon which a monkey had been scribbling with a pen.

In other respects the cell exhibited a general appearance of neglect and dilapidation; and from the state of the utensils it might
be inferred that the master had long been diverted from his usual
pursuits by other occupations.

This master, meanwhile, bending over a vast manuscript adorned
by grotesque paintings, appeared to be tormented by an idea which
incessantly obtruded itself upon his meditations. So at least Jehan
judged on hearing him utter this soliloquy, with the pensive pauses
of one in a brown study who thinks aloud:

"Yes, so Manou asserted and Zoroaster taught. The sun is the offspring of fire, the moon of the sun; fire is the soul of the universe.
Its elementary atoms are incessantly overflowing and pouring upon
the world in innumerable currents. At the points where these
currents intersect one another in the atmosphere they produce light;
at their points of intersection in the earth they produce gold. Light,

1. Whence? Thence? Man is a monster to men. —The stars my camp, the name,
my god.—The bigger the book, the greater the evil. —To learn, listen. —It bloweth
where it listeth.

gold—one and the same thing! From the state of fire to the concrete state. The difference between the visible and palpable, between the fluid and solid in the same substance, between steam and ice, nothing more. This is not a dream—'tis the general law of nature. But how is science to set about detecting the secret of this general law? Why, this light which floods my hand is gold! These same atoms, which expand according to a certain law, need but be condensed according to a certain other law. How is this to be done? Some have proposed to effect it by burying a ray of the sun. Averroes—yes, it was Averroes—buried one under the first pillar on the left, in the sanctuary of the Koran, in the grand mosque at Cordova; but the vault must not be opened to see whether the operation has been successful for the space of eight thousand years."

"By Jupiter! 'tis a long while to wait for a crown!" said Jehan to himself.

"Others have thought," continued the archdeacon, "that it would be better to operate upon a ray of Sirius. But it is very difficult to obtain one of his rays pure, on account of the simultaneous presence of the other stars, whose light mingles with it. Flamel conceives that it is more simple to operate upon terrestrial fire. Flamel! what a name for an adept! *Flamma*—yes, fire. That is all. The diamond is in charcoal, gold is in fire. But how is it to be extracted? Magistri affirms that there are certain names of women possessing so sweet and so mysterious a charm, that it is sufficient to pronounce them during the operation. Let us see what Manou says on the subject: 'Where women are honored the gods are pleased; where they are despised it is useless to pray to the gods. The mouth of a woman is constantly pure; it is a running water, a ray of sunshine. The name of a woman ought to be agreeable, soft, imaginary; to terminate with long vowels, and to be like words of blessing.' Yes, the philosopher is right; thus, La Maria, La Sophia, La Esmeral— Perdition! always—always—that thought."

He closed the book with violence. He passed his hand over his brow, as if to chase away the idea which annoyed him; and then took up a nail and a small hammer, the handle of which was curiously painted with cabalistic letters.

"For some time past," said he, with a bitter smile, "I have failed in all my experiments. One fixed idea haunts me and pierces my brain like a red-hot iron. I have not even been able to discover the secret of Cassiodorus, who made a lamp to burn without wick and without oil. A simple matter, nevertheless!"

"*Peste!*" muttered Jehan.

"One single miserable thought, then," continued the priest, "is sufficient to make a man weak or mad! Oh! how Claude Pernelle would laugh at me! She who could not for a moment divert Nicholas Flamel from the prosecution of the great work! But have I not in my hand the magic hammer of Zechiele! At every blow which the dread rabbi, in the recesses of his cell, struck upon this nail with this hammer, some one of his enemies whom he had doomed to destruction sunk into the earth which swallowed him up. The King of France himself, having one night knocked for a frolic at his door, sunk up to his knees in the pavement of Paris. This happened not three centuries ago. Well, I have the hammer and the nail: but then these tools are not more formidable in my hands than a rule in the hands of a carpenter. And yet I should possess the same power could I but discover the magic word pronounced by Zechiele while striking the nail."

"Nonsense!" thought Jehan.

"Let's see! let's try!" resumed the archdeacon, with vehemence. "If I succeed, a blue spark will fly from the head of the nail—Emen Hetan! Emen Hetan! That's not it—Sigeani! Sigeani! May this nail open a grave for every man named Phœbus. . . . Curses on it! forever and ever the same idea!"

He angrily threw down the hammer, and then sunk forward in his arm-chair upon the table, so that the enormous back completely hid him from Jehan's sight. For a few minutes he saw no part of him but his hand convulsively clinched upon a book. All at once Dom Claude rose, took up a pair of compasses, and engraved in silence on the wall in capital letters, the Greek word

ANA'TKH.[1]

"My brother is mad," said Jehan to himself. "It would have been much more simple to write *Fatum.* Everybody is not obliged to understand Greek."

The archdeacon returned, seated himself again in his arm-chair, and laid his head on both his hands, like one whose head aches to such a degree that he cannot hold it up.

The student watched his brother with astonishment. He, who carried his heart in his hand, who observed no other law in the world but the good law of nature, who let his passions run off by his inclinations, and in whom the lake of powerful emotions was always dry, so assiduous was he every morning in making new channels to drain it—he knew not how furiously this sea of human passions ferments and boils when it is refused any outlet; how it swells, how it

1. Destiny, fatality.

rises, how it overflows; how it heaves in inward convulsions, till it
has broken down its dikes and burst its bed. The austere and icy
envelope of Claude Frollo, that cold surface of inaccessible virtue,
had always deceived Jehan. The jovial scholar never dreamed of
the lava, deep and furious, which boils beneath the snowy crest of
Etna.

We know not whether these ideas occurred to him at the moment; but, volatile as he was, he apprehended that he had seen
more than he ought to have seen, that he had surprised the soul of
his elder brother in one of its most secret attitudes, and that he must
take good care not to let Claude perceive it. Perceiving that the archdeacon had relapsed into his former stupor, he softly drew back his
head and took several steps outside the door, that his footfall might
apprise the archdeacon of his arrival.

"Come in," cried his brother, from within the cell; "I have been
waiting for you. Come in, Master Jacques."

The scholar boldly entered. The archdeacon, to whom such a
visitor in such a place was anything but welcome, started at the
sight of him. "What! is it you, Jehan?"

"'Tis a J, at any rate," said the student, with his ruddy, impudent,
jovial face.

The countenance of Dom Claude resumed its stern expression.
"What brings you hither?"

"Brother," replied the scholar, assuming as humble, modest, and
decorous an air as he could, and twirling his cap on his fingers with
a look of innocence, "I am come to ask of you—"

"What?"

"A little wholesome advice, which I much need." Jehan durst not
add—"and a little money which I need still more." This last member
of the sentence he forebore to utter.

"Sir," said the archdeacon, in an austere tone, "I am highly displeased with you."

"Alas!" sighed the student.

Dom Claude made his chair describe one-fourth of a circle, and
looked steadfastly at Jehan. "I wanted to see you," said he.

This was an ominous exordium. Jehan prepared himself for a
fierce attack.

"Every day, Jehan, complaints are brought to me of your mis-
conduct. What have you to say for yourself about that beating
which you gave to the young Viscount Albert de Ramonchamp?"

"Oh!" replied Jehan, "a mere bagatelle! The scurvy page amused himself with making his horse run in the mud for the purpose of splashing the scholars."

"And what excuse have you to make," resumed the archdeacon, "about that affair with Mahiet Targel, whose gown you tore? *Tunicam dechiraverunt*[1] says the complaint."

"Pooh! only one of the sorry Montaigu hoods! that's all!"

"The complaint says *tunicam* and *capettam*. Have you not learned Latin?"

Jehan made no reply.

"Yes," continued the priest, "the study of letters is at a low ebb now. The Latin language is scarcely understood, the Syriac unknown, the Greek so hateful that it is not accounted ignorance even in the greatest scholars to skip a Greek word without pronouncing it, and to say *Græcum est non legitur*."[2]

Jehan boldly raised his eyes. "Brother," said he, "would you like me to explain in simple French the Greek word written there upon the wall?"

"Which word?"

"*ANA'TKH!*"

A slight flush tinged the pallid cheek of the archdeacon, like the puff of smoke which betokens the secret commotion of a volcano. The student scarcely perceived it.

"Well, Jehan," stammered the elder brother with some effort, "what is the meaning of that word?"

"FATALITY."

Dom Claude turned pale, and the scholar carelessly continued: "And that word underneath, engraven by the same hand, 'Ανάγνεια, signifies impurity. You see, I do know something of Greek."

The archdeacon was silent. This Greek lesson had made him thoughtful. Young Jehan, who had all the art of a spoiled child, deemed it a favorable moment for hazarding his request. Assuming, therefore, as soothing a tone as possible, he thus began: "My good brother, surely you will not look morose and take a dislike to me merely on account of a few petty bruises and thumps given in fair fight to a pack of little chits and monkeys—*quibusdam marmosetis*. You see, I do know something of Latin, Brother Claude."

But this canting hypocrisy had not its accustomed effect upon the stern senior. It did not remove a single wrinkle from the brow of the archdeacon. "Come to the point," said he, dryly.

"Well, then," replied Jehan, screwing up his courage; "it is this—I want money."

At this straightforward declaration the countenance of the arch-

---

1. "They have torn the robe."
2. "It is Greek, it is not read."

deacon all at once assumed a magisterial and paternal expression.

"You know, Monsieur Jehan," said he, "that our fief of Tirechappe produces no more, deducting ground rent and other outgoings for the twenty-one houses, than thirty-nine livres, eleven sous, six deniers parisis. This is half as much again as in the time of the Paclets, but 'tis no great deal."

"I want money," repeated Jehan, stoically.

"You know that the official decided that our twenty-one houses are liable to the payment of fines to the bishopric, and that to relieve ourselves from this homage we must pay the most reverend bishop two marks in silver gilt at the rate of six livres parisis. Now I have not yet been able to save these two marks, as you well know."

"I know that I want money," repeated Jehan, for the third time.

"And what would you do with it?"

At this question a glimmer of hope danced before the eyes of Jehan. He resumed his soft and fawning manner.

"Look you, my dear brother Claude, it is not for any bad purpose that I make this application. It is not to play the gallant in taverns with your unzains, or to parade the streets of Paris in a suit of gold brocade with a lackey at my heels. No, brother; it is for an act of charity."

"What act of charity?" inquired Claude, with some surprise.

"There are two of my friends who have proposed to purchase baby-linen for the child of a poor widow in Haudry's almshouses: it is a real charity. It would cost three florins, and I wish to contribute my share."

"A likely story!" observed the sagacious Claude. "What sort of baby-linen must it be to cost three florins—and that too for the infant of one of the Haudry widows! Since when have those widows had young infants to provide clothes for?"

"Well, then," cried Jehan, once more arming himself with his usual impudence, "I want money to go at night to see Isabeau la Thierrye."

"Dissolute wretch!" exclaimed the priest.

" 'Αναγνεία," said Jehan.

This word which stared the scholar in the face on the wall of the cell, produced an extraordinary effect on the priest. He bit his lips, and his anger was extinguished in a deep blush.

"Get you gone!" said he to Jehan; "I expect some one."

Jehan made another attempt: "Brother Claude, give me at least one petit parisis to get something to eat."

"Where are you in Gratian's decretals?" asked Dom Claude.

"I have lost my exercises."

"Where are you in the Latin humanities?"

"Somebody has stolen my Horace."

"Where are you in Aristotle?"

"By my fay, brother! which of the fathers of the church is it who says that heretics have in all ages sought refuge under the briers of Aristotle's metaphysics? Faugh upon Aristotle! I will not tear my religion to rags against his metaphysics."

"Young man," replied the archdeacon, "at the last entry of the king there was a gentleman called Philippe de Comines who had embroidered on the trappings of his horse this motto, which I counsel you to ponder well: *Qui non laborat non manducet.*" [He that will not work neither shall he eat.]

The scholar continued silent for a moment, with his finger on his ear, his eye fixed upon the floor, and a look of vexation. All at once turning toward Claude with the brisk motion of a water-wagtail, "Then, my good brother," said he, "you refuse me a sou to buy me a crust at the baker's?"

"Qui non laborat non manducet."

At this inflexible answer of the archdeacon's, Jehan covered his face with his hands, sobbed like a woman, and cried in a tone of despair: "Ο το το το το τοῖ!"

"What is the meaning of that?" asked Claude, surprised at this vagary.

"Why," said the scholar, after rubbing his eyes with his knuckles to give them the appearance of weeping—"it is Greek—'tis an anapest of Æschylus, which expresses grief to the life."

He then burst into a laugh so droll and so ungovernable that the archdeacon could not help smiling. It was in fact Claude's fault: why had he so utterly spoiled the boy?

"Nay now, my good brother Claude," resumed Jehan, "only look at my wornout buskins. Did you ever see a more lamentable sight?"

The archdeacon had quickly resumed his former sternness. "I will send you new buskins, but no money."

"Only one poor petit parisis, brother!" besought Jehan. "I will learn Gratian by heart, I will be a good Christian, a real Pythagoras of learning and virtue. One petit parisis, pray! Would you let me fall a prey to hunger which is staring me in the face?"

Dom Claude shook his wrinkled brow. *"Qui non laborat——"*

"Well, then," cried Jehan, interrupting him, "jollity forever! I will game, I will fight, I will go to the tavern and the bordel!"

So saying, he threw up his cap and snapped his fingers like castanets. The archdeacon eyed him with gloomy look.

"Jehan," said he, "you are on a very slippery descent. Know you whither you are going?"

"To the tavern," said Jehan.

"The tavern leads to the pillory."

"'Tis a lantern like any other; and it was perhaps the one with which Diogenes found his man."

"The pillory leads to the gallows."

"The gallows is a balance which has a man at one end and all the world at the other. 'Tis a fine thing to be the man."

"The gallows leads to hell."

"That is a rousing fire."

"Jehan, Jehan, the end will be bad."

"The beginning at least will have been good."

At this moment the sound of a footfall was heard on the stairs.

"Silence!" said the archdeacon; "here is Master Jacques. Hark ye, Jehan," added he, in a lower tone, "be sure not to mention what you shall have seen and heard here. Quick! hide yourself under this furnace, and don't so much as breathe."

The scholar crept under the furnace. Here an excellent idea occurred to him: "By the bye, brother Claude, I must have a florin for not breathing."

"Silence! you shall have it."

"But give it me now."

"There, take it!" said the archdeacon, angrily, throwing him his pouch. Jehan crawled as far as he could under the furnace, and the door opened.

CHAPTER V

THE TWO MEN IN BLACK

THE PERSON who entered had a black gown and a gloomy look. Our friend Jehan, who had contrived to arrange himself in his hiding-place in such a manner as to hear and see all that passed, was struck at the first glance by the perfect sadness of the garb and the countenance of the visitor. A certain gentleness at the same time overspread that face, but it was the gentleness of a cat or a judge. The man was very gray, wrinkled, and hard upon sixty, with white eye-brows, hanging lip, and large hands. When Jehan saw that it was no-body, that is to say, in all probability some physician or magistrate, and that his nose was at a great distance from his mouth, a sure sign of stupidity, he shrunk back in his hole, vexed at the prospect of having to pass an indefinite time in so confined a posture and in such scurvy company.

The archdeacon meanwhile had not even risen to this personage. He motioned to him to be seated on a stool near the door, and, after a few moments' silence, in which he seemed to be pursuing a pre-vious meditation, he said with the tone of a patron to his client, "Good-morrow, Master Jacques."

"Good-morrow, master," replied the man in black.

In the two ways of pronouncing on the one hand that Master Jacques, and on the other that master by way of eminence, there was as much difference as between monseigneur and monsieur; it clearly bespoke the teacher and the disciple.

"Well," resumed the archdeacon, after another silence, which Master Jacques took care not to interrupt, "have you succeeded?"

"Alas! master," said the other, with a sorrowful smile, "I keep puffing away. More ashes than I want, but not an atom of gold."

A gesture of displeasure escaped Dom Claude.

"I was not talking of that, Master Jacques Charmolue, but of the proceedings against your sorcerer, Marc Cenaine, I think you called him, the butler of the Court of Accompts. Doth he confess his guilt? Has the torture produced the desired effect?"

"Alas! no," replied Master Jacques, still with his sad smile; "we have not that consolation. The man is as hard as a flint. We might boil him in the Swine Market before he would confess. However, we are sparing no pains to get the truth; his joints are all dislocated. We are trying everything we can think of, as old Plautus says:

> "'Advorsum stimulos, laminas, crucesque, compedesque,
> Nervos, catenas, carceres, numellas, pedicas, bolas——'

but all to no purpose. Oh! he is a terrible fellow. He fairly puzzles me."

"Have you found nothing further in his house?"

"Yes," said Master Jacques, groping in his pouch; "this parchment. There are words upon it which pass our comprehension: and yet Monsieur Philippe Lheulier, the criminal advocate, knows some-thing of Hebrew, which he picked up in the affair of the Jews at Brussels."

As he thus spoke Master Jacques unrolled the parchment.

"Give it to me," said the archdeacon. He threw his eye over it. "Pure magic, Master Jacques!" he exclaimed. "*Emen Hetan*—that is the cry of the witches on their arrival at their sabbath meetings. *Per ipsum, et cum ipso, et in ipso*—that is the command which chains down the devil in hell. *Hax, pax, max*—that belongs to medicine— a form against the bite of mad dogs. Master Jacques, you are the king's proctor in the ecclesiastical court: this parchment is abominable."

"We will apply the torture again. But here is something else," added Master Jacques, fumbling a second time in his pouch, "that we have found at Marc Cenaine's."

It was a vessel of the same family as those which covered Dom Claude's furnace. "Aha!" said the archdeacon; "a crucible of alchemy!"

"I must confess," resumed Master Jacques, with his timid and awkward smile, "that I tried it upon the furnace, but with no better luck than with my own."

The archdeacon examined the vessel. "What has he engraved on his crucible? *Och, och*—the word that drives away fleas. This Marc Cenaine is an ignoramus. I can easily believe that you will not make gold with this. 'Tis fit to put in your alcove in summer, and that is all."

"Talking of blunders," said the king's proctor, "I have been examining the porch below before I came up. Is your reverence quite sure that the one of the seven naked figures at the feet of Our Lady, with wings at his heels, is Mercury?"

"Certainly," replied the priest; "so it is stated by Augustin Nypho, the Italian doctor, who had a bearded demon that revealed everything to him. But we will go down presently, and I will explain this to you to be the text."

"Many thanks, master," said Charmolue, with a very low obeisance. "But I had well-nigh forgotten—when doth it please you that I should order the young sorceress to be apprehended?"

"What sorceress?"

"That Bohemian, you know, who comes every day to dance in the Parvis, in despite of the prohibition of the official. She has a goat which is possessed, and has the devil's own horns, and reads, and writes, and understands mathematics, and would be enough to bring all Bohemia to the gallows. The indictment is quite ready. A handsome creature, upon my soul, that dancer! the brightest black eyes! a pair of Egyptian carbuncles! When shall we begin!"

1. By itself, and with itself, and in itself.

The archdeacon turned pale as death. "I will tell you," stammered he, with a voice scarcely articulate. Then with an effort he added: "For the present go on with Marc Cenaine."

"Never fear," said Charmolue, smiling; "as soon as I get back, I will have him strapped down again to the leathern bed. But 'tis a devil of a fellow: he tries Pierrat Torterue himself, and his hands are bigger than mine. As saith the good Plautus:

"'Nudus vinctus centum pondo, es quando pendes per pedes.'

The windlass will be the best thing to set to work upon him."

Dom Claude appeared to be absorbed in gloomy reverie. Suddenly turning to Charmolue: "Master Pierrat—Master Jacques, I would say, go on with Marc Cenaine."

"Ay, ay, Dom Claude. Poor man, he will have suffered a martyrdom. But then what an idea, to go to the sabbath! a butler of the Court of Accompts, who ought to know the text of Charlemagne's ordinance, *Stryga vel masca!* As for the girl—'Smeralda, as they call her—I shall await your orders—Ah, true! and when we are at the porch you will also explain to me what the gardener in low relief at the entrance of the church is meant for! Is it not the Sower? Hey, master! What think you?"

Dom Claude, engrossed by his own reflections, attended not to the speaker. Charmolue, following the direction of his eye, perceived that it was mechanically fixed upon a large spider's web stretched across the window. At that moment a giddy fly, attracted by the March sun, flew into the net and became entangled in it. At the shock given to his web, an enormous spider rushed forth from his central cell, and then with one leap, sprung upon the fly, which he doubled up with his fore-legs, while with his hideous sucker he attacked the head. "Poor fly!" said the proctor, and raised his hands to rescue it. The archdeacon, suddenly starting up, held back his arm with convulsive violence.

"Master Jacques!" cried he, "meddle not with fatality!"

The proctor turned about in alarm: it seemed as if his arm was held by iron pincers. The eye of the priest was fixed, wild, glaring, and gazed intently upon the horrible little group of the fly and the spider.

"Oh, yes, yes!" resumed the priest, with a voice that seemed to proceed from his very bowels—"this is an emblem of the whole affair. It is young, it flies about, it is merry, it seeks the open air, the spring sunshine, liberty. Oh, yes! But it is stopped at the fatal window; it is caught in the toils of the spider! Poor dancing-

girl! poor predestined fly! Be quiet, Master Jacques! it is fatality!
Alas, Claude! thou art the spider. Claude, thou art the fly, too! Thou
didst seek science the light, the sunshine; thou desiredst only to
reach the free air, the broad daylight of eternal truth; but, while
darting toward the dazzling window which opens into the other
world, a world of brightness, intelligence, and science, blind fly, silly
doctor, thou didst not perceive that subtle spider's web spread by
Fate between the light and thee; thou rushedst into it, and now,
with mangled head and broken wings, thou strugglest in the iron
grip of fatality! Master Jacques! Master Jacques! let the spider
alone!"

"I assure you," said Charmolue, who stared at him without com-
prehending his meaning, "that I will not meddle with it. But for
mercy's sake, master, loose my arm: you have a hand like a vise."

The archdeacon heard him not. "Oh, fool! fool!" he again began, without taking his eyes for a moment off the window. "And if
thou couldst have broken through those formidable meshes with
thy delicate wings, dost thou imagine that thou couldst then have
attained the light? How wouldst thou have passed that glass, which
is beyond it, that transparent obstacle, that wall of crystal harder
than brass, which separates all philosophies from truth? Oh, vanity
of science! how many sages come fluttering from afar to dash their
heads against it! how many systems come buzzing to rush pell-mell
against this eternal window!"

He paused. The concluding reflections, which had insensibly diverted his mind from himself to science, appeared to have restored him to a degree of composure. Jacques Charmolue brought
him back completely to a feeling of reality by asking him this
question: "By the bye, master, when will you come and help me to
make gold? I am not lucky at it."

The archdeacon shook his head with a bitter smile. "Master
Jacques," he replied, "read the 'Dialogus de Energia et Operatione
Dæmonum,'[1] by Michael Psellus. What we are about is not abso-
lutely innocent."

"Speak low, master," said Charmolue. "I thought as much myself. But a man may be allowed to dabble a little in hermetics when
he is but king's proctor in the ecclesiastical court at thirty crowns
tournois per annum. Only let us speak lower."

At that moment, sounds resembling those made in mastication,
proceeding from beneath the furnace, struck the alarmed ear of
Charmolue.

"What is that?" he asked.

1. *Dialogue upon the Powers and Works of Demons.*

It was the scholar who, cramped in his hiding-place, and heartily weary of it, had there found a hard crust and a cube of moldy cheese, and fallen foul of them without ceremony, by way of consolation and breakfast. As he was very hungry he made a great noise, and smacked his chops so audibly at every munch as to excite alarm in the proctor.

"'Tis only my cat," said the archdeacon, sharply, "regaling herself under there with a mouse."

This explanation satisfied Charmolue. "In fact, master," he replied, with a respectful smile, "every great philosopher has had his familiar animal. As Servius says, you know: *Nullus enim locus sine genio est.*" [1]

Dom Claude, apprehensive of some new prank of Jehan's, reminded his worthy disciple that they had some figures on the porch to study together; and both left the cell, to the great relief of the scholar, who began seriously to fear that his knees and his chin would grow together.

CHAPTER VI

CAPTAIN PHŒBUS DE CHATEAUPERS

"*Te Deum laudamus!*" exclaimed Master Jehan, sallying forth from his hole; "the two screech-owls are gone. Och! och!—Hax! pax! max! —the fleas!—the mad dogs!—the devil!—I've had quite enough of their talk! my head rings like a belfry. Let us be off, too, and turn my good brother's moneys into bottles!"

He cast a look of kindness and admiration into the interior of the precious pouch, adjusted his dress, wiped his buskins, brushed the ashes from his sleeves, whistled a tune, cut a caper, looked round to see if there was anything else in the cell that he could make free with, picked up here and there on the furnace some amulet of glass, fit to be given by way of trinkets to Isabeau la Thierrye, opened the door which his brother as a last indulgence had left unlocked, and which he in his turn left open as the last trick he could play him, and descended the winding stairs, hopping like a bird.

He stamped with his foot when he found himself again on the ground. "Oh, good and honorable pavement of Paris!" he exclaimed

1. "There is no place without its genius."

—"cursed stairs that would give a breathing to the angels of Jacob's ladder themselves! What was I thinking of to squeeze myself into that stone gimlet which pierces the sky, and all to eat moldy cheese and to see the steeples of Paris through a loop-hole!"

He had moved but a few steps when he perceived the two screech-owls, *alias* Dom Claude and Master Jacques Charmolue, contemplating one of the sculptures of the porch. He approached them on tiptoe, and heard the archdeacon say in a very low tone to his companion: "It was William of Paris who had a Job engraved upon that stone of the color of lapislazuli, and gilt on the edges. Job represents the philosopher's stone, which must be tried and tortured in order to become perfect, as saith Raymond Lully: *Sub conservatione formæ specificæsalva anima.*"

"What is that to me?" said Jehan to himself—"I have got the purse."

At this moment he heard a loud and sonorous voice behind him pour forth a formidable volley of oaths: "*Sang Dieu! Ventre Dieu! Bedieu Corps de Dieu! Nombril de Belzebuth! Nom d'un pape! Corne et tonnere!*"

"Upon my soul," cried Jehan, "that can be nobody but my friend Captain Phœbus!"

The name of Phœbus struck the ear of the archdeacon at the moment when he was explaining to the king's proctor the dragon hiding his tail in a bath whence issue smoke and a royal head. Dom Claude shuddered, stopped short, to the great surprise of Charmolue, turned around, and saw his brother Jehan accosting a tall officer at the door of the Gondelaurier mansion.

It was in fact Captain Phœbus de Chateaupers. He was leaning against the angle of the house and swearing like a pagan.

"By my fay! Captain Phœbus," said Jehan, grasping his hand, "you swear with marvelous emphasis."

"Blood and thunder!" replied the captain.

"Blood and thunder to you!" rejoined the scholar. "But, I say, gentle captain, what has occasioned this overthrow of fair words?"

"I beg your pardon, my good comrade Jehan," cried Phœbus, shaking him by the hand, "a horse at the top of his speed can not stop short. Now I was swearing at full gallop. I have just come from those affected prudes, and whenever I leave them I have my throat full of oaths; I am forced to turn them out or they would choke me outright."

"Will you come and drink with me?" asked the scholar.

This proposal pacified the captain. "I fain would," said he, "but I have no money."

"Well, but I have."

"Aha! let us see!"

Jehan exhibited the pouch to the wondering gaze of the captain. Meanwhile, the archdeacon, who had left Charmolue quite astonished, had approached and stopped within a few paces of them, watching both without their being aware of it, so entirely was their attention engrossed by the pouch.

"A purse in your pocket, Jehan," cried Phœbus, "is like the moon in a bucket of water. You see it, but it is not there; 'tis only the shadow. Nothing but pebbles in it, I would wager."

"There are the pebbles that I pave my pocket with," replied Jehan, dryly; and so saying, he emptied the pouch upon a post close by, with the air of a Roman saving his country.

"By Heaven!" muttered Phœbus; "real moneys! 'tis absolutely dazzling."

Jehan retained his grave and dignified attitude. A few liards had rolled into the mud; the captain, in his enthusiasm, stooped to pick them up. He counted the pieces, and, turning with a solemn look toward his companion, "Do you know, Jehan," said he, "that there are twenty-three sous parisis? Whom have you had the luck to lighten last night in the Rue Coupe-Gueule?"

Jehan threw back the light hair that curled about his face, and half closed his disdainful eyes. "'Tis a good thing," said he, "to have a brother who is an archdeacon and a simpleton."

"*Corne de Dieu!*" exclaimed Phœbus. "The worthy fellow!"

"Let us go and drink," said Jehan.

The two friends then bent their steps toward the tavern known by the sign of *La Pomme d'Eve*. It is superfluous to say that they had first picked up the money, and that the archdeacon followed them.

The archdeacon followed them with a wild and gloomy look. Was this the Phœbus whose accursed name had, ever since his interview with Gringoire, haunted all his thoughts? He knew not, but at any rate it was a Phœbus, and this magic name sufficed to lure the archdeacon to follow the two reckless companions with stealthy step, listening to their conversation and watching their slightest gestures with intense anxiety. Indeed, nothing was more easy than to hear all they said, so loud was the tone in which they carried on their conversation about duels, flagons, and drunken frolics.

At the turning of the street, the sound of a tambourine was wafted to them from a crossing at a little distance. Dom Claude heard the officer say to his brother: "Come, let us quicken our pace!"

"Why, Phœbus?"

"I am afraid lest the Bohemian should see me."

"What Bohemian?"

"The girl with the goat."

"La 'Smeralda?"

"The same, Jehan. I always forget her name. Let us make haste; she would know me again. I don't wish that girl to speak to me in the street."

"Are you then acquainted with her, Phœbus?"

Here the archdeacon saw Phœbus grin, stoop to Jehan's ear, and whisper a few words in it. The captain then burst into a loud laugh and tossed his head with a triumphant air.

"Indeed!" said Jehan.

"Upon my soul!" replied Phœbus.

"To-night?"

"This very night."

"Are you sure she will come?"

"You must be silly, Jehan. Not the least doubt of it."

"Captain Phœbus, you are a lucky fellow!"

The archdeacon heard every syllable of this conversation. His teeth chattered. A shudder, visible to the eye, thrilled his whole frame. He paused for a moment, leaned against a post, like a drunken man, and again followed the two boon companions.

CHAPTER VII

THE GOBLIN MONK

THE CELEBRATED TAVERN called La Pomme d'Eve was situated in the University, at the corner of Rue de la Rondelle and Rue du Batonnier. It was a very spacious but very low room, with a double roof, the central return of which was supported by a massive wooden pillar painted yellow; the floor covered with tables, bright tin jugs hanging up against the wall, plenty of topers, plenty of profligate women, a window next to the street, a vine at the door, and over the door a creaking square of sheet-iron, upon which were painted a woman and an apple, rusted with rain and turning upon an iron spike. This kind of weathercock, which looked toward the pavement, was the sign of the house.

It was nightfall, and the tavern, full of candles, glared at a distance like a forge in the dark; the sounds of carousal, swearing, altercation, mixed with the jingle of glasses issued from the broken panes. Through the haze which covered the window, in consequence of the heat of the room, might be discerned swarms of confused figures, from which burst from time to time roars of laughter. The pedestrians whose business called them that way, passed this noisy window without casting their eyes on it; but at intervals some little ragged urchin would stand on tiptoe to look in, and shout the old doggerel couplet with which it was usual in those days to greet drunkards:

> "Aux Houls,
> Saouls, saouls, saouls!"

One man, however, kept incessantly walking to and fro before the noisy tavern, narrowly watching all goers and comers, and never moving further from it than a sentry from his box. He was muffled up in a cloak to the very eyes. This cloak he had just bought at a shop contiguous to the tavern, no doubt as a protection from the cold of the March evening, perhaps also to conceal his dress. From time to time he paused before the window, looked through the small lozenge-shaped panes bordered with lead, listened and stamped.

At length the tavern door opened. It was this that he appeared to be waiting for. Two persons who had been drinking there came out. The ray of light which escaped at the door fell for a moment upon their jovial faces. The man in the cloak stationed himself under a porch on the other side of the street to watch them.

"The clock has just struck seven," exclaimed one of the topers: "that is the time for my appointment."

"I tell you," replied his companion, with an articulation far from distinct, "that I don't live in the Rue des Mauvaises Paroles—*indignus qui inter verba mala habitat.*[1] I lodge in the Rue Jean Pain Mollet. You are more horned than a unicorn if you say to the contrary."

"Jehan, my friend, you are drunk," said the other.

His companion rejoined, staggering: "That is what you are pleased to say, Phœbus; but it is proved that Plato had the profile of a hound."

The reader has no doubt already recognized in the two jolly top-

1. He is unworthy who dwelleth among evil words.

ers the captain and the scholar. The man who was watching them in the dark appeared also to have recognized them; for, with slow step, he followed all the zigzags into which the captain was drawn by his companion. The former, more inured to tippling, was none the worse for liquor. The man in the cloak, listening to them attentively, was enabled to catch the whole of the following interesting conversation:

"Body o' Bacchus! Mr. Bachelor, try to walk straight; you know I must leave you. It is seven o'clock, I tell you, and I have an appointment."

"Then go, leave me! I see the stars and darts of fire. You are like the Castle of Dampmartin, bursting with laughter."

"By my grandmother's warts! Jehan, the nonsense you talk is too absurd. By the bye, Jehan, have you any money left?"

"Mr. Rector, there is no fault—the little shambles, *perox boucheria.*"

"Jehan, my friend Jehan, you know I have an assignation with that damsel at the end of the Pont St. Michel. Surely, Jehan, we have not drunk all the parson's money. See if you have not one parisis left."

"The consciousness of having well spent the other hours is an excellent sauce to the table."

"Fire and fury! A truce to cross purposes, Jehan. Tell me, have you any money left? I must have some, or, by Heaven! I will rifle your pockets."

"Why, sir, the Rue Galiache is a street that has the Rue de la Verrerie at one end, and the Rue de la Tixeranderie at the other."

"Quite right, my dear friend Jehan, so it has. But, for Heaven's sake! rally your senses. It is seven o'clock, and I want but one sou parisis."

"Silence, now—silence to the song, and attention to the chorus:

> "'When it shall befall the cats
> To be eaten up by rats,
> Then the King of Arras city
> Shall be master—more's the pity!
> When at St. John's tide the sea,
> Wide and warm although it be,
> Shall be frozen firm and fast,
> As if done by winter's blast;
> Then the folks from Arras, they
> O'er the ice shall trudge away.'"

"Scholar of Antichrist!" cried Phœbus, "may thy brains be dashed out with thine own books!" At the same time he gave the intoxicated student a violent push which sent him reeling against the wall, where he presently sunk gently upon the pavement of Philip Augustus. From a relic of that brotherly compassion which is never wholly banished from the heart of a toper, Phœbus rolled Jehan with his foot upon one of those pillows of the poor which Providence keeps ready in the corners of all the streets of Paris, and which the wealthy disdainfully stigmatize with the name of dung-hills. The captain placed Jehan's head on an inclined plane of cabbage-stalks and the scholar instantly began to snore in a magnificent bass. Yet was not the captain's heart wholly free from animosity. "So much the worse for thee if the devil's cart picks thee up as it passes!" said he to the sleeping scholar, and away he went.

The man in the cloak, who had kept following him, paused for a moment before the helpless youth, as if undecided what to do; then, heaving a deep sigh, he continued to follow the captain.

Like them, we will leave Jehan sleeping beneath the canopy of heaven, and speed after them, if it so please the reader.

On reaching the Rue St. Andre des Arcs, Captain Phœbus perceived that some one was following him. Chancing to turn his eyes, he saw a kind of shadow creeping behind him along the walls. He stopped; the figure stopped; he walked on; the figure walked on too. He felt but little alarm at this discovery. "Pooh!" said he to himself, "I have not a single sou."

He halted in front of the College of Autun, where he had commenced what he called his studies, close to the statue of Cardinal Pierre Bertrand, on the right of the porch, and looked around him. The street was absolutely deserted. Nothing was to be seen but the figure, which approached him with slow steps, so slow that he had abundant time to observe that it had a cloak and a hat. When very near to him it stopped and remained motionless as the statue of Cardinal Bertrand, intently fixing upon him, however, a pair of eyes glaring with that vague light which issues at night from those of a cat.

The captain was brave and would not have cared a rush for a robber with a cudgel in his fist. But this walking statue, this petrified man, thrilled him with horror. There were at that time in circulation a number of stories of a goblin monk who haunted at night the streets of Paris; these stories crowded confusedly upon his memory. He stood stupefied for some minutes, and at length broke silence by a forced laugh. "If you are a robber, as I hope," said he, "you are somewhat like a heron attacking a nut-shell. I am the hopeful sprig of a ruined family, my dear fellow. Seek some better game. In the chapel of that college there is some wood of the true cross, which is kept in the treasure-room."

The hand of the figure was stretched from beneath the cloak, and grasped the arm of Phœbus with the force of an eagle's talons. "Captain Phœbus de Chateaupers!" said the specter at the same moment.

"What, the devil!" cried Phœbus; "you know my name!"

"Not only your name," replied the mysterious stranger in a sepulchral tone: "you have an assignation this evening."

"I have," answered the astounded Phœbus.

"At the hour of seven."

"In a quarter of an hour."

"At Falourdel's at the Pont St. Michel."

"Precisely so."

"To meet a female."

"I plead guilty."

"Whose name is——"

"La 'Smeralda," said Phœbus, gayly, having by degrees recovered his levity.

At that name the specter shook the captain's arm with violence. "Captain Phœbus de Chateaupers, thou liest!"

Whoever could have seen at that moment the flushed face of the captain, the backward bound which he made with such force as to disengage his arm from the gripe in which it was held, the fierce look with which he clapped his hand to the hilt of his sword, and the motionless attitude of the cloaked figure—whoever had witnessed this would have been frightened. It was something like the battle between Don Juan and the statue.

"Fire and fury!" cried the captain. "This is a word to which the ear of a Chateaupers is not accustomed. Thou darest not repeat it."

"Thou liest!" said the specter, dryly.

The captain gnashed his teeth. Goblin monk, phantom, superstitious tales—were all forgotten at the moment. In his eyes it was but a man and an insult. "Bravely said!" stammered he, half choked with rage. He drew his sword, and in a faltering voice—for rage makes one tremble, as well as fear—cried, "Here! on the spot! this very moment! draw—draw! The blood of one of us must dye this pavement!"

Meanwhile the other neither flinched nor stirred. When he saw his adversary on guard and ready for the combat: "Captain Phœbus," said he, in a tone tremulous with vexation, "you forget your engagement."

In men like Phœbus gusts of passion are like boiling milk, the ebullition of which a drop of cold water is sufficient to allay. At those few simple words the captain dropped the weapon which glistened in his hand.

"Captain," continued the stranger, "to-morrow, the day after to-morrow, a month, a year, ten years hence, you will find me ready to cut your throat; but first go to your assignation."

"In fact," said Phœbus, as if seeking to capitulate with himself, "a sword and a girl are two delightful things to encounter in a meeting; but I don't see why I should give up one for the other when I may have both."

He returned his sword to the scabbard.

"Go to your assignation," repeated the unknown.

"Many thanks, sir, for your courtesy," replied Phœbus with some embarrassment. "It is very true that it will be time enough to-morrow to slash and cut button-holes in Father Adam's doublet. I am beholden to you for allowing me one more agreeable quarter of an hour. I did hope, to be sure, to put you to bed in the kennel, and yet be in time for my appointment, especially as in such cases it is genteel to make the damsels wait a little. But you appear to be a hearty fellow, and it is safest to put off our meeting till to-morrow. So I shall go to my assignation, which is for the hour of seven, as you know." Here Phœbus tapped his forehead. "Ah! I forgot! I must have money, and I have not a single sou left."

"Here is money," said the stranger.

Phœbus felt the cold hand of the unknown slip into his a large piece of money. He could not help taking the coin and pressing that hand.

"By Heaven!" he exclaimed, "you are a good fellow!"

"On condition!" said the stranger. "Prove to me that I was wrong, and that you spoke the truth. Conceal me in some corner where I may see whether the girl is really the same whose name you mentioned."

"Oh!" replied Phœbus, "that will make no difference to me."

"Come along, then," rejoined the figure.

"At your service," said the captain. "For aught I know, you may be the devil in *propriâ personâ;* but let us be good friends to-night; to-morrow I will pay you my debts, both of the purse and the sword."

They walked away with hasty steps. In a few minutes the noise of the river apprised them that they were on the bridge of St. Michel, at that time covered with houses. "I will first introduce you," said Phœbus to his companion, "and then go and fetch the wench, who is to wait for me near the Petit Chatelet."

His companion made no reply; since they had been walking side by side he had not uttered a word. Phœbus stopped before a low door, against which he kicked violently. A light glimmered through the crevices of the door.

"Who's there?" cried a mumbling voice.

"*Corps Dieu? Tete Dieu! Ventre Dieu!*" replied the captain.

The door instantly opened and discovered an old woman and a lamp, both of which trembled. The hag was bent almost double, and dressed in rags. Her head shook, and her hands, face and neck were covered with wrinkles. She had very small eyes; her lips receded owing to the loss of her teeth, and all round her mouth she had long white hairs resembling the whiskers of a cat. The interior of her dwelling corresponded with herself. The walls were of plaster; the ceiling was formed of the black rafters and floor of the room above; the fireplace was dismantled, and every corner displayed a drapery of cob-webs. Two or three rickety tables and stools occupied the middle of the floor; a dirty boy was playing in the ashes, and at the further end the stairs, or rather ladder, led up to a trap-door in the ceiling. On entering this den, the captain's mysterious companion drew his cloak up to his eyes, while Phœbus kept swearing like a Turk. He put into the hand of the old woman, the coin which had been given to him by the stranger. The crone, who called him monseigneur at every other word, deposited the crown in a drawer. When her back was turned, the ragged urchin rose from the hearth, slyly went to the drawer, took out the piece of money, and put a dry leaf which he had pulled from a fagot in its place.

The hag beckoned to the two gentlemen, as she called them, to follow, and ascended the ladder before them. On reaching the room above, she set the lamp upon a coffer, and Phœbus opened a door that led to a dark closet. "This way, my good fellow," said he to his companion. The man in the cloak complied without uttering a word; the door closed upon him; he heard Phœbus bolt it, and a moment afterward go downstairs with the old woman. The light disappeared along with them.

CHAPTER VIII

UTILITY OF WINDOWS LOOKING TOWARD THE RIVER

CLAUDE FROLLO—for we presume that the reader, more intelligent than Phœbus, has discovered that the specter monk was no other than the archdeacon—Claude Frollo groped about for a few moments in the dark hole in which the captain had bolted him. It was, in fact, a loft such as builders sometimes leave in the roof above the outer walls of a house. The vertical section of this kennel, as Phœbus had aptly called it, would have given a triangle. It had neither window nor loop-hole, and the inclined plane of the roof would not permit a person to stand upright in it. Claude, therefore, crouched in the dust and mortar that crunched under him. His brain seemed to be on fire: but what passed at that moment in the dark soul of the archdeacon none but God and himself could ever know.

In what fatal order did he arrange in imagination La Esmeralda, Phœbus, Jacques Charmolue, his younger brother, whom he so loved, yet whom he had left in the mud, his archdeacon's gown, his reputation perhaps, staked as it was at Falourdel's—all these images, all these adventures? I can not tell. But it is certain that these ideas formed in his mind a horrible group.

He waited a full quarter of an hour. To him this interval appeared an age. All at once he heard the stairs creak; some one was coming up. The trap-door opened; a light was discernible. In the crazy door of the loft there was a crevice to which he applied his eye. It was wide enough to allow him to see all that passed in the adjoining room. The hag first made her appearance, with the lamp in her hand, then Phœbus, turning up his whiskers, then a third face, that of the beautiful and graceful Esmeralda. The priest saw it rise above the floor like a dazzling apparition. Claude trembled; a cloud darkened his eyes; his arteries beat with violence; he was stunned with a rushing as of a mighty wind; everything about him seemed to whirl round, and presently sight and hearing forsook him.

When he came to himself Phœbus and La Esmeralda were alone, sitting on the wooden coffer by the side of the lamp, which threw a strong light upon their two youthful faces, and enabled the archdeacon to discover a truckle-bed at the further extremity of the garret.

Beside this bed was a window, through the panes of which, broken like a spider's web by a shower of rain, he could see a patch of sky and the moon couched on a bed of light fleecy clouds.

The damsel was flushed, confused, palpitating. Her long, downcast eyelashes shaded her crimsoned cheeks. The face of the officer, to which she durst not raise her eyes, was radiant with delight. Unconsciously, and with a charming semblance of childishness, she traced unmeaning lines on the lid of the coffer with tip of her finger, and then looked at the finger which had been thus employed. Her feet could not be seen: the little goat was cowering upon them.

An amorous chit-chat is a very commonplace sort of thing. It is a perpetual "I love you"—a phrase musical enough to the parties concerned, but exceedingly bald and insipid to indifferent persons, when not adorned with a few *fiorituri*. Claude, however, was not an indifferent listener.

"Oh! despise me not, Monseigneur Phœbus," said the girl, without raising her eyes. "I fear that what I am doing is wrong."

"Despise you, my pretty dear!" replied the officer, with a consequential air of gallantry; "despise you! and why?"

"For having accompanied you."

"I perceive, my beauty, that we don't understand each other. I ought, by rights, not to despise you, but to hate you."

The girl looked at him in alarm.

"Hate me! What then have I done?"

"For wanting so much solicitation."

"Alas!" said she, "I am breaking a vow. . . . I shall never find my parents again. . . . The charm will lose its virtue. But no matter! What need have I at present of father or mother?"

As she thus spoke, she fixed on the captain her large dark eyes, moist with delight and tenderness.

"I declare I do not comprehend you!" exclaimed Phœbus.

La Esmeralda was silent for a moment; a tear then trickled from her eye, a sigh burst from her lips, and she said:

"Oh, monseigneur, I love you!"

There was around this young female such an odor of chastity, such a charm of virtue, that Phœbus did not feel quite at ease by her side. This confession, however, emboldened him. "You do love me!" said he with transport, throwing his arm round the waist of the Egyptian, having only waited for such an occasion.

"Phœbus," resumed the Bohemian, gently removing from her waist the tenacious hand of the captain, "you are kind, you are generous, you are handsome; you saved me, who am but a poor foundling. I have long been dreaming about an officer saving my life. It was you that I dreamed of before I knew you; the officer of my dreams had a handsome uniform like you, the look of a gentleman, and a sword. Your name is Phœbus; 'tis a fine name; I love your name, I love your sword. Draw your sword, Phœbus—let me look at it."

"Strange girl!" said the captain, unsheathing his sword, with a smile. The Egyptian looked at the handle and at the blade, examined with especial curiosity the cipher on the hilt, and kissed the weapon, saying: "You belong to a brave man."

As she bent over it, Phœbus availed himself of this opportunity to imprint a kiss upon her beautiful neck. The girl suddenly raised her head, with a face crimsoned like a cherry. The priest gnashed his teeth in the dark.

"Captain Phœbus," the Egyptian again began, "let me talk to you. Just stand up and walk, and let me hear your spurs rattle. Gemini! how handsome you are!"

The captain rose in compliance with her wish, and said in a tone of rebuke, yet with a smile of satisfaction, "Why, how childish you are! . . . But, my dear, did you ever see me in my state uniform?"

"Ah, no!" replied she.

"You would say that is handsome."

Phœbus went and again seated himself beside her, but much closer than before.

"Hark you, my dear——"

The Egyptian patted his lips with her pretty hand, with the grace and playfulness of a child.

"No, no, I won't hearken to you. Do you love me? I want you to tell me if you love me."

"Do I love thee, angel of my life?" exclaimed the captain, half sinking upon his knee. "I love thee, and never loved any but thee."

The captain had so often repeated this declaration in many a similar conjuncture, that he brought it out without bungling or making a single blunder. At this impassioned apostrophe the Egyptian raised her eyes with a look of angelic happiness toward the dirty ceiling which here usurped the place of heaven.

"Oh!" she softly murmured, "this is the moment at which one ought to die!"

Phœbus thought it a seasonable moment for stealing another kiss, which inflicted fresh torment upon the miserable archdeacon in his hiding-place.

"To die!" cried the amorous captain. "What are you talking of, my angel! Why, 'tis the very time to live, or Jupiter is a cheat! Die at such a moment as this! A good joke, by the devil's horns! No, no, that won't do. Hark ye, my dear Similar—I beg pardon, Esmenarda —but you have such a prodigiously outlandish name that I can't beat it into my head."

"Good God!" said the poor girl, "and I thought it a pretty name for its singularity. But, since you dislike it, I will change it to whatever you please."

"Nay, my darling, don't think about such trifles! 'tis a name one must get used to, that's all. When once I have learned it by heart, I shall say it off-hand. But listen, my dear Similar, I passionately adore you. I can not tell how much I love you; and I know a damsel who is bursting with rage about it."

"Who is that?" inquired the jealous girl.

"That is nothing to the purpose," said Phœbus. "Do you love me?"

"Do I?" said she.

"Well, that is enough. You shall see how I love you too. May the great devil Neptunus spit me upon his prong if I don't make you the happiest girl in the world! We will have a pretty little box somewhere or other. My archers shall parade under your windows. They are all on horseback, and Captain Mignon's are fools to them. I will take you to the Grange de Rully—'tis a magnificent sight. Eighty thousand stand of arms; thirty thousand suits of bright armor, cuirasses or brigandines; the sixty-seven banners of the trades; the standards of the parliament; the chamber of accounts; the workers of the mint—in short, a devil of a train. I will take you to see the lions in the king's hotel, which all the women are very fond of."

For some moments the damsel, absorbed in her own charming thoughts, was drinking in the intoxicating tones of his voice, without attending to the meaning of his words.

"Oh! you shall be so happy!" continued the captain, at the same time examining the buckle of her belt.

"What are you about?" said she, sharply, roused from her reverie.

"Nothing," replied Phœbus; "I was only saying that you must lay aside this strange mountebank dress when you are with me."

"When I am with you, my Phœbus!" said the girl, affectionately; and again she became silent and thoughtful. All at once she turned toward him. "Phœbus," said she, with an expression of infinite love, "instruct me in thy religion."

"My religion!" cried the captain, bursting into a hoarse laugh. "I instruct you in my religion! Blood and thunder! what do you want with my religion?"

"That we may be married," replied the Egyptian.

The captain's face assumed a mixed expression of surprise, disdain, and licentious passion.

"Pooh!" said he; "what should we marry for?"

The Bohemian turned pale, and sorrowfully drooped her head.

"My sweet one," resumed Phœbus, tenderly, "these are silly notions. Of what use is marriage? Do people love one another the less for not having mangled Latin in the shop of a priest?" As he thus spoke in his kindest tones, his eye glistened more and more.

Dom Claude, meanwhile, was watching all that passed. The planks of which the door was made were so decayed as to leave large chasms for his hawk's eyes. The priest quivered and boiled at the scene. The sight of the beauteous girl thus *tête-à-tête* with the ardent officer seemed to infuse molten lead into his veins. An extraordinary commotion took place within him. Whoever could have seen, at that moment, the face of the unhappy man pressed against the crevices of the door would have taken it for the face of a tiger looking through the bars of a cage at some jackal devouring a gazelle. His eyes flamed like a candle through the chasms.

All at once Phœbus snatched away the neckerchief of the Egyptian. The poor girl, who had continued pale and thoughtful, started up, and hastily retreated from the enterprising officer. Casting a glance at her bare shoulders, blushing, confused, and dumb with shame, she crossed her two finely turned arms over her bosom to conceal it. But for the flush that crimsoned her cheeks, whoever had seen her thus silent, motionless, and with downcast eyes, would have taken her for a statue of Modesty.

This attack of the captain's upon her toilet had uncovered the mysterious amulet which she wore about her neck.

"What is that?" said he, seizing this pretext for approaching the beautiful creature whom his vehemence had just alarmed.

"Touch it not," answered she, sharply; "'tis my protector. It is this that will enable me to find my family, if I do nothing unworthy of it. Oh, leave me, captain, I beseech you! Ah, mother! my poor mother! where art thou? Help, help thy child! Pray, Captain Phœbus, give me my neckerchief!"

"Oh, mademoiselle!" said Phœbus, stepping back, in a tone of indifference, "I see plainly that you love me not."

"Not love him!" exclaimed the unhappy girl, at the same time clinging to the captain, and making him sit down by her. "Not love thee, my Phœbus? Naughty man to say so! Wouldst thou break my heart? . . . I am thine. Of what use to me is the amulet? what need have I of a mother? To me thou art father and mother, since I love thee! Phœbus, my beloved Phœbus, look at me; thou wilt not put away from thee one who comes to place herself in thy hands! My soul, my life, my all, are thine. So I am but loved, I shall be the proudest and the happiest of women. And when I am grown old and ugly, Phœbus, when I shall be no longer fit for thee to love, then permit me to be thy servant. Others shall then embroider scarfs for thee, but thou wilt let me clean thy boots and thy spurs, and brush thy uniform. Thou wilt grant me that indulgence, wilt thou not, my Phœbus? Meanwhile, take me: let me belong to thee and be the only object of thy love! We Egyptians want nothing else but air and love."

As she thus spoke, she threw her arms around the neck of the officer, and with a sweet smile and tearful eye fixed upon him a beseeching look. The captain pressed his burning lips to her bosom.

All at once above the head of the captain she beheld another head—a livid, green, convulsive face, with the look of one of the damned: close to this face was a hand holding a dagger; it was the face and the hand of the priest. Unperceived by them, he had contrived to break open the crazy door, and there he was!

The girl was struck speechless and motionless with horror by this terrible apparition, like a dove raising her head at the moment when a falcon with glaring eyes is looking into her nest. She had not even the power to shriek. She saw the dagger descend upon the captain, and rise again reeking. "Perdition!" he exclaimed, and fell. She swooned.

At the moment when her eyes closed, and her senses were forsaking her, she thought she felt a kiss, burning as a hot iron, impressed upon her lips. On coming to herself, she was surrounded by soldiers belonging to the watch. The captain was carried away bathed in his blood. The priest was gone. The window at the further end of the chamber, which looked toward the river, was wide open. A cloak, supposed to belong to the officer, was picked up, and she heard the men saying to one another: " 'Tis a sorceress who has stabbed a captain."

Book Seven

CHAPTER I

THE CROWN TRANSFORMED INTO A DRY LEAF

FOR UPWARD of a month Gringoire and the whole of the crew in the Cour des Miracles had been in a state of extreme anxiety. La Esmeralda was missing. They knew neither what had become of her, which sorely grieved the Duke of Egypt and his vagabond subjects, nor what had become of her goat, which redoubled Gringoire's sorrow. One night the girl had disappeared, and all researches had proved bootless; no traces of her could be discovered. Some of the mendicant tribe had told Gringoire that they had met her that evening, near the Pont St. Michel, walking along with an officer; but this husband, after the fashion of Bohemia, was an incredulous philosopher; and, besides, he knew better than any one else how well his wife could defend herself. He had had abundant opportunities of judging what invincible chastity resulted from the two combined virtues of the amulet and the Egyptian, and had mathematically calculated the resistance of that chastity to the second power. He was, therefore, quite easy on that point.

But for this very reason he was the more puzzled to account for her disappearance. So deeply did he take it to heart that he would have fretted the flesh off his bones had it been possible for him to become thinner than he was. He had forgotten everything else, even his literary pursuits, not excepting his great work, "De Figuris regularibus et irregularibus," which he intended to get printed with the first money he should have. For he was over head and ears in love with printing, ever since he had seen the "Didaskalon" of Hugo St. Victor printed with the celebrated types of Vindelin of Spire.

One day, while sorrowfully passing the Tournelle, a prison for criminals, he perceived a concourse of people about one of the doors of the Palace of Justice.

"What is going forward here?" he asked a young man who was coming out.

"I do not know, sir," answered the young man. "I am told that they are trying a woman for murdering an officer of the king's ordnance. As there seems to be something of sorcery in the business, the bishop and the official have interfered, and my brother, the Archdeacon of Josas, devotes all his time to it. I wanted to speak to him, but could not get at him for the crowd, which vexed me exceedingly, as I am in great need of money."

"Alas, sir!" said Gringoire, "I wish it was in my power to lend you some; but my pockets are all in holes, not with crowns or any other coin, I can assure you."

He durst not tell the young man that he knew his brother, the archdeacon, whom he had never called upon since the scene in the church—a neglect of which he felt ashamed.

The scholar went his way, and Gringoire followed the crowd who were ascending the great staircase. In his estimation there was nothing like a criminal trial for dispelling melancholy, the judges being in general so amusingly stupid. The people with whom he had mingled moved on and elbowed one another in silence. After a slow and tiresome shuffling along an endless passage, which ran winding through the palace like the intestinal canal of the old structure, he arrived at a low door opening into a hall, which, from his tall stature, he was enabled to overlook above the undulating heads of the crowd.

The hall was spacious and dark, which made it appear still larger. The day was declining; the tall pointed windows admitted but a faint light, which expired before it reached the vaulted roof, an enormous trellis of carved wood-work, the thousand figures of which seemed to move confusedly in the dusk. There were already several lighted candles here and there upon the tables, which threw their rays upon the heads of clerks poring over heaps of papers. The anterior part of the hall was occupied by the crowd; on the right and left were lawyers seated at tables; at the further end, upon a raised platform, a great number of judges, men with immovable and sinister-looking faces, the last rows of whom were scarcely discernible for the darkness. The walls were sprinkled with an abundance of *fleurs-de-lis*. A large crucifix was indistinctly seen above the judges, and on every side an array of pikes and halberds, which the light of the candles seemed to tip with fire.

"Sir," said Gringoire to one of his neighbors, "who are all those persons ranged in rows yonder, like prelates in council?"

"Sir," answered the neighbor, "those are the counselors of the great chamber on the right, and the counselors of inquiry on the left; the masters in black gowns, and the messires in red ones."

"And who is that great red porpoise above them?" inquired Gringoire.

"That is Monsieur the President."

"And those rams behind him?" continued Gringoire, who, as we have already observed, was not fond of magistrates, perhaps owing to the grudge which he bore the Palace of Justice ever since his dramatic miscarriage.

"They are the masters of requests of the king's hotel."

"And that boar in front of them?"

"The clerk to the Court of Parliament."

"And that crocodile on the right?"

"Master Philip Lheulier, advocate extraordinary to the king."

"And that great black cat on the left?"

"Master Jacques Charmolue, the king's proctor in the ecclesiastical court, with the gentlemen of the officiality."

"But, I pray you, sir, what are all these worthy folks about here?"

"They are trying somebody."

"Who is it? I do not see the accused."

"It is a young woman, sir. She stands with her back toward us, and we can't see her for the crowd. Why, there she is, where you see that group of halberds."

"Do you know her name?" asked Gringoire.

"No, sir; I am but just come: but I presume that there is sorcery in the case, as the official attends the trial."

"Come on!" said our philosopher, "let us watch all these lawyers banqueting on human flesh! 'Tis a sight as well as any other."

Here the by-standers imposed silence on the interlocutors. An important witness was under examination.

"Gentlemen," said an old woman in the middle of the hall, who was so muffled up as to walk like a bundle of rags—"gentlemen, it is as true as that my name is Falourdel, and that I have kept house for forty years at the Pont St. Michel, and regularly paid rent, taxes, and rates. A poor old woman now, gentlemen, but once reckoned handsome, though I say it. One night I was spinning, when there comes a knock at my door. I asked 'Who's there?' and there was such a swearing! I opened the door; two men came in; a man in black, with a comely officer. Nothing was to be seen of the man in black but his eyes, for all the world like two burning coals; all the rest of him was cloak and hat. 'St. Martha's room!' said they to me. That is my room upstairs, gentlemen, my best room. They gave me a crown. I put it into my drawer, saying to myself: It will serve to-morrow to buy tripe with at the shambles of the Gloriette. Well, we went upstairs, and while my back was turned the man in black was gone. This staggered me a little. The officer, as handsome a gentleman as you would wish to set eyes on, went downstairs with me, and out he goes. By the time I had spun a quarter of a bobbin, in he comes again with a pretty poppet of a damsel, who would have dazzled you like the sun if she had been properly attired. She had with her a goat, a large goat: it might be black, it might be white; I don't recollect now. The girl—that was no concern of mine —but the goat put me out, I must say. . . . I don't like those animals; they have got a beard and horns . . . too like a man . . . and then the thing smells of witchcraft. However, I said nothing, and why should I? Had I not got the crown? And all right too, my lord, wasn't it? So I took the captain and the girl to the room upstairs, and left them alone, that is to say, with the goat. I went down, and fell to spinning again. . . . But I ought to tell you that my house has a ground floor and a floor above; the back of it looks to the river, like all the other houses on the bridge, and the windows, both of the ground floor and the chamber, open toward the water. Well, as I said just now, I began spinning again. I can't tell, not I, why I thought of the goblin monk, which the goat had put into my head —and then the girl was dressed in such a strange fashion! Well, all at once I heard such a scream upstairs, and something fall upon the floor, and the window open. I ran to mine, which is below, and saw a black figure drop before my eyes, and tumble into the water. It was a specter in the habit of a priest. The moon was shining bright, so I saw it as plain as I see you now. It swam away toward the city. I was all over of a tremble, and called the watch. When those gentlemen came in they did not know what to make of it at first, and, being rather fuddled, they fell to beating me. I soon set them right. We went up, and what should we find but my best chamber drenched with blood, the captain laid in full length with a dagger in his bosom, the girl shamming dead, and the goat frightened out of its wits! 'A pretty job,' said I; 'it will take me a fortnight to get the floor clean again—scour and scrub it as I will.' They carried away the officer—poor young man!—and the girl with her bosom all bare. But, worse than all, next day when I went to the drawer for the crown to buy tripe, lo and behold! I found nothing but a withered leaf where I had left it!"

The old woman ceased speaking. A murmur of horror arose from the auditory. "The specter, the goat and all that, look very like sorcery," said Gringoire to a neighbor. "Ay, and the withered leaf," added another. "No doubt," observed a third, "it was a witch colleagued with the goblin monk to rob the officer." Gringoire himself could scarcely help thinking that there was some probability in the conjecture.

"Witness," said the president, in a dignified manner, "have you nothing further to communicate to the court?"

"No, my lord," replied the old woman, "only that in the report my house is called a crazy, filthy hovel, which is a scandalous falsehood. To be sure, the houses on the bridge are not so goodly as some, but yet the butchers like to live in them, and they are people well to do in the world, and their wives are as proper, comely women as you would wish to see."

The magistrate whom Gringoire had likened to a crocodile now rose. "Silence!" said he. "I beg you, my lord and gentlemen, to bear in mind that a dagger was found upon the accused. Witness, have you brought with you the leaf into which the crown given you by the demon was changed?"

"Yes, sir," she replied; "here it is."

An usher handed the dead leaf to the crocodile, who gave a sinister shake of the head, and passed it to the president; and the president sent it to the king's proctor in the ecclesiastical court; so that it went the round of the hall. "Upon my word, a birch leaf!" ejaculated Master Jacques Charmolue: "a fresh proof of sorcery!"

A counselor then rose and spoke. "Witness," said he, "two men went upstairs together at your house: a man in black who immediately disappeared, and whom you afterward saw swimming in the Seine, in the habit of a priest, and the officer. Which of the two gave you the crown?"

The old woman considered for a moment. "It was the officer," said she.

A murmur again ran through the court. "Aha!" thought Gringoire, "that alters the case materially."

Master Philip Lheulier, advocate extraordinary to the king, again interposed. "Let me remind you, my lord and gentlemen, that the officer, in his deposition, taken in writing by his bedside, while admitting that he had a confused idea, at the moment when he was accosted by the man in black, that it might be the goblin monk, added, that the phantom had strongly pressed him to keep his appointment with the accused; and when the said captain observed that he had no money, he gave him the crown with which the officer paid the witness Falourdel. The crown, therefore, is a coin of hell."

This conclusive observation appeared to dispel all the lingering doubts of Gringoire and the other skeptics among the audience.

"Gentlemen are in possession of the papers," added the king's advocate, sitting down; "they can refer to the deposition of Captain Phœbus de Chateaupers."

At that name the accused rose. Her head was seen above the crowd. To his horror, Gringoire recognized La Esmeralda.

She was pale; her hair, once so gracefully plaited, and studded with sequins, was disheveled; her lips were livid, her eyes hollow. Alas! what a change!

"Phœbus!" exclaimed she, wildly, "where is he? Oh, my lords, before you put me to death, for mercy's sake tell me if he still lives!"

"Silence, prisoner!" replied the president; "we have nothing to do with that."

"If you have any pity, tell me if he is alive!" she resumed, clasping her attenuated hands; and her chains were heard to rustle along her dress.

"Well," said the king's advocate, dryly, "he is dying. Are you satisfied?"

The unhappy girl sunk down again upon her seat, voiceless, tearless, white as a waxen image.

The president stooped toward a man placed at his feet, who had a gold-laced cap, a black gown, a chain about his neck, and a wand in his hand. "Usher, bring in the second prisoner."

All eyes turned toward a small door which opened, and, to the extreme agitation of Gringoire, in walked a pretty goat with gilt horns and hoofs. The elegant creature stopped for a moment on the threshold, stretching out her neck, as if, perched on the point of some rock, she was overlooking a vast plain beneath her. All at once she descried the Bohemian, and, springing over the table and the head of a clerk of the court, in two leaps she was at her knees; she then nestled gracefully on the feet of her mistress, soliciting a word or a caress; but the prisoner remained motionless, and poor Djali herself could not obtain even a look.

"Nay, by my fay! 'tis the same nasty beast," cried old Falourdel. "I could swear positively to them both."

"If it so pleaseth you, my lord and gentlemen," began Charmolue, "we will proceed to the examination of the second prisoner."

The second prisoner was the goat, sure enough. Nothing was more common in those days than to indict animals for sorcery. In the accounts of the provosty for 1466, we find, among others, the curious details of the costs of the trial of Gillet-Soulart and his sow, "executed for their crimes at Corbeil." Every item is there: the charge for the place of confinement made for the sow, the five hundred bundles of wood carried to the port of Morsant, the three quarts of wine and the bread, the last meal of the sufferer, fraternally shared by the executioner, even to the eleven days' keep and subsistence of the sow at eight deniers parisis each. Sometimes, indeed, our pious ancestors went still further than animals. The capitularies of Charlemagne and Louis le Debonnaire decree the infliction of severe punishment upon those luminous phantoms which have the audacity to appear in the air.

The proctor of the ecclesiastical court then pronounced this solemn denunciation: "If the demon which possesses this goat, and which has withstood all the exorcisms that have been tried, persists in his wicked courses, and shocks the court with them, we forewarn him that we shall be forced to demand that he be sentenced to the gallows or the stake."

Cold perspiration covered the face of Gringoire. Charmolue took from the table the tambourine of the Egyptian, held it in a particular way to the goat, and asked, "What hour is it?"

The goat eyed him with intelligent look, raised her gilt foot and struck seven strokes. It was actually seven o'clock. A shudder of terror thrilled the crowd. Gringoire could no longer contain himself.

"The creature will be her own destruction!" he exclaimed aloud. "See you not that she knows not what she does?"

"Silence among the lieges in the court!" cried the usher, sternly.

Jacques Charmolue, by shifting the tambourine in various ways, made the goat exhibit several other tricks respecting the day of the month, the month of the year and so forth, which the reader has already witnessed; and, from an optical illusion peculiar to judicial proceedings, the very same spectators who had perhaps many a time applauded the innocent pranks of Djali in the streets, were horror-stricken at them within the walls of the Palace of Justice. The goat was decidedly the devil.

But when the king's proctor had emptied out upon the table a little leathern bag filled with detached letters which Djali had about her neck, and the goat was seen sorting out with her foot the separate letters of the fatal name PHŒBUS; the spells to which the captain had fallen a victim appeared to be irresistibly demonstrated in the opinion of all; and the Bohemian, the exquisite dancer who had so often enchanted the gazers with her graceful performances, was an odious witch.

The poor girl, meanwhile, exhibited not the least sign of life: neither the fond evolutions of her Djali, nor the threats of the judges, nor the muttered imprecations of the audience, were noticed by her. In order to rouse her, a sergeant went to her, and shook her most unmercifully, while the president, raising his voice in a solemn tone, thus spoke: "Girl, you are of Bohemian race, addicted to unrighteous deeds. In company with the bewitched goat, your accomplice, implicated in this indictment, you did, on the night of the 29th of March last, in concert with the powers of darkness, and by the aid of charms and unlawful practices, stab and slay Phœbus de Chateaupers, captain of the archers of the king's ordnance. Do you persist in denying this?"

"Oh, horror of horrors!" exclaimed the prisoner, covering her face with her hands. "Oh, my Phœbus! This is hell indeed!"

"Do you persist in denying it?" asked the president, coldly.

"Do I deny it!" said she, in a fearful tone, and with flashing eye, as she rose from her seat.

"Then," proceeded the president, calmly, "how do you explain the facts laid to your charge?"

In broken accents she replied: "I have already told you. I know not. It was a priest—a priest, a stranger to me—an infernal priest who haunts me!"

"There it is!" resumed the judge—"the goblin monk."

"Oh, sirs, have pity upon me! I am but a poor girl——"

"Of Egypt," continued the judge.

Master Jacques Charmolue, in his gentlest, softest tone, then said, "In consequence of the painful obstinacy of the prisoner, I demand the application of the torture."

"Granted," said the president.

The unhappy girl shook all over. She rose, however, at the order of the halberdiers, and, preceded by Charmolue and the officers of the officiality, walked with tolerably firm steps, between two files of partisans, toward a low door which suddenly opened and closed after her. To Gringoire it seemed as though she had been swallowed up by the gaping jaws of the monster. As soon as she disappeared, a plaintive bleating was heard. It was the poor goat, bewailing the loss of her mistress.

The proceedings were suspended. A counselor observed that the judge must be fatigued, and that they would be detained a long time if they waited for the conclusion of the torture; to which the president replied that a magistrate ought to have learned to sacrifice personal convenience to his duty.

"The provoking hussy!" said an old judge, "to bring the torture upon herself just now, when we ought to be at supper!"

CHAPTER II

SEQUEL TO THE CROWN TRANSFORMED INTO A DRY LEAF

HAVING ASCENDED and descended some steps in passages so dark that they were lighted in broad day by lamps, La Esmeralda, still surrounded by her dismal escort, was thrust by the sergeants of the palace into a room of sinister aspect. This room, of circular shape, occupied the ground floor of one of the towers that at the present day still perforate the stratum of modern edifices with which new Paris has covered the old city. There were no windows in this dungeon, neither was there any other aperture than the low entrance closed by a strong iron door. At the same time there was no want of light: in the massive substance of the wall there was a furnace, in which burned a large fire that threw a red glare over the den, and quite eclipsed the light of a miserable candle placed in a corner. The iron portcullis, which served as a door to the furnace, was drawn up at that moment, so that at its flaming mouth there were to be seen only the lower extremities of its bars, resembling a row of black, sharp, parted teeth, which made the furnace look like the mouth of one of those dragons of the legends vomiting fire and smoke. By the light which it diffused the prisoner perceived around the room a variety of instruments, the uses of which were unknown to her. In the middle was a leathern mattress laid almost flat upon the floor, on which hung a thong with a buckle, fastened to a copper ring, which a grotesque monster sculptured in the keystone of the vaulted ceiling held between his teeth. Tongs, pincers, broad plowshares, lay pell-mell, heating in the fire in the interior of the furnace. Its blood-red flare presented to the eye in the whole circumference of the chamber naught but an assemblage of fearful objects. This Tartarus was merely called the Chamber of the Question.

On the bed was carelessly seated Pierrat Torterue, the "sworn tormentor." His assistants, two square-faced gnomes, with leathern aprons and linen breeches, were stirring the coals under the iron implements.

The poor girl had need to muster her courage: on entering this den she was struck with horror. The sergeants of the bailiff of the

palace ranged themselves on one side, and the priests of the officiality on the other. In one corner was a table, at which sat a clerk
with pen, ink, and paper.

Master Jacques Charmolue approached the Egyptian with one of
his kindest smiles. "My dear girl," said he, "do you persist in your
denial?"

"Yes," she replied, in a voice scarcely audible.

"In that case," rejoined Charmolue, "it will be very painful to us
to *question* you more urgently than we would. Take the trouble to
sit down on this bed. Master Pierrat, give place to this young woman,
and shut the door."

Pierrat rose, growling. "If I shut the door," muttered he, "my fire
will go out."

"Well, then, my good fellow," replied Charmolue, "leave it open."

Meanwhile, La Esmeralda remained standing. That leathern bed,
on which so many wretched creatures had writhed in agony, frightened her. Horror thrilled the very marrow of her bones: there she
stood bewildered, stupefied. At a sign from Charmolue, the two assistants laid hold of her, and placed her in a sitting posture on the
bed. Those men did not hurt her, but when they grasped her, when
the leather touched her, she felt all her blood flow back to her heart.
She looked wildly around the room. She fancied that she saw those
ugly implements of torture—which were, among the instruments of
all kinds that she had hitherto seen, what bats, millipedes, and
spiders are among the birds and reptiles—quitting their places and
advancing from every part of the room toward her, to crawl over
her, and to bite, pinch, and sting her.

"Where is the doctor?" asked Charmolue.

"Here," answered a man in a black gown whom she had not yet
noticed.

She shuddered.

"Damoiselle," resumed the smooth tongue of the proctor of the
ecclesiastical court, "for the third time, do you persist in denying
the charges preferred against you?"

This time her voice failed: she was able only to nod an affirmative.

"You persist," cried Charmolue. "I am very sorry for it, but I am
obliged to perform the duty of my office."

"Mr. Proctor," said Pierrat, abruptly, "what shall we begin with?"

Charmolue paused for a moment, with the ambiguous grimace of
a poet at a loss for a rhyme. "With the buskin," he at length replied.

The unfortunate girl felt herself so totally abandoned by God and
man, that her head sunk upon her bosom, like something inert and

destitute of animation. The tormentor and the physician approached her together: at the same time the two assistants began to rummage in their hideous arsenal. At the clanking of the horrible irons, the unhappy girl shivered like a dead frog subjected to the action of galvanism. "Oh, my Phœbus!" murmured she, in so low a tone as to be inaudible. She then relapsed into her former insensibility and death-like silence. This sight would have rent any other heart than the hearts of judges. The wretched being to whom all the tremendous apparatus of saws, wheels and pulleys was about to be applied, the being about to be consigned to the iron gripe of executioners and pincers, was that gentle, tender, frail creature—poor grain of millet given up by human justice to be ground in the horrible mill of the torture!

Meanwhile the horny hands of Pierrat's men had brutally stripped that beautiful leg and that elegant foot which had so often delighted the by-standers with their gracefulness and agility in the streets of Paris. "'Tis a pity!" muttered the tormentor, surveying those graceful and delicate forms. Had the archdeacon been present, he would assuredly have bethought him at that moment of his symbol of the spider and the fly. Presently the poor girl saw through the cloud that spread itself before her eyes the buskin approaching; presently her foot was hidden from sight in the iron-bound apparatus. Terror then restored her strength. "Take it off!" cried she, wildly, at the same time starting up. "For mercy's sake!" She sprung from the bed with the intention of throwing herself at the feet of the king's proctor; but, her leg being confined in the heavy block of oak sheathed with iron, she sunk down powerless as a bee having its wings loaded with lead. On a sign from Charmolue, she was replaced on the bed, and two coarse hands fastened round her slender waist the thong that hung from the ceiling.

"For the last time," said Charmolue, with his imperturbable benignity, "do you confess the crimes laid to your charge?"

"I am innocent."

"Then how do you explain the circumstances alleged against you?"

"Alas, sir, I know not."

"You deny them?"

"Everything!"

"Begin," said Charmolue to Pierrat.

Pierrat turned a screw; the buskin became more and more contracted, and the wretched sufferer gave one of those horrible shrieks which baffle the orthography of every human language.

"Hold!" said Charmolue to Pierrat—"Do you confess?" he then asked the Egyptian.

"Everything?" cried the miserable girl. "I confess—mercy! mercy!"

In defying the torture she had not calculated her strength. Poor thing! her life had till then been so bright, so cheery, so joyous!—the first pang overcame her.

"Humanity obliges me to inform you," observed the king's proctor, "that, though you confess, you have nothing but death to expect."

"I wish for it," said she. And she sunk back upon the leathern bed, suspended, as if lifeless, by the thong buckled round her waist.

"So, my pretty—hold up a little!" said Master Pierrat, raising her. "You look like the golden sheep about the neck of Monsieur of Burgundy."

Jacques Charmolue again raised his voice.

"Clerk, write: Bohemian girl, you confess your participation in the feasts, sabbaths, and practices of hell with demons, sorcerers, and witches? Answer."

"Yes," said she in so low a tone as to be scarcely heard.

"You confess that you have seen the ram which Beelzebub displays in the clouds to summon his children to their sabbath, and which is seen only by sorcerers?"

"Yes."

"You confess that you have had commerce with the devil in the shape of the goat implicated in the proceedings?"

"Yes."

"Lastly, you declare and confess that, instigated by, and with the assistance of the devil and the goblin monk, you did, on the night of the 29th of March last, kill and slay a captain named Phœbus de Chateaupers?"

She fixed her glazed eyes upon the magistrate and replied, as if mechanically, without shock or convulsion, "Yes." It was evident that her spirit was utterly broken.

"Write, clerk," said Charmolue. Then turning to Pierrat's men: "Loose the prisoner," he proceeded, "and let her be taken into court." When the buskin was removed, the proctor examined her foot, still numbed with the pain. "Come, come," said he; "'tis not much the worse. You cried out in time. You would soon be able to dance as well as ever, my beauty!" Then, addressing the priests of the officiality: "Justice is enlightened at last," said he. "'Tis a consolation, gentlemen! and the damsel will bear witness that we have shown her all possible lenity."

CHAPTER III

CONCLUSION OF THE CROWN
TRANSFORMED INTO A DRY LEAF

WHEN SHE AGAIN entered the court, pale and halting, she was greeted
with a general buzz of pleasure. On the part of the auditory it arose
from that feeling of gratified impatience which is experienced at
the theater, at the conclusion of the last interlude of a play, when
the curtain rises and the fifth act begins; and on the part of the
judges, from the prospect of being soon dismissed to their suppers.
The poor little goat, too, bleated for joy. She would have run to her
mistress, but she had been tied to a bench.

It was now dark night. The candles, having received no accession to their number, gave so faint a light that the walls of the
court were not discernible. The darkness enveloped objects in a sort
of haze. A few unfeeling faces of judges alone were with difficulty
distinguishable. Opposite to them, at the other extremity of the
long hall, they could perceive an undefined patch of white moving
along the dark floor. It was the prisoner.

She advanced with faltering steps to her place. When Charmolue
had magisterially resumed possession of his, he sat down. Presently
rising again, he said, without too strongly betraying the vanity of
success: "The accused has confessed the crime."

"Bohemian girl," began the president, "you have confessed, then,
all your misdeeds of magic, of prostitution, and murder committed
on the body of Phœbus de Chateaupers?"

Her heart was wrung, and she was heard to sob in the dark.
"Whatever you please," she answered, faintly; "only put me to death
soon!"

"Mr. Proctor," said the president, "the court is ready to hear your
requisitions."

Master Charmolue produced a tremendous roll of paper, from
which he began to read with abundant gesticulation, and the exag-
gerated emphasis of the bar, a Latin oration in which all the evidence was built upon Ciceronian periphrases, flanked by quotation
from Plautus, his favorite comic writer. We are sorry that we can

not treat the reader to this delectable composition. The orator delivered it with wonderful action. Before he had finished the exordium, big drops of perspiration trickled from his brow, and his eyes appeared to be starting from his head. All at once, he stopped short in the middle of a sentence. His look, which was wont to be so bland, nay, even so stupid, became terrific. "Gentlemen," he cried—now deigning to speak in French, for it was not in his manuscript—"to such a degree is Satan mixed up in this business, that yonder he is personally present at our proceedings, and making a mock of their majesty!" As he thus spoke he pointed with his finger at the little goat, which observing the gesticulations of Charmolue, had seated herself upon her haunches, and was imitating as well as she could, with her fore-paws and her bearded head, the pathetic pantomime of the king's proctor in the ecclesiastical court. The reader will recollect that this was one of her most diverting tricks. This incident, the last proof, produced a powerful effect. To put an end to this scandal, the goat's legs were bound, and the king's proctor resumed the thread of his eloquent harangue. He concluded with requiring that the prisoner be condemned, in the first place to pay a certain pecuniary indemnity; in the second, to do penance before the grand porch of Notre Dame; and thirdly, to be taken with her goat to the Place de Grève, and there executed.

He put on his cap and sat down.

A man in a black gown, near the prisoner, then rose: it was her advocate. The judges, feeling in want of their supper, began to murmur.

"Be brief," said the president.

"My lord," replied the advocate, "since the prisoner has confessed the crime, I have but a few words to offer. In the Salic law there is this clause:—'If a witch have eaten a man, and she be convicted of it, she shall pay a fine of eight thousand deniers, which make two hundred sous in gold.' May it please the court, then, to sentence my client to pay this fine."

"That clause is become obsolete," said the advocate extraordinary to the king.

"Nego!" replied the advocate of the prisoner.

"To the vote!" said a counselor: "the crime is proved, and it is late."

The question was put to the vote without leaving the court. The judges decided off-hand: they were pressed for time. Their capped heads were seen uncovered one after another in the dusk, as the question was put to them successively in a low tone by the judge. The poor prisoner appeared to be looking at them; but her dim eye no longer saw the objects before it.

The clerk of the court began writing, and then handed a long parchment to the president. The unhappy girl heard a bustle among the people, pikes clashing together, and a chilling voice pronounced these words:

"Bohemian girl, on such a day as it shall please our lord the king, at the hour of noon, you shall be drawn in a tumbril, stripped to your shift, barefoot, with a rope about your neck, to the great porch of the Church of Notre Dame, and shall there do penance, holding in your hand a wax taper of two pounds' weight: and thence you shall be taken to the Place de Grève, and there hanged by the neck on the gallows of the city; and this your goat likewise: and you shall pay to the official three gold lions in reparation of the crimes by you committed and by you confessed, of sorcery, magic, incontinence, and murder done upon the body of Sieur Phœbus de Chateaupers. God receive your soul!"

"Oh! 'tis a dream!" murmured the prisoner, and she felt rough hands bearing her away.

CHAPTER IV

LASCIATE OGNI SPERANZA [1]

IN THE MIDDLE AGES, when a building was complete there was almost as much of it under ground as above. A palace, a fortress, a church, had always a double basement, unless it stood upon piles like Notre Dame. Under a cathedral there was a kind of subterraneous church, low, dark, mysterious, blind and mute, beneath the upper nave, which was resplendent with light and rang with the pealing of organs and bells, night and day: sometimes it was catacomb. In palaces, in bastiles, it was a prison, sometimes a sepulcher, and sometimes both together. The mighty edifices, the mode of whose formation and vegetation we have elsewhere described, had not merely foundations, but, as it were, roots, which shot out into the soil in chambers, in galleries, in staircases, like the buildings above them. Thus churches, palaces, bastile, were buried up to the middle in the ground. The vaults of a building were another building, to

1. Hope no more.

which you descended instead of ascending, and which clapped its subterraneous stories beneath the exterior stories of the edifice, like those woods and mountains which appear reversed in the mirror of a lake beneath the woods and mountains rising from its banks.

At the Bastile St. Antoine, at the Palace of Justice, at the Louvre, these subterraneous edifices were prisons. The stories of these prisons became more and more contracted and gloomy the lower you descended. They were so many zones pervaded by different shades of horror. Dante could not find anything more suitable for his hell. These funnels of dungeons usually terminated in a deep hole gradually widening from the bottom upward, in which Dante has placed his Satan, but where society confined culprits under sentence of death. When once a miserable wretch was thus buried, farewell to light, to air, to life, to every hope: there was no leaving the place but for the gallows or the stake. Sometimes the prisoner was left to molder there: human justice called this forgetting. The condemned felt himself cut off from his kind by a superincumbent mountain of stones and a host of jailers: and the entire prison, the massive bastile, was but an enormous complicated lock which shut him out from the living world.

Into a dungeon of this kind—the *oubliettes* dug by St. Louis, the *in pace* of the Tournelle—La Esmeralda was thrust after her condemnation, no doubt for fear of escape, with the colossal Palace of Justice over her head. Poor girl! she could not have stirred the smallest of the stones of which it was built. There needed not such a profusion of misery and torture to crush so frail a creature.

There she was, wrapped in darkness, buried, entombed, immured. Whoever had beheld her in this state, after having seen her sporting and dancing in the sun, would have shuddered. Cold as night, cold as death, not a breath of air in her dark locks, not a human sound in her ear, not a glimmer of light in her eyes, weighed down with chains, bent double, crouched beside a pitcher and a loaf of bread, on a little straw, in the pool formed beneath her by the water that dripped from the walls of her dungeon, motionless and scarcely breathing—what more could she suffer? Phœbus, the sun, the daylight, the free air, the streets of Paris, the dances which had won her such applause; her love-prattle with the officer; then the priest, the dagger, the blood, the torture, the gallows; all this had again passed before her mind, sometimes like a gay and golden vision, at others like a hideous nightmare: but it was now no more than a horrible and indistinct struggle, which was veiled in darkness, or than distant music played above on the earth, and which was not heard at the depth into which the unfortunate creature was sunk. Since she had been there she had not waked, she had not slept. In this profound wretchedness, in the gloom of this dungeon, she could no more distinguish waking from sleeping, dream from reality, than night from day. She had ceased to feel, to think; at the utmost she mused. Never had living creature been plunged so deeply into nothingness.

Thus torpid, frozen, petrified, she had scarcely noticed the noise of a trap-door, which had opened twice or thrice somewhere near her, but without admitting a glimmer of light, and at which a hand had thrown down to her a crust of black bread. It was, nevertheless, the sole communication still left to her with mankind—the periodical visit of the jailer. Her ear was mechanically directed to the only sound that now engaged it; above her head the wet filtered through the mossy stones of the vaulted roof, and a drop of water fell from it at equal intervals. She listened stupidly to the noise made by this drop falling into the pool of water by her side. This was the only motion still perceptible around her, the only clock that marked the lapse of time, the only noise that reached her of all the noises that are made on the face of the earth. Not but that she did indeed feel from time to time, in this dark and disgusting abode, something cold crawling about on her foot or her arm, and she could not help shuddering.

How long she had been in this place she knew not. She had a recollection of a sentence of death passed somewhere upon somebody; she remembered that she had then been borne away, and that she had awoke chilled with cold, in darkness and in silence. She had crawled about on her hands: iron rings had then galled her ankle and chains had rattled. She had ascertained that there was a solid wall all around her, that under her there was a pavement covered with water, and a bundle of straw. She had then seated herself on this straw, and sometimes, for change of posture, on the lowest of the stone steps that led down to her dungeon. At one time she had tried to count the dark minutes measured by the drop of water; but presently her mind discontinued of itself this melancholy task imposed by a diseased brain, and it left her in a state of stupor.

At length, one day, or one night—for midnight and noonday were of the same color in this sepulcher—she heard above her a louder noise than that usually made by the jailer when he brought her loaf and her pitcher of water. She raised her head, and saw a reddish ray entering through a cranny in a kind of trap-door placed in the vaulted roof of the *in pace*. At the same time the heavy iron bars rattled; the door grated on its rusty hinges; it turned, and she saw a lantern, a hand, and the nether extremities of two figures, the door being too low for her to perceive their heads. The light so painfully affected her that she closed her eyes.

When she opened them again the door was shut, a lantern was placed on one of the steps, and something like a human form stood before her. A black wrapper descended to its feet; a hood of the same color concealed the face. Nothing was to be seen of the person, not even the hands. The figure looked like a long, black winding-sheet standing upright, under which something might be perceived moving. For some minutes she kept her eyes intently fixed on this spectral shape. Neither spoke. You would have taken them for two statues confronting each other. Two things only gave signs of life in the dungeon: the wick of the lantern which crackled, owing to the dampness of the atmosphere, and the drip of the roof breaking this irregular crepitation by its monotonous plash, which caused the light of the lantern to dance in concentric rings on the oily surface of the pool.

At length the prisoner broke silence.

"Who are you?"

"A priest."

The word, the accent, the voice made her shudder.

"Are you prepared?" asked the priest, in a low tone.

"For what?"

"To die."

"Oh!" said she; "will it be soon?"

"To-morrow."

Her head, which she had raised with a look of joy, again sunk upon her bosom. "'Tis a long time till then," murmured she. "Why not to-day? What difference could it have made to them?"

"You must be very unhappy, then?" said the priest, after a moment's silence.

"I am very cold," she replied. She clasped her feet with her hands, and her teeth chattered.

The priest seemed from beneath the hood to cast his eyes around the dungeon. "Without light! without fire! in the water! 'Tis horrible!"

"Yes," answered she, with that air of timidity which suffering had imparted: "everybody enjoys the light. Why should I be thrust into darkness?"

"Do you know," resumed the priest, after another pause, "why you are here?"

"I think I did know," said she, passing her attenuated fingers over her brow, as if to assist her memory, "but I don't now."

All at once she burst out a-crying like a child. "I want to leave this place, sir. I am cold, I am afraid, and there are loathsome things which crawl upon me."

"Well, come along with me."

With these words the priest took hold of her arm. The wretched girl was chilled to her inmost vitals, yet that hand produced a sensation of cold.

"Oh!" murmured she, "it is the icy hand of Death! Who are you, then?"

The priest pushed back his hood. She looked at him. It was that sinister face which had so long haunted her, that demon head which had appeared to her at Falourdel's above the head of her adored Phœbus, that eye which she had last seen glistening near a dagger.

This apparition, always so baneful to her, and which had thus hurried her on from misery to misery, roused her from her stupor. The thick veil which seemed to have spread itself over her memory was rent asunder. All the circumstances of her dismal adventure, from the night scene at Falourdel's to her condemnation at La Tournelle, rushed at once upon her mind, not vague and confused as at the time of their occurrence, but distinct, fresh, palpitating, terrible. These recollections, almost obliterated by the excess of her sufferings, were revived by the somber figure before her, as the invisible words written with sympathetic ink upon white paper are brought out quite fresh on its being held to the fire. All the wounds of her heart seemed to be torn open afresh, and to bleed at once.

"Ha!" cried she, with a convulsive tremor, and holding her hands over her eyes, "it is the priest!" Presently dropping her enfeebled arms, she remained sitting, her head bent forward, her eyes fixed on the ground, mute and trembling. The priest looked at her with the eye of a hawk, which has long been descending in silence from the topmost height of the heavens, in circles gradually more and more contracted around a poor lark squatting in the corn, and, having suddenly pounced like winged lightning upon his prey, clutches the panting victim in his talons.

She began to murmur in a faint tone: "Finish! finish! Give the last blow!" and she bowed down her head with terror, like the lamb awaiting the fatal stroke from the hand of the butcher.

At length he asked, "Are you afraid of me, then?"

She made no reply.

"Are you afraid of me?" he repeated.

Her lips were compressed as though she smiled.

"Yes," said she, "the executioner jeers the condemned. For months he has been haunting, threatening, terrifying me! But for him, oh, God! how happy I should be! 'Tis he who has hurled me into this abyss—'tis he who killed him—who killed my Phœbus!" Sobbing vehemently, she raised her eyes to the priest. "Who are you, wretch?" she exclaimed. "What have I done to you? Why should you hate me thus? What grudge have you against me?"

"I love thee!" said the priest.

Her tears suddenly ceased. She eyed him with the vacant stare of an idiot. He had meanwhile sunk upon his knees, and gazed upon her with eye of fire.

"Dost thou hear? I love thee!" he repeated.

"Ah! what love!" ejaculated the unhappy creature, shuddering.

"The love of the damned," he replied.

Both remained silent for some minutes, overwhelmed by their emotions; he frantic, she stupid.

"Listen," at length said the priest, who had all at once recovered a wonderful degree of composure; "thou shalt know all. I will tell thee what hitherto I have scarcely dared tell myself, when I secretly examined my conscience, in those hours of night on which rests such thick darkness that it seems as if God could no longer see us. Listen: Before I saw thee I was happy."

"And I!" she sighed forth faintly.

"Interrupt me not. Yes, I was happy, or at least I fancied that I was so. I was innocent. No head was lifted so high and so proudly as mine. Priests and doctors consulted me. Science was all in all to me: it was a sister, and a sister sufficed me. In spite, however, of my determination to acknowledge no other influence, that power of nature which, silly youth as I was, I had hoped to crush for life, had more than once convulsively shaken the chain of those iron vows which bind me, miserable man that I am, to the cold stones of the altar. But fasting, prayer, study, the mortification of the cloister, re-stored to the spirit the dominion over the passions. I shunned the sex. Besides, I needed but to open a book, and all the impure vapors of my brain were dispelled by the splendor of science. In a few minutes the dark things of earth fled far away and I found myself calm and serene in the soothing light of everlasting truth. So long as the demon sent only vague shadows of women to attack me, so long as they passed casually before my eyes, at church, in the streets, in the fields, and scarcely recurred to my thoughts, I vanquished him with ease. Alas! if victory has not remained with me, it is the fault of God, who has not made man equal in strength to the demon. List to me: One day——"

The priest paused, and deep sighs burst from his bosom. He resumed:

"One day I was sitting at the window of my cell. I was reading. The window looked upon an open place. I heard the sound of a tambourine. Vexed at being disturbed in my reverie, I cast my eyes upon the place. What I there saw, and what others saw besides me, was not a sight made for human eyes. There, in the middle of the pavement—it was noon—brilliant sunshine—a creature was dancing —a creature so beautiful that she might have served as a model for the mother of the Graces. Her eyes were black and splendid: amid her dark hair there were locks, which, saturated, as it were, by the sun's beams, shone like threads of gold. Around her head, in her black tresses, there were pieces of metal which sparkled in the sun and formed a coronet of stars for her brow. Her azure robe, besprinkled with a thousand spangles, glistened like a summer night. Her feet, in their rapid movements, appeared indistinct, like the spokes of a wheel that is whirling quickly round. Her brown and supple arms were tied and untied around her body like two scarfs. Her figure was of surpassing beauty. Oh! the resplendent form, which had something luminous about it even in the broad sunlight! Surprised, charmed, intoxicated, I could not forbear watching thee: I looked till I shuddered: I felt the hand of Fate was upon me."

The priest, oppressed by emotion, again paused for a moment. He then proceeded:

"Half fascinated already, I endeavored to grasp at something to break my fall. I recollected the snares which Satan had previously spread for me. The creature before me possessed that superhuman beauty which can proceed only from heaven or from hell. She was not a mere girl, molded of our common clay, and faintly lighted within by the flickering ray of a female spirit. It was an angel, but an angel of darkness—of fire, not of light. At the moment when these thoughts were crossing my brain I saw near her a goat, a beast which associates with witches. It looked at me and laughed. The noontide sun tipped its horns with flame. I then perceived the snare of the demon and had no further doubt that thou wert come from hell, and come for my perdition. I believed so."

The priest here looked steadfastly in the face of the prisoner, and coldly added, "I believe so still."

"Meanwhile, the charm began to operate by degrees. Thy dancing turned my brain. I felt the mysterious spell upon me. All that would have waked in my soul was lulled to sleep; and, like men perishing in the snow, I took pleasure in yielding to this slumber. All at once I heard thee begin to sing. What could I do? Thy singing was more fascinating than thy dancing. I would have fled. Impossible. I was riveted, rooted to the spot. I was forced to remain till thou hadst finished. My feet were ice, my head a furnace. At length, perhaps in pity to me, thy song ceased, and I saw thee depart. The reflection of the dazzling vision, the sounds of the enchanting music, vanished by degrees from my eyes, and died away in my ears. I then sunk into the corner of the window, stiff and helpless as a fallen statue. The vesper bell awoke me. I fled; but, alas! something had fallen within me which I could not raise up; something had come upon me from which I could not flee!"

He made another pause and thus proceeded:

"Yes, from that day I was possessed with a spirit that was strange to me. I had recourse to my remedies—the cloister, the altar, occupation, books. Follies! Oh, how hollow science sounds when you dash against it in despair a head filled with passions! Knowest thou, maiden, what thenceforth I always saw between the book and me? Thee, thy shadow, the image of the luminous apparition which had one day passed before me. But that image had no longer the same color; it was somber, dark, gloomy, like the black circle which long dances before the eye that has been imprudent enough to gaze at the sun.

"Haunted by it incessantly, incessantly hearing thy song ringing in my ears, incessantly seeing thy feet dancing upon my breviary, my dreams by night, as well as my thoughts by day, being full of thee, I was desirous to behold thee again, to touch thee, to know who thou wert, to ascertain whether thou resembledst the ideal image impressed upon my mind, to dispel perhaps the phantasm by the reality. At all events, I hoped that a new impression would efface the first, for the first had become intolerable to me. I sought thee. Again I beheld thee. When I had seen thee twice, I wished to see thee a thousand times, to have thee always in my sight. Then —who can stop himself on the steep descent to perdition?—then I was no longer my own master. I became a vagrant, like thyself. I waited for thee beneath porches; I lurked at the corners of streets; I watched thee from my tower. Each night, on examining myself, I found that I was more helpless, more spell-bound, more bewitched, more undone.

"I learned who thou wert; Egyptian, Bohemian, gitana, zingara.

How could I longer doubt that there was witchcraft in the case? I hoped that the law would break the charm. A sorceress had bewitched Bruno d'Ast: he caused her to be burned, and was cured. I knew him. I resolved to try the same remedy. In the first place I obtained an ordinance forbidding thee to appear in the precincts of our church, hoping to forget thee if I should see thee no more. Reckless of this prohibition, thou camest as usual. Then did I conceive the idea of carrying thee off. One night I attempted to put it into execution. There were two of us. We had thee already in our clutches when that odious officer came up and rescued thee. Thus did he commence thy sufferings, mine, and his own. At length, not knowing what to do, I denounced thee to the officials. I thought that I should be cured, as Bruno d'Ast was. I had also a confused notion that a judicial process would deliver thee into my power; that in a prison I should have thee, should hold thee; that there thou couldst not escape me. When one is doing evil 'tis madness to stop half-way. The extremity of guilt has its delirium of rapture.

"I should perhaps have renounced my design; my hideous idea would perhaps have evaporated from my brain without producing any result. I imagined that it would depend on me to follow up or to stop the proceedings whenever I pleased. But every wicked thought is inexorable, and hurries to become a fact; and where I fancied myself all-powerful, Fate proved more mighty than I. Alas! alas! it was Fate that caught thee and threw thee among the terrible works of the machine which I had secretly constructed. List to me. I have nearly done.

"One day—another day of lovely sunshine—I saw a man walking before me who pronounced thy name, who laughed, and whose eyes glistened with unhallowed fire. I followed him—thou knowest the rest."

He ceased speaking. "Oh, my Phœbus!" was all that the poor girl could utter.

"Not that name!" said the priest, seizing her arm with violence. "Name not that name! Wretched as we are, 'tis that name which has undone us; or rather, we are undoing each other through the unaccountable freaks of fatality! . . . Thou art suffering; I know it. Thou art chilled; the darkness blinds thee; the dungeon clasps thee: but perhaps thou hast still some light in the recesses of thy soul, were it but thy childish love for that empty man who plays with thy heart—while I, I carry a dungeon within me; within me is the chill of winter, the chill of despair; darkness inwraps my soul. Knowest thou all that I have suffered? I was present at thy trial. Yes, one of those priest's cowls covered torments unequaled but by those of the damned. I was there when that savage beast—oh! I foreboded not the torture!—bore thee off to his den. I saw thee stripped, and thy delicate limbs grasped by the infamous hands of the executioner. I saw thy foot, which I would have given an empire to kiss, that foot by which to have been trampled upon had been to me happiness, I saw it incased in the horrible buskin which converts the members of a living being into a bloody jelly. At the shriek which was forced from thee I plunged into my bosom a dagger that I carried beneath my wrapper. Look, it still bleeds."

He threw open his cassock. His breast was lacerated as by the claw of a tiger. The prisoner recoiled in horror.

"Oh, maiden!" said the priest, "take pity on me. Thou deemest thyself miserable. Alas! thou knowest not what misery is. It is to love a woman—to be a priest—to be hated—to love with all the energies of your soul—to feel that you would give for the least of her smiles your blood, your life, your character, your salvation, immortality and eternity, this world and the next—to regret that you are not a king, an emperor, an archangel, that you might throw a greater slave at her feet; to clasp her night and day in your sleeping and in your waking dreams—to see her fond of a soldier's uniform, and to have nothing to offer her but the squalid cassock, which is to her an object of fear and disgust—to be present, with a heart bursting with jealousy and rage, while she lavishes on a silly braggart the treasures of love and beauty—to think of that delicious form till you writhe for whole nights on the floor of your cell, and to see all the endearments which you have reserved for her in imagination end in the torture—these, these are pincers heated in the fire of hell. Happy in comparison is he who is sawn asunder between two planks, or quartered by horses. Knowest thou what agony it is when, during the long nights, your arteries boil, your heart is bursting, your head splitting, and your teeth tear your own flesh; when you are turned incessantly as upon a red-hot gridiron by those inexorable tormentors, love, jealousy, despair. Mercy, maiden! relax for a moment; or, if it must be so, torture me with one hand, but fondle me with the other. Have pity on me, girl! have pity on me!"

The priest rolled in the water on the floor, and dashed his head against the stone steps of the dungeon. The Egyptian listened to him, looked at him. When he ceased speaking, breathless and exhausted, she repeated, in a low tone: "Oh, my Phœbus!"

The priest crawled toward her upon his knees. "I implore thee," he cried, "if thou hast any compassion, repulse me not. I love thee—I am miserable. When thou utterest that name, it is as if thou wert rending all the fibers of my heart. Only have pity. If thou goest to perdition, I must go with thee. All that I have done, I have done for this. The place where thou art will be to me a paradise; the sight of thee is more entrancing than that of Heaven. Oh, say, wilt thou not have me? I should have thought that the day when a woman could reject such love the mountains would dissolve. Oh, if thou wouldst, how happy might we yet be! We would flee . . . I would enable thee to escape . . . we would seek that spot where there are the most trees, the most sunshine, the most azure sky."

She interrupted him with a loud, thrilling laugh. "Look, father, you have blood upon your fingers!"

The priest, motionless for some moments, as if petrified, looked steadfastly at his hand.

"Why, yes," he at length replied, with unwonted mildness, "abuse me, jeer me, overwhelm me!—but come, come! Let us lose no time. It will be to-morrow, I tell thee. The gibbet of the Grève—thou knowest the gibbet—it is always ready. It is horrible—to see thee drawn in that cart! Oh, mercy, mercy! Never did I feel as at this moment how dearly I love thee! Oh, come along with me. Thou shalt take thine own time to love me after I have saved thee. Thou shalt hate me as long as thou wilt. Only come. To-morrow! to-morrow! the gallows! Oh, save thyself—spare me!"

In a state approaching to madness he seized her arm and would have hurried her along. She fixed her eyes intently upon him. "What is become of my Phœbus?" she inquired.

"Ah!" said the priest, loosing her arm from his grasp, "you have no pity!"

"What is become of Phœbus?" repeated she, coldly.

"He is dead," replied the priest.

"Dead!" said she, still cold and passionless; "then why persuade me to live?"

He heard her not. "Oh, yes!" said he, as if talking to himself, "he must be dead. I struck home. The point must have reached his heart."

The girl rushed upon him like an enraged tigress and thrust him toward the steps with supernatural force: "Begone, monster! begone, murderer! leave me to die! May the blood of us both mark thy brow with an everlasting stain! . . . Be thine, priest! Never never! Nothing shall bring us together, not even hell itself. Avaunt, accursed!—never!"

The priest had stumbled upon the steps. Silently disengaging his feet from the skirt of his cassock, he picked up his lantern and began slowly to ascend to the door; he opened it and went forth. The prisoner gazed after him. All at once his head again appeared stooping over the stairs. His face was ghastly. With a rattle of rage and despair, he cried, "I tell thee he is dead!"

She fell with her face to the ground, and no sound was then to be heard in the dungeon save the splash of the dropping water, which rippled the pool amid the profound darkness.

CHAPTER V

THE MOTHER

I CAN NOT conceive anything in the world more delightful than the ideas awakened in the heart of a mother at the sight of her child's little shoe, especially if it be a holiday, a Sunday, a baptismal shoe; a shoe embroidered down to the very sole; a shoe upon which the infant has never stepped. This shoe is so small and so pretty; it is so impossible for it to walk, that it seems to the mother as though she saw her child. She smiles at it, she kisses it, she talks to it; she asks herself if a foot can really be so small; and if the infant should be absent, the pretty shoe is sufficient to set the sweet and tender creature before her eyes. She fancies she sees it—she does see it—all alive, all joyous, with its delicate hands, its round head, its pure lips, its serene eyes, the white of which is blue. If it be winter, there it is, crawling upon the carpet, climbing laboriously upon a stool, and the mother trembles lest it should approach too near the fire. If it be summer, it is creeping about in the courtyard or in the garden, looking innocently and fearlessly at the big dogs and the big horses, pulling up the grass growing between the stones, playing with the shells and the flowers, and making the gardener scold on finding sand on his borders and mold on his paths. All about it is bright, joyous, and playful, like itself, even to the very breeze and the sunshine, which sport together in the locks of its soft hair. All this the little shoe sets before the mother, and it makes her heart melt like wax before the fire.

But when the child is lost, these thousand images of joy, delight, and affection which crowd around the little shoe are transformed into as many frightful things. The pretty little embroidered shoe then becomes but an instrument of torture, which is incessantly racking the heart of the mother. It is still the same fiber that vibrates—the deepest and the most keenly sensitive fiber—not under the caresses of an angel, but in the grip of a demon.

One morning when the sun of May was rising in one of those deep-blue skies, beneath which Garofalo loved to picture the taking down from the cross, the recluse of Roland's Tower heard the rumbling of wheels, the tramp of horses, and the clanking of iron in the Place de Grève. The noise scarcely roused her; she tied her hair over her ears that she might not hear it, and again fell upon her knees to gaze at the inanimate object which she had thus adored for fifteen years. To her this shoe was, as we have already observed, the universe. Her thoughts were wrapped up in it, never to be parted from it but by death. How many bitter imprecations, how many touching complaints, how many earnest prayers she had addressed to Heaven on the subject of this charming little shoe of rose-colored satin was known to the cell of Roland's Tower alone. Never were keener sorrows poured forth over object so pretty and so delicate. On this particular morning her grief seemed to burst forth with greater violence than usual; and she was heard from without bewailing herself with a loud and monotonous voice which wrung the heart.

"Oh, my child!" said she, "my child! my poor, dear little child!—never, no, never shall I see thee more!—and still it seems as if it had happened but yesterday. Oh, my God! my God! better she had not been given to me at all than to have her taken from me so soon. And yet Thou must know that our children are a part of ourselves, and that a mother who has lost her child is tempted to—

". . . Ah! wretch that I was, to go out that day. . . . Oh, Lord, Lord! to snatch her from me thus, Thou couldst never have seen me with her, when I warmed her, all glee, before the fire, when she ceased sucking to laugh in my face, when I made her little feet step up my bosom to my very lips! Hadst Thou seen this, oh, my God! Thou wouldst have had pity on my joy; Thou wouldst not have ravished from me the only love that was left in my heart. Was I then so vile a wretch, oh, Lord! that Thou couldst not look at me before condemning me? Alas, alas! there is the shoe but where is the foot? where is the child? My child, my own child! what have they done with thee? Oh, Lord! give me back my child. My knees have been flayed for these fifteen years in praying to Thee; is not this enough? Restore her to me for a day, an hour, a minute, only

one minute, oh, Lord! and then cast me forth to the Evil One to all
eternity. Oh, did I but know where to find Thee, I would grasp the
skirts of Thy garments with both these hands, and not let Thee go
till Thou hadst given me back my child. Behold her pretty little
shoe! Hast Thou no compassion? Canst Thou doom a wretched
mother to fifteen years of such torment as this? Blessed Virgin of
heaven! they have stolen my child; they have devoured her on the
moor; they have drunk her blood; they have gnawed her bones.
Kind Virgin, have pity on me! My child! I want my child! What is
it to me that she is in Paradise? I want none of your angels; I want
my child. Oh, I will writhe upon the ground, I will dash my head
against the stones, I will gladly seal my own perdition, so thou wilt
but restore to me my child! Thou seest how these arms are torn!
Has then the good God no compassion? Oh, let them give me but
black bread and salt, provided I have my daughter. She will be to
me both meat and drink, and warmth and sunshine. I confess that
I am but a vile sinner, but my child was making me pious. Out of
love to her I was amending my life, and I saw Thee through her
smile as through the opened heavens. . . . Oh, that I could but once
more, only once, put this pretty shoe on her rosy little foot, I would
die blessing thee, Holy Virgin! But no—fifteen years!—she must be
grown up now! Unfortunate girl! 'tis too certain that I shall never
see thee more, not even in heaven, for there I shall never enter.
Oh, what anguish!—to say, there is her shoe, and that is all."

The wretched creature threw herself upon that shoe, a source of
solace and of sorrow for so many years; and she sobbed as though
her heart would break, just as she had done on the very first day.
Grief like this never grows old. Though the garments of mourning
become threadbare and lose their color, the heart remains as black
as ever.

At this moment the brisk and merry voices of boys passed before
her cell. At this sight or the sound of children, the unhappy mother
would always dart into the darkest nook of her sepulcher with such
precipitation that you would think she was striving to bury her head
in the wall, in order that she might not hear them. On this occasion,
contrary to her custom, she started up and listened attentively. One
of the boys was just saying to another "They are going to hang an
Egyptian to-day."

With the sudden bound of the spider, that we lately saw rushing
upon the fly entangled in his net, she sprung to the aperture which
looked, as the reader knows, toward the Place de Grève. A ladder
was actually reared against the permanent gallows, and the hang-

man was engaged in adjusting the chains, which had become rusty with the wet. A few people were standing around.

The laughing troop of boys was already far off. The recluse looked about for some passenger whom she might question. She perceived close to her cell a priest, who feigned to be reading in the public breviary, but whose thoughts were much less engaged by the book than by the gibbet, toward which he glanced from time to time with wild and gloomy look. She recognized in him the Archdeacon of Josas, an austere and holy man.

"Father," she inquired, "whom are they going to hang yonder?"

The priest looked at her without answering. She repeated the question.

"I know not," said he.

"Some boys," rejoined the recluse, "said just now that it was an Egyptian."

"I believe so," said the priest.

Paquette la Chantefleurie burst into an hysterical laugh.

"Sister," said the archdeacon, "you seem to hate the Egyptians with all your heart."

"Hate them!" cried the recluse; "why, they are witches, child-stealers! They devoured my little girl, my child, my only child! They eat my heart along with her—I have none now!"

The priest eyed her coldly.

"There is one in particular," she resumed, "that I hate and that I have cursed; a young girl about the same age that my child would have been now had they not eaten her. Whenever this young viper passes my cell she sets all my blood a-boiling."

"Well, then, sister, rejoice," said the priest, cold as the statue on a sepulcher; "'tis for her that these preparations are making."

His head sunk upon his bosom and he slowly withdrew.

The recluse waved her arms in triumph. "Thanks, Sir Priest," cried she. "I told her what she would come to."

She then began, with hurried step, to pace to and fro before her window, her hair disheveled, her eye glaring, dashing against the wall with her shoulder, with the wild air of a caged she-wolf which has long been hungry, and is aware that the hour for her repast is approaching.

CHAPTER VI

THREE HUMAN HEARTS DIFFERENTLY CONSTITUTED

PHŒBUS, MEANWHILE, was not dead. Men of that kind are hard to kill. When Master Philip Lheulier, advocate extraordinary to the king, said to poor Esmeralda, "He is dying"—he was either misinformed or joking. When the archdeacon repeated to her, after condemnation, "He is dying"—the fact was that he knew nothing about the matter; but he believed it, he had no doubt of it, he made sure of it, he hoped it. It would have gone too much against the grain to give good tidings of his rival to the female of whom he was enamored. Every man in his place would have done the same.

Not that Phœbus's wound was not severe, but the injury was less serious than the archdeacon flattered himself it was. The master surgeon to whose house the soldiers of the watch had immediately carried him, was for above a week under apprehensions for his life, and had even told him so in Latin. Youth, however, enabled him to get the better of it; and, as it frequently happens, notwithstanding prognostics and diagnostics, Nature had amused herself in saving the patient in spite of the doctor's teeth. It was while lying on the master surgeon's truckle-bed that he had undergone the first interrogatories of Philip Lheulier and the inquisitors of the officials, which had annoyed him exceedingly. One fine morning, therefore, finding himself better, he had left his gold spurs in payment at the surgeon's and decamped without beat of drum. This circumstance, however, had not in the least affected the judicial proceedings. Justice in those days cared but little about propriety and accuracy in a criminal process; provided that the accused were hung, it was perfectly satisfied. Now, the judges had evidence sufficient against Esmeralda. They believed Phœbus to be dead, and that was quite enough.

Phœbus, on his part, had not fled far. He had merely rejoined his company, in garrison at Queue-en-Brie, in the Isle of France, a few relays from Paris. He felt no inclination whatever to come forward personally in this process. He had a vague impression that he should cut a ridiculous figure in it. At bottom, he knew not what to think of the whole affair. Irreligious and superstitious, like every soldier who is nothing but a soldier, when he called to mind all the circumstances of this adventure, he could not tell what to make of the goat, of the odd way in which he had first met with La Esmeralda, of the not less strange manner in which she had betrayed her love, of her being an Egyptian, and lastly, of the goblin monk. He imagined that in his history there was much more of magic than of love, probably a sorceress, perhaps the devil; in short, a comedy, or to use the language of those days, a mystery, of a very disagreeable nature, in which he played an extremely awkward part—that of the butt for blows and laughter. The captain was quite dashed; he felt the sort of shame which La Fontaine so admirably compares with that of a fox caught by a hen. He hoped, besides, that the affair would not be bruited about, that in his absence his name would scarcely be mentioned in connection with it, or at any rate not beyond the pleadings at the Tournelle. Neither was he far wrong in this expectation; there were then no newspapers; and as scarcely a week passed but there was some coiner boiled, some witch hanged, or some heretic burned, at one of the numberless *justices* of Paris, people were so accustomed to see the old feudal Themis, with bare arms and tucked-up sleeves, performing her office at the gallows and the pillory, that they scarcely took any notice of such events. In those days the higher classes scarcely knew the name of the sufferer who was carried past the corner of the street, and the populace at most regaled itself with this coarse fare. An execution was a familiar incident in the public ways, like the oven of a baker or the butcher's slaughter-house. The hangman was but a kind of butcher a shade darker than the other.

Phœbus, therefore, set his mind at ease respecting the sorceress Esmeralda, or Similar, as he called her, the wound inflicted by the Bohemian or the goblin monk—he cared not which—and the issue of the proceedings. But no sooner was his heart vacant on this score than the image of Fleur-de-lys returned thither. The heart of Captain Phœbus, like the philosophy of those times, abhorred a vacuum.

Besides, Queue-en-Brie was a very stupid place, a village of blacksmiths and dairy women with chapped hands, a long line of crazy cottages bordering both sides of the high-road for a mile. Fleur-de-lys was his last passion but one, a handsome girl with a good dower. One fine morning, therefore, being quite convalescent, and presuming that the affair with the Bohemian must, after the lapse of two months, be completely blown over and forgotten, the amorous cavalier came swaggering to the door of the Gondelaurier mansion. He took no notice of a numerous concourse assembled in the Place du Parvis, before the porch of Notre Dame; he recollected that it was the month of May, and, supposing that the people might be drawn together by some religious holiday or procession, he fastened his horse to the ring at the gate and gayly went upstairs to his fair betrothed.

She was alone with her mother. Fleur-de-lys had always felt sore about the scene with the sorceress, her goat, her cursed alphabet, and the long absences of Phœbus; nevertheless, at the entrance of her truant, he looked so well, had such a new uniform, such a smart shoulder-belt, and so impassioned an air, that she reddened with pleasure. The noble damoiselle was herself more charming than ever. Her magnificent light hair was admirably plaited; she was attired completely in sky-blue, which so well suits females of a fair complexion—a piece of coquetry which she had been taught by Colombe—and her eye swam in that languor of love which suits them so much better.

Phœbus, who had so long set eyes on nothing superior in beauty to the wenches of Queue-en-Brie, was transported with Fleur-de-lys; and this imparted such a warmth and such a tone of gallantry to his manner that his peace was instantly made. Mme. de Gondelaurier herself, maternally seated as usual in her great arm-chair, had not the heart to scold him; and as for the reproaches of Fleur-de-lys, they expired in accents of tenderness.

The young lady was seated near the window, still working away at her grotto of Neptune. The captain leaned over the back of her chair, and in an under-tone she commenced her half-caressing, half-scolding inquiries.

"What have you been doing with yourself for these two months, you naughty man?"

"I swear," replied Phœbus, who did not relish the question, "you are so beautiful that an archbishop could not help falling in love with you."

She could not forbear smiling. "Beautiful, forsooth! My beauty is nothing to the purpose, sir. I want an answer to my question."

"Well, then, my dear cousin, I was ordered away to keep garrison."

"Where, if you please? and why not come to bid me adieu?"

"At Queue-en-Brie."

Phœbus was delighted that the first question enabled him to shirk the second.

"But that is close by, sir. How is it that you have not been once to see me?"

Here Phœbus was seriously embarrassed. "Why . . . our duty . . . and, besides, charming cousin, I have been ill."

"Ill!" she exclaimed in alarm.

"Yes, wounded."

"Wounded!"

The poor girl was thunder-struck.

"Oh, you need not frighten yourself about that," said Phœbus, carelessly; "it was nothing. A quarrel, a scratch with a sword. How can that concern you?"

"Not concern me?" cried Fleur-de-lys, raising her beautiful eyes swimming in tears. "Oh, in saying so you do not say what you think. How came you by the scratch you talk of? I insist on knowing all."

"Well, then, my fair cousin, I had a squabble with Mahe Fedy—you know him—the lieutenant of St. Germain-en-Laye, and each of us ripped up a few inches of the other's skin. That is all."

The mendacious captain well knew that an affair of honor always raises a man in the estimation of a female. Accordingly, Fleur-de-lys turned about and looked him in the face with emotions of fear, pleasure, and admiration. Still she was not completely satisfied.

"Ah, Phœbus," said she, "how I rejoice that you are quite well again! I do not know your Mahe Fedy—but he is a scurvy fellow. And what was the cause of this quarrel?"

Here Phœbus, whose imagination was not the most fertile, began to be puzzled how to get out of the dilemma.

"Oh, I hardly recollect—a mere nothing, a word about a horse. But, fair cousin," cried he, in order to change the conversation, "what is the occasion of this bustle in the Parvis? Only look," he continued, stepping to the window, "what a crowd there is in the place!"

"I know not," replied Fleur-de-lys. "I did hear that a witch is to do penance this morning before the church, and to be hung afterward."

The captain made so sure that the affair with La Esmeralda was long since over that he took but little interest in the information given to him by Fleur-de-lys. He nevertheless asked her one or two questions.

"What is the name of this witch?"

"I know not," answered she.

"And what do they say she has done?"

"I know not," said she, with another shrug of her fair shoulders.

"Oh, my God!" said the mother, "there are nowadays so many

sorcerers and witches that they burn them, I verily believe, without knowing their names. You might as well ask the name of every cloud in the sky. But what need we care? God Almighty will be sure to keep a correct list." Here the venerable lady rose and advanced to the window. "Bless me! there is indeed a crowd, as you say, Phœbus. Why, the very roofs are covered with the populace! Do you know, Phœbus, this reminds me of my young days, of the entry of King Charles VII., when there was as great a crowd as this—only the people were much more comely then than now. Every spot was thronged with them, even the battlements of the Gate of St. Antoine. The king had the queen on the crupper behind him, and after their highnesses came all the ladies riding in the same way behind their lords. A procession of all the gentlemen of France with their banners waving in the air. Ah! well-a-day! 'tis sad to think that all this pomp has been, and that nothing of it is now left!"

The lovers were not listening to the worthy dowager. Phœbus had again planted himself behind his betrothed, and was leaning over the back of her chair, wandering over so much of her neck as was not covered by her dress. Dazzled by that skin which shone like satin, the captain said within himself: "How can one love any but a fair woman?" Both kept silence. The lady gave him from time to time a look of delight and fondness, and their hair mingled together in the spring sunshine.

"Phœbus," said Fleur-de-lys, abruptly, in a low tone, "we are to be married in three months. Swear that you never loved any other but me."

"I do swear it, beautiful angel!" replied Phœbus, and his impassioned look concurred with the emphatic accent of his words to convince Fleur-de-lys. It is possible that at the moment he himself believed what he asserted.

Meanwhile the good mother, pleased to see the young people on such excellent terms, had left the apartment to attend to some domestic matter, or other. Phœbus perceived her absence, which emboldened the enterprising captain. Fleur-de-lys loved him; she was betrothed to him; she was alone with him; his former fondness for her was revived, if not in all its freshness, at any rate in all its ardor. I know not precisely what ideas crossed his mind; but so much is certain, that Fleur-de-lys became suddenly alarmed at the expression of his countenance. She looked around her—her mother was gone!

"Bless me!" said she, flushed and agitated. "I am very hot."

"Why," replied Phœbus, "I dare say it is almost noon. The sun is troublesome. I will draw the curtains."

"No, no!" cried the trembling damsel; "on the contrary I have need of air;" and rising, she ran to the window and stepped out on the balcony. Phœbus followed her thither.

The Place du Parvis in front of Notre Dame, into which, as the reader knows, this balcony looked, exhibited at this moment a sinister and singular spectacle, which quickly changed the nature of the timid Fleur-de-lys's alarm. An immense crowd which flowed back into all the adjacent streets covered the place properly so-called. The low wall which encompassed the Parvis would not have been sufficient to keep it clear, had it not been thickly lined by sergeants of the Onzevingts and arquebusiers, with their pieces in their hands. The wide portals of the church were closed, contrasting with the numberless windows around the place, which, thrown open up to the very roofs, displayed thousands of heads heaped one above another, nearly like piles of cannon-balls in a park of artillery. The surface of this crowd was gray, squalid, dirty. The sight which it was awaiting was evidently one of those which have the privilege of calling together all that is most disgusting in the population. Nothing could be more hideous than the noise that arose from this assemblage of sallow caps and unkempt heads. In this concourse there were more women than men, more laughing than crying.

Ever and anon some harsh or shrill voice was heard above the general din to this effect:

"I say, Mahiet Baliffre, is she to be hanged yonder?"

"No, simpleton—only to do penance there in chemise—the priest is going to fling Latin in her face. 'Tis always done here at noon precisely. If you want to see the hanging, you must e'en go to the Grève."

"I will go afterward."

      *   *   *   *   *   *   *

"Is it true, La Boucandry, that she has refused a confessor?"

"I am told so, La Bechaigne."

"Only think! the pagan!"

      *   *   *   *   *   *   *

"It is the custom, sir. The bailiff of the palace is bound to deliver over the culprit for execution, if of the laity, to the Provost of Paris; but if a clerk, to the official of the bishopric."

"I thank you, sir."

      *   *   *   *   *   *   *

Such were the dialogues carried on at that moment among the spectators collected by the ceremony.

"Oh, my God! the poor creature!" exclaimed Fleur-de-lys, surveying the populace with a sorrowful look. The captain was too much engaged with her to notice the rabble.

At this moment the clock of Notre Dame slowly struck twelve. A murmur of satisfaction pervaded the crowd. Scarcely had the last vibration of the twelfth stroke subsided, when the vast assemblage of heads was broken into waves like the sea in a gale of wind, and one immense shout of, "There she is!" burst simultaneously from pavement, windows, and roofs.

Fleur-de-lys covered her eyes with her hands that she might not see.

"Will you go in, charmer?" asked Phœbus.

"No," she replied; and those eyes which had shut for fear she opened again out of curiosity.

A cart drawn by a strong Norman bay, and completely surrounded by horsemen in purple livery, marked with white crosses, had just issued from the Rue St. Pierre aux Bœufs and entered the place. The sergeants of the watch opened a passage for it through the populace with staves, with which they laid lustily about them. Beside the cart rode certain officers of justice and police, who might be known by their black dress, and the awkward manner in which they sat their horses. At their head paraded Master Jacques Charmolue. In the fatal vehicle was seated a young female, with her hands tied behind her, and no priest at her side. She was stripped to her chemise: her long black hair—for it was not then customary to cut it off till the culprit was at the foot of the gallows—fell loosely over her bosom and her half-uncovered shoulders.

Through this flowing hair, more glossy than a raven's plumage, might be seen twisting a gray, knotty cord, which fretted her delicate skin, and twined itself around the neck of the poor girl like an earth-worm upon a flower. Beneath this cord glistened a little amulet adorned with green beads, which had been left her no doubt because it is usual to refuse nothing to those who are going to die. The spectators in the windows could see at the bottom of the cart her naked legs, which she strove to conceal beneath her, as if by a last instinct of female modesty. At her feet there was a little goat also bound. The prisoner held with her teeth her chemise, which was not properly fastened. Her misery seemed to be greatly aggravated by her being thus exposed nearly naked to the public gaze. Alas! it is not for such tremors that modesty is made.

"Only look, fair cousin," said Fleur-de-lys, sharply, to the captain—"'tis that Bohemian hussy with the goat."

As she thus spoke she turned round toward Phœbus. His eyes were fixed on the cart. He was unusually pale.

"What Bohemian with the goat?" said he, faltering.

"What!" rejoined Fleur-de-lys; "don't you recollect—"

"I know not what you mean," said Phœbus, interrupting her.

He was stepping back to return to the room; but Fleur-de-lys, whose jealousy, some time since so strongly excited by this same Egyptian, was anew awakened, cast on him a look full of penetration and mistrust. She had a confused recollection at the moment of having heard that a captain was implicated in the proceedings against this sorceress.

"What ails you?" said she to Phœbus; "one would suppose that the sight of this creature had given you a shock."

"Me! not the least in the world!" stammered Phœbus, with a forced grin.

"Then stay!" rejoined she, imperiously, "and let us look on till all is over."

The unlucky captain was obliged to stay. He recovered somewhat of his assurance on observing that the prisoner never raised her eyes from the bottom of the cart. It was too surely La Esmeralda. On this last step of misfortune and ignominy she was still beautiful; her large black eyes appeared still larger, on account of the hollowness of her cheeks; her livid profile was pure and sublime. She resembled what she had been, as a Virgin of Masaccio's resembles a Virgin of Raphael's—feebler, thinner, more attenuated.

For the rest, there was nothing about her, excepting her modesty, but was left, as it were, to chance, so deeply was she overwhelmed by stupor and despair. At each jolt of the cart her form rebounded like an inanimate thing: her look was dull and silly. A tear glistened in her eye, but it was motionless, and looked as if it was frozen.

Meanwhile, the somber cavalcade had passed through the crowd, amid shouts of joy and attitudes of curiosity. In order to deserve the character of faithful historians, we must nevertheless record that many of the mob, ay, and of the hardest-hearted too, on seeing her so beautiful and so forlorn, were moved with pity. The cart had now reached the Parvis.

It stopped before the central porch. The escort ranged itself on either side. The mob kept silence; and amid this silence, full of solemnity and anxiety, the folding-doors of the great porch turned as if spontaneously upon their hinges, which creaked with a shrill

sound like that of a fife, affording a view of the whole length of the
church, vast, gloomy, hung with black, dimly lighted by a few tapers
glimmering in the distance upon the high altar, and opening like
the mouth of a cavern upon the place resplendent with the glorious
sunshine. At the furthest extremity, in the dusk of the chancel, was
faintly seen a colossal silver cross relieved upon black cloth which
fell behind it from the roof to the pavement. The whole nave was
vacant. Heads of priests were, however, seen confusedly moving
about in the distant stalls of the choir; and at the moment when the
great door opened, there burst from the church a grave, loud and
monotònous chant, hurling, as it were, in gusts, fragments of doleful
psalms at the head of the condemned one:

"Non timebo millia populi circumdantis me: exsurge, Domine; salvum
me fac, Deus!
"Salvum me fac, Deus, quoniam intraverunt aquæ usque ad animam
meam.
"Infixus sum in limo profundi; et non est substantia." [1]

At the same time another voice singly struck up on the steps of
the high altar this melancholy offertory:

"Qui verbum meum audit, et credit et qui misit me, habet vitam
æternam et in judicum non venit; sed transit a morte in vitam." [2]

These chants sung by aged men, lost in the darkness, over that
beautiful creature full of youth and life, caressed by the warm air
of spring, and inundated with sunlight, belonged to the mass for
the dead. The populace listened devoutly.

The terrified girl, fixing her eyes on the dark interior of the
church, seemed to lose both sight and thought. Her pale lips moved
as if in prayer: and when the executioner's man went to assist her
to alight from the cart, he heard her repeating in a faint voice the
word, Phœbus!

Her hands were unbound, and she alighted, accompanied by her
goat, which had also been untied, and bleated for joy on finding
itself at liberty; and she was then made to walk barefoot on the
hard pavement to the foot of the steps leading to the porch. The
rope which was fastened about her neck trailed behind her: you
would have taken it for a snake that was following her.

The chanting in the church ceased. A large gold crucifix and a
file of tapers began to move in the dusk. The sound of the halberds
of the parti-colored Swiss was heard; and in a few moments a long
procession of priests in copes, and deacons in dalmatics, slowly ad-

1. "I shall not fear though thousands compass me about; arise, Lord, and save me.
Save me, O Lord, for the waters have overwhelmed my very soul. I am caught in
the deep mire, and my goods are gone from me."
2. " Whoso heareth my words, and believeth in Him that sent me, he shall have everlasting life, and does not come to judgement, but passes from death to life."

vanced chanting toward the prisoner, and expanded itself before her eyes and those of the mob. But hers were riveted on him who walked at its head immediately after the bearer of the crucifix. "Oh!" she muttered to herself shuddering, "there he is again! the priest!"

It was actually the archdeacon. On his left was the subchanter, and on his right the chanter bearing the staff of his office. He advanced with head thrown back, and eyes fixed and open, chanting with a loud voice:

"De ventre inferi clamavi, et exaudisti vocem meam.

"Et projecisti me in profundum, in corde maris, et flumen circumdedit me."[1]

At the moment when he appeared in the broad daylight beneath the lofty pointed arch of the portal, covered with an ample cope of silver marked with a black cross, he was so pale that sundry of the crowd imagined it must be one of the marble bishops kneeling on the sepulchral monuments in the choir, who had risen and come to receive on the brink of the tomb her who was about to die.

She, not less pale, nor less statue-like, was scarcely aware that a heavy lighted taper of yellow wax had been put into her hand; she had not heard the squeaking voice of the clerk reading the form of the penance; when told to say Amen, she had said Amen. Neither did she recover any life or strength till she saw the priest make a sign to those who had her in custody to retire, and advance alone toward her. She then felt the blood boil in her head, and a spark of indignation was rekindled in that soul, already cold, benumbed, stupefied.

The archdeacon approached her slowly; even in this extremity she saw him survey her nearly naked form with an eye sparkling with pleasure, love, and jealousy. In a loud voice he thus addressed her: "Bohemian girl, have you prayed to God to pardon your crimes and misdemeanors?" Then stooping—as the spectators imagined, to receive her last confession—he whispered, "Wilt thou be mine? I can even yet save thee!"

She eyed him steadfastly. "Go to the fiend, thy master, or I will inform of thee!"

He grinned horribly a ghastly smile. "They will not believe thee," he replied. "Thou wilt but add scandal to guilt. Answer quickly; wilt thou have me?"

"What hast thou done with my Phœbus?"

"He is dead," said the priest.

1. "I called from the deep and Thou heardest my voice; Thou didst plunge me into the deep, in the heart of the sea, and floods compassed me about."

At that moment the wretched archdeacon raised his head mechanically, and saw on the other side of the place the captain standing in the balcony with Fleur-de-lys. He shuddered, passed his hand over his eyes, looked again, muttered a malediction, and all his features were violently contracted.

"Well, then, die!" said he. "No one shall have thee." Then, lifting his hand over the Egyptian, he pronounced these words in a loud and solemn tone: "*I nunc anima anceps, et sit tibi Deus misericors!*" [1]

This was the dreadful form with which it was customary to conclude these gloomy ceremonies. It was the signal given by the priest to the executioner. The populace fell on their knees.

"*Kyrie Eleison!*" said the priests, who stopped beneath the porch.

"*Kyrie Eleison!*" repeated the crowd, with a murmur that rose above their heads like the rumbling of an agitated sea.

"Amen!" said the archdeacon.

He turned his back on the prisoner; his head sunk upon his bosom; his hands crossed each other; he rejoined the train of priests, and presently receded from sight with the crucifix, the tapers, and the copes, beneath the dusty arches of the cathedral; and his sonorous voice expired by degrees in the choir, while chanting this verse of anguish: "*Omnes gurgites tui et fluctus tui super me transierunt.*" [2]

At the same time the intermitting stamp of the ironshod shafts of the halberds of the Switzers, dying away between the intercolumniations of the nave, produced the effect of a clock-hammer striking the last hour of the doomed one.

Meanwhile, the doors of Notre Dame were left open, displaying to view the church empty, deserted, in mourning, taperless, and voiceless. The condemned girl stood motionless in her place, awaiting what was to be done with her. One of the vergers was obliged to intimate as much to Master Charmolue, who, during the whole of this scene, had been studying the basso-relievo of the great porch, representing, according to some, the sacrifice of Abraham, according to others the alchemical operation, the angel being typified by the sun, the fire by the bundle of sticks, and the operator by Abraham. It was with some difficulty that he was roused from this contemplation: but at length he turned about, and at a sign which he made, two men in yellow dresses, the executioner's assistants, approached the Egyptian to tie her hands again.

The unfortunate creature, at the moment for reascending the fatal cart and setting out on her last stage, was probably seized by some keen repining after life. She raised her dry but inflamed eyes toward heaven, toward the sun, toward the silvery clouds, studded

1. "Go, wavering soul! And may God be merciful unto thee!"
2. "All thy whirlpools, O Lord, and all Thy waves, have gone over me!"

here and there with trapeziums and triangles of azure, and then cast them down around her upon the earth, upon the crowd, upon the houses.

All at once, while the men in yellow were pinioning her arms, she gave a startling scream—a scream of joy. In the balcony at the corner of the place she had descried him, her friend, her lord, her Phœbus, just as he looked when alive. The judge had told her a falsehood! the priest had told her a falsehood! 'twas he himself—she could not possibly doubt it. There he stood, living, moving, habited in his brilliant uniform, with the plume on his head and the sword by his side.

"Phœbus," she cried; "my Phœbus!"—and she would have stretched out toward him her arms, trembling with love and transport, but they were bound.

She then saw the captain knit his brow; a young and handsome female who leaned upon him looked at him with disdainful lip and angry eye; Phœbus then uttered a few words, which she was too far off to hear; both hastily retired from the balcony into the room, and the window was immediately closed.

"Phœbus!" cried she, wildly, "dost thou too believe it?" A horrible idea had just flashed upon her. She recollected that she had been condemned for the murder of Captain Phœbus de Chateaupers. She had borne up thus far against everything. This last shock was too violent. She fell senseless upon the pavement.

"Come!" said Charmolue, "carry her to the cart, and let us make an end of the business!"

No person had yet observed in the gallery of the royal statues, immediately above the pointed arches of the porch, a strange-looking spectator, who had till then been watching all that passed, with attitude so motionless, head so outstretched, visage so deformed, that, but for his apparel, half red and half purple, he might have been taken for one of those stone monsters at whose mouths the long gutters of the cathedral have for these six hundred years disgorged themselves. This spectator had not lost a single incident of the tragedy that had been acting ever since noon before the porch of Notre Dame; and in the very first moments he had, unobserved, securely tied to one of the small pillars of the gallery a knotted rope, the end of which reached the pavement. This done, he had set himself to watch as quietly as before, hissing from time to time at the jackdaws as they flew past him. All at once, at the moment when the executioner's assistants were preparing to obey the phlegmatic order of Charmolue, he strode across the balustrade of the gallery, seized the rope with feet, knees and hands, glided down the façade like a drop of rain down a pane of glass, ran up to the two men with the swiftness of a cat that has fallen from a roof, felled both of them to the ground with his enormous fists, bore off the Egyptian on one arm, as a girl would her doll, and at one bound he was in the church, holding up the young girl above his head and shouting with a terrific voice—"Sanctuary! sanctuary!" This was all done with the rapidity of lightning.

"Sanctuary! sanctuary!" repeated the mob, and the clapping of ten thousand hands caused Quasimodo's only eye to sparkle with joy and exultation.

This shock brought La Esmeralda to her senses. She opened her eyes, looked at Quasimodo, and instantly closed them again as if horror-stricken at the sight of her deliverer.

Charmolue stood stupefied—so did the executioners and the whole escort. Within the walls of Notre Dame the prisoner was secure from molestation. The cathedral was a place of refuge. Human justice dare not cross its threshold.

Quasimodo paused under the great porch. His large feet seemed as firmly rooted in the pavement of the church as the massive Roman pillars. His huge head, with its profuse covering of hair, appeared to be thrust down into his shoulders, like that of the lion, which, too, has a copious mane and no neck. He held the damsel, palpitating all over, hanging from his horny hands like a white drapery; but he carried her with as much care as if he was fearful of bruising or disturbing her.

He felt, you would have thought, that a thing so delicate, so exquisite, so precious, was not made for such hands as his. At times he looked as though he dared not touch her even with his breath. Then, all at once, he would clasp her closely in his arms, against his angular bosom, as his treasure, as his all, as the mother of that girl would herself have done. His Cyclops eye, bent down upon her, shed over her a flood of tenderness, of pity, of grief, and was suddenly raised, flashing lightning. At this sight the women laughed and cried, the crowd stamped with enthusiasm, for at that moment Quasimodo was really beautiful. Yes, he was beautiful—he, that orphan, that foundling, that outcast; he felt himself august and strong; he looked in the face that society from which he was banished, and from which he had made so signal a conquest; that human justice from which he had snatched its victim; those judges, those executioners, all that force of the king's, which he, the meanest of the mean, had foiled with the force of God!

And then, how touching was that protection afforded by a being so deformed, to a being so unfortunate as the girl condemned to die and saved by Quasimodo! It was the two extreme miseries of Nature and society meeting and assisting each other.

After a triumph of a few minutes, however, Quasimodo hastened into the interior of the church with his burden. The people, fond of daring deeds, followed him with their eyes along the dusky nave, regretting that he had so soon withdrawn himself from their acclamations. All at once he was again descried at one of the extremities of the gallery of the kings of France: he ran along it like a maniac, holding up his prize in his arms, and shouting, "Sanctuary!" The populace greeted him with fresh applause. Having traversed the gallery, he again penetrated into the interior of the church. Presently afterward he again appeared on the upper platform, still bearing the Egyptian in his arms, still running like one frantic, still shouting, "Sanctuary!" Again the mob applauded. At length he made his third appearance on the top of the tower of the great bell: there he seemed to show proudly to the whole city her whom he saved, and his thundering voice—that voice which was heard so seldom, and which he himself never heard—made the air ring with the thrice-repeated shout of "Sanctuary! Sanctuary! Sanctuary!"

"Huzza! huzza!" cried the populace on their part; and this prodigious acclamation was heard on the other side of the river by the crowd collected in the Place de Grève, and by the recluse, who was still waiting with her eyes riveted on the gallows.

Book Eight

CHAPTER I

A HIGH FEVER

CLAUDE FROLLO was no longer in Notre Dame when his foster-son cut thus abruptly the fatal noose in which the unhappy archdeacon had caught the Egyptian, and was himself caught. On returning to the sacristy he had stripped off the alb, the cope, and the stole, thrown them all into the hands of the stupefied bedel, hurried out at the private door of the cloisters, ordered a boatman of the Terrain to carry him across the river, and wandered among the hilly streets of the University, meeting at every step parties of men and women, hastening joyously toward the Pont St. Michel, "in hopes of being in time to see the sorceress hanged!" Pale and haggard, blinded and more bewildered than an owl let loose and pursued by a troop of boys in broad daylight, he knew not where he was, what he did, whether he was awake or dreaming. He walked, he ran, heedless whither, taking any street at random, still driven onward by the Grève, the horrible Grève, which he vaguely knew to be behind him.

In this manner he pursued his way along the Hill of St. Genevieve, and left the town by the gate of St. Victor. So long as he could see, on turning round, the line of towers inclosing the University, and the scattered houses of the suburb, he continued to flee; but when, at length, the inequality of the ground had completely shut out that hateful Paris from his view, when he could fancy himself a hundred leagues off, in the country, in a desert, he paused, and felt as though he breathed once more.

A crowd of frightful ideas then rushed upon his mind. He saw plainly into the recesses of his soul, and shuddered. He thought of that unhappy girl who had undone him, and whom he had undone. With haggard eye he followed the double winding way along which fatality had urged their two destinies to the point of intersection, where it had pitilessly dashed them against one another. He thought of the folly of eternal vows, of the vanity of chastity, science, religion, and virtue. He willfully plunged into evil thoughts, and as he immersed himself in them he felt a satanic laugh arising within him.

And when, while thus diving into his soul, he saw how large a space nature had there prepared for the passions, he laughed still more bitterly. He stirred up from the bottom of his heart all its hatred and all its malignity; and he perceived, with the cold indifference of a physician examining a patient, that this hatred and this malignity were but vitiated love; that love, the source of very virtue in man, was transformed into horrid things in the heart of a priest, and that one so constituted as he in making himself a priest made himself a demon. He then laughed more hideously than ever, and all at once he again turned pale on considering the darkest side of his fatal passion, that corroding, venomous, rancorous, implacable love which had consigned the one to the gallows, the other to perdition.

And then he laughed again on bethinking him that Phœbus was not dead; that he was still alive, gay, and joyous; that he had a smarter uniform than ever, and a new mistress whom he took to see the old one hanged. He laughed still more heartily on reflecting that, among all the living beings whose death he had wished for, the Egyptian, the only creature whom he did not hate, was also the only one who had not escaped him.

He bethought him of the plight in which the female whom he loved had been exposed to the gaze of the crowd, of the entire population of Paris. He wrung his hands on reflecting how that female, that beauteous girl, that virgin lily, that being all modesty and purity, whom he durst not approach without trembling, and a glimpse of whom to himself alone would have been supreme happiness, had been exhibited in the broad face of day to the populace, to the vilest of the rabble of Paris, to lackeys, vagabonds, mendicants, thieves. He wept for rage at the miseries of love exposed, profaned, sullied, withered forever.

And when he strove to picture to himself the felicity which he might have found upon earth if she had not been a Bohemian, and if he had not been a priest, if Phœbus had not existed, and if she had not loved him; when he considered that a life of serenity and affection might have been possible for him also, even for him; that at that very moment there were here and there on the earth happy couples engaged in fond converse in orange groves, on the banks of murmuring streams, in the presence of a setting sun or of a starry sky; and that, had it pleased God, he might have formed with her one of those blessed couples, his heart dissolved in tenderness and despair.

She formed the subject of his every thought. It was this fixed idea that haunted him incessantly, that tortured him, that racked his brain and gnawed his vitals. He felt not regret; he felt not remorse: all that he had done he was ready to do again: he would rather see her in the hands of the hangman than in the arms of the captain. But so acute was his anguish that at times he tore off his hair by handfuls.

There was one moment among others when it came into his mind that possibly at that very instant the hideous chain which he had seen in the morning might be drawing its iron noose around that neck so slender and so graceful. This idea made the perspiration start from every pore.

There was another moment when, laughing diabolically at himself the while, his imagination represented to him at once La Esmeralda, as on the first day he had seen her, all life, all mirth, all joy, dressed and adorned, agile, dancing, harmonious, and La Esmeralda of the last hour, stripped, the rope about her neck, slowly ascending with bare feet the rough ladder to the gibbet. This twofold picture was drawn before him with such force as to extort from him a terrible shriek.

While this hurricane of despair was bending, breaking, shivering, overthrowing, uprooting everything in his soul, his eye ranged over the scene around him. At his feet the fowls were ferreting among the bushes, and picking up the burnished insects that were running about in the sun; overhead groups of dapple-gray clouds were sprinkled upon an azure sky; at the horizon, the steeple of the Abbey of St. Victor pierced the curve of the hill with its slated obelisk, and the miller of Copeaux watched, whistling, the laboring sails of his mill turning round. All this active, organized, tranquil life displayed around him in a thousand forms, gave him pain. Again he began to flee.

This flight from Nature, from life, from himself, from man, from God, from everything, lasted till evening. Sometimes he threw himself on his face upon the earth and tore up the young corn with his fingers; at others he paused in some lone village street, and his thoughts were so insupportable that he grasped his head with both hands, as though striving to wrench it from his shoulders in order to dash it upon the ground.

The sun was near setting when, on examining himself afresh, he found that he was almost mad. The storm which had been raging within him from the moment when he had lost the hope and the will to save the Egyptian had not left in his mind a single sound thought or idea. His reason was laid prostrate, nay, almost utterly destroyed. His mind retained but two distinct images, La Esmeralda and the gibbet; all the rest was black. These two images formed a horrible group; and the more he fixed on them so much attention and thought as he was yet master of, the more they seemed to increase, according to a fantastic progression, the one in charm, in grace, in beauty, in light—the other in horror: so that at last La Esmeralda appeared like a star, the gibbet like an enormous flesh- less arm.

It is remarkable that, during the whole of this torture, he never conceived any serious idea of putting an end to himself. The wretched man was tenacious of life. It is possible that he really saw hell ready to receive him afterward.

The day, meanwhile, continued to decline. The living principle which still existed within him began to think confusedly of return- ing. He conceived that he was far from Paris, but, on examining the objects around, he found that he had turned short after passing the bounds of the University. The steeple of St. Sulpice and the three tall spires of St. Germain des Près shot up above the horizon on his right. He proceeded in that direction. When he heard the challenge of the men at arms of the abbot round the embattled circumvallation of St. Germain, he turned off, took a path which presented itself between the abbey mill and the lazar-house of the hamlet, and presently found himself on the margin of the Prè aux Clercs. This meadow was celebrated for the squabbles which took place there night and day; it was, so saith the chronicler, the *hydra* of the poor monks of St. Germain. The archdeacon was apprehen- sive lest he should meet some one; he was afraid of every human face; he had avoided the University and the hamlet of St. Germain; he wished to make it as late as possible before he entered the streets. He proceeded along the Prè aux Clercs, took the lonely path which separated it from the Dieu Neuf, and at length reached the bank of the river. There Dom Claude found a boatman who for a few deniers took him up the Seine to the point of the city, and set him ashore upon that vacant tongue of land where the reader has already seen Gringoire pondering, and which extended beyond the king's gardens parallel with the isle of the cattle-ferryman.

The monotonous rocking of the boat and the murmur of the water had somewhat lulled the wretched Claude. When the boatman had left him he remained standing stupidly upon the strand, looking straight forward. All the objects he beheld seemed to dance before his eyes, forming a sort of phantasmagoria. It is no uncommon thing for the fatigue of excessive grief to produce this effect upon the mind.

The sun had set behind the tall tower of Nesle. It was just twilight. The sky was white; the water of the river was white; and between these the left bank of the Seine, upon which his eyes were fixed, extended its somber mass, which, gradually diminished by the perspective, pierced the haze of the horizon like a black arrow. It was covered with houses, of which nothing was distinguishable but the obscure profile, standing out in strong relief in the dark from the light ground of the sky and the water. Lights began to glimmer here and there in windows. This immense black obelisk, thus bounded by the two white sheets of the sky and the river, of great breadth at this place, produced on Dom Claude a singular effect, which may be compared with that which would be experienced by a man lying down on his back at the foot of the steeple of Strasburg Cathedral, and looking at its enormous shaft piercing above his head the penumbra of the twilight: only in this case Claude was standing and the obelisk lying. But as the river, in reflecting the sky, lengthened the abyss beneath him, the immense promontory shot forth into space like any church steeple, and the impression was the same. That impression was rendered the more striking and extraordinary by the circumstance that this steeple was two leagues high —a colossal, immeasurable, unparalleled object; a Tower of Babel; an edifice such as human eye never beheld. The chimneys of the houses, the battlements of the walls, the angles of the roofs, the steeple of the Augustines, the Tower of Nesle, all those salient points which indented the profile of the immense obelisk, heightened the illusion by presenting to the eye a grotesque semblance of the fretwork of a rich and fantastic sculpture. Claude, in the state of hallucination in which he then was, fancied that he saw—saw with his bodily eyes—the tower of hell: the thousand lights gleaming from bottom to top of this frightful tower appeared to him so many entrances to the immense furnace within; and the voices and sounds which issued from it, the shrieks and moans of the damned. A deep fear came over him; he covered his ears with his hands that he might not hear, turned his back that he might not see, and hurried away from the terrible vision. But the vision was within him.

On entering the streets, the passengers who jostled one another by the light of the shop-fronts appeared like specters incessantly going and coming around him. Strange noises rang in his ears, extraordinary fancies disturbed his mind. He saw neither houses nor pavement, neither men, women, nor carriages, but a chaos of confused objects blending one with another. At the corner of the Rue de la Barillerie there was a grocer's shop, the pent-house of which was hung all along, according to immemorial custom, with tin hoops, to which were attached imitation candles of wood; these, being shaken by the wind, clattered like castanets. He imagined that he heard the skeletons of Montfaucon clashing together in the dark.

"Oh!" muttered he, "the night-wind is driving them one against another, and mingling the clank of their chains with the rattling of their bones. She is there too, perhaps, among them!"

Distracted, he knew not whither he went. Presently he was upon the Pont St. Michel. He perceived a light in the window of a ground-floor room; he approached it. Through a cracked pane he beheld a mean apartment, which awakened confused recollections in his mind. In this apartment, faintly lighted by a lamp, he saw a fair, fresh-colored, jovial-looking youth, loudly laughing with a young female; and near the lamp was seated an old woman spinning and singing, or rather squalling, a song. In the intervals when the laughter ceased, snatches of the old woman's song reached the ear of the priest; the tenor of it was frightful and not very intelligible.

The old woman was Falourdel, the girl was a stranger, and the youth was his brother Jehan. He continued to watch them. He saw Jehan go to the window at the further end of the room, open it, and look out on the quay, where a thousand illumined windows glanced in the distance; and he heard him say while shutting the window—"'Pon my soul, 'tis dark night. The citizens are lighting up their candles, and Night her stars."

Jehan then went back to his companion, and held up a bottle which stood on the table. "Zounds!" he cried, "empty already!—and I have no more money." So saying, he came forth from the house. Dom Claude had but just time to throw himself on the ground that he might not be met, looked in the face, and recognized by his brother. Luckily the street was dark and the scholar not sober. "Oho!" said he; "here is one who has been enjoying himself to-day." With his foot he shook Dom Claude, who held in his breath.

"Dead drunk!" resumed Jehan. "Full enough, it seems. A proper leech loose from a cask. Bald too!" added he, stooping—"an old man! *Fortunate senex!*" [1]

Dom Claude then heard him move away, saying—"Never mind! Reason is a fine thing, though; and very lucky is my brother the archdeacon in being prudent and having money."

The archdeacon then rose, and ran without stopping toward Notre Dame, the enormous towers of which he saw lifting themselves in

1. Fortunate old man!

the dark above the houses. At the moment when, quite breathless, he reached the Place du Parvis, he paused, and durst not raise his eyes to the fatal edifice. "Oh!" said he, in a low tone, "is it true then that such a thing could have happened here to-day?—this very morning?"

He ventured, however, to look at the church. The façade was dark, the sky behind it glistened with stars. The crescent of the moon, which had not been long above the horizon, was seen at that moment on the top of the right-hand tower, and seemed to be perched like a luminous bird on the edge of the parapet, cut out into large trefoils.

The door of the cloisters was shut, but the archdeacon always carried about him the key of the tower in which was his laboratory. Availing himself of it, he entered the church. He found the interior dark and silent as the grave. From the large shadows which fell from all sides in broad sheets, he knew that the hangings put up for the morning's ceremony had not been removed. The great silver cross glistened amid the gloom, dotted with sparkling points, like the milky-way of this sepulchral night. The tall windows of the choir showed above the black drapery the upper extremity of their pointed arches, the panes of which, admitting a faint ray of moonlight, had but those doubtful colors of night, a sort of violet, white, and blue, the tint of which is elsewhere found only on the faces of the dead. The archdeacon, perceiving all around the choir these livid points of arches, fancied that he beheld a circle of ghastly faces staring at him.

With hurried step he began to flee across the church. It then seemed to him that the church too moved, breathed, lived; that each massive column was transformed into an enormous leg, stamping the ground with its broad stone foot, and that the gigantic cathedral was but a sort of prodigious elephant, puffing and walking, with pillars for legs, the two towers for trunks, and the immense sheet of black cloth for a caparison.

Thus the fever or the frenzy of the wretched priest had attained such a degree of intensity that to him the external world was but a kind of Apocalypse visible, palpable, terrific. For a moment he felt somewhat relieved. On entering one of the aisles he perceived a reddish light behind a cluster of pillars. He ran toward it as toward a star. It was the petty lamp which night and day threw a dim light on the public breviary of Notre Dame, beneath its iron grating. He hurried to the sacred book, in hopes of finding in it some consolation or encouragement. It was open at this passage of Job, which caught his fixed eye, "Then a spirit passed before my face, and the hair of my flesh stood up."

On reading this fearful text he felt much the same as a blind man whose fingers are pricked by the staff which he has picked up. His knees failed him, and he sunk upon the pavement, thinking of her who had that day suffered death. Such volumes of blasting vapors enveloped his brain that it seemed as if his head had been turned into one of the chimneys of hell.

He must have remained for a long time in this attitude, neither thinking nor feeling, helpless and passive in the hand of the demon. At length, recovering some degree of consciousness, he thought of seeking refuge in the tower, near his trusty Quasimodo. He rose, and, being afraid, he took the lamp of the breviary to light him. This was a sacrilege, but he no longer regarded such a trifle as that.

He slowly ascended the staircase of the tower, filled with a secret dread, which was communicated to the passengers who now and then crossed the Parvis, on seeing the mysterious light of his lamp mounting so late from loop-hole to loop-hole to the top of the tower.

All at once he felt a cool air upon his face, and found himself under the doorway of the uppermost gallery. The night was cold. The sky was mottled with clouds, the large white masses of which, overlapping each other at the edges, and being compressed at the corners, resembled the ice of a river that has broken up in winter. The crescent moon, imbedded in those clouds, looked like a celestial ship surrounded by these aerial sheets of ice.

He cast down his eye between the iron railing of the dwarf colonnade which unites the two towers, and for a moment contemplated through the veil of mist and smoke the vast extent of the roofs of Paris, sharp, countless, crowded together, and small as the ripples of a calm sea in a summer night. The moon gave but a faint light which imparted an ashy tint to earth and sky.

At this moment the clock raised its loud and solemn voice. It was midnight. The priest thought of noon; it was again twelve o'clock. "Oh!" muttered he to himself, "she must be cold by this time!"

All at once a gust of wind extinguished his lamp, and at the same moment he saw something white, a shade, a human form, a female, appear at the opposite angle of the tower. He shuddered. By the side of this female there was a little goat, which mingled her bleating with the last tones of the bell. He had the courage to look at her—'twas she herself!

She was pale; she was sad. Her hair fell over her shoulders, as in the morning; but there was no rope about her neck; her hands were not bound; she was free; she was dead.

She was habited in white, and had a white veil over her head. She came toward him slowly, looking up at the sky, and followed by the supernatural goat. He was petrified: he would have fled, but was unable. All he could do was to recede a step for every one that she advanced. He retreated in this manner till he was beneath the dark vault of the staircase. His blood curdled at the idea that she might perhaps come that way too; if she had, he must have died of fright.

She did in fact approach so near as the door of the staircase, where she paused for a few moments; she cast a fixed look into the darkness, but without appearing to discern the priest, and passed on. She seemed to him taller than when alive; he saw the moonshine through her white robe; he heard her breathe.

When she was gone he began to descend the stairs as slowly as he had seen the specter move. Horror-stricken, his hair erect, still holding the extinguished lamp in his hand, he fancied himself a specter; and while descending the winding stairs he heard a voice laughing and repeating distinctly in his ear, "A spirit passed before my face, and the hair of my flesh stood up."

CHAPTER II

THE SANCTUARY

IN THE MIDDLE AGES every town, and till the time of Louis XII. every town in France, had its sanctuaries. Amid the deluge of penal laws and barbarous jurisdiction which inundated that division of Paris which we have specially called the City, these sanctuaries were a kind of islands, which rose above the level of human justice. Every criminal who took refuge there was saved. There were in a district almost as many sanctuaries as places of execution. It was the abuse of impunity going hand in hand with the abuse of punishment—two bad things which strove to correct each other. The palaces of the king, the hotels of the princes, but above all, the churches, had the right of sanctuary. Sometimes that right was conferred for a time on a whole city which needed repeopling. Louis XI. made Paris a sanctuary in 1467.

When he had once set foot in the sanctuary, the criminal was sacred, but he was obliged to beware of leaving it; one step out of the island asylum plunged him again into the sea. The wheel, the gallows, the rack, kept strict guard around his retreat, and watched their prey incessantly as sharks prowl around a ship. Condemned persons thus rescued have been known to grow gray in a cloister, on the staircase of a palace, in the garden of an abbey, in the porch of a church: in this way the sanctuary was a prison as well as any place that bore the name. It sometimes happened that a solemn ordinance of the parliament violated the sanctuary, and gave up the condemned to the executioner; but the case was rare. The parliaments were jealous of the bishops, and, when the gowns of the two professions chanced to come into collision, that of the churches generally had the worst of it. At times, however, as in the affair of the assassins of Petit Jean, the executioner of Paris, and in that of Emery Rousseau, the murderer of Jean Valleret, justice overleaped the church, and passed on to the execution of its sentences; but, unless authorized by an ordinance of the parliament, woe to him who forcibly violated a sanctuary. Everybody knows what was the fate of Robert de Clermont, Marshal of France, and Jean de Chalons, Marshal of Champagne; and yet the party, in whose case they had interfered, one Berrin Marc, was but a money-changer's man and a scurvy assassin; but then the two marshals had broken open the doors of St. Mery. There was the enormity!

Such was the respect with which sanctuaries were invested, that, according to tradition, it occasionally extended to brute animals. Aymoin relates that a stag, hunted by Dagobert, having taken refuge near the tomb of St. Denis, the dogs stopped short, merely barking at him.

The churches had in general a cell appropriated to the reception of fugitives. In 1307, Nicolas Flamel had built for such persons, in the Church of St. Jacques de la Coucherie, a chamber which cost him four livres six sous sixteen deniers parisis.

At Notre Dame it was a small cell on the top of the aisle, under the flying buttresses, facing the cloisters, on the very spot where the wife of the present keeper of the towers has made herself a garden, which is to the hanging gardens of Babylon what a lettuce is to a palm tree, or a portress to Semiramis.

Here it was that, after his wild and triumphant course through towers and galleries, Quasimodo deposited La Esmeralda. So long as this race lasted, the damsel had not recovered her senses: half stupefied, half awake, she was sensible of nothing but that she was mounting into the air, that she was floating, flying in it, that something was lifting her above the earth. From time to time she heard the loud laugh and the harsh voice of Quasimodo at her ear; she opened her eyes, and then beneath her she confusedly saw Paris speckled with its thousand roofs of slate and tile, like red and blue mosaic-work, and above her head the hideous but joyful face of Quasimodo. Again her eyes closed: she imagined that all was over, that she had been executed during her swoon, and that the deformed spirit who had governed her destiny had seized and borne her away.

But when the panting bell-ringer had laid her down in the cell of the sanctuary, when she felt his huge hands gently loosing the cord that galled her arms, she experienced that kind of shock which abruptly wakens those on board a ship that runs aground in the middle of a dark night. Her ideas awoke also and returned to her one by one. She saw that she was in the church; she recollected having been snatched out of the hand of the executioner; that Phœbus was alive, and that he no longer loved her; and these two ideas, one of which imparted such bitterness to the other, presenting themselves at once to the poor girl, she turned toward Quasimodo, who remained standing beside her, and whose aspect frightened her, saying, "Why did you save me?"

He looked anxiously at her, as if striving to guess what she said. She repeated the question. He then cast on her a look deeply sorrowful, and withdrew. She was lost in astonishment.

A few moments afterward he returned, bringing a bundle which he laid at her feet. It contained apparel which charitable women had left for her at the door of the church. She then cast down her eyes at herself, saw that she was almost naked, and blushed. Life had fully returned. Quasimodo seemed to participate in this feeling of modesty. Covering his face with his large hand, he again retired, but with slow step.

She hastened to dress herself. It was a white robe with a white veil—the habit of a novice of the Hotel Dieu. She had scarcely finished before Quasimodo returned. He brought a basket under one arm and a mattress under the other. The basket contained a bottle, bread, and some other provisions. He set down the basket and said, "Eat!" He spread the mattress on the floor and said, "Sleep!" It was his own dinner, his own bed, that the bell-ringer had brought her.

The Egyptian lifted her eyes to his face to thank him; but she could not utter a word. The poor fellow was absolutely hideous. She drooped her head with a thrill of horror.

"Ah!" said he, "I frighten you, I see. I am ugly enough, God wot. Do not look at, but only hearken to me. In the day-time you shall stay here; at night you walk about all over the church. But stir not a step out of it, either by night or by day, or they will catch you, and kill you, and it will be the death of me."

Moved at this address, she raised her head to reply, but he was gone. Once more she was alone, pondering on the singular words of this almost monstrous being, and struck by the tone of his voice, at once so harsh and so gentle.

She then began to examine her cell. It was a chamber some six feet square, with a small aperture for a window, and a door opening upon the slightly inclined plane of the roof, composed of flat stones. Several gutters, terminating in heads of animals, seemed to bend down over it, and to stretch out their necks to look in at the hole. On a level with its roofs she perceived a thousand chimney-tops, disgorging the smoke of all the fires of Paris. Melancholy prospect for the poor Egyptian, a foundling, rescued from the gallows; an unfortunate young creature who had neither country, nor family, nor home!

At the moment when the idea of her forlorn situation wrung her heart more keenly than ever, she felt a hairy, shaggy head rubbing against her hands and knees. She shuddered—everything now alarmed her—and looked. It was the poor goat, the nimble Djali, which had escaped along with her at the moment when Quasimodo dispersed Charmolue's brigade, and had been at her feet nearly an hour, lavishing caresses on her mistress without obtaining a single glance. The Egyptian covered the fond animal with kisses. "Oh, Djali!" said she, "how I have forgotten thee! And yet thou thinkest of me. Thou, for thy part, at least, art not ungrateful." At the same time, as if an invisible hand had removed the obstruction which had so long repressed her tears, she began to weep, and as the big drops trickled down her cheeks, she felt the keenest and bitterest portion of her sorrows leaving her along with them.

Evening came on. The night was so beautiful, the moonlight so soft, that she ventured to take a turn in the high gallery which runs round the church. She felt somewhat refreshed by her walk, so calm did the earth appear to her, beheld from that elevation.

CHAPTER III

A HUMAN HEART IN A FORM SCARCELY HUMAN

NEXT MORNING she perceived on awaking that she had slept. This singular circumstance surprised her—it was so long that she had been unaccustomed to sleep! The sun, peeping in at her window, threw his cheering rays upon her face. But besides the sun she saw at this aperture an object that affrighted her—the unlucky face of Quasimodo. She involuntarily closed her eyes, but in vain; she still fancied that she saw through her rosy lids that visage so like an ugly mask. She kept her eyes shut. Presently she heard a hoarse voice saying very kindly: "Don't be afraid. I am your friend. I came to see you sleep. What harm can it do to you if I come to look at you when your eyes are shut. Well, well, I am going. There, now, I am behind the wall. Now you can open your eyes."

There was something still more plaintive than these words in the accent with which they were uttered. The Egyptian, affected by them, opened her eyes. He was actually no longer at the window. She went to it, looked out, and saw the poor hunchback cowering under the wall, in an attitude of grief and resignation. She made an effort to overcome the aversion which he excited. "Come!" said she kindly to him. Observing the motion of her lips, Quasimodo imagined that she was bidding him go away. He then rose and retired, with slow and halting step and drooping head, without so much as daring to raise his eyes, filled with despair, to the damsel.

"Come, then!" she cried; but he continued to move off. She then darted out of the cell, ran to him, and took hold of his arm. On feeling her touch, Quasimodo trembled in every limb. He lifted his supplicating eye, and, finding that she drew him toward her, his whole face shone with joy and tenderness. She would have made him go into her cell, but he insisted on staying at her threshold. "No, no," said he; "the owl never enters the nest of the lark."

She then seated herself gracefully on her bed, with her goat at her feet. Both remained for some minutes motionless, contemplating in silence, he so much beauty, she so much ugliness. Every moment she discovered in Quasimodo some new deformity. Her look wandered from his knock-knees to his hunchback, from his hunchback to his only eye. She could not conceive how a creature so awkwardly put together could exist. At the same time an air of such sadness and gentleness pervaded his whole figure that she began to be reconciled with it.

He was the first to break silence.

"Did you not call me back?" said he.

"Yes!" replied she with a nod of affirmation.

He understood the sign.

"Alas!" said he, as if hesitating to finish, "you must know, I am deaf."

"Poor fellow!" exclaimed the Bohemian, with an expression of pity.

He smiled sadly.

"You think nothing else was wanting, don't you? Yes, I am deaf. That is the way in which I am served. It is terrible, is it not?—while you—you are so beautiful!"

The tone of the poor fellow conveyed such a profound feeling of his wretchedness that she had not the heart to utter a word. Besides, he would not have heard her. He then resumed:

"Never till now was I aware how hideous I am. When I compare myself with you, I cannot help pitying myself, poor unhappy monster that I am! I must appear to you like a beast. You, you are a sunbeam, a drop of dew, a bird's song! I, I am something frightful, neither man nor brute; something harder, more shapeless, and more trampled upon than a flint."

He then laughed, and scarcely could there be aught in the world more cutting than this laugh. He continued:

"Yes, I am deaf: but you will speak to me by gestures, by signs. I have a master who talks to me that way. And then I shall soon know your meaning from the motion of your lips, from your look."

"Well then," replied she, smiling, "tell me why you have saved me?"

He looked steadfastly at her while she spoke.

"I understand," rejoined he: "you ask me why I saved you. You have forgotten a wretch who attempted one night to carry you off, a wretch to whom, the very next day, you brought relief on the ignominious pillory. A draught of water and a look of pity are more than I could repay with my life. You have forgotten that wretch —but he has not forgotten."

She listened to him with deep emotion. A tear started into the eye of the bell-ringer, but it did not fall. He appeared to make a point of repressing it.

"Look you," he again began, when he no longer feared lest that tear should escape him, "we have very high towers here; a man falling from one of them would be dead almost before he reached the pavement. When you wish to be rid of me, tell me to throw myself from the top—you have but to say the word; nay, a look will be sufficient."

He then rose. Unhappy as was the Bohemian, this grotesque being awakened compassion even in her. She made him a sign to stay.

"No, no," said he, "I must not stay too long. I do not feel comfortable. It is out of pity that you do not turn your eyes from me. I will seek some place where I can look at you without your seeing me: that will be better."

He drew from his pocket a small metal whistle.

"Take this," said he: "when you want me, when you wish me to come, when you have the courage to see me, whistle with this. I shall hear that sound."

He laid the whistle on the floor and retired.

CHAPTER IV

EARTHENWARE AND CRYSTAL

TIME PASSED ON. Tranquillity returned by degrees to the soul of La Esmeralda. Excessive grief, like excessive joy, is too violent to last. The human heart cannot continue long in either extremity. The Bohemian had suffered so much that, of the feelings she had lately experienced, astonishment alone was left.

Along with security, hope began to revive within her. She was out of society, out of life, but she had a vague feeling that it might not be impossible for her to return to them. She was like one dead, keeping in reserve a key to her tomb.

The terrible images which had so long haunted her were leaving her by degrees. All the hideous phantoms, Pierrat Torterue, Jacques Charmolue, had faded from her mind—all of them, even the priest himself. And then Phœbus was yet living: she was sure of it; she had seen him. To her the life of Phœbus was everything. After the series of fatal shocks which had laid waste all her affections, she had found but one sentiment in her soul which they had not over-thrown—her love for the captain. Love is like a tree: it shoots of itself; it strikes its roots deeply into our whole being, and frequently continues to be green over a heart in ruins. And there is this unaccountable circumstance attending it, that the blinder that passion, the more tenacious it is. Never is it stronger than when it is most unreasonable.

No doubt La Esmeralda did not think of the captain without pain. No doubt it was terrible that he too should have made such a mistake, that he too should have thought the thing possible, that he too should have believed the wound to be inflicted by one who would have given a thousand lives for his sake. Still there was no great reason to be angry with him: had she not confessed the crime? had she not, frail creature as she was, yielded to the torture? All the fault was hers. She ought to have suffered them to tear her in pieces rather than make such an admission. After all, could she see Phœbus but once more for a single minute; a word, a look would suffice to undeceive him and to bring back the truant. This she had not the least doubt of. There were, at the same time, several singular circumstances about which she puzzled herself—the accident of Phœbus's presence at the penance; the young female in whose company he was. She was, no doubt, his sister. An improbable explanation, but she was satisfied with it, because she must needs believe that Phœbus still loved her, and loved but her. Had he not sworn it? What more could she require, simple and credulous as she was? And then, in this affair, were not appearances much more against her than against him? She waited therefore—she hoped.

We may add too that the church, that vast church which saved her, which enveloped her on all sides, which guarded her, was itself a sovereign anodyne. The solemn lines of that architecture, the religious attitude of all the objects around her, the serene and pious thoughts which transpired, as it were, through all the pores of that pile, acted upon her unknown to herself. The edifice, moreover, had sounds of such majesty and such blessing that they soothed her broken spirit. The monotonous chant of the officiating priests; the response of the congregation, sometimes inarticulate, sometimes thundering; the harmonious shiver of the windows; the organ bursting forth like a hundred trumpets; the three belfries buzzing like hives of immense bees; all that orchestra, with its gigantic gamut incessantly ascending and descending from a crowd below to a bell-tower above, lulled her memory, her imagination, her sorrows. The bells more especially had this soothing effect. It was like a mighty magnetism which those vast engines poured over her in broad waves. Accordingly, each successive sunrise found her more serene, more comfortable, and less pale. In proportion as her inward wounds healed, her face recovered its grace and beauty, but chastened with more sedateness, more repose. Her former character returned also— even somewhat of her cheerfulness, her pretty pout, her fondness for her goat and for singing, and her modesty. In the morning she shrunk into a corner of her cell to dress herself, lest any inmate of the neighboring garrets should espy her through the window.

When the thoughts of Phœbus allowed her time, the Egyptian would sometimes think of Quasimodo. He was the only bond, the only link, the only communication, that was left her with mankind, with the living. The unfortunate girl was more completely cut off from the world than Quasimodo. As for the strange friend whom chance had given her, she knew not what to make of him. She would frequently reproach herself for not feeling sufficient gratitude to blind her to his imperfections; but decidedly she could not accustom herself to the poor bell-ringer. He was too hideous.

She had left on the floor the whistle that he had given her. Quasimodo, nevertheless, looked in from time to time on the succeeding days. She strove as much as she could to conceal her aversion when he brought her the basket of provisions or the pitcher of water; but he was sure to perceive the slightest movement of that kind, and then he went sorrowfully away.

One day he came just at the moment when she was fondling Djali. For awhile he stood full of thought before the graceful group of the goat and the Egyptian. At length, shaking his huge, misshapen head: "My misfortune," said he, "is that I am too much like a human creature. Would to God that I had been a downright beast, like that goat!"

She cast on him a look of astonishment. "Oh!" he replied to that look—"well do I know why," and immediately retired.

Another time, when he came to the door of the cell, which he never entered, La Esmeralda was singing an old Spanish ballad: she knew not the meaning of the words, but it dwelt upon her ear because the Bohemian women had lulled her with it when quite a child. At the abrupt appearance of that ugly face the damsel stopped short, with an involuntary start, in the middle of her song. The unhappy bell-ringer dropped upon his knees at the threshold of the door, and with a beseeching look clasped his clumsy, shapeless hands. "Oh!" said he, sorrowfully, "go on, I pray you, and drive me not away." Not wishing to vex him, the trembling girl continued the ballad. By degrees her alarm subsided, and she gave herself up entirely to the impression of the melancholy tune which she was singing; while he remained upon his knees, with his hands joined as in prayer, scarcely breathing, his look intently fixed on the sparkling orbs of the Bohemian. You would have said that he was listening to her song with his eyes.

On another occasion, he came to her with an awkward and bashful air. "Hearken to me," said he, with effort; "I have something to say to you."

She made a sign to him that she was listening. He then began to sigh, half opened his lips, appeared for a moment ready to speak, looked at her, shook his head, and slowly retired, pressing his hand to his brow, and leaving the Egyptian in amazement.

Among the grotesque heads sculptured in the wall there was one for which he showed a particular predilection, and with which he seemed to exchange brotherly looks. The Egyptian once heard him address it in these words: "Oh! why am I not of stone, like thee?"

At length, one morning, La Esmeralda, having advanced to the parapet of the roof, was looking at the place over the sharp roof of St. Jean le Rond. Quasimodo was behind her. He stationed himself there on purpose to spare the damsel the disagreeable spectacle of his ungainly person. On a sudden the Bohemian shuddered: a tear and a flash of joy sparkled at once in her eyes: she fell on her knees and extended her arms in anguish toward the place, crying, "Phœbus! come! come! one word, a single word, for God's sake! Phœbus! Phœbus!" Her voice, her face, her attitude, her whole figure, had the agonizing expression of a shipwrecked person who is making signals of distress to a distant vessel sailing gayly along in the sunshine.

Quasimodo, bending forward, perceived that the object of this wild and tender appeal was a young and handsome horseman, a captain, glistening with arms and accoutrements, who passed caracoling through the place, and bowing to a fair lady smiling in her balcony. The officer was too far off to hear the call of the unhappy girl.

But the poor deaf bell-ringer understood it. A deep sigh heaved his breast; he turned round; his heart was swollen with the tears which he repressed; he dashed his convulsive fists against his head, and when he removed them there was in each of them a handful of red hair.

The Egyptian paid no attention to him. Gnashing his teeth, he said, in a low tone, "Perdition! That is how one ought to look, then! One need but have a handsome outside!"

She continued meanwhile upon her knees, and cried, with vehement agitation, "Oh! there he alights! He is going into that house! Phœbus! Phœbus! He does not hear me! Phœbus! Oh! the spiteful woman, to talk to him at the same time that I do! Phœbus! Phœbus!"

The deaf bell-ringer watched her. He comprehended this pantomime. The poor fellow's eyes filled with tears, but he suffered none of them to escape. All at once he gently pulled her sleeve. She turned round. He had assumed a look of composure, and said to her, "Shall I go and fetch him?"

She gave a cry of joy. "Oh! go, go! run! quick! that captain! that captain! bring him to me! I will love thee!" She clasped his knees. He could not help shaking his head sorrowfully.

"I will go, and bring him to you," said he, in a faint voice. He then retired and hurried down the staircase, stifled with sobs.

When he reached the place nothing was to be seen but the fine horse fastened to the gate of the Gondelaurier mansion. The captain had just entered. He looked up to the roof of the church. La Esmeralda was still at the same place, in the same posture. He made her a sad sign with his head, and leaned with his back against one of the pillars of the porch, determined to await the captain's departure.

In that house it was one of those festive days which precede a wedding. Quasimodo saw many persons enter, but nobody came out. Every now and then he looked up at the roof; the Egyptian did not stir any more than he. A groom came and untied the horse and led him to the stable. The whole day passed in this manner—Quasimodo at the pillar, La Esmeralda on the roof, and Phœbus no doubt at the feet of Fleur-de-lys.

At length night arrived; a night without a moon, a dark night. To no purpose did Quasimodo keep his eye fixed on La Esmeralda; she soon appeared to be but a white spot in the twilight, which became more and more indistinct, till it was no longer discernible amid the darkness.

Quasimodo saw the front windows of the Gondelaurier mansion lighted up from top to bottom; he saw the other windows of the place lighted up one after another; he saw them darkened again to the very last of them, for he remained the whole evening at his post. Still the officer came not forth. When all the passengers had retired to their homes, and not a light was to be seen in any of the windows, Quasimodo was left alone, in absolute darkness.

The windows of the Gondelaurier mansion, however, continued lighted, even after midnight. Quasimodo, motionless and attentive, saw a multitude of living and dancing shadows passing over the many-colored panes. Had he not been deaf, in proportion as the noises of Paris subsided, he would have heard more and more distinctly sounds of festivity, mirth and music within the mansion.

About one in the morning the company began to break up. Quasimodo, enveloped in darkness, watched all the guests as they came out under the porch lighted with torches. The captain was not among them.

He was filled with sad thoughts. Ever and anon he looked up at the sky, as if tired of waiting. Large, heavy, ragged black clouds hung like crape hammocks beneath the starry cope of night. You would have said that they were the cobwebs of the firmament. In one of those moments he all at once saw the glazed door of the balcony mysteriously open. Two persons came forth, and shut it after them without noise. It was with some difficulty that Quasimodo recognized in the one the handsome captain, in the other the young lady whom he had seen in the morning welcoming the officer from the window. The place was quite dark, and a double crimson curtain, which had collapsed again behind the door at the moment of its shutting, scarcely suffered a gleam of light from the apartment to reach the balcony.

The young captain and the lady, as far as our deaf watcher could judge—for he could not hear a word they said—appeared to indulge in a very tender *tête-à-tête*. The young lady seemed to have permitted the officer to throw his arm around her waist, and feebly withstood a kiss.

Quasimodo witnessed from below this scene, which it was the more delightful to see inasmuch as it was not intended to be witnessed. He, however, contemplated that happiness, that beauty, with bitterness of soul. After all, Nature was not silent in the poor fellow, deformed as he was, his heart nevertheless had affections. He thought of the miserable portion which Providence had allotted to him; that woman, love and its pleasures would be forever passing before his eyes, but that he should never do more than witness the felicity of others. But what afflicted him most in this sight, and mingled anger with his vexation, was to think what the Egyptian must suffer if she beheld it. To be sure, the night was very dark; La Esmeralda, if she had stayed in the same place—and he had no doubt of that—was at a considerable distance; and it was quite as much as he could do himself to distinguish the lovers in the balcony. This was some consolation.

Meanwhile, their conversation became more and more animated. The young lady appeared to address the officer in a beseeching attitude. Quasimodo could discern her fair hands clasped, her smiles mingled with tears, her looks uplifted to heaven, and the eager eyes of the captain bent down upon her. The door of the balcony suddenly opened; an aged lady appeared; the fair one looked confused, the officer vexed, and all three went in.

A moment afterward, a horse was prancing beneath the porch, and the brilliant officer, wrapped in his cloak, passed swiftly before Quasimodo. The bell-ringer suffered him to turn the corner of the street, and then ran after him with the agility of a monkey, crying: "Ho! captain!"

The captain pulled up. "What would the varlet with me?" said he, on spying in the dark the uncouth figure limping toward him.

Quasimodo, on coming up to him, boldly laid hold of the horse's bridle. "Follow me, captain," said he; "there is one who would speak with you."

"By Mahound's horns!" muttered Phœbus, "methinks I have seen this rascally scarecrow somewhere or other. Halloo! fellow! let go the bridle."

"Captain," replied the deaf bell-ringer, "ask me not who it is."

"Loose my horse, I tell you," cried Phœbus, angrily. "What means the rogue, hanging thus from my bridle rein? Dost thou take my horse for a gallows, knave?"

Quasimodo, so far from relaxing his hold of the bridle, was preparing to turn the horse's head the contrary way. Unable to account for the opposition of the captain, he hastened to give him this explanation—"Come, captain; 'tis a female who is waiting for you—a female who loves you."

"A rare varlet," said the captain, "to suppose that I am obliged to go to all the women who love me, or say they do. After all, perhaps she is like thyself with that owl's face. Tell her who sent thee that I am going to be married, and that she may go to the devil."

"Hark ye, monseigneur," cried Quasimodo, thinking with a word to overcome his hesitation: " 'tis the Egyptian whom you are acquainted with."

This intimation made a strong impression upon Phœbus, but not of the kind that the speaker anticipated. It will be recollected that our gallant officer had retired with Fleur-de-lys a few moments be-

fore Quasimodo rescued the condemned girl from the clutches of
Charmolue. In all his subsequent visits to the logis Gondelaurier he
had carefully abstained from mentioning that female, the recollection of whom was, besides, painful to him; and Fleur-de-lys, on her
part, had not deemed it politic to tell him that the Egyptian was
alive. Phœbus believed, therefore, that poor "Similar" was dead,
and that she must have been so for a month or two. Add to this that
for some moments the captain had been pondering on the extreme
darkness of the night, on the supernatural ugliness and sepulchral
voice of the strange messenger: it was past midnight; the street was
as lonely as on the evening that the specter monk had accosted
him, and his horse snorted at the sight of Quasimodo.

"The Egyptian?" he exclaimed, with almost a feeling of terror.
"What, then, art thou from the other world?" At the same time he
clapped his hand to the hilt of his dagger.

"Quick! quick!" said the dwarf, striving to lead the horse; "this
way."

Phœbus dealt him a smart stroke with his whip across the arm.
Quasimodo's eye flashed. He made a movement as if to rush upon
the captain; but instantly restraining himself he said, "Oh! how
happy you are since there is somebody who loves you!" laying particular emphasis on the word somebody. "Get you gone!" added he,
loosing the bridle.

Phœbus clapped spurs to his horse, at the same time swearing
lustily. Quasimodo looked after him till he was lost in the darkness.
"Oh!" said the poor fellow—"to refuse such a trifle as that!"

He returned to Notre Dame, lighted his lamp, and ascended the
tower. As he expected, the Bohemian was still in the same place.
The moment she saw him she ran to meet him. "Alone!" she exclaimed, sorrowfully, clasping her hands.

"I could not meet with him," said Quasimodo, dryly.

"You should have waited all night," she replied, angrily.

He saw her look of displeasure, and comprehended the reproach.
"I will watch him better another time," said he, drooping his head.

"Go thy way!" cried she.

He left her. She was dissatisfied with him. He had rather be ill-
used by her than give her pain. He therefore kept all the mortification to himself.

From that day he avoided the presence of the Egyptian. He
ceased to come to her cell. At most she sometimes caught a glimpse
of the bell-ringer on the top of a tower, with his eye fixed in melan-

choly mood upon her; but the moment he was aware that she saw him, he was gone.

Truth obliges us to state that she grieved very little about this voluntary absence of the poor hunchback. At the bottom of her heart she was glad of it. Quasimodo did not deceive himself on this point.

She saw him not, but she felt the presence of a good genius around her. Her fresh supplies of provisions were brought by an invisible hand while she was asleep. One morning she found over her window a cage with birds. Above her cell there was a sculptured figure which frightened her, as she had more than once signified to Quasimodo. One morning—for all these things were done at night— it was gone; it had been broken off. Whoever had clambered up to this piece of sculpture must have risked his life.

Sometimes, in the evening, she heard the voice of some unseen person beneath the pent-house of the belfry singing a wild, sad strain, as if to lull her to sleep. They were verses without rhyme, such as a deaf man might make.

One morning, on opening her eyes, she saw two nosegays standing in her window. One was in a bright, handsome crystal vase, but cracked. The water with which it was filled had run out, and the flowers were faded. The other was a pot of coarse common stone-ware, but which retained all the water, and the flowers in it were fresh and fragrant. I know not whether it was done intentionally, but La Esmeralda took the faded nosegay, and carried it all day at her bosom. On that day she heard not the voice singing from the tower—a circumstance that gave her very little concern. She passed whole days in fondling Djali, in watching the door of the logia Gon-delaurier, in talking to herself of Phœbus, and in feeding the swallows with crumbs of bread.

For some time she had neither seen nor heard Quasimodo. The poor bell-ringer seemed to have entirely forsaken the church. One night however, unable to sleep for thinking of her handsome captain, she heard a sigh near her cell. Somewhat alarmed, she rose, and by the light of the moon she saw a shapeless mass lying outside across the door-way. It was Quasimodo asleep upon the stones.

CHAPTER V

THE KEY OF THE PORTE ROUGE

MEANWHILE, PUBLIC RUMOR had communicated to the archdeacon the miraculous manner in which the Egyptian had been saved. When apprised of this, he knew not how he felt. He had made up his mind to the death of La Esmeralda, and was therefore easy on that point; he had drained the cup of misery to the dregs. The human heart—Dom Claude had deeply meditated on these matters—can not contain more than a certain quantity of despair. When a sponge is thoroughly soaked, the sea may pass over it without introducing into it one additional drop.

Now the sponge being filled by the death of La Esmeralda, Dom Claude could not experience keener suffering in this world. But to know that she was living, and Phœbus, too, was to be exposed anew to the vicissitudes, the shocks, the torments of life; and Claude was weary of them all.

On hearing these tidings he shut himself up in his cell in the cloisters. He attended neither the conferences of the chapter nor the usual offices. He closed his door against all, not excepting the bishop, and continued to seclude himself in this manner for several weeks. It was reported that he was ill. So he really was.

What was he doing while thus shut up? Under what thoughts was the wretched archdeacon struggling? Was he engaged in a last conflict with his indomitable passion? Was he combining a final plan of death for her and perdition for himself?

His Jehan, his beloved brother, his spoiled child, came to his door, knocked, swore, entreated, mentioned his name ten times over—Claude would not open to him.

He passed whole days with his face close to the panes of his window. From that window, situated as we have said in the cloisters, he could see the cell of La Esmeralda; he perceived the girl herself with her goat, sometimes with Quasimodo. He remarked the little attentions of the scurvy hunchback, his respectful manners and his submissive demeanor toward the Egyptian. He recollected—for he had a good memory, and memory is the tormentor of the jealous—

he recollected the extraordinary look of the bell-ringer at the dancing-girl on a particular evening. He asked himself what motive could have instigated Quasimodo to rescue her. He witnessed a thousand little scenes between the Bohemian and the hunchback, the pantomime of which, beheld at a distance, and commented on by his passion, appeared to him exceedingly tender. He then vaguely felt awakening within him a jealousy such as he had no conception of, a jealousy which made him blush for shame and indignation. For the captain, it was not surprising; but for such an object as that! The idea distracted him.

His nights were terrible. Since he knew that the Egyptian was alive, the cold ideas of specter and tomb which haunted him for a whole day were dispelled, and passion regained its dominion over him. He writhed upon his bed when he reflected that the lovely brunette was so near a neighbor to him.

Every night his frenzied imagination pictured to him La Esmeralda in all those attitudes which had made the blood boil most vehemently in his veins. He saw her stretched upon the wounded captain, her eyes closed, her beautiful bosom covered with his blood, at the moment of transport, when the archdeacon had imprinted on her pale lips that kiss which had felt to the unfortunate girl, though half dead, like the touch of a burning coal. Again he saw her stripped by the rough hands of the torturers; he saw them expose her finely shaped leg and her white supple knee while they incased her delicate little foot in the screw buskin. He further saw that ivory knee alone left uncovered by the horrible apparatus. Lastly he figured to himself the forlorn damsel, the rope about her neck, with bare feet, bare shoulders, bare bosom, as he had seen her on the day of penance. These images made his blood boil and a thrill run through his whole frame.

One night, among others, they inflamed him to such a degree that, leaping out of his bed, he threw a surplice over him and quitted his cell, with his lamp in his hand, wild, and his eyes glaring like fire.

He knew where to find the key of the Porte Rouge, the communication between the cloisters and the church; and, as the reader knows, he always carried about him a key of the staircase to the towers.

CHAPTER VI

SEQUEL TO THE KEY OF THE PORTE ROUGE

ON THAT NIGHT La Esmeralda had fallen asleep in her lodge, forgetful of the past, and full of hope and pleasing thoughts. She had slept for some time, dreaming, as she was wont, of Phœbus, when she seemed to hear a kind of noise about her. Her sleep was always light and unquiet—a bird's sleep; the least thing awoke her. She opened her eyes. The night was very dark. She nevertheless saw at the window a face looking at her: there was a lamp which threw a light upon this apparition. At the moment when the figure saw that it was perceived by La Esmeralda, it blew out the lamp. The girl, however, had had time to get a glimpse of it; her eyes closed with affright. "Oh!" she cried, in a faint voice—"the priest!"

All her past miseries flashed upon her again like lightning. She fell back on her bed frozen with horror. A moment afterward, she felt something touch her which made her shudder. She raised herself furiously into a sitting posture. The priest clasped her in both his arms. She would have shrieked, but could not.

"Begone, murderer! begone, monster!" said she, in a voice faint and tremulous with rage and terror.

"Mercy! mercy!" muttered the priest, pressing his lips to her shoulders.

Seizing with both hands the hair remaining on his bald head, she strove to prevent his kisses.

"Mercy! mercy!" repeated the wretched priest. "If thou didst but know what my love for thee is!—it is fire; it is molten lead; it is a thousand daggers in my heart!" And he held her two arms with superhuman force.

"Loose me!" she cried, distractedly, "or I will spit in thy face!"

He loosed his hold. "Strike me; heap indignities upon me; do what thou wilt; but, for mercy's sake, love me!"

She then struck him with childish rage. "Begone, demon!" said she, while her taper fingers bent in order to scratch his face.

"Love me! for pity love me!" cried the wretched priest, grappling her, and returning her blows with kisses.

She soon found that he was too strong for her. "'Tis time to put an end to this!" said he, gnashing his teeth.

Palpitating, exhausted, vanquished, she made a last effort, and began to cry, "Help! help!—a vampire! a vampire!"

No one came. Djali alone was awakened, and bleated with affright.

"Be silent," said the panting priest.

All at once, having fallen on the floor in the struggle, the hand of the Egyptian touched something cold, that felt like metal. It was Quasimodo's whistle. She seized it with a convulsion of hope, lifted it to her lips, and whistled with all the force she had left. The whistle gave out a clear, shrill, piercing sound.

"What is that?" inquired the priest.

Almost at the same moment he felt himself grasped by a vigorous arm. The cell was dark; he could not discern who held him thus; but he heard teeth gnashing with rage, and there was just sufficient light scattered amid the darkness to enable him to see the broad blade of a cutlass glistening above his head.

The priest imagined that he perceived the figure of Quasimodo. He supposed that it could be no other. He recollected having stumbled on entering against a bundle of something lying across the doorway outside. Still, as the new-comer uttered not a word, he knew not what to believe. He caught the arm which held the cutlass, crying, "Quasimodo!"—forgetful, in this moment of distress, that Quasimodo was deaf.

In the twinkling of an eye the priest was stretched upon the floor, and felt a leaden knee pressing upon his breast. From the angular pressure of that knee he recognized Quasimodo; but what could he do? how was he to make himself known to the assailant? night rendered the deaf monster blind. He gave himself up for lost. The girl, with as little pity as an enraged tigress, interposed not to save him. The cutlass was descending upon his head. The moment was critical. All at once his adversary appeared to hesitate. "No," said a muttering voice—"no blood upon her!" It was actually the voice of Quasimodo.

The priest then felt a huge hand dragging him by the leg out of the cell; it was there that he was to die. Luckily for him, the moon had just burst forth. When they were past the door, her pale beams fell upon the head of the priest. Quasimodo looked at his face, was seized with a trembling, relaxed his grasp, and started back.

The Egyptian, who had advanced to the threshold of the cell, saw with surprise the actors suddenly exchanging characters. It was now the priest's turn to threaten, Quasimodo's to supplicate. The priest, having furiously assailed the hunchback with gestures of anger and reproach, at length motioned him to retire. Quasimodo stood for a moment with bowed head, and then, falling on his knees before the door of the Egyptian, "Monseigneur," said he, in a tone of gravity and resignation, "kill me first, and do what you please afterward."

As he thus spoke he offered his cutlass to the priest. Beside himself with rage, the priest clutched at the weapon; but La Esmeralda was too quick for him. Snatching the cutlass from the hand of Quasimodo and bursting into an hysteric laugh, "Come on!" said she to the priest.

She held the blade uplifted. The priest wavered. She would certainly have struck. "Thou darest not approach now, coward!" she cried. Then, with unpitying look, and well aware that she should pierce the heart of the priest as with a thousand red-hot irons, she added, "Ah! I know that Phœbus is not dead!"

The priest with a violent kick overthrew Quasimodo, and rushed, quivering with rage, to the vaulted staircase. When he was gone, Quasimodo picked up the whistle which had been the means of saving the Egyptian. "It was getting rusty," said he handing it to her. He then left her to herself.

The damsel, vehemently agitated by this violent scene, sunk exhausted upon her bed and sobbed aloud. Her horizon had again become overcast.

The priest, on his part, groped his way back to his cell. The thing was conclusive: Dom Claude was jealous of Quasimodo! With pensive look he repeated the fatal phrase, "Nobody shall have her!"

Book Nine

CHAPTER I

GRINGOIRE HAS SEVERAL CAPITAL IDEAS, ONE AFTER ANOTHER, IN THE RUE DES BERNARDINS

AS SOON AS Gringoire perceived the turn which this whole affair was taking, and that decidedly halter, gibbet, and other unpleasant things would be the lot of the principal characters of this comedy, he felt no sort of inclination to interfere in it. The Vagabonds, with whom he had remained, considering that after all they were the best company in Paris, had continued to interest themselves for the Egyptian. This he thought perfectly natural in people who, like her, had no other prospect than Charmolue and Torterue, and who never soared like him into the regions of imagination between the two wings of Pegasus. From them he learned that she whom he had espoused over the broken jug had taken sanctuary in Notre Dame, and he was very glad of it. He thought sometimes of the little goat, and that was all. In the day-time he performed mountebank tricks for a livelihood, and at night he elucubrated a memorial against the Bishop of Paris, for he remembered the drenching he had got from his mills, and bore him a grudge for it. He was also engaged in a commentary upon the admired work of Baudry le Rouge, Bishop of Noyon and Tournay, "De Cupa Petrarum," which had awakened in him a violent passion for architecture—a passion which had superseded in his heart the passion for hermetics; the one indeed was but a natural corollary to the other, since there is an intimate connection between hermetics and masonry. Gringoire had passed from the love of an idea to the love of the form of an idea.

One day he had stopped near St. Germain l'Auxerrois, at the corner of a building called the Fort l'Eveque, which faced another named the Fort le Roi. At this Fort l'Eveque there was a beautiful chapel of the fourteenth century, the choir of which looked toward the street. Gringoire was intently examining the sculptures on the outside. It was one of those moments of absorbing, exclusive, supreme enjoyment when the artist sees nothing in the world but his art, and sees the world in his art. All at once he felt a hand fall heavily upon his shoulder. He turned about. It was his old friend, his old master, the archdeacon.

He was stupefied. It was a long time since he had seen the archdeacon, and Dom Claude was one of those solemn and impassioned personages, the meeting with whom always deranges the equilibrium of the skeptical philosopher.

The archdeacon kept silence for a few moments, during which Gringoire had leisure to observe him. He found Dom Claude greatly altered—pale as a winter morning, his eyes sunk, his hair almost white. The priest at length broke this silence, saying, but in a grave, freezing tone: "How goes it with you, Master Pierre?"

"As to my health?" said Gringoire, "why, I may say, so-so. Upon the whole good. I take everything in moderation. You know, master, the secret of health recommended by Hippocrates—*cidi, potus, somni, omnia moderata sint.*" [1]

"Then you have no troubles, Master Pierre?" rejoined the archdeacon, looking steadfastly at Gringoire.

"No, i' faith, not I."

"And what are you doing now?"

"You see, master, I am examining the cut of these stones, and the way in which that basso-relievo is chiseled."

The priest smiled. It was one of those bitter smiles which lift up but one of the corners of the mouth. "And that amuses you?"

" 'Tis paradise!" exclaimed Gringoire. And turning to the sculptures, with the dazzled look of a demonstrator of living phenomena: "Don't you think," said he, "that this metamorphosis in low relief, for example, is executed with great skill, patience, and delicacy? Look at this little pillar. About what capital did you ever see foliage more elegant and highly finished? Look at those three medallions by Jean Maillevin. They are not first-rate works of that great genius; nevertheless, the truth to nature, and the sweetness of the faces, the gayety of the attitudes and draperies, and that inexplicable charm which is blended with all the defects, render the miniature figures exceedingly lively and exceedingly delicate—perhaps too much so. Do you not think that this is amusing?"

"Yes, I do," said the priest.

"And if you were to see the interior of the chapel!" resumed the poet, with his garrulous enthusiasm; "sculptures all over; tufted like a cauliflower. The choir is in a right goodly style, and so peculiar that I never saw anything like it."

Dom Claude interrupted him. "You are happy, then?"

"Yes, upon my honor," replied Gringoire, with warmth. "At first

1. "In food, drink, sleep, love, let there be moderation."

I was fond of women, then of beasts, now of stones. They are quite as amusing as women and beasts, and much less treacherous."

The priest raised his hand to his brow. It was his habitual gesture. "Indeed!"

"Stay," said Gringoire; "you shall see that a man need not want pleasure." He took the arm of the priest, who made no resistance, and drew him into the staircase turret of the Fort l'Eveque. "There is a staircase for you! whenever I look at it I am happy. It is the simplest of its kind, and yet the most exquisite in Paris. Every step is rounded off underneath. Its beauty and simplicity consist in the overlapping parts, which for a foot or thereabout are let in, mortised, imbedded, enchained, enchased, dove-tailed one into another, and bite in such a way as to be not less solid than goodly."

"And you wish for nothing?"

"No."

"And regret nothing?"

"Neither wishes nor regrets. I have arranged my life."

"Man arranges," said Claude; "circumstances derange."

"I am a Pyrrhonian philosopher," replied Gringoire, "and I keep everything in equilibrium."

"And how do you earn a livelihood?"

"I still make epics and tragedies now and then; but what brings in most money is the trade you have seen me follow—carrying pyramids of chairs and so forth between my teeth."

"A scurvy trade for a philosopher."

"It has to do with the equilibrium," said Gringoire. "When you take an idea into your head, you find it in everything."

"I know it," replied the archdeacon.

After a pause the priest resumed:

"You are nevertheless as poor as ever?"

"Poor enough, I grant you, but not unhappy."

At this moment the dialogue was interrupted by the trampling of horses, and a company of archers of the king's ordnance, with raised lances, and an officer at their head, passed the end of the street. The cavalcade was brilliant, and the pavement rang beneath their tread.

"How you eye that officer!" said Gringoire to the archdeacon.

"I rather think I know him."

"What is his name?"

"I believe," said Claude, "his name is Phœbus de Chateaupers."

"Phœbus; a curious name! There is also a Phœbus Comte de Foix. I once knew a girl who never swore but by Phœbus."

"Come this way!" said the priest; "I have something to say to you."

Ever since the appearance of the archers, some agitation was perceptible under the frozen exterior of the archdeacon. He walked on, followed by Gringoire, who was wont to obey him, like all who had ever approached him, such was the ascendency which he exercised. They proceeded in silence to the Rue des Bernardins, where a casual passenger only was at times to be seen. Here Dom Claude stopped short.

"What have you to say to me, master?" inquired Gringoire.

"Don't you think," said the archdeacon, with a look of deep reflection, "that the dress of those archers who have just passed is finer than yours or mine?"

Gringoire shook his head.

"By my fay! I like my red and yellow jacket better than those shells of iron and steel. A sorry pleasure, to make at every step the same noise that the Ironmongers' Quay would do in an earthquake!"

"Then, Gringoire, you have never envied those comely fellows in their habiliments of war?"

"Envied them!—for what, Mr. Archdeacon?—for their strength, their armor, their discipline? Far preferable are philosophy and independence in rags. I had rather be the head of a fly than the tail of a lion."

"That is singular," said the priest, thoughtfully. "A goodly uniform is nevertheless goodly."

Gringoire, seeing him absorbed in thought, left him, and went up to the porch of a neighboring house.

Presently he returned, clapping his hands.

"If you were not so deeply engaged with the goodly uniforms of the men at arms, Mr. Archdeacon, I would beg you to go and look at that door. I always said that the entrance to the Sieur Aubrey's house is not to be matched all the world over."

"Pierre Gringoire," said the archdeacon, "what have you done with the young Egyptian dancing-girl?"

"La Esmeralda? Why, how abruptly you change the conversation!"

"Was she not your wife?"

"Yes, after a fashion; by means of a broken jug we were joined together for four years. By the bye," added Gringoire, with a half-bantering tone and look, "you seem to be always thinking of her."

"And do you never think of her now?"

"Very little. I am so busy! . . . But what a charming little goat that was!"

"Did not that Bohemian save your life?"

"True enough, by'r Lady!"

"Well, what is become of her? What have you done with her?"

"I can't tell. I believe they hanged her!"

"You believe?"

"I am not sure. When I saw that they were determined to hang somebody, I got out of the way."

"Is that all you know about the matter?"

"Stop a moment! I was told that she had taken sanctuary in Notre Dame, and that she was safe there, which I was very glad to hear; but I have not been able to ascertain whether her goat was saved along with her—and that is all I know about the matter."

"I can tell you more, then," cried Dom Claude, his voice, hitherto low almost to a whisper, rising to the loudness of thunder. "She has actually taken sanctuary in Notre Dame. But in three days justice will again seize her, and she will be hanged in the Grève. The parliament has issued a decree."

"That is a pity!" said Gringoire.

In the twinkling of an eye the priest had relapsed into his former coldness and tranquillity.

"And," resumed the poet, "who the devil has amused himself with soliciting an order of restitution? Why could they not let the parliament alone? What harm is there in it if a poor girl does seek shelter among the swallows' nests under the flying buttresses of Notre Dame?"

"There are satans in the world," rejoined the archdeacon.

"'Tis infernally cross-grained!" observed Gringoire.

"Then she did save your life?" resumed the archdeacon, after a pause.

"That was among my very good friends, the Vagabonds. She came in the nick of time, or I should have been hanged. They would have been sorry for it now."

"Will you then not try to do something for her?"

"I desire no better, Dom Claude; but perhaps I may get my own neck into an ugly noose!"

"What signifies that?"

"What signifies it! You are exceedingly kind, master! I have just begun two great works."

The priest struck his forehead. Notwithstanding the composure which he affected, a violent gesture from time to time betrayed his inward convulsions. "What can be done to save her?"

"Master," said Gringoire, "I answer, *Il padelt*, which is Turkish for God is our hope."

"What can be done to save her?" repeated Claude, thoughtfully.

Gringoire, in his turn, struck his brow. "Hark ye, master: I have no lack of imagination; I will devise expedients. Suppose we solicit the king's pardon."

"Pardon! of Louis XI.!"

"Why not?"

"Take the bone from the hungry tiger!"

Gringoire cast about for other expedients.

"Well, stop! Shall we make declaration that the girl is pregnant, and demand an examination of matrons?"

The pupils of the priest's hollow eyes sparkled. "Pregnant, dolt! Knowest thou aught to that purpose?"

His look alarmed Gringoire. "Oh, no, not I!" he hastily replied. "Our marriage was literally *foris-maritagium*—for I was shut out. At any rate, we should obtain a respite."

"Stupid oaf! hold thy tongue!"

"Nay, don't be angry," muttered Gringoire. "One might obtain a respite; that would harm nobody, and would put forty deniers parisis into the pockets of the matrons, who áre poor women."

The priest heard him not. "At any rate," he muttered, "she must away! The order must be executed in three days! Besides, if there were no order, that Quasimodo! Who can account for the depraved tastes of women!" Then, raising his voice: "Master Pierre," said he, "I have well weighed the matter; there is but one way to save her."

"And which? I can see none for my part."

"Hark ye, Master Pierre; recollect that to her you owe your life. I will tell you frankly my idea. The church is watched night and day; only such persons as have been seen to enter are suffered to go out again. Of course you would be allowed to go in. You must come; I will take you to her. You must change clothes with her."

"So far, so good," observed the philosopher. "And then?"

"Why, then she will go away in your clothes, and you will remain in hers. You will be hanged perhaps, but she will escape."

Gringoire rubbed his brow with a profoundly serious look.

"I declare," said he, "that is an idea which would never have come into my head of itself."

At this unlooked-for proposition of Dom Claude's, the open and good-humored countenance of the poet was overcast, like a smiling landscape of Italy when some unlucky blast dashes a cloud upon the sun. "Well, Gringoire, what do you say to this expedient?"

"I say, master, they will not hang me perhaps, but they will hang me to a certainty."

"That does not concern us."

"The deuce!" exclaimed Gringoire.

"She saved your life. You are only paying a debt."

"How many of my debts besides that are unpaid!"

"Master Pierre, you absolutely must comply."

The archdeacon spoke imperatively.

"Hark ye, Dom Claude," replied the dismayed poet, "you cling to this idea; but you are quite wrong. I see no reason why I should thrust my head into the halter instead of another."

"What is there, then, that so strongly attaches you to life?"

"Why, a thousand things."

"What are they? I would ask."

"What are they? The fresh air, the blue sky, morning and evening, the warm sunshine and the moonlight, my good friends the Vagabonds, our romps with the good-natured damsels, the beautiful architectural works of Paris to study, three thick books to write—one of them against the bishop and his mills—and I know not what besides. Anaxagoras said that he was in the world to admire the sun. And then I have the felicity to pass all my days from morn to even-tide with a man of genius, to wit myself, which is exceedingly agreeable."

"A head fit for a bell!" muttered the archdeacon. "Well, but tell me, who saved this life which is so charming to thee? To whom is it owing that thou yet breathest this air, beholdest that sky, and canst amuse thy lark's spirit with extravagances and follies? What wouldst thou be but for her? And yet thou canst suffer her to die —her, to whom thou owest thy life—her, that beautiful, lovely, adorable creature, almost as necessary to the light of the world as the sun himself; while thou, half sage, half madman, rough sketch of something or other, a species of vegetable, who imaginest thou canst walk and think, thou wilt continue to live with the life of which thou hast robbed her, as useless as a candle at noonday! Nay, nay, have some feeling, Gringoire: be generous in thy turn. It was she who set the example."

The priest was warm. Gringoire listened to him at first with a look of indecision; presently he began to soften, and at last he put on a tragic grimace, which made his wan face look like that of a newborn infant which has the colic.

"You are pathetic," said he, brushing away a tear. "Well, I will think of it. 'Tis a droll idea, this of yours!" Pausing awhile, he continued: "After all, who knows! perhaps they will not hang me. Betrothal is not always followed by marriage. When they find me up yonder in the little cell, so grotesquely attired in cap and petticoat, perhaps they will only laugh. And then, if they do hang me, why, death by the halter is like any other death, or, more correctly speaking, is not like any other death. It is a death worthy of the sage who has oscillated all his life; a death which is neither fish nor flesh, like the soul of the downright skeptic; a death impressed all over with Pyrrohonism and hesitation, which holds the middle place between heaven and earth, which leaves one in suspense. It is a philosophic death, and perhaps I was predestined to it. 'Tis magnificent to die as one has lived."

The priest interrupted him. "Are we agreed?"

"After all, what is death?" continued Gringoire, in the warmth of his excitement. "An unpleasant moment, a toll, a passage from little to nothing. When some one asked Cercidas of Megalopolis if he should like to die—'Why not?' he replied; 'for, after death, I shall see those great men, Pythagoras among the philosophers, Hecatæus among the historians, Homer among the poets, and Olympus among the musicians.'"

The archdeacon held out his hand. "It is settled then; you will come to-morrow?"

This gesture, and the question which accompanied it brought Gringoire back from his digression. "Beshrew me, no!" said he, in the tone of a man awakening from sleep. "Be hanged!—too absurd! —I beg to be excused."

"Farewell, then!" and the archdeacon added, muttering between his teeth, "I will find thee out again!"

"I don't wish that fellow to find me again," thought Gringoire, running after Dom Claude. "Hold, Mr. Archdeacon: no malice between old friends! You take an interest in that girl, my wife, I would say—quite right! You have devised a stratagem to withdraw her in safety from Notre Dame, but to me your expedient is extremely disagreeable. A capital idea has just occurred to me. If I could propose a method of extricating her from the dilemma without entangling my own neck in the smallest running noose whatever, what would you say to it? would that satisfy you? or must I absolutely be hanged before you are content?"

The priest tore off the buttons of his cassock with irritation. "Eternal blabber! what is thy proposal?"

"Yes," resumed Gringoire, talking to himself, and clapping his forefinger to his nose in the attitude of meditation—"that's it! She is a favorite with the dark race. They will rise at the first word. Nothing easier. A sudden attack. In confusion, carry her away! To-morrow night . . . they will desire nothing better."

"Your proposal! Let us hear!" said the priest, shaking him.

Gringoire turned majestically toward him. "Leave me alone! you see I am composing." Having considered for a few moments longer, he clapped his hands in exultation, exclaiming, "Admirable! sure to succeed!"

"But the means?" inquired Claude, angrily. Gringoire's face beamed with triumph.

"Come hither, then, and lend me your ear. 'Tis a right bold counter-mine, which will get all of us out of our trouble. By Heaven! it must be confessed that I am no fool." He stopped short. "By the bye, is the little goat with the girl?"

"Yes!"

"They meant to have hanged her too, did they not?"

"What is that to me?"

"Yes, they meant to hang her. Why, it was only last month that they hanged a sow. The hangman likes that—he eats the meat afterward. Hang my pretty Djali! Poor, dear little lamb!"

"Malisons upon thee!" cried Dom Claude. "Thou thyself art the hangman. What means, dolt, hast thou devised for saving her? Must one tear thine idea from thee with pincers?"

"Gentle, master; I will tell you."

Gringoire bent his lips to the archdeacon's ear and whispered very softly, at the same time casting an uneasy look from one end of the street to the other, though not a creature was passing. When he had finished, Dom Claude grasped his hand, and said, coldly, "Good! to-morrow?"

"To-morrow," repeated Gringoire. The archdeacon retired one way, while he went the other, saying to himself, in an under-tone, "A rare business this, Monsieur Pierre Gringoire! No matter! It shall not be said, that because one is little, one shrinks from great undertakings. Bito carried a full-grown bull on his shoulders: the wagtail, the nightingale, the swallow, cross the ocean."

CHAPTER II

"TURN VAGABOND"

THE ARCHDEACON, on his return to the cloisters, found his brother Jehan waiting for him at the door of his cell. The youth had amused himself, while waiting, by drawing with a piece of charcoal upon the wall a profile of his elder brother, enriched with an enormous nose.

Dom Claude scarcely looked at Jehan: his thoughts were otherwise engaged. The reckless, jovial countenance of Jehan, the radiance of which had so often restored serenity to the gloomy physiognomy of the priest, was now incapable of dispelling the mist which thickened daily over his corrupt, mephitic, and stagnant soul.

"Brother," said Jehan, shyly, "I am come to see you."

"What then?" replied the archdeacon, without so much as lifting his eyes to him.

"Brother," resumed the young hypocrite, "you are so kind to me, and give me such good advice, that I can not stay away from you."

"What then?" repeated Dom Claude.

"Alas, brother! you had great reason to say to me, 'Jehan, conduct yourself discreetly. Jehan, attend to your studies. Jehan, pass not the night out of college, without legitimate occasion and the leave of the master. Beat not the Picards. Rot not, like an unlettered ass, upon the straw of the school. Jehan, submit to punishment at the discretion of the master. Jehan, go to the chapel every evening and sing an anthem, with collect and prayer, to the blessed Virgin Mary.' Ah! what excellent counsels were these!"

"What more?"

"Brother, you see before you a sinner, a grievous sinner, a wretch, a libertine, a criminal, a reprobate. My dear brother, Jehan has trodden underfoot your gracious counsels like straw and litter. Severely am I punished for it: God Almighty is rigidly just. So long as I had money I made merry, reveled in folly, and led a joyous life. How fascinating is debauchery in front, but, oh! how ugly and deformed behind! Now I have not a coin left; I have sold my linen. My joyous life is over. The bright taper is put out; and I have but a scurvy tallow candle which stinks in my nostrils. People make a mock at me. I have only water to drink. I am dunned by remorse and creditors."

"What more?" said the archdeacon.

"Alas! my dear brother, I would fain turn me to a better life. I come to you full of contrition. I am penitent. I confess my faults. I have great reason to wish that I may one day become licentiate and sub-monitor of the College of Torchi. At this moment I feel an irresistible vocation to that office. But I have no ink, I have no pens, I have no paper, I have no books. I must buy more. To this end I am in great need of a little money, and I am come to you, brother, with a heart full of contrition."

"Is that all?"

"Yes," said the scholar. "A little money."

"I have none."

"Well, then, brother," replied Jehan, with a grave and at the same time a determined look, "I am sorry to have to inform you that very fair offers have been made to me from another quarter. You will not give me some money?"

"No."

"Then I will turn Vagabond." In uttering this monstrous resolution, he assumed the look of Ajax expecting the thunder-bolt to descend upon his head.

"Turn Vagabond," coldly replied the archdeacon.

Jehan made a low obeisance, and skipped whistling down the cloister stairs.

At the moment when he was passing through the court of the cloisters, beneath the window of his brother's cell, he heard it open, and, looking up, saw the stern face of the archdeacon protruded through the aperture. "Get thee gone!" said Dom Claude; "that is the last money thou shalt have from me."

At the same time the priest threw at Jehan a purse which made a great bump on the scholar's forehead, and with which Jehan went his way, at once growling and pleased, like a dog that is pelted with marrow-bones.

CHAPTER III

IL ALLEGRO

THE READER has not perhaps forgotten that part of the Cour des Miracles was inclosed by the ancient wall surrounding the Ville, many of the towers of which had begun so early as this period to fall to ruin. One of these towers had been converted into a place of entertainment by the Vagabonds. At the bottom was a tavern, and the upper floors were appropriated to other purposes. This tower was the busiest and consequently the most disgusting part of this resort of the crew. It was a kind of monstrous hive, where an incessant buzz was kept up night and day. At night, when all the rest of the colony was buried in sleep, when not a single light was to be seen in the windows of the crazy buildings encompassing the place, when no sound was to be heard issuing from the innumerable dens swarming with thieves and dissolute persons of both sexes, the jovial tower might always be known by the noise that was made there, by the crimson light which, gleaming at once from the chimneys, the windows, and the crevices in the cracked walls, issued, as it were, from every pore.

The cellar, therefore, was the tavern. The descent to it was by a low door and stairs as rugged as a classic Alexandrine. Over the door there was by way of sign a wondrous daubing representing a number of new sous and dead chickens (*des sous neufs et des poulets tues*) with this pun underneath: *Aux sonneurs pour les trepasses.*[1]

One evening, at the moment when the curfew bell was ringing in every belfry in Paris, the sergeants of the watch, had they chanced to enter the redoubtable Cour des Miracles, might have remarked that there was a greater tumult than usual in the tavern of the Vagabonds, and that the inmates were both drinking and swearing more lustily. In the open space without were numerous groups conversing in a subdued tone, as when some important enterprise is planning; and here and there a varlet was crouching and whetting some rusty weapon or other upon a paving-stone.

In the tavern itself, however, wine and gaming were so powerful a diversion to the ideas which on that evening engrossed the vaga-

1. "To the bell–ringers for the dead."

bond crew, that it would have been difficult to discover from the conversation of the topers the nature of their project. They merely appeared to be in higher spirits than ordinary, and between the legs of each was seen glistening some weapon or other—a billhook, a hatchet, a thick bludgeon, or the supporter of an old arquebuse.

The room, of circular form, was very spacious; but the tables were so close and the customers so numerous that all the contents of the tavern, men and women, benches and beer-jugs, those who were drinking, those who were sleeping, those who were gaming, the able-bodied and the cripple, seemed to be tumbled together pell-mell, with just as much order and harmony as a heap of oyster-shells. A few tallow candles were burning on the tables, but the real luminary of the tavern, that which performed the part of the chandelier at the opera-house, was the fire. This cellar was so damp that the fire was never suffered to go out, even in summer. It was an immense fire-place, with carved mantel, bristling with clumsy andirons and other culinary apparatus, containing one of those large fires of wood and turf mixed, which at night in the village streets produce, by their glare on the opposite walls, the appearance of the windows of a smithy. A large dog, squatted in the ashes, was turning a spit laden with viands before the fire.

Notwithstanding the confusion, after the first glance there might be distinguished in this multitude three principal groups crowding around three personages with whom the reader is already acquainted. One of these personages, grotesquely bedizened with many a piece of eastern frippery, was Matthias Hunyadi Spicali, Duke of Egypt and Bohemia. The varlet was seated on a table, his legs crossed, his finger uplifted, imparting in a loud voice sundry lessons in black and white magic to many a gaping face around him. Another party had drawn closely about our old friend, the valiant King of Thunes, who was armed to the very teeth. Clopin Trouille-fou, with grave look and in a low voice, was superintending the pillage of a hogshead full of arms, which stood with head knocked out before him, and from which stores of hatchets, swords, coats of mail, hunting-knives, spear-heads, saws, augers, were disgorged like apples and grapes from a cornucopia. Each took from the heap what he pleased—one a helmet, another a long rapier, a third a cross or basket-hilted dagger. The very children armed themselves, and there were even little urchins cuirassed and accoutered, running between the legs of the topers like large beetles.

Lastly, a third party, the most noisy, the most jovial, and the most numerous, occupied the benches and tables amid which a treble voice was swearing and holding forth from beneath a heavy suit of armor complete from head to heel. The individual who had thus incased himself was so impanoplied by his martial accoutrements, that no part of his person could be seen, save a saucy, red, snub nose, a lock of light hair, rosy lips and daring eyes. He had his belt stuck full of daggers, a long sword at his thigh, a rusty arbalest on his left, and a large jug of wine before him, from which ever and anon he took a copious draught. Every mouth around him was laughing, cursing, drinking.

Add to these twenty secondary groups, the attendants, male and female, running about with plates and jugs, the gamesters lolling over the billiards, the merils, the dice, and the impassioned game of the tringlet; the quarrels in one corner, the kisses in another; and you will have some idea of the whole, over which flickered the glare of a huge blazing fire, which made a thousand broad, grotesque shadows dance on the walls of the tavern.

As for the noise, it was like that within a bell in a grand peal.

Amid all this din, upon the bench in the chimney-corner, was seated a philosopher absorbed in meditation, his feet in the ashes, and his eye fixed on the burning brands. It was Pierre Gringoire.

"Come, make haste, arm yourselves! We shall start in an hour!" said Clopin Trouillefou to his crew.

Two card-players were quarreling. "Knave," cried the more rubicund of the two, holding up his fist at the other, "I will mark thee with the club. Thou shalt be qualified to succeed Mistigri in the card-parties of Monseigneur the King."

"Oaf," roared a Norman who might easily be known by his nasal twang, "we are crammed together here like the saints of Callouville!"

"My sons," said the Duke of Egypt to his auditors, in his falsetto, "the witches of France go to the sabbath without broom or aught else to ride on, merely with a few magical words: those of Italy always have a goat at the door awaiting for them. They are all obliged to go out of the house through the chimney."

The voice of the young warrior in armors was heard above the uproar. "Huzza! Huzza!" cried he; "my first feat of arms to-day! A Vagabond! Zounds! what am I but a Vagabond! Pour me out some drink! My friends, my name is Jehan Frollo du Moulin, and I am a gentleman. I could lay any wager that if Jupiter were a gendarme, he would be fond of plunder. We are going, brothers, on a rare expedition. We are valiant fellows. Lay siege to the church, break open the doors, carry off the damsel, rescue her from the judges, save her from the priests, dismantle the cloisters, burn the bishop in his palace—why, we shall do it in less time than a burgomaster takes to eat a basin of soup. Our cause is a righteous one; we'll plunder Notre Dame; that's flat. We'll hang Quasimodo. Do you know Quasimodo, fair gentlewomen? Have ye seen him puffing upon the great bell on Whit-Sunday? By Beelzebub's horns, that is grand! you would take him for a devil astride of a ghoul. I say, my friends, I am a Vagabond to my heart's core, a Canter in my soul, a cadger born. I have been well off, and have run through my fortune. My father wanted to make me an officer, my mother sub-dean, my aunt a counselor of inquisition, my grandmother prothonotary to the king, my grandaunt keeper of the short robe: while I—I have chosen to be a Vagabond. I told my father so; he flung his malison in my face; and my mother, who—poor old lady—began to cry and sputter like that steak on the fire. A merry life though a short one, say I! Taverniere, my darling, let us change our wine; I have some money left yet. I don't like the Surene; it cuts my throat. Corbœuf! I'd almost as lief swallow knives."

Meanwhile, the rabble applauded with bursts of laughter; and as the tumult swelled around him, the scholar shouted, "How delightful!—*populi debacchantis populosa debacchatio!*"[1] His eyes swimming in ecstasy, he then fell a-chanting, in the tone of a canon at vespers; but, suddenly stopping short, he cried, "Here, you devil's taverner, give me some supper!"

Then followed a moment of comparative quiet, during which the Duke of Egypt raised his shrill voice while instructing his Bohemians. "The weasel is called Aduine; the fox, Bluefoot; the wolf, Grayfoot, or Goldfoot; the bear, the old man, or the grandfather. The cap of a gnome renders you invisible, and enables you to see invisible things. Every toad that is baptized ought to be dressed in red or black velvet, with a bell about its neck and a bell at each foot. The godfather must take hold of the head; the godmother, of the feet."

Meanwhile the crew continued to arm themselves at the other end of the tavern, amid such whispers as these:

"Poor Esmeralda!" said a Bohemian. "She is our sister. We must release her."

"Is she still in Notre Dame?" asked a Jew-looking peddler.

"Ay, by the mass!"

"Well, then comrades!" cried the peddler, "to Notre Dame! the sooner the better! In the chapel of St. Fereol and St. Ferrutien there are two statues, one of St. John Baptist, the other of St. Anthony, both of gold, weighing together seventeen marks fifteen esterlings,

1. "The ravings of the people, popular fury."

and the pedestals of silver gilt seventeen marks five ounces. I know this to a certainty—I am by trade a goldsmith."

By this time Jehan's supper was set before him. Falling to with an excellent appetite, he exclaimed, "By St. Voult de Lucques!—the people call him St. Goguelu—I am the happiest fellow in Paris, though I have renounced the half of a house situate, lying, and being in paradise, promised me by my brother the archdeacon. Look at that simpleton, gazing at me with the smooth look of an archduke. There is another on my left with tusks so long that they hide his chin. Body o'Mahound! comrade, thou hast the very air and odor of a bone-dealer, and yet hast the assurance to clap thyself down so near me! I am noble, my friend. Trade is incompatible with nobility. Go thy ways! Soho! you there! what are ye fighting for? What, Baptiste Croque Oison, art not afraid to risk thy goodly nose against the clumsy fists of that booby? Knowest thou not, simpleton, *non cuiquam datum est habere nasum?*[1] Thou wouldst be absolutely divine, Jacqueline Rouge Orelle, if thou couldst add a few inches to thine. Girls, keep those mischievous brats quiet, and snuff the candles. By Mahound! what have I got here? Goodly hostelry of Beelzebub!"

So saying, he dashed his plate on the pavement, and began singing with all his might one of the peculiar songs of the lawless crew of whom he had become a worthy associate.

Clopin Trouillefou had meanwhile finished his distribution of arms. He went up to Gringoire, who, with his feet on the andiron, appeared to be in a brown study. "Friend Pierre," said the King of Thunes, "what the devil art thou thinking of?"

Gringoire turned toward him with a melancholy smile. "I am fond of the fire, my dear sir," said he; "not for the trivial reason that it warms our feet or cooks our soup, but because there are sparks in it. Sometimes I pass whole hours watching those sparks. I discover a thousand things in those stars which sprinkle the black chimneyback. Those stars are worlds too."

"Thunder and death, if I understand thee!" cried the King of Thunes. "Dost know what hour it is?"

"Not I," answered Gringoire.

Clopin then went to the Duke of Egypt. "Comrade Matthias," said he, "it lacks not quite one quarter of an hour. I am told the king is in Paris."

"One reason more why we should get our sister out of their clutches," replied the old Bohemian.

"Thou speakest like a man, Matthias," rejoined Trouillefou. "Be-

1. It is not given to everyone to have a nose.

sides, we shall get on swimmingly. No resistance to fear in the church. The canons are mere hares, and we are strong. The officers of the parliament will be finely taken in to-morrow when they go to look for her. By the pope's nose! they shall not hang the comely damsel."

With these words Clopin sallied forth from the tavern.

Gringoire, roused from his meditations, had begun to contemplate the wild and noisy scene around him, muttering between his teeth, "*Luxuriosa res vinum et tumultuosa ebrietas.*' What good reason have I to abstain from liquor! and admirably St. Benedict observes, '*Vinum apostatare facit etiam sapientes.*'" [2]

At that moment Clopin returned, and shouted with a voice of thunder, "Midnight!"

At this signal, which had the effect of the sound To horse! upon a regiment in halt, all the vagabond crew, men, women and children, poured in a torrent out of the tavern, with a loud noise of arms and the clanking of iron implements.

The moon was overcast. The Cour des Miracles was quite dark. Not a light was to be seen. It was nevertheless filled with a multitude of both sexes, who talked in low tones together. A vast buzz was to be heard, and all sorts of weapons were seen glistening in the dark. Clopin mounted a huge stone. "To your ranks, ye men of Cant!" he cried. "To your ranks, Egypt! To your ranks, Galilee!" A bustle ensued amid the darkness. The immense multitude appeared to be forming in column. In a few minutes the King of Thunes again raised his voice: "Now, silence in passing through the streets! No torch is to be lighted till we are at Notre Dame. March!"

In less than ten minutes the horsemen of the watch fled panic-stricken before a long black procession descending in profound silence toward the Pont au Change, along the winding streets which run in all directions through the massive quarter of the Halles.

CHAPTER IV

A MISCHIEVOUS FRIEND

THAT SAME NIGHT Quasimodo slept not. He had just gone his last round in the church. He had not remarked that, at the moment

1. " Wine is a thing of luxury, drunkness of tumult."
2. "To abjure wine also makes wise men."

when he was fastening the doors, the archdeacon had passed, or the ill-humor he had shown on seeing him employed in carefully bolting and padlocking the immense iron bars, which gave to the large folding doors the solidity of a wall. Dom Claude appeared that night to be more deeply absorbed in thought than usual. Ever since the nocturnal adventure in the cell, he had treated Quasimodo with great harshness, but, in spite of this usage, nay, even though he sometimes went so far as to strike him, nothing could shake the submission, the patience, the devoted resignation, of the faithful bell-ringer. From the archdeacon he would take anything, abuse, threats, blows, without murmuring a reproach, without uttering a complaint. The utmost that he did was to watch the archdeacon with anxiety when he ascended the staircase of the tower; but Claude had of himself cautiously abstained from appearing again in the presence of the Egyptian.

That night, then, Quasimodo, after taking a glance at his bells, at Mary, at Jacqueline, at Thibault, whom he had lately so miserably neglected, went up to the top of the northern tower, and there, placing his well-closed dark-lantern on the leads, he began to take a survey of Paris.

The night, as we have already said, was very dark. Paris, which, at this period, was scarcely lighted at all, presented to the eye a confused aggregate of black masses, intersected here and there by the whitish curve of the Seine. Quasimodo could discern no light but in the window of a distant building, the vague and somber outline of which was visible above the roofs in the direction of the Gate of St. Antoine. There too was some one who watched.

While his eye ranged over this expanse of haze and darkness, an unaccountable feeling of apprehension and uneasiness gained upon him. For several days past he had been upon his guard. He had observed suspicious-looking men prowling incessantly about the church, and keeping their eyes fixed on the young girl's asylum. He imagined that some plot against the unfortunate refugee might be on foot, and that the hatred of the people might be directed against her as it was against himself. So he stood on the watch, upon his tower, *revant dans son revoir,*[1] as Rabelais expresses it, gazing by turns at the cell and at the city, making sure guard, like a good dog, with a heart full of distrust.

All at once, while he was scrutinizing the great city with the eye which Nature, by way of compensation, had made so piercing that it almost supplied the deficiency of the other organs, it seemed to him that the outline of the quay of La Vielle Pelleterie had an ex-

1. Dreaming in his dream–place.

traordinary appearance; that there was a motion at that point; that the black line of the parapet, defined upon the white surface of the water, was not straight and steady like that of the other quays, but that it undulated to the eye, like the waves of a river, or like the heads of a moving multitude. This struck him as strange. He redoubled his attention. The movement appeared to be toward the city. It lasted some time on the quay, then subsided by degrees, as if that which caused it were entering the interior of the isle; it afterward ceased entirely, and the outline of the quay again became straight and motionless.

While Quasimodo was forming all sorts of conjectures, the movement seemed to reappear in the Rue du Parvis, which runs into the city, perpendicularly to the façade of Notre Dame. At last, notwithstanding the intense darkness, he perceived the head of a column approaching through this street, and the next moment a crowd spread itself over the Place du Parvis, where nothing could be distinguished but that it was a crowd.

The sight was alarming. It is probable that this singular procession, which seemed to make a point of avoiding observation, was equally careful to maintain profound silence; yet it could not help making some noise, were it only by the trampling of the feet. But even this sound reached not the ear of Quasimodo; and this vast multitude, of which he could scarcely see anything, and of which he heard absolutely nothing, though all was bustle and motion so near to him, must have had the effect of an army of the dead, mute, impalpable, and shrouded in vapor. It appeared to him as if a mist full of human beings was approaching, and that what he saw moving were shadows of the shades.

Then were his apprehensions revived, and the idea of an attempt against the gypsy girl again occurred to his mind. He had a confused foreboding of mischief. At this critical moment he began to consider what course he had best pursue, and with more judgment and decision than might have been expected from a brain so imperfectly organized. Ought he to wake the Egyptian? to assist her to escape? How? which way? the streets were invested; the church was backed by the river. There was no boat, no outlet. He had, therefore, but one course—to die on the threshold of Notre Dame; at any rate to make all the resistance in his power until succor should arrive, and not to disturb the slumber of La Esmeralda; the unfortunate creature would be awakened time enough to die. This resolution once taken, he set about examining the enemy with greater composure.

The crowd seemed to increase every moment in the Parvis. He presumed, however, that the noise they made must be very slight, because the windows in the streets and the place remained closed. All at once a light appeared, and in an instant seven or eight lighted torches rose above the heads of the multitude, shaking their tufts of flame amid the darkness. Then did Quasimodo distinctly perceive a frightful rabble of men and women in rags, armed with scythes, pikes, pick-axes, and halberds, with their thousand glistening heads. Here and there black forks projected like horns over hideous faces. He had some vague recollection of this mob, and fancied that he had seen those faces some months before, when he was elected Pope of Fools. A man, who held a torch in one hand and a cudgel in the other, got upon a post, and appeared to be haranguing them. At the same time this strange army made some evolutions, as if certain divisions were taking their respective stations about the church. Quasimodo picked up his lantern and went down to the platform between the towers, to obtain a nearer view and to arrange his means of defense.

Clopin Trouillefou, on his arrival before the lofty portal of Notre Dame, had, in fact, ranged his troops in order of battle. Though he expected no resistance, yet he resolved, like a prudent general, to preserve such order as would enable him to face about in case of need against any sudden attack of the watch or of the *onze-vingts*. Accordingly, he drew up his brigade in such a way that, had you seen it from above or at a distance, you would have taken it for the Roman triangle at the battle of Ecnomus, the boar's head of Alexander, or the famous wedge of Gustavus Adolphus. The base of this triangle rested upon the furthest side of the place, so as to block up the Rue du Parvis; one of its sides faced the Hotel Dieu, and the other the Rue Saint Pierre aux Bœufs. Trouillefou had placed himself at the apex, with the Duke of Egypt, our friend Jehan, and the boldest of the Vagabonds.

An enterprise of this kind was by no means uncommon in the towns of the Middle Ages. Police, as we understand the term, there was none. Neither was there in populous cities, and in capitals more particularly, any sole, central, regulating power. The feudal system had constituted these large communities after a strange fashion. A city was an assemblage of a thousand seigneuries, which cut it up into compartments of all forms and all dimensions. Hence a thousand contradictory polices, that is to say, no police at all. In Paris, for instance, independently of the one hundred and forty-one seigneurs claiming manorial rights, there were twenty-five who claimed the right of administering justice, from the Bishop of Paris, who had five hundred streets, down to the prior of Notre Dame des Champs, who had four. The paramount authority of the king was but nominally recognized by all these feudal justiciaries. Louis XI., that indefatigable workman, who so largely commenced the demolition of the feudal edifice, continued by Richelieu and Louis XIV. for the interest of royalty, and completed by Mirabeau for the benefit of the people—Louis XI. had certainly endeavored to break this web of seigneuries spread out over Paris, by violently hurling against it at random two or three ordinances of general police. Thus, in 1465, the inhabitants were ordered as soon as it was dark to place lighted candles in their windows, and to shut up their dogs, upon pain of the gallows. The same year they were enjoined to block the streets at night with iron chains, and forbidden to carry daggers or offensive weapons out-of-doors after dark; but, in a short time, all these attempts at municipal legislation fell into neglect. The old structure of feudal jurisdictions was left standing. Bailiwicks and seigneuries without number carved out the city among them, crossing, jostling, entangling themselves with, and dove-tailing into one another. There was an endless confusion of watches, under-watches, and counter-watches, in defiance of which robbery, plunder, and sedition were carried on by main force. Amid this disorder, then, it was no uncommon thing for a part of the rabble to make an attack upon a palace, a mansion, a house, in the most populous parts of the city. The neighbors in general abstained from interfering in the affair, unless the pillage extended to their own property. They shut their ears to the firing, closed their shutters, barricaded their doors, left the quarrel to be settled by or without the watch; and the next morning the talk in Paris would be, "Stephen Barbette's was broken open last night," or "the Maréchal de Clermont was seized," etc. Thus not only the royal habitations, the Louvre, the Palace, the Bastile, Les Tournelles, but the mere seignorial residences, the Petit Bourbon, the Hotel de Sens, and the Hotel d'Angoulême, had their walls and their battlements, their portcullises and their gates. The churches were protected by their sanctity. Some of them, however, were fortified; but Notre Dame was not of the number. The Abbey of St. Germain des Près was embattled like a baronial castle, and it expended more brass on cannon than on bells. But to return to Notre Dame.

As soon as the first arrangements were terminated—and we must say, for the honor of the Vagabond discipline, that Clopin's orders were executed in silence, and with admirable precision—the worthy chief of the band mounted upon the parapet of the Parvis, and raised his harsh and husky voice, turning his face toward Notre Dame, and at the same time waving his torch, the flame of which, blown about by the wind, and ever and anon almost drowned in its own smoke, now reddened the façade of the church, and presently left it buried in darkness.

"To thee, Louis de Beaumont, Bishop of Paris, counselor to the court of parliament, I, Clopin Trouillefou, King of Thunes, Grand Coesre, Prince of Slang, Bishop of Fools, give this notice: Our sister, falsely condemned for magic, has taken sanctuary in thy church. Thou owest her safeguard and protection. Now, the court of parliament wishes to lay hold of her again, and thou consentest thereto; therefore, oh, bishop, are we come to thee. If thy church is sacred, our sister is sacred also; if our sister is not sacred, neither is thy church. We summon thee, then, to surrender the girl to us if thou wouldst save thy church; or, we will take the girl ourselves and plunder thy church. This will be still better. In testimony whereof I here plant my banner. So God keep thee, Bishop of Paris!"

Unluckily, Quasimodo could not hear these words, which were pronounced with a sort of wild and somber majesty. One of the Vagabonds delivered his banner to Clopin, who solemnly planted it between two paving-stones. It was a pitchfork, on the tines of which hung a lump of bleeding carrion.

This done, the King of Thunes turned round and surveyed his army, a savage throng, whose eyes glistened almost as much as their pikes. After a moment's pause he gave the word of onset. "Forward! my lads! To your business, blackguards!" was the cry of Clopin Trouillefou.

Thirty stout men, fellows with brawny limbs and the faces of blacksmiths, sprung from the ranks, bearing sledge-hammers, pincers, and crow-bars in their hands and on their shoulders. They made for the great door of the church, ascended the steps, and were presently crouching down beneath the arch, at work with their pincers and their levers. A crowd of the Vagabonds followed to assist or to look on. The eleven steps of the porch were thronged by them. The door, however, held firm. "Devil!" said one, "it is tough and obstinate!"—"'Tis old, and its joints are stiff," said another—"Courage, comrades!" replied Clopin. "I'll wager my head against an old shoe that you will have opened the door, taken the girl, and stripped the high altar before there is a beadle awake. Hold! I think the lock is giving away."

Clopin was interrupted at this moment by a tremendous crash

behind him. He turned round. An enormous beam had fallen from
the sky; it had crushed a dozen of the Vagabonds on the steps of
the church, and rebounded on the pavement with the noise of a cannon, breaking a score or two of legs among the crowd of beggars,
who, with cries of horror, scampered off in every direction. The
area of the Parvis was cleared in a twinkling. The blacksmiths,
though protected by the depth of the porch, abandoned the door,
and Clopin himself fell back to a respectful distance from the
church. "I have had a narrow escape," cried Jehan. "I was in the
wind of it, by Jove! but Peter the Butcher is butchered."

It is impossible to describe the fright and consternation which fell
with that beam upon the banditti. For some minutes they stood staring up at the sky, more astounded at the piece of timber than they
would have been by the arrival of twenty thousand of the king's
archers. "The devil!" exclaimed the Duke of Egypt; "this does look
like magic!"—"It must surely be the moon that has thrown us this
log," said Andry the Red. "Why, then, methinks the moon is a good
friend to our Lady the Virgin," observed François Chanteprune.—
"Thousand popes!" cried Clopin, "ye are a parcel of fools!" But still
he knew not how to account for the fall of the beam.

Meanwhile, nothing was to be seen on the façade, the top of which
was too high for the light of the torches to reach it. The ponderous
beam lay in the middle of the Parvis, and nothing was heard save
the groans of the wretches who had been mangled by its shock upon
the steps. The first panic over, the King of Thunes at length fancied
that he had made a discovery, which appeared plausible to his companions. "*Ventre Dieu!*" cried he; "are the canons defending themselves? If so, sack! sack!"—"Sack! sack!" responded the whole crew,
with a tremendous hurrah; and a furious discharge of cross-bows
and arquebuses was leveled at the façade of the church.

The report of the fire-arms awoke the peaceful inhabitants of the
neighboring houses; sundry windows might be seen opening, night-
caps popping out, and hands holding candles. "Fire at the windows!" roared out Clopin. The windows were shut in an instant, and
the poor citizens, who had scarcely had time to cast a hasty and
timid glance upon this scene of flash and tumult returned to perspire
with fright by the sides of their spouses, asking themselves whether
the witches' sabbath was now held in the Parvis, or whether there
was another attack of the Burgundians, as in '64. The men were apprehensive of robbery, the women of violence, and all trembled.

"Sack! sack!" repeated the men of Slang, but they durst not advance. They looked first at the church and then at the beam. The

beam did not stir, and the church retained its calm and lonely air, but something had frozen the courage of the Vagabonds.

"To work, then, scoundrels!" cried Trouillefou. "Force the door!" Not a soul moved a finger. "Pretty fellows, these," said Clopin, "who are frightened out of their wits by a bit of wood!"

"Captain," rejoined an old smith, "it is not the bit of wood that frightens us; but the door is all clamped with iron bars. The pincers are of no use."

"What want you then to break it open?" inquired Clopin.

"We want a battering-ram."

"Here it is then," cried the King of Thunes, stepping boldly up to the formidable beam, and setting his foot upon it: "the canons themselves have sent you one. Thank you, canons," he added, making a mock obeisance toward the church.

This bravado produced the desired effect. The charm of the beam was broken; picked up like a feather by two hundred vigorous arms, it was dashed with fury against the great door, which the Vagabonds had in vain attempted to force. In the dim light thrown by a few torches upon the place, this long beam and its supporters might have been taken for an immense beast with hundreds of legs butting at a giant of stone.

At the shock of the beam the half-metallic door resounded like an immense drum: it yielded not, but the whole cathedral shook, and the innermost cavities of the edifice were heard to groan. At the same instant a shower of stones began to rain upon the assailants. "This is no joke!" cried Jehan: "are the towers shaking their balustrades upon us?" But the impulse was given; the King of Thunes was right; it was decidedly the bishop defending the citadel, and the Vagabonds only battered the door with the more fury, in spite of the stones which were cracking skulls in all directions. It is remarkable that these stones fell one by one, but so closely did they follow each other that the assailants always felt two at a time, one at their legs, the other at their heads. There were few of them that did not tell: already a large heap of killed and wounded lay bleeding and palpitating under the feet of their comrades, who, nothing daunted, filled up their ranks as fast as they were thinned. The long beam continued to batter at regular intervals, the door to groan, and the stones to shower down. The reader need not be told that this unexpected resistance, which so exasperated the Vagabonds, proceeded from Quasimodo. Chance had unluckily favored the courageous hunchback.

When he had descended to the platform between the towers his brain was all in confusion. For some minutes he ran along the gallery to and fro like a maniac, looking down at the compact mass of banditti ready to burst into the church, and calling upon saints and angels to save the Egyptian. He had a thought of mounting to the southern belfry and ringing the alarm bell; but before he could have made big Mary utter a single sound, the church might have been broken open ten times over. It was just at this moment that the smiths were coming up to the door with their tools. What was to be done?

All at once he recollected that workmen had been engaged the whole day in repairing the wall, timbers, and roof, of the southern tower. To that tower Quasimodo hastened. The lower rooms were full of materials. There were piles of stones, rolls of lead, bundles of lath, massive beams and heaps of gravel: it was, in short, a complete arsenal.

There was no time to be lost. The crow-bars and hammers were at work below. With a strength increased tenfold by the sense of danger, he hoisted up the heaviest and longest beam he could find, shoved it out of a small window, and over the angle of the balustrade surrounding the platform, and fairly launched it into the abyss. The enormous mass, in this fall of one hundred and sixty feet, grazed the wall, breaking the sculptures, and turned over and over several times in its descent. At length it reached the ground; horrid shrieks succeeded; and the black beam, rebounding on the pavement, looked like a serpent writhing and darting upon its prey.

Quasimodo saw the Vagabonds scattered by the fall of the beam, like ashes before the wind. He took advantage of their consternation, and while they fixed a superstitious stare upon the log fallen as they thought from the sky, and put out the eyes of the stone saints of the porch by the discharge of their arrows and fire-arms, Quasimodo fell to work in silence to carry stones, rubbish, gravel, and even the bags of tools belonging to the masons, to the edge of the balustrade over which he had already hoisted the beam. As soon as they commenced battering the door the shower of stones began to fall, and the Vagabonds imagined that the church was tumbling about their ears. Any one who could have seen Quasimodo at that moment would have been seized with dread. Besides the projectiles, which he had piled upon the balustrade, he had carried a heap of stones to the platform itself, so that as soon as the former were exhausted he might have recourse to the latter. There he was, then, stooping and rising, stooping and rising again, with an activity absolutely inconceivable. His huge head, more like that of a gnome than a human being, was at times bent over the balustrade; then an enormous stone would fall, then another and another. From time to time, too, he would follow a thumping stone with his eye, and when it did good execution he would grunt out, "Hun!"

The Vagabonds, however, were nothing daunted. More than twenty times the massive door against which their attack was directed had trembled under the weight of the oaken ram, multiplied by the force of a hundred men. The panels were cracking, the carving flew off in shivers, the hinges at every blow sprung up from the pivots, the planks began to start, and the wood was pounded to powder between the braces of iron: luckily for Quasimodo there was more iron than wood. He was aware, nevertheless, that the door could not hold out long. Though he could not hear it, yet every stroke of the ram reverberated in the caverns and in the inmost recesses of the church. From his lofty station he saw the assailants, flushed with triumph and with rage, shaking their fists at the gloomy façade, and, for his own sake as well as for the Egyptian's, he coveted the wings of the daws which flew off in flocks above his head. His ammunition was not effective enough to repel the assailants.

At this moment of anguish he remarked, a little lower down than the balustrade from which he crushed the men of Slang, two long gutters of stone which disgorged themselves immediately over the great door. The inner orifice of these gutters opened on the level of the platform. An idea struck him. He ran to his bell-ringer's lodge for a fagot, placed it over the hole of the two spouts, laid upon it several bundles of lath and rolls of lead, a kind of ammunition to which he had not yet resorted: and as soon as all was arranged, he set fire to the fagot with his lantern.

During this interval, as the stones had ceased falling, the Vagabonds no longer looked up; and the ruffians, panting like dogs baying the wild boar in his den, crowded tumultuously round the great door, shattered by the battering engine, but still standing. They awaited with a thrill of impatience the last grand blow, the blow that was to shiver it in pieces. Each was striving to get nearest to the door, that he might be first to dart into the rich magazine of treasures, which had been accumulating in the cathedral for three centuries. They roared with joy as they reminded one another of all the beautiful silver crucifixes, the rich copes of brocade, the monuments of silver gilt, the magnificence of the choir, the Christmases sparkling with torches, the Easters dazzling in the sun—all those splendid solemnities when shrines, chandeliers, pyxes, tabernacles, reliquaries embossed the altars with a crest of gold and diamonds.

Assuredly at this moment the canters and whiners, the limpers, and tremblers, and tumblers, thought much less of the rescue of the Egyptian than of the plunder of Notre Dame. For our own part, we verily believe that with a great proportion of them La Esmeralda was merely a pretext, if, however, robbers need any pretext.

All on a sudden, while they were grouping themselves for a last effort about the engine, each holding his breath and stiffening his muscles to throw all his strength into the decisive blow, a howling more hideous than that which followed the fall of the fatal beam burst from among them. Those who were not yelling and yet alive looked round. Two streams of molten lead were pouring from the top of the building upon the thickest part of the crowd. This sea of men had subsided beneath the boiling metal, which had made, at the points where it fell, two black and smoking holes in the rabble, such as hot water would make in a snow-drift. Here the dying were writhing half calcined and roaring with agony. All around these two principal streams a shower of this horrible rain was scattered over the assailants, and the drops pierced their skulls like gimlets of fire. The clamor was horrible. The Vagabonds, throwing the beam upon the dead and dying, fled, pell-mell, the bold and the timid together, and the Parvis was cleared a second time.

All eyes were raised to the top of the building. They beheld a sight of an extraordinary kind. In the uppermost gallery, above the central rose window, a vast body of flame, accompanied by showers of sparks, ascended between the two towers—a fierce and irregular flame, patches of which were every now and then carried off by the wind along with the smoke. Below this fire, below the somber balustrade, with its glowing red open-work ornaments two spouts, in the shape of the jaws of monsters, vomited without cessation those silver streams, which stood out distinctly against the dark mass of the lower façade. As they approached the ground, those two streams spread like water poured through the holes of the spout of a watering pot. Above the flames the enormous towers, each showing two sides deeply contrasted, the one quite black, the other quite red, appeared still larger from the immense shadows which they threw toward the sky. Their numberless sculptures of devils and dragons assumed a doleful aspect. The flickering of the flame gave to them the appearance of motion. Gorgons seemed to be laughing, water-spouts yelping, salamanders puffing fire, and griffins sneezing in the smoke. And among the monsters thus wakened from their sleep of stone by the flames and by the din, there was one that moved from place to place, and passed from time to time in front of the fire, like a bat before a candle.

A silence of terror fell upon the army of the Vagabonds, during which might be heard the cries of the canons shut up in their cloisters, and more alarmed than horses in a stable that is on fire, together with the sound of windows stealthily opened and more quickly shut, a bustle in the interior of the houses and in the Hôtel Dieu, the wind in the flame, the last rattle of the dying, and the continuous pattering of the leaden rain upon the pavement.

Meanwhile, the principals of the Vagabonds had retired to the porch of the Gondelaurier mansion, and were holding consultation. The Duke of Egypt, seated on a post, contemplated with religious awe the resplendent blaze burning at the height of two hundred feet in the air. Clopin Trouillefou struck his clumsy fists together with rage. "Impossible to break in!" muttered he to himself.

"An enchanted church!" grumbled the old Bohemian, Matthias Hunyadi Spicali.

"By the pope's whiskers!" exclaimed a gray-headed ragamuffin who had been a soldier, "those two church gutters beat the portcullis of Lectoure at spewing lead, out and out!"

"Do you see that demon passing to and fro before the fire?" cried the Duke of Egypt.

"Egad," said Clopin, "'tis that cursed bell-ringer, that Quasimodo."

"And I tell you," replied the Bohemian, shaking his head, "it is the spirit of Sabnac, the demon of fortification. He appears in the form of an armed soldier with a lion's head. He changes men into stones, and builds towers with them. He has the command of fifty legions. I know him well—'tis he, sure enough."

"Is there then no way of forcing that infernal door?" cried the King of Thunes, stamping violently on the pavement. The Duke of Egypt pointed mournfully to the two streams of boiling lead, which still continued to stripe the dark façade.

"Churches have been known," observed he with a sigh, "to defend themselves in this manner, without the aid of man. It is now about forty years since St. Sophia at Constantinople threw down three times running the crescent of Mohammed by shaking her domes, which are her heads. William of Paris, who built this, was a magician."

"Shall we then give it up for a bad job, like a scurvy set of poltroons?" said Clopin. "Shall we leave our sister behind, to be hanged to-morrow by these cowled wolves?"

"And the sacristy too, where there are cartloads of gold?" added a rapscallion whose name we regret our inability to record.

"Beard of Mahound!" ejaculated Trouillefou.

"Let us make one more trial," said the preceding speaker.

Again Matthias Hunyadi shook his head. "We shall not get in at the door, that's certain."

"I shall go back," said Clopin. "Who will come with me? By the bye, where is little Jehan, the student, who had cased himself up to the eyes in steel?"

"Dead, no doubt," replied some one. "I have not heard his laugh for some time."

The King of Thunes knit his brow. "More's the pity! He carried a bold heart under that iron shell. And Master Pierre Gringoire, what is become of him?"

"Captain Clopin," said Andry the Red, "he sneaked off as soon as we had reached the Pont aux Changeurs."

Clopin stamped. "'Sdeath! the coward! To urge us into this affair and then leave us in the lurch!"

"Captain," cried Andry the Red, who was looking down the Rue du Parvis, "yonder comes the little scholar."

"Thanks be to Pluto!" rejoined Clopin. "But what the devil is he dragging after him?"

It was actually Jehan, who was advancing as expeditiously as he could for his heavy, war-like accouterments and a long ladder which, with the aid of half a dozen of the gang, he was trailing along the pavement, more out of breath than a pismire dragging a blade of grass twenty times as long as itself.

"Victory! *Te Deum!*" shouted the scholar.

Clopin went up to him. "What, in the devil's name, are you going at with that ladder?"

"I have got it," replied Jehan, panting and blowing. "I knew where it was kept—under the shed belonging to the lieutenant's house. I am acquainted with one of the maids there, who thinks me a perfect Cupid. The poor girl came down half naked to let me in—and here is the ladder."

"I see," said Clopin; "but what are you going to do with it?"

Jehan eyed him with a look of spite and importance, and snapped his fingers like castanets. At that moment he was really sublime. His head was cased in one of those surcharged helmets of the fifteenth century, which daunted the enemy by their fantastic appendages. He was bestudded with ten iron beaks, so that he might have disputed the formidable epithet δεχεμβολος with Nestor's Homeric ship.

"What am I going to do with it, august King of Thunes? Do you see that row of statues which look so like idiots, there, above the three porches?"

"Yes; what then?"

"That is the gallery of the kings of France."

"And what of that?" said Clopin.

"Just listen. At the end of that gallery there is a door which is always on the latch. With this ladder I will mount to it, and then I am in the church."

"Let me go up first, boy."

"No, no, comrade. I brought the ladder. You shall be second if you will."

"May Beelzebub strangle thee!" cried Clopin, peevishly. "I will not be second to any man."

"Then, my dear fellow, seek a ladder for yourself."

Jehan started again, dragging his ladder along and shouting, "This way, my lads!"

In an instant the ladder was raised and placed against the balustrade of the lower gallery, above one of the side doors, amid loud acclamations from the crowd of the Vagabonds, who thronged to the foot of it to ascend. Jehan maintained his right to go up first. The gallery of the kings of France is at this present time about sixty feet above the pavement. The eleven steps up to the porch increased the height. Jehan mounted slowly, being impeded by his heavy armor, laying hold of the ladder with one hand, and having his arbalest in the other. When he was about half-way up he cast a melancholy look at the dead bodies that covered the steps and the pavement. "By my fay!" said he, "a heap of carcasses that would not disgrace the fifth book of the Iliad." He then continued to ascend, followed by the Vagabonds. Had you seen this line of cuirassed backs undulating in the dark, you would have taken it for an immense serpent with iron scales raising itself against the church.

The scholar at length touched the balcony and nimbly leaped upon it. He was greeted by a general shout from the whole gang. Thus master of the citadel, he joined in the hurrahs, but all at once he was struck dumb with horror. He perceived Quasimodo crouching in the dark behind one of the royal statues and his eye flashing fire.

Before a second of the besiegers could set foot on the gallery, the formidable hunchback sprung to the top of the ladder, and, without uttering a word, caught hold of the two sides with his nervous hands, and pushed them from the wall with superhuman force. The long ladder, bending under the load of the escalading party, whose piercing shrieks rent the air, stood upright for a moment, and seemed to hesitate; then, all at once taking a tremendous lurch, it fell with its load of banditti more swiftly than a draw-bridge when the chains that held it have broken. An immense imprecation ensued. Presently all was silent, and here and there a mangled wretch crawled forth from beneath the heap of dead. Quasimodo, leaning with his two elbows upon the balustrade looked quietly on.

Jehan Frollo found himself in a critical situation. Separated from his comrades by a perpendicular wall of eighty feet, he was alone in the gallery with the formidable bell-ringer. While Quasimodo was playing with the ladder, the scholar had run to the postern, which he expected to find upon the latch. He was disappointed. The dwarf had locked it after him when he went down to the gallery. Jehan then hid himself behind one of the stone kings, holding his breath, and eying the monstrous hunchback with a look of horror, like the man who, having scraped acquaintance with the wife of a keeper of wild beasts, went one night in pursuance of an assignation, and, climbing over the wrong wall, found himself all at once face to face with a prodigious white bear. For some moments he was not observed by Quasimodo, who at length chancing to turn his head, and perceiving the scholar, suddenly started up.

Jehan prepared himself for a rude encounter, but the hunchback stood stock still, merely fixing his eye intently upon the scholar. "Hoho!" said Jehan; "why dost thou look at me so spitefully?" With these words the hare-brained youth slyly adjusted his arbalest. "Quasimodo," cried he, "I will change thy surname; instead of the deaf thou shalt henceforth be called the blind." The feathered shaft whizzed and pierced the left arm of the bell-ringer. Quasimodo heeded it no more than he would have done the scratch of a pin. He laid hold of the quarrel, drew it from his arm, and calmly broke it upon his massive knee; he then dropped rather than threw the pieces over the balustrade. Jehan had not time to discharge a second. Quasimodo, having broken the arrow, suddenly drew in his breath, leaped like a grasshopper, and fell upon the scholar, whose armor was flattened against the wall by the shock. A tremendous sight was then seen in the clare-obscure produced by the faint light of the torches.

Quasimodo grasped with his left hand the two arms of the scholar, who forbore even to struggle, so completely did he feel himself overpowered. With his right the hunchback took off in silence, and with ominous deliberation, the different parts of his armor, one after

another—helmet, cuirass, arm-pieces, sword, daggers. He looked for
all the world like an ape picking a walnut. He threw the iron shell
of the scholar, piece by piece, at his feet.

When Jehan found himself stripped, disarmed, powerless, in the
hands of his irresistible antagonist, he began to laugh him impudently in the face, with all the thoughtless gayety of a boy of sixteen.
But he did not laugh long. Quasimodo was seen standing upon the
parapet of the gallery, holding the scholar by the leg with one hand,
and swinging him round over the abyss like a sling. Presently was
heard a sound like that of a cocoanut broken by being dashed
against a wall; something was seen falling, but it was stopped one
third of the way down by a projecting part of the building. It was a
dead body that stuck there, bent double, the back broken, and the
skull empty.

A cry of horror burst from the Vagabonds. "Revenge!" shouted
Clopin. "Sack! sack!" responded the multitude. "Storm! storm!" Then
followed prodigious yells, intermingled with all language, all dia-
lects, all accents. The death of poor Jehan kindled a fury in the
crowd. They were filled with shame and indignation at having been
so long held in check before a church by a hunchback. Rage found
ladders and multiplied the torches; and, in a few moments, Quasimodo beheld with consternation a fearful rabble mounting on all
sides to the assault of Notre Dame. Some had ladders, others knotted
ropes, while such as could not procure either, scrambled up by the
aid of the sculptures, holding by one another's rags. There were no
means of withstanding this rising tide of grim faces, to which rage
gave a look of twofold ferocity. The perspiration trickled down their
begrimmed brows; their eyes flashed; all these hideous figures were
now closing in upon Quasimodo. You would have imagined that
some other church had sent its gorgons, its demons, its dragons, its
most fantastic monsters, to the assault of Notre Dame.

Meanwhile, the place was illumined with a thousand torches. A
flood of light suddenly burst upon the scene of confusion, which had
till then been buried in darkness. The fire kindled on the platform
was still burning, and illumined the city to a considerable distance.
The enormous outline of the two towers, projected afar upon the
roofs of the houses, formed a large patch of shadow amid all this
light. The city seemed to be in a bustle.

Distant alarm-bells were proclaiming that there was something
amiss. The Vagabonds were shouting, yelling, swearing, climbing:
and Quasimodo, powerless against such a host of enemies, shudder-

ing for the Egyptian, seeing so many ferocious faces approaching nearer and nearer to the gallery, prayed to Heaven for a miracle, at the same time wringing his hands in despair.

CHAPTER V

THE RETREAT WHERE MONSIEUR LOUIS OF FRANCE SAYS HIS PRAYERS

THE READER has perhaps not forgotten that Quasimodo, the moment before he perceived the nocturnal band of the Vagabonds, while surveying Paris from the top of his tower, had discovered but a single light, which illumined a window in the uppermost floor of a lofty and gloomy building by the Gate of St. Antoine. This building was the Bastile. The light was the candle of Louis XI.

The king had actually been for two days past in Paris. He was to leave it again on the day after the morrow for his fortress of Montilz lez Tours. His visits to his good city of Paris were rare and short; for there he felt that he had not trap-doors, gibbets, and Scottish archers enough about him.

He had come that day to sleep in the Bastile. He disliked the great chamber which he had at the Louvre, five fathoms square, with its great chimney-piece adorned with twelve great beasts and thirteen great prophets, and its great bed, twelve feet by eleven. He was lost amid all this grandeur. This burgher king gave the preference to the Bastile, with a humble chamber and suitable bed. Besides, the Bastile was stronger than the Louvre.

This chamber which the king had reserved for himself in the famous state-prison was spacious, and occupied the top-most floor of a turret in the keep. It was an apartment of circular form, the floor covered with shining straw-matting, the rafters of the ceiling adorned with *fleurs-de-lis* of pewter gilt, the spaces between them colored, wainscoted with rich woods, sprinkled with rosettes of tin, painted a fine lively green composed of orpine and wood.

There was but one long and pointed window, latticed with brass wire and iron bars, and somewhat darkened besides by beautiful stained glass, exhibiting the arms of the king and those of the queen, each pane of which cost twenty-two sous.

There was but one entrance, a modern door, with elliptic arch, covered on the inside with cloth, and having without one of those porches of Irish wood, frail structures of curious workmanship, which were still very common in old buildings one hundred and fifty years ago. "Though they disfigure and encumber the places," says Sauval, peevishly, "yet will not our ancient folk put them away, but they preserve them in spite of every one."

In this chamber was to be seen none of the furniture of ordinary apartments, neither tables upon trestles, nor benches, nor forms, nor common stools in the shape of a box, nor those of a better sort, standing upon pillars and counter-pillars, at four sous apiece. Nothing was to be seen there, save a very magnificent folding arm-chair. The wood-work was adorned with roses painted on a red ground, and the seat was of scarlet Spanish leather, garnished with silk fringe, and studded with a thousand golden nails. This solitary chair indicated that one person only had a right to sit down in that apartment. Near the chair and close to the window was a table covered with a cloth, on which were the figures of birds. On this table were a portfolio spotted with ink, sundry parchments, pens, and a chased silver mug. At a little distance stood a chafing-dish, and a desk for the purpose of prayer, covered with crimson velvet embossed with studs of gold. Lastly, at the furthest part of the room there was a simple bed, of yellow and flesh-colored damask, without lace or any trimming but plain fringe. This bed, famed for having witnessed the sleep or the sleeplessness of Louis XI., was to be seen two hundred years ago in the house of a councilor of state.

Such was the chamber commonly called "The retreat where Monsieur Louis of France said his prayers."

At the moment of our ushering the reader into this retreat it was very dark. An hour had elapsed since the tolling curfew: it was night, and there was only one flickering wax candle upon the table, to light five persons who formed several groups in the chamber.

The first on whom the light fell was a personage superbly dressed in hose, scarlet close-bodied coat striped with silver, and a surtout of cloth of gold with black designs, and trimmed with fur. This splendid costume, upon which the light played, seemed to be braided with flame at all its folds. The wearer had his arms embroidered at the breast in gaudy colors; a chevron, with a deer passant in the base of the shield. The escutcheon was supported on the dexter side by an olive branch, and on the sinister by a buck's horn. This personage carried in his belt a rich dagger, the hilt of which, of silver gilt, was chased in the form of a crest, and terminated in a count's coronet.

He carried his head high, had a haughty bearing, and an ill-natured look. At the first glance you discovered in his countenance an expression of arrogance; at the second, of cunning.

He stood bareheaded, with a long paper in his hand, before the arm-chair, on which was seated a person, shabbily dressed, his body ungracefully bent, one knee crossed over the other, and his elbow upon the table. Figure to yourself, on the seat of rich Cordova leather, a pair of slender thighs and spindle-shanks, appareled in black knitted woolen stuff; a body wrapped in a surtout of fustian trimmed with fur, which showed much more leather than hair; lastly, to crown all, an old greasy hat of the coarsest black cloth, in the band of which were stuck a number of small leaden figures. This, with a dirty skull-cap, which suffered scarcely a hair to struggle from beneath it, was all that could be seen of the seated personage. His head was so bent forward upon his breast as to throw into the shade the whole of his face, excepting the tip of his nose, on which a ray of light fell: it was evidently a long one. The wrinkled, attenuated hand indicated that he was old. It was Louis XI.

At some distance behind the two persons we have described, two men, dressed in the Flemish fashion, were conversing in a low voice. It was not so dark where they stood but that one who attended the representation of Gringoire's mystery would have recognized in them two of the principal Flemish envoys, Guillaume Rym, the sagacious pensionary of Ghent, and Jacques Coppenole, the popular hosier. It will be recollected that these two persons were mixed up with the secret politics of Louis XI.

Lastly, at the opposite end of the room, near the door, stood motionless as a statue, a short, thick-set man in military attire, with coat of arms embroidered on the breast, whose square face without brow, eyes on a level with the top of the head, and ears hidden by two large pent-houses of straight hair, partook at once of the dog's and the tiger's.

All were uncovered excepting the king.

The nobleman standing near the king was reading to him a long memorial, to which his majesty seemed to listen attentively. The two Flemings were whispering together.

"By the rood!" muttered Coppenole, "I am tired of standing. Are no chairs allowed here?"

Rym answered by a shake of the head, accompanied by a discreet smile.

"By the mass!" resumed Coppenole, who was quite miserable to be obliged to speak in so low a tone, "I have a good mind to clap myself down on the floor, as I might do at home."

"Nay, Master Jacques, prithee do no such thing."

"Hey-day, Master Guillaume! must one keep on one's legs all the while one is here, then?"

"Even so, or on your knees," replied Rym.

At that moment the king raised his voice. They were silent.

"Fifty sous the gowns of our serving men, and twelve livres the cloaks of the clerks of our crown! Why, 'tis throwing gold away by tons! Are you distraught, Olivier?"

As he thus spoke, the old king raised his head. About his neck might then be seen glistening the golden balls of the collar of St. Michael. The rays of the candle fell full upon his skinny and morose face. He snatched the paper from the hands of the reader.

"You will ruin us!" he cried, running his hollow eye over it. "What means all this? What need have we for such a prodigious establishment? Two chaplains, at the rate of ten livres each per month, and a clerk of the chapel at one hundred sous! A valet-de-chambre, at ninety livres by the year! Four esquires of the kitchen, at six score livres by the year, each! An overseer of the roast, another of the vegetables, another of the sauces, a head cook, a butler, and two assistants, at ten livres each per month! Two scullions at eight livres! A groom and his two helpers at twenty-four livres the month! A porter, a pastry cook, a baker, two carters, at sixty livres by the year each! And the marshal of the forges, six score livres! And the master of the chamber of our exchequer, twelve hundred livres! And the controller, five hundred! And I know not how many more! 'Tis enough to drive one mad! To pay the wages of our servants, France is plundered. All the ingots in the Louvre will melt away before such a fire of expense! We will sell our plate! And next year, if God and our Lady" [here he lifted his hat] "grant us life, we will take our diet-drink out of a pewter pot."

As he thus spoke he cast a look at the silver mug which glistened upon the table. He coughed and then proceeded: "Master Olivier, the princes who rule over great countries, such as kings and emperors, ought never to suffer habits of expense to creep into their households; for that fire runs further and catches the provinces. Give me not occasion to repeat this, Master Olivier. Our expenditure increases every year. The thing likes us not. Why, *Pasque Dieu!* till '79 it never exceeded thirty-six thousand livres; in '80 it amounted to forty-three thousand six hundred and nineteen livres— I have the exact sum in my head; in '81, to sixty-six thousand six hundred and eighty; and this year, by the faith of my body, it will not be under eighty thousand! Doubled in four years; monstrous!"

He paused to take breath, and then began again with warmth: "I see about me none but people who fatten upon my leanness. Ye suck crowns out of me at every pore!"

All present maintained profound silence. It was one of those paroxysms which must be left to themselves. He continued:

"It is like that petition in Latin from the nobles of France, that we would re-establish what they call the great charges of the crown! Charges, in good sooth! crushing charges! Ah, gentlemen, ye say that we are not a king to reign *dapifero nullo, buticalario nullo!*[1] We will show you, *Pasque Dieu!* whether we are not a king."

Here he smiled in the feeling of his power: his wrath was softened, and he turned toward the Flemings.

"Look you, Compere Guillaume, the grand master of the pantry, the grand chamberlain, the grand seneschal, are of less use than the meanest serving-man. Remember that, Compere Coppenole! They are good for nothing. Such useless attendants on a king are very like the four evangelists about the dial of the great clock of the palace, which Philip Brille has lately beautified. They are gilt, but they mark not the hour, and the hand can go without them."

For a moment he appeared thoughtful, and then, shaking his old head, he added: "No, no; by our Lady, I am not Philip Brille, and I will not new-gild the grand vassals. Go on, Olivier." The person to whom he spoke took up the paper, and began reading again with a loud voice:

"To Adam Tenon, clerk to the keeper of the seals of the provosty of Paris, for silver, making and engraving said seals, which have been new made, because the former could no longer be used, by reason of their being old and worn out—twelve livres parisis.

"To Guillaume Frere, the sum of four livres four sous parisis, as his salary and wages for feeding the pigeons in the two dove-cotes of the Hotel des Tournelles, in the months of January, February, and March of this present year; and for this there have been given seven quarters of barley.

"To a Gray Friar, for confessing a criminal, four sous parisis."

The king listened in silence. He coughed from time to time; he would then lift the mug to his lips and swallow a mouthful, at the same time making a wry face.

"In this year there have been made by order of justice, by sound of trumpet, in the public places of Paris, fifty-six proclamations— the account to be settled.

1."No footman, no butler."

"For having made quest and search in certain places, both in Paris and elsewhere, after moneys which were said to be concealed there, but none found, forty-five livres parisis."

"Bury a crown to dig up a soul!" said the king.

"For putting six panes of white glass in the place where the iron cage is at the Hotel des Tournelles, thirteen sous.

"For two new sleeves to the king's old doublet, twenty sous.

"For a pot of grease to grease the king's boots, fifteen deniers.

"For new-making a sty for the king's black hogs, thirty livres parisis.

"For sundry partitions, planks, and doors, made to shut up the lions at St. Pol, twenty-two livres."

"Costly beasts those!" said Louis XI. "No matter: 'tis a seemly magnificence in a king. There is a great red lion which I am very fond of for his engaging ways. Have you seen him, Master Guillaume? It is right that princes should keep extraordinary animals. We kings ought to have lions for our dogs and tigers for our cats. What is great befits crowns. In the time of Jupiter's pagans, when the people offered to the churches a hundred oxen and a hundred sheep, the emperors gave a hundred lions and a hundred eagles. That was proud and magnificent. The kings of France have always had these bellowings around their thrones: nevertheless, people must do me the justice to say that I spend less money in that way than my predecessors, and that I am exceedingly moderate on the score of lions, bears, and elephants, and leopards. Go on, Master Olivier. We wished to say thus much to our Flanders friends."

Guillaume Rym made a profound obeisance, while Coppenole, with his sulky mien, looked like one of those bears which his majesty had been talking of. The king did not notice this. He sipped at the mug, and spitting out the drink, exclaimed: "Faugh! the horrid ptisan!" The reader proceeded:

"For the feed of a walking knave shut up for these six months in the lodge of the slaughter-house, till it is settled what to do with him, six livres four sous."

"What is that?" said the king—"feed what ought to hang! Pasque Dieu! not another sou will I give for that feed. Olivier, settle that business with Monsieur d'Estouteville, and this very night make me the needful preparations for wedding this gallant with the gallows. Go on."

Olivier made a mark with his thumb-nail against the last item, and proceeded:

"To Henriet Cousin, master executioner of Paris, the sum of sixty sous parisis, to him adjudged and ordered by Monseigneur the Provost of Paris, for that he did buy, at the command of the said Sieur the Provost, a great sword for executing and beheading persons condemned by justice for their misdeeds, and did provide a sheath and all thereunto appertaining, and likewise did get the old sword ground and repaired, by reason that it was broken and notched in doing justice upon Messire Louis of Luxembourg, as may more fully appear—"

The king interrupted the reader. "That is enough; I order that sum with all my heart. Those are expenses which I think not of. I never grudge moneys so laid out. Go on."

"For new-making a great cage—"

"Ah!" said the king, grasping the arms of his chair with both hands, "I knew that I had come to this Bastile for something. Stop, Master Olivier; I will look at that cage myself. You shall read the items while I examine it. Gentlemen of Flanders, come and look at it—'tis a curious thing."

He then rose, leaned upon the arm of the reader, motioned to the kind of mute standing before the door to precede him, and the two Flemings to follow, and left the chamber.

The royal party was re-enforced at the door of the retreat by men at arms encumbered with iron, and slender pages bearing torches. It pursued its way for some time through the interior of the somber keep, perforated with staircases and corridors even into the substance of the walls. The captain of the Bastile went first, to get the wickets opened for the old king, who, bent with age and infirmity, coughed as he walked along. At each wicket every head was obliged to stoop excepting that of the old monarch. "Hum!" muttered he between his gums—for he had lost all his teeth—"we are already not far from the door of the tomb. At a low door the passenger must stoop."

At length, having passed the last wicket, so encumbered with locks and fastenings that it took nearly a quarter of an hour to open it, they entered a lofty and spacious hall, in the middle of which was discovered by the light of the torches a massive cube of masonry, iron, and timber. The interior was hollow. It was one of those famous cages for prisoners of state which were called "the king's daughter." In the sides of it were two or three small windows, so closely latticed with thick iron bars that the glass could not be seen. The door was a large stone slab, like those which are laid upon graves, one of those doors which are never used but to enter: only in this case the buried person was yet living.

The king began to walk slowly round the little edifice, examining it with care, while Master Olivier, who followed him, read aloud to this effect: "For having new-made a great wooden cage of thick joists, girders, and planks, being nine feet long by eight wide, and seven feet from floor to ceiling, planed and clamped with strong iron clamps, the which hath been set in a chamber situate in one of the towers of the Bastile St. Antoine, in which cage is put and kept, by command of our lord the king, a prisoner who aforetime dwelt in a cage that was old, crazy, and decayed. There were used for the said new cage ninety-six joists, fifty-two uprights, ten girders, three fathoms in length; and there were employed nineteen carpenters in squaring, cutting, and working all said timber in the court of the Bastile for twenty days——"

"Capital heart of oak!" said the king, rapping the wood with his knuckle.

"There were used for this cage," continued the reader, "two hundred and twenty thick iron clamps of nine and eight feet, the rest of middling length, with the screws, nuts, and bands to the said clamps; the whole of the said iron weighing three thousand seven hundred and thirty-five pounds; besides eight stout holdfasts to fasten the said cage, with the nails, weighing together two hundred and eighteen pounds; without reckoning the iron grating to the windows of the chamber in which the cage is placed, the iron door of that chamber, and other things——"

"A great deal of iron," said the king, "to repress the levity of one mind!"

"The whole amounts to three hundred and seventeen livres five sous seven deniers."

"*Pasque Dieu!*" exclaimed the king. At this imprecation, which was the favorite oath of Louis XI., some person appeared to rouse up within the cage. Chains were heard trailing upon the floor, and a faint voice, which seemed to issue from a tomb, cried, "Mercy, sire! mercy!" The person who thus spoke could not be seen.

"Three hundred and seventeen livres five sous seven deniers!" repeated Louis XI.

The lamentable voice which issued from the cage had thrilled all present, including Master Olivier himself. The king alone appeared not to have heard it. At his command, Master Olivier began reading again, and his majesty coolly continued his examination of the cage.

"Besides the above, there has been paid to a mason who made the holes to receive the bars of the windows, and the floor of the chamber where the cage is, because the floor could not have borne this cage by reason of its weight—twenty-seven livres fourteen sous parisis."

The voice again began moaning: "Mercy, for Heaven's sake, sire! I assure your majesty that it was the Cardinal of Angers who did the treason, and not I."

"The mason is high," said the king. "Proceed."

Olivier continued:

"To a joiner for windows, bedstead, and other things, twenty livres two sous parisis."

The voice likewise continued: "Alas! sire! will you not hear me? I protest that it was not I who wrote that thing to Monseigneur de Guyenne, but Cardinal Balue!"

"The joiner is dear," observed the king. "Is that all?"

"No, sire. To a glazier, for the windows of the said chamber, forty-six sous eight deniers parisis."

"Pardon, sir! pardon! Is it not enough that all my goods have been given to my judges, my plate to Monsieur de Torcy, my library to Master Pierre Doriolle, my tapestry to the Governor of Roussillon? I am innocent. For fourteen years I have pined in an iron cage. Mercy, sire! mercy! You will be rewarded for it in heaven."

"Master Olivier," said the king, "the total?"

"Three hundred and sixty-seven livres eight sous three deniers parisis."

"By our Lady!" exclaimed the king, "an extravagant cage."

Snatching the paper from the hand of Master Olivier, he looked by turns at the account and at the cage, and began to reckon up himself upon his fingers. Meanwhile, the prisoner continued wailing and sobbing. It was truly doleful in the dark. The by-standers looked at one another and turned pale.

"Fourteen years, sire! fourteen long years! ever since the month of April, 1469. In the name of the Blessed Mother, sire, hearken to me. Your majesty has all this time been enjoying the warmth of the sun. Am I never more to see the daylight? Be merciful, sire! Clemency is a right royal virtue which turneth aside the current of wrath. Doth your majesty believe that at the hour of death it is a great consolation to a king not to have left any offense unpunished? Besides, sire, it was not I, but Monsieur d'Angers, who was guilty of the treachery against your majesty. Would that you saw the thick chain fastened to my leg, and the great iron ball at the end of it, much heavier than it need be! Ah! sire! take pity on me!"

"Olivier," said the king, shaking his head, "I perceive that I am charged twenty sous by the load for lime, though it may be bought for twelve. Send back this account."

Turning from the cage, he began to move toward the door of the chamber. The wretched prisoner judged from the receding torches and noise that the king was going. "Sire! sire!" cried he in tones of despair. The door shut. He saw nothing, he heard nothing save the husky voice of the jailer chanting a stanza of a song of that day on the subject of his own misfortunes:

> "Maitre Jean Balue
> A perdu la vue
>   De ses évèches.
> Monsieur de Verdun
> N'en a plus pas un,
>   Tous sont dépèches." [1]

The king returned in silence to his retreat, followed by his train, who were thrilled by the last heart-rending wailings of the prisoner. His majesty turned abruptly toward the governor of the Bastile.

"By the bye," said he, "was there not some one in that cage?"

"In good sooth, sire, there was," replied the governor, astonished at the question.

"Who, then?"

"The Bishop of Verdun."

The king knew that better than anybody else, but this was his way.

"Ah!" said he, as naturally as if he had but just thought of it; "Guillaume de Harancourt, a friend of Monsieur de Balue. A good fellow of a bishop!"

The door of the retreat presently opened and again closed upon the five personages to whom the reader was introduced at the beginning of this chapter, and who resumed their places, their whispering conversation, and their attitudes.

During the king's absence, several dispatches had been laid upon his table. He broke the seals of them himself and hastily ran over one after another. He then made a sign to Master Olivier, who appeared to perform the office of minister, to take a pen, and, without communicating to him the contents of the dispatches, began in a low tone to dictate his answers, which Olivier wrote kneeling very incommodiously at the table.

Guillaume Rym watched him closely. The king spoke so low that the Flemings could catch no more than a few detached and scarcely intelligible fragments of his dictation, such as: "To maintain the

[1].Master Jean Balue has no more / The bishoprics he had before, / My Lord of Verdun / He hath not one.

fertile places by commerce, the barren by manufactures." "To show the English lords our four pieces of ordnance, the London, the Brabant, the Bourg-en-Bresse, and the St. Omer." "The artillery causes war to be now carried on more judiciously." "To our friend, Monsieur Bressuire." "Armies cannot be kept without taxes——"

By and by he raised his voice. "*Pasque Dieu!* Monsieur the King of Sicily seals his letters with yellow wax, like a king of France. Perhaps we are wrong to permit this. The greatness of houses is assured by the integrity of their prerogatives. Note this, Compere Olivier."

Presently, "Oho!" said he, "the big message! What would our brother the emperor?" Running his eye over the missive, he ever and anon interrupted his reading by interjections—"Certes, the Allmains are so great and so mighty that 'tis scarcely credible."—"But we forget the old saying: the finest county is Flanders; the finest duchy, Milan; the finest kingdom, France."—"Is it not so, my Flemish friends?"

This time Coppenole bowed as well as Rym. The patriotism of the hosier was tickled.

The last dispatch made M. Louis knit his brow. "What is this!" he exclaimed. "Grievances and complaints against our garrison in Picardy! Olivier, write forthwith to Monsieur the Marshal de Roualt that discipline is relaxed—that the gendarmes of the guard, the nobles of the ban, the yeoman-archers, the Switzers, do infinite mischief to our lieges—that the soldier, not content with the provisions which he finds in the houses of the farmers, drives them out with grievous blows of sticks and staves to the city in quest of wine, fish, groceries and other luxurious things—that Monsieur the King is acquainted with these proceedings—that it is our intention to protect our people from molestation, robbery, and plunder—that it is our will, by our Lady!—that, moreover, it pleaseth us not that any musician, surgeon, or man at arms shall be attired like a prince in velvet, silks, and rings of gold—that these vanities are hateful to God—that we ourself, who are a gentleman, are content with a doublet of cloth at sixteen sous the Paris ell—that messieurs the soldiers' boys may even come down to that price too—Order and command—To Monsieur de Roualt, our friend—Right!"

This letter he dictated aloud, in a firm tone, and by fits and starts. At the moment when he had finished, the door opened, and a personage whose look bespoke vehement terror rushed into the chamber, crying: "Sire! sire! there is a sedition of the populace in Paris!"

The stern features of M. Louis were contracted, but all the visible signs of his emotion passed away like lightning. He restrained himself, and observed with calm austerity. "Compere Jacques, you come in rather abruptly!"

"Sire! sire! the mob is in rebellion!" replied Compere Jacques, breathless with haste and alarm.

The king, who had risen, seized him roughly by the arm and whispered so as to be heard by him alone, with concentrated anger and a sidelong glance at the Flemings: "Be silent or speak low."

The new-comer comprehended his meaning, and began in a low tone as coherent a narrative as his fears would permit. The king listened with composure, while Guillaume Rym directed the attention of Coppenole to the face and the dress of the speaker, to his furred hood, his short cloak, and his black velvet gown, which bespoke a president of the Court of Accompts.

No sooner had this personage communicated a few particulars to the king than M. Louis burst into a loud laugh, exclaiming:

"Is that all? Speak up, Compere Coictier! Be not afraid to open your mouth. Our Lady knows that I have no secrets from our good friends of Flanders."

"But, sire——"

"Speak up, I tell you, man!"

Compere Coictier was dumbfounded.

"Come!" resumed the king—"speak, sir!—there is a riot of the rabble in our good city of Paris?"

"Yes, sire."

"Directed, you say, against Monsieur the Bailiff of the Palace of Justice?"

"It is, apparently," said the compere, still stammering, quite disconcerted at the abrupt and unaccountable change which had taken place in the sentiments of the king.

"Where did the watch fall in with the mob?" inquired Louis.

"Going along the great Truanderie toward the Pont aux Changeurs. I met it myself as I was coming hither in obedience to the commands of your majesty. I heard some of them shouting: 'Down with the bailiff of the palace!'"

"And what complaint have they to make against the bailiff?"

"Why," said Compere Jacques, "he is their liege lord."

"Indeed!"

"Yes, sire. They are the ragamuffins of the Cour des Miracles: they have long been complaining of the bailiff, whose vassals they are. They will not acknowledge his authority either in criminal or civil matters."

"Ay, marry!" ejaculated the king, with a smile of satisfaction which he strove in vain to disguise.

"In all their petitions to the parliament," replied the Compere Jacques, "they pretend that they have but two masters, your majesty and their God—who, I verily believe, is the devil."

"Eigh! eigh!" said the king.

He rubbed his hands with an inward exultation which beamed forth from his face; he could not dissemble his joy, though he endeavored at times to compose himself. He completely puzzled all present, not excepting Master Olivier himself. He kept silence for a moment, with a look of deep thought, but also of satisfaction.

"Are they numerous?" he all at once inquired.

"Indeed they are, sire," answered Compere Jacques.

"How many?"

"Six thousand at least."

The king could not help ejaculating, "Good!" He then asked, "Are they armed?"

"With scythes, pikes, spades, arquebuses—all sorts of very dangerous weapons."

The king appeared not at all uneasy at this recapitulation. Compere Jacques deemed it his duty to add, "If your majesty send not prompt succor to the bailiff, he is lost."

"We will send," said the king, with a look of affected gravity. " 'Tis well. Certes, we will send. Monsieur the Bailiff is our friend. Six thousand! They are saucy rascals. Their boldness is marvelous, and hath sorely offended us. But we have few people about us to-night. It will be time enough in the morning."

"Instantly, sir!" exclaimed Compere Jacques, "or they will have leisure to plunder the bailiff's house, to pull down the seigneurie, and to hang the bailiff twenty times over. For the love of God, sire, send before morning!"

The king looked him full in the face—"I tell you, in the morning." It was one of those looks to which there is no replying.

For some moments Louis was silent. "Tell me, Compere Jacques," he again began, "for you must know, what was"—he corrected himself—"what is the feudal jurisdiction of the bailiff."

"Sire, the bailiff of the palace has the Rue de la Calandre, as far as the Rue de l'Herberie, the Place St. Michel, and the places vulgarly called the Mureaux, situate near the church of Notre Dame des Champs"—here the king lifted the brim of his hat—"which hotels are thirteen in number; also the Cour des Miracles, the lazar-house called La Banlieue, and the whole line of causeway commencing at this lazar-house and ending at the Gate of St. Jacques. Of all these parts he is the liege lord, with the right of administering high, middle and low justice."

"Hey-day!" said the king, rubbing the side of his nose with his forefinger; "'tis a good slice of my fair city. So Monsieur the Bailiff was king of all that!"

He asked no more questions, but remained absorbed in thought, and talking to himself. "Very fine, Monsieur the Bailiff; you had there between your teeth a nice piece of our Paris!"

All at once he burst forth; "*Pasque Dieu!* what mean those men who pretend to be liege lords, judges, and masters here, who have their toll-bar at the end of every field, their gibbet and their hangman at every cross street among our people? So that, like the Greek who believed in as many dogs as there were fountains, and the Persian, as he saw stars, the French have as many kings as they see gibbets. Egad! this is a frightful state of things. I like not the confusion. I would fain know if it be by the grace of God that there is at Paris any other liege lord beside the king, any other justice beside our parliament, any other emperor beside ourself in this empire? By the faith of my soul! there must come a day when there shall be in France but one king, one liege lord, one judge, one headsman, as in paradise there is but one God!"

Again he lifted his hat, and, still musing, continued, with the look and accent of a huntsman letting slip and urging on his dogs—"Good, my people! well done! Down with these false lords! On them! on them! Sack, plunder, hang! You would fain be kings, messeigneurs, would you?"

Here he stopped short, bit his lips as if to catch the thought which had half escaped him, fixed his piercing eye on each of the five personages around him in succession, and, suddenly seizing his hat with both hands and looking steadfastly at it, he exclaimed: "Oh, I would burn thee if thou knewest what there is in my head!"

Then casting his eyes again around him, with the keen and restless look of a fox slyly returning to his den: "It matters not; we will send succors to Monsieur the Bailiff. Unluckily, we have but few troops here at this moment against such a mob. We must wait till morning. Order shall be restored in the city, and they shall hang out of the way all who are taken."

"By the bye, sire," said Compere Coictier, "I forgot in my first alarm—the watch has taken two stragglers of the band. If your majesty pleases to see them, they are below."

"Will I see them?" cried the king. "*Pasque Dieu!* how couldst thou forget that! Run quick, Olivier, and fetch them!"

Master Olivier left the room, and presently returned with the two prisoners surrounded by archers of the ordnance. The first had a bloated face and stupid, idiot-like, drunken look. He was dressed in rags, and, in walking, he bent his knees and shuffled his feet. With the pale and smiling countenance of the other the reader is already familiar.

The king scrutinized them for a moment without saying a word, and then abruptly asked the first: "What is thy name?"

"Gieffroy Pincebourde."

"Thy profession?"

"A Vagabond."

"What wert thou going to do in that damnable sedition?"

The varlet stared at the king, swinging his arms with a besotted look. His was one of those misshapen heads in which the understanding is almost as much cramped as a light beneath an extinguisher.

"I know not," said he. "The others went! so I went along."

"Were ye not bound to attack with violence and to plunder your liege lord the bailiff of the palace?"

"I know that we were going to take something from somebody—that is all!"

A soldier brought to the king a hedging-bill which had been found upon the prisoner.

"Ownest thou that weapon?" inquired the king.

"Yes; 'tis my bill; I am a vine-dresser."

"Knowest thou this man?" pointing to the other prisoner. "Was he one of thy companions?"

"No; I know him not."

" 'Tis enough," said the king; and, beckoning to the silent personage stationed near the door, "Compere Tristan," said he, "there is a man for you."

Tristan the Hermit bowed. He gave some directions in a low tone to two archers, who took the wretched prisoner away.

The king, meanwhile, turned to the second prisoner whose brow was covered with a cold perspiration: "Thy name?"

"Sire, Pierre Gringoire."

"Thy trade?"

"A philosopher, sire."

"How darest thou, knave, to go and assault our friend Monsieur the Bailiff of the Palace, and what hast thou to say to this riot?"

"Sire, I had no hand in it."

"How now, varlet! Hast thou not been apprehended by the watch in this goodly company?"

"No, sire; 'tis a mistake; it was quite an accident. I make tragedies. Sire, I conjure your majesty to hear me. I am a poet. Men of my profession are addicted to walking the streets at night. It was the greatest chance in the world. I have been wrongfully apprehended; I am innocent of this commotion. Your majesty found that I am not known to yon Vagabond. I beseech your majesty——"

"Silence!" said the king between two gulps of his diet-drink. "Thou stunnest one."

Tristan the Hermit stepped forward, and pointing to Gringoire; "Sire," he asked, "may we take him too?" It was the first audible word that he had uttered.

"Why," replied the king, "I see no reason to the contrary."

"Alas, sire! I see a great many!" ejaculated Gringoire.

Our philosopher was at that moment greener than an olive. From the cold and indifferent look of the king he perceived that he had no resource but in something unusually pathetic, and throwing himself at his feet, he cried with vehement gesticulation: "Sire, your majesty will deign to hear me. Ah, sire! let not your wrath fall upon so humble an object as I am! The thunder-bolts of God are not hurled against a lettuce. You, sire, are an august and most puissant monarch; have pity on a poor but honest man, who would be more puzzled to kindle a sedition than an icicle to give out a spark. Most gracious sovereign, clemency is a kingly virtue, while severity only exasperates the minds of men. The fierce blasts of the north cannot make the traveler throw off his cloak; the sun, gradually pouring forth his rays, warms him to such a degree that he is glad to strip himself to his shirt. I avouch to you, my sovereign lord, and master, that I am not of the Vagabond crew, a thief, or a disorderly person. Sedition and robbery belong not to the train of Apollo. I am not a man to rush into those clouds which burst in thunders of insurrection. I am a faithful liege of your majesty. The same jealousy which a husband has for the honor of his wife, the love which a son feels in return for the affection of a father, a good subject ought to have for the glory of his king; he ought to burn with zeal for his person, his house, his prosperity, to the exclusion of every other passion. Such, sire, is my political creed. Judge me not, then, for this coat out at elbows, to be an accomplice in sedition and plunder. Pardon me, sire, and on my knees will I pray to God, night and morning, for you. I am not very rich, it is true: indeed I am rather poor, but not vicious for all that. It is not my fault. Every one knows that great wealth is not to be gained by letters, and that the most learned have not always the largest fire in winter. The lawyers run away with all the grain, and leave nothing but the straw for the other scientific professions. I could repeat to you forty excellent proverbs on the ragged cloak of the philosopher. Oh, sire! clemency is the only light that can illumine the interior of a great soul. Clemency bears the torch before all other virtues. Without it they are blind, and grope about in the dark for God. Mercy, which is the same thing as clemency, produces love in subjects, which is the most effective guard for the person of the prince. What harm can it do to your majesty, who dazzles all eyes, that there is one poor man more upon earth—one poor innocent philosopher, floundering in the darkness of calamity, with empty pocket and empty stomach! Besides, sire, I am one of the learned. Great kings add a pearl to their crown by protecting letters. Hercules disdained not the title of Musagetes; Matthias Corvinus patronized Jean de Monroyal, the ornament of the mathematics. Now it is a bad way of patronizing letters to hang those who cultivate them. What a stain upon Alexander if he had hanged Aristotle! That trait would not be a spot on the face of his reputation, heightening its beauty, but a foul ulcer disfiguring it. Sire, I have composed a most pertinent epithalamium for Mademoiselle of Flanders and Monseigneur the most august Dauphin. That is not a brand of rebellion. Your majesty perceives that I am not an ignorant varlet, that I have studied deeply, and that I have great natural eloquence. Have mercy, then, sire! In so doing you will perform an act of gallantry to our Lady; and I protest to you that I have a strong dislike to the idea of being hanged!"

As he thus spoke, the disconsolate Gringoire kissed the king's slippers, and Guillaume Rym whispered Coppenole: "He does right to crawl the floor. Kings are like the Cretan Jupiter: they have no ears but in their feet." The hosier, without bestowing a thought on the Cretan Jupiter, replied with a grim smile, and his eye fixed on Gringoire: "Capital, by the rood! Methinks I hear the Chancellor Hugonet begging his life of me!"

When Gringoire at length ceased, out of breath with his harangue, he lifted his eyes, trembling, toward the king, who was scratching with his nail a spot on the knee of his breeches; his majesty then sipped at his drink. He uttered not a word, however, and in his silence kept Gringoire on the rack. At length the king fixed his eye upon him. "What an eternal prater!" said he. Then, turning to Tristan the Hermit: "Bah! let the varlet go!"

Gringoire fell backward, overpowered with joy.

"Let him go!" grumbled Tristan. "Will it not please your majesty to have him shut up awhile in a cage?"

"Compere," rejoined Louis XI., "dost think it is for such birds that we make cages costing three hundred and sixty-seven livres eight sous three deniers? Dismiss me incontinently this paillard"—M. Louis was fond of this term, which with *Pasque Dieu,* constituted the whole stock of his jocularity—"and turn him out with a sound drubbing."

"Ah!" ejaculated Gringoire, "what a magnanimous king!" and, for fear of a counter-order, he hastened toward the door, which Tristan opened for him with a very ill grace. The soldiers went out with him, driving him before them with kicks and thumps, which Pierre bore like a genuine stoic.

The good humor of the king, ever since he had been informed of the insurrection against the bailiff, manifested itself in all he did. This unusual clemency was no slight sign of it. Tristan the Hermit looked as surly in his corner as a dog when you have shown him a bone and taken it away again.

The king, meanwhile, was playfully drumming the march of Pont Audemer with his fingers on the arm of his chair. This prince was a dissembler, but he could conceal his troubles much better than his joy. These external manifestations of delight at any agreeable tidings were sometimes carried to a great length; as at the death of Charles the Bold, when he vowed to present a silver balustrade to St. Martin of Tours; and at his accession to the throne, when he forgot to give directions for the funeral of his father.

"Eh, sire!" suddenly exclaimed Jacques Coictier, "what is become of the acute fit of illness for which your majesty commanded my services?"

"Oh!" said the king, "I am really in great pain, compere. I have a ringing in my ears, and rakes of fire are harrowing my breast."

Coictier took the hand of the king and felt his pulse with a most self-sufficient look.

"See, Coppenole," said Rym, in a low tone, "there he is between Coictier and Tristan. These are his whole court. A physician for himself, a hangman for all besides."

While feeling the king's pulse, Coictier assumed a look of more and more alarm. Louis eyed him with some anxiety. Coictier's countenance assumed a darker and darker shade. The worthy man had nothing to live upon but the ill health of the king; this resource he cultivated with his utmost skill.

"Indeed!" he at length muttered: "but this is serious!"

"Is it not?" said the king in alarm.

"Pulse quick, irregular, intermittent," continued the physician. "*Pasque Dieu!*"

"In less than three days this might prove fatal."

"Our Lady!" ejaculated the king. "And what remedy, compere?"

"I will consider of it, sire."

He desired the king to put out his tongue, shook his head and made a rueful face. In the midst of these grimaces, "Egad, sire!" he abruptly began, "I have to tell you that a receivership of vacant benefices has fallen in, and to remind you that I have a nephew."

"Thy nephew shall have my receivership, Compere Jacques," replied the king; "but relieve me from this fire in my chest."

"Since your majesty is so gracious," rejoined the physician, "you will not refuse me a little aid toward the building of my house in the Rue St. André des Arcs."

"Eh!" said the king.

"My money is all run out," continued the doctor, "and it were indeed a pity that the house should lack a roof: not for the sake of the house, which is quite simple and burgher-like; but for the paintings of Jehan Fourbault wherewith the ceilings are enlivened. There is a Diana flying in the air, but so excellent, so delicate, with action so natural, head-gear so neat and crowned with a crescent, and flesh so white, that she is enough to tempt them that examine her too closely. There is a Ceres too—another goddess of rare beauty. She is seated upon sheaves of wheat, having upon her head a gay garland of ears intwined with salsify and other flowers. Nothing was ever seen more lovely than her eyes, more neatly turned than her limbs, more noble than her air, or more graceful than her drapery. She is one of the most innocent and perfect beauties that the pencil hath ever produced."

"Bloodsucker!" muttered the king, "what is it thou wouldst have?"

"I lack a roof for these paintings, sire; the cost will be trifling, but I have no money."

"How much will it cost?"

"Why—a roof of copper, embellished with figures and gilt—two thousand livres at the utmost."

"Ah! the murderer!" exclaimed the king. "He never draws me a tooth but he makes a diamond of it for himself?"

"Shall I have my roof?" said Coictier.

"Yes, and go to the devil!—but cure me first."

Jacques Coictier made a profound obeisance.

"Sire," said he, "nothing but a repellent can save you. We will rub your loins with that fine specific composed of cerate, Armenian bole, white of egg, oil, and vinegar. You must continue your drink, and we will answer for your majesty."

A lighted candle attracts more than one moth. Master Olivier, seeing the liberality of the king, and deeming it a favorable opportunity, approached in his turn. "Sire——"

"How now?" said Louis XI.

"Sire, your majesty knows that Simon Radin is dead."

"What then?"

"He was Councilor of Justice to the Exchequer."

"Well?"

"His place is vacant, sire."

As he thus spoke, the haughty face of Master Olivier had relinquished its arrogant expression and assumed a cringing air—the only change of which a courtier's features are susceptible. The king looked him full in the face. "I understand," said he, dryly.

"Master Olivier," he again began, after a brief pause, "Marshal de Boucicaut used to say, 'There are no gifts to be got but from the king, no fish to be caught but in the sea.' I perceive that you are of the same way of thinking as Monsieur de Boucicaut. Now listen to this: We have a good memory. In '68, we made you groom of our chamber; in '69, keeper of the castle of the bridge of St. Cloud, at a salary of one hundred livres tournois; you wanted them to be parisis. In November, '73, by letters issued at Gergeaule, we appointed you keeper of the wood of Vincennes, in the room of Gilbert Acle, Esquire; in '75, ranger of the forest of Rouvray lez St. Cloud, in the room of Jacques le Maire; in '78, we were graciously pleased, by letters patent with double seal of green wax, to grant a yearly sum of ten livres parisis to you and your wife, upon the Place aux Marchands, situate at the School of St. Germain; in '79, we made you ranger of the forest of Senart, in the room of poor Jehan Daiz; then captain of the Castle of Loches; then Governor of St. Quentin; then captain of the Bridge of Meulan, from which you have taken the style of count. Out of the fine of five sous paid by every barber who shaves on a holiday, three sous go to you, and we have your leavings. We have been pleased to change your name from Le Mauvais, which accorded but too well with your mien. In '74 we granted you, to the great displeasure of our nobility, coat armor of a thousand colors, which makes you a breast like a peacock's. *Pasque Dieu!* are you not content yet? Is not the draught of fishes miraculous enough? Are you not afraid lest another salmon should sink your boat? Pride will be your downfall, compere. Pride always has ruin and shame close at its heels. Think of this, and be quiet."

These words, uttered with a stern look, caused the angry visage of Master Olivier to resume its former insolence. " 'Tis plain," murmured he almost aloud, "that the king is ill to-day. He gives everything to the physician."

Louis, so far from being exasperated at this impertinence, again began with a degree of mildness: "Hold! I forgot that I made you my embassador to Ghent to Madame Marie. Yes, gentlemen," added the king, turning toward the Flemings, "this man was my embassador. There now, compere," continued he, addressing Master Olivier, "we will not fall out: we are old friends. It is very late: we have finished our business. Shave me."

Our readers were probably not prepared till this moment to recognize in "Master Olivier" that terrible Figaro whom Providence, the great dramatist, so curiously mixed up with the long and bloody comedy of Louis XI. We shall not here attempt to portray that singular face. This royal barber had three names. At court he was politely called Olivier de Daïm; by the people, Olivier the Devil. His real name was Olivier le Mauvais.

Olivier le Mauvais, then, stood motionless, looking doggedly at the king, and stealing sidelong glances at Jacques Coictier. "Yes, yes! the physician!" he muttered between his teeth.

"Ah, yes, the physician!" repeated Louis XI. with singular mildness—"the physician has more influence than thou. And very naturally. He has our whole body in his gripe, whilst thou layest hold of us by the chin only. Come my poor barber, think no more of it. What wouldst thou say, and what would become of thy office, if I were a king like Chilperic, who had a beard which he was in the habit of grasping in his hand? Now, compere, fetch your things, and shave me."

Olivier, seeing that the king was determined not to be put out of temper, left the room, grumbling, to comply with his orders.

The king rose, went to the window, and hastily opening it, cried, clapping his hands, and with extraordinary agitation, "Ah, yes! the sky over the city is all in a glow. The bailiff's house must be on fire. It cannot be anything else. Well done, my good people!—at length ye lend me a hand to crush their lordships." Then, turning toward the Flemings—"Only come and look, gentlemen. Is not that a fire yonder?"

The two citizens of Ghent approached. " 'Tis a great fire too," said Guillaume Rym.

"By the rood!" cried Coppenole, whose eyes all at once sparkled, "that reminds me of the burning of the Seigneur d'Hymbercourt's house. There must be a fine insurrection yonder."

"Think you so, Master Coppenole?" said the king, with a look of scarcely less delight than that of the hosier. "'Twill be difficult to quell, no doubt."

"By the mass! sire, your majesty will get a great many companies of men at arms thinned in doing it."

"Ah!—I!—that alters the case!" rejoined the king. "If I pleased——"

"If this riot be what I suppose," boldly replied the hosier, "your pleasing will be to no purpose."

"Compere," said Louis XI., "with two companies of my guard and one piece of ordnance, one might soon put down the rabble."

The hosier, regardless of the signs made to him by his colleague, appeared determined to contradict the king. "The Switzers too were rabble," said he. "The Duke of Burgundy, being a proud gentleman, held this rabble dog-cheap. At the battle of Grandson he cried: 'Gunners, fire on yon base-born varlets!' and he swore by St. George. But Scharnachthal, the avenger, rushed upon the goodly duke with his mace and his men; and at the onslaught of peasants clad in buffalo-hides the shining Burgundian army was shivered like a pane of glass by a stone. I know not how many knights were slain by the rabble; and Monsieur de Chateau Guyon, the most illustrious of the Burgundian nobles, was found dead with his tall gray charger in a small meadow."

"My friend," rejoined the king, "you are talking of a battle: we have to do with a riot. Why, I would put an end to it in the twinkling of an eye."

"It may be, sire," replied the other with indifference; "but in that case the people's time had come."

Guillaume Rym thought it right to interfere.

"Master Coppenole, you are speaking to a mighty monarch."

"I know it," gravely replied the hosier.

"Let him talk away, my friend Rym," said the king. "I like his frankness. My father, Charles VII., was accustomed to say that truth was sick. Now I fancied that she was dead, and had not found a confessor. Master Coppenole is making me sensible of my mistake."

Then, laying his hand familiarly upon Coppenole's shoulder, he proceeded: "You were saying, Master Jacques——"

"I was saying, sire, that perhaps you are right—that the hour of the people here is not yet come."

Louis fixed upon him his piercing eye: "And when will that hour arrive?"

"You will hear it strike."

"By what clock, pray?"

Coppenole, with grave but tranquil look, drew the king close to the window. "Listen, sire. Here is a castle-keep, there a bell-tower, cannon, burghers, soldiers. When the bell-tower shall buzz, when the cannon shall roar, when the keep shall fall with a mighty crash, when the burghers and the soldiers shall shout and slay one another, then shall the hour have struck."

The face of Louis XI. became gloomy and thoughtful. For a moment he was silent; he then patted with his hand the thick wall of the tower, as though it had been the flank of a favorite charger. "Oh, no!" said he, "thou wilt not fall so easily, my good Bastile!" Then turning sharply toward the bold Fleming, "Master Jacques," said he, "have you seen an insurrection?"

"I have made one," answered the hosier.

"How do you set about making an insurrection?" inquired the king.

"Why," replied Coppenole, "the thing is not at all difficult. There are a hundred ways. In the first place, the city must be discontented. That is not a rare circumstance. And then the character of the inhabitants. Those of Ghent are disposed to sedition. They are always attached to the son of the reigning prince, but never to the prince himself. Well, I will suppose that some morning, some one comes into my shop and says to me: 'Father Coppenole, here is this, that, and the other; the damoiselle of Flanders is determined to save her ministers; the high bailiff had doubled the toll for grinding corn'—or anything else—no matter what. Incontinently I leave my work, and out I go into the street and shout—'To arms!' There is always some cask or hogshead lying about. I leap upon it, and I tell, in the first words that come, what I have upon my heart; and when one belongs to the people, sire, one always has something upon his heart. Then the lieges assemble, they shout, they ring the alarm-bell, they arm themselves with weapons taken from the soldiers, the market people join them, and they fall to work. And this will always be the way while there are lords in the seignories, burghers in the burghs, and peasants in the country."

"And against whom do ye thus rebel?" inquired the king. "Against your bailiffs? against your liege lords?"

"Sometimes one, sometimes the other, just as it happens; sometimes, too, against the duke."

M. Louis returned to his chair. "Aha!" said he, with a smile; "here they have got no further than the bailiffs!"

At that moment Olivier le Daim returned. He was followed by two pages bearing the requisites for the king's toilet; but what struck Louis XI. was the circumstance of his being accompanied also by the Provost of Paris and the officer of the watch, whose countenances bespoke alarm. The face of the spiteful barber also wore a look of dismay, but an expression of pleasure lurked beneath it. He it was who spoke. "Begging your majesty's pardon," he said, "I bring calamitous tidings."

The king, turning sharply round, tore the mat on the floor with the legs of his chair. "What have you to say?"

"Sire," replied Olivier le Daim, with the malignant look of a man who rejoices in the opportunity of striking a severe blow, "it is not against the bailiff of the palace that the insurrection of the populace is directed."

"And against whom, then?"

"Against yourself, sire!"

The aged monarch started upon his feet, upright as a young man. "Explain. Olivier, explain! And beware of thy head, compere; for I swear by the cross of St. Lo that if thou liest, the sword which cut off the head of Monsieur de Luxembourg is not so notched but it shall hack off thine!"

This was a formidable oath. In all his life Louis XI. had sworn but twice by the cross of St. Lo. Olivier opened his lips to reply. "Sire——"

"Down on thy knees!" cried the king, vehemently, interrupting him. "Tristan, look to this man!"

Olivier fell on his knees. "Sire," said he, coldly, "a witch has been sentenced to death by your court of parliament. She has taken sanctuary in Notre Dame. The people have risen to remove her by force. The provost and the officer of the watch, who have just come from the spot, are here to contradict me if I speak not the truth. It is to Notre Dame that the rabble are laying siege."

"Soho!" ejaculated the king, in a low tone, pale and trembling with rage. "Notre Dame, is it? They are besieging our Lady, my good mistress, in her own cathedral! Rise, Olivier. Thou art right. I give thee Simon Radin's place. Thou art right. It is myself whom they are assailing. The witch is under the safeguard of the church, the church is under my safeguard. I verily believed that the bailiff was the object of their attack. It is myself, after all!"

Then, as if his passion had suddenly restored to him the vigor of youth, he began to pace the floor with hasty strides. He no longer laughed; he was terrible to behold as he stalked to and fro. The fox was turned into a hyena. He seemed to be choked, and incapable of utterance; his lips moved and his scraggy fists were clinched. All at once he raised his head; his hollow eye glared, and his voice burst forth like the blast of a trumpet: "Cut them in pieces, Tristan! cut all those knaves in pieces! Go, my friend Tristan! slay, and spare not!"

This explosion over, he returned to his seat, and said with cold, concentrated rage: "Here, Tristan! We have with us in this Bastile the Vicomte de Gif's fifty lances, making together three hundred horse; take them. There is also Captain de Chateaupers's company of the archers of our ordnance; take them. You are provost of the farriers; you have your own people; take them. At the Hotel St. Pol you will find forty archers of the new guard of Monsieur the Dauphin; take them. And with all this force hasten forthwith to Notre Dame. So, so, messieurs of the mob of Paris, it is at the crown of France, at the sanctity of our Lady, and at the peace of this commonwealth, that your blows are aimed! Exterminate, Tristan! exterminate! Spare not one of them but for Montfaucon!"

Tristan bowed. "It shall be done, sire." After a pause he asked: "What shall I do with the sorceress?"

"Ah!" said he, musing at this question—"the sorceress! Monsieur d'Estouteville, what would the people with her?"

"Sire," replied the Provost of Paris, "I should imagine that, as the people are gone to take her from her sanctuary in Notre Dame, they are offended because she is unpunished, and mean to hang her."

For a while the king appeared to be lost in thought; then, turning to Tristan: "Compere," said he, "exterminate the people and hang the sorceress."

"Excellent!" whispered Rym to Coppenole; "punish the people for the intention, and carry that intention into effect!"

"'Tis enough, sire," answered Tristan. "But if the sorceress be still in Notre Dame, is she to be removed in despite of sanctuary?"

"Pasque Dieu! sanctuary!" ejaculated the king, rubbing his forehead. "And yet the witch must be hanged."

Here, as if actuated by a sudden idea, he fell upon his knees before his chair, took off his hat, laid it upon the seat, and devoutly fixed his eyes on one of the leaden figures with which it was garnished. "Oh!" he began with clasped hands, "my gracious patroness, our Lady of Paris, forgive me! I will do it but this once. That criminal must be punished. I assure you, Holy Virgin, my good mistress, that she is a sorceress who is not worthy of your kind protection. You know, madame, that many very pious princes have transgressed the privileges of churches for the glory of God and the necessity of the state. St. Hugh, a bishop of England, allowed King Edward to take a magician in his church. St. Louis of France, my master, violated for the same purpose the Church of Monsieur St. Paul; and Monsieur Alphonse, son of the King of Jerusalem, the Church of the Holy Sepulcher itself. Forgive me then for this time, our Lady of Paris! I will never do so again, and I will give you a goodly statue of silver, like that which I gave last year to our Lady of Ecouys. Amen!"

He made the sign of the cross, rose, put on his hat, and said to Tristan: "Lose not a moment, compere. Take Monsieur de Chateaupers along with you. Let the alarm-bell be rung. Quell the rabble. Hang the sorceress. That is settled. I expect to bear the costs of the execution. Report to me upon it. Come, Olivier; I shall not get to bed to-night. Shave me."

Tristan the Hermit bowed and retired. The king then motioned Rym and Coppenole to withdraw. "God keep you, my good friends of Flanders. Go, take a little rest; the night is far spent; indeed we are nearer to morning than evening."

Both accordingly retired, and on reaching their apartments, to which they were escorted by the captain of the Bastile, Coppenole said to Guillaume Rym: "By the rood! I have had enough of this coughing king. I have seen Charles of Burgundy drunk; he was not so ill-conditioned as Louis XI. sick."

"Master Jacques," replied Rym, "'tis because the wine of kings is not so cruel as their diet-drink."

CHAPTER VI

A NARROW ESCAPE

ON LEAVING the Bastile, Gringoire scudded down the Rue St. Antoine with the swiftness of a runaway horse. When he had reached the Baudover Gate, he walked straight up to the stone cross which stood in the middle of the open space, as though he had been able to discern in the dark the figure of a man in a black dress and cowl seated on the steps of the cross. "Is it you, master?" said Gringoire.

The black figure started up. "Death and perdition! You make my blood boil, Gringoire. The warder on the tower of St. Gervais has just cried half-past one."

"Why," replied Gringoire, "'tis not my fault, but that of the watch and the king. I have had a narrow escape. I was on the point of being hanged. I am predestined to it, I fancy."

"Thou art never in time for anything," said the other; "but let us be gone. Hast thou the watchword?"

"Only think, master—I have seen the king! I have just come from him. He wears fustian breeches. 'Tis quite an adventure!"

"Eternal babbler! What care I for thy adventure! Hast thou the watchword of the Vagabonds?"

"Be easy; I have."

"'Tis well. We should not else be able to reach the church. The rabble block up all the streets. Luckily, they seem to have met with resistance. We shall perhaps yet arrive in time."

"Yes, master. But how are we to get into the church?"

"I have the key to the towers."

"And how shall we get out?"

"Behind the cloisters there is a postern opening upon the Terrain, and so to the river. I have taken the key of it, and I moored a boat there this morning."

"I have had a most lucky escape from the gallows indeed!" said Gringoire, exultingly.

"Never mind that now! come along, quick!" rejoined the other.

Both then proceeded at a rapid pace toward the city.

CHAPTER VII

CHATEAUPERS TO THE RESCUE!

THE READER probably recollects the critical situation in which we left Quasimodo. The brave hunchback, assailed on all sides, had lost, if not all courage, at least all hope of saving, not himself—he never once thought of himself—but the Egyptian. He ran in consternation to the gallery. The church was on the point of being carried by the mob. All at once the tramp of horses in full gallop was heard in the neighboring streets; and presently a wide column of horsemen riding at speed and a long file of torches poured with a tremendous noise into the place like a hurricane. "France! France forever! Chateaupers to the rescue! Down with rascals!" The affrighted Vagabonds faced about.

Quasimodo, who could not hear the din, saw the naked swords, the torches, the pike-heads, the whole column of cavalry, at the head of which he recognized Captain Phœbus. He observed the confusion of the rabble, the consternation of some, and the alarm of the stoutest; and at the sight of this unexpected succor, he mustered strength enough to throw down the foremost of the assailants, who was already striding over into the gallery.

The mob defended themselves with the valor of despair. Taken in flank by the Rue St. Pierre aux Bœufs and in rear by the Rue du Parvis, with their backs toward Notre Dame, which they were still assailing and which Quasimodo defended, at once besiegers and besieged, they were in the singular situation in which Count Henri d'Harcourt subsequently found himself at the famous siege of Turin, in 1640, between Prince Thomas of Savoy, whom he was besieging, and the Marquis de Leganez, who was blockading him; *Taurinum obsessor idem et obessus,*[1] as his epitaph has it.

The conflict was terrible. As Father Mathieu observes, "Wolf's flesh requires dogs' teeth." The king's troops, amid whom Phœbus de Chateaupers conducted himself valiantly, gave no quarter: what escaped the point of the sword was cut down by the edge. The rabble, badly armed, foamed and bit. Men, women, children, darting at the flanks and chests of the horses, clung to them like cats with tooth and nail. Some thrust torches into the faces of the archers; while others, catching them by the neck with iron hooks, pulled them from their horses and cut them in pieces. One in particular was remarked with a huge scythe, mowing away at the legs of the horses. It was a fearful sight. Snuffling a stave with nasal twang, he kept his scythe incessantly going. At each stroke he formed about him a large semicircle of dismembered limbs. In this manner he wrought his way into the thickest of the cavalry with the deliberate movement, the swaying of the head, and the regular expiration of a mower cutting a field of clover. It was Clopin Trouillefou. The fire of an arquebuse laid him prostrate.

Meanwhile, windows were thrown open. The neighbors, hearing the shouts of the men at arms, took part in the affair, and showers of balls were discharged from every story upon the rabble. The Parvis

1. He oppressed the people of Turin and was oppressed by them.

was filled with a dense smoke, which the musketry streaked ever and anon with fire. Through this smoke was faintly seen the façade of Notre Dame, and the decrepit Hotel Dieu, with a number of pale-faced patients gazing from the top of its roof studded with dormer windows.

The Vagabonds at length gave way, discomfited by weariness, the want of proper weapons, the consternation of their surprise, the firing from the windows, and the furious onslaught of the king's troops. Forcing the line of their assailants, they fled in all directions, leaving the Parvis strewed with dead.

When Quasimodo, who had been busily engaged the whole time, perceived their defeat, he fell on his knees and lifted his hands to heaven; then, frantic with joy, he flew with the swiftness of a bird to the little cell, the access to which he had so gallantly defended. He had now but one thought—to throw himself at the feet of her whom he had saved for the second time. When he reached the cell he found it empty.

Book Ten

CHAPTER I

THE LITTLE SHOE

AT THE MOMENT when the Vagabonds attacked the church, La Esmeralda was asleep. It was not long before she was roused by the constantly increasing noise around the cathedral and the uneasy bleating of her goat, which had awoke before her. She sat up, listening and looking about; then, alarmed by the light and the uproar, she hurried out of the cell to see what was the matter. The aspect of the place, the scene exhibited there, the confusion of this nocturnal assault, the hideous appearance of the rabble, hopping about like a host of frogs, faintly discerned in the dark, the harsh croaking of this coarse mob, the few torches dancing to and fro in the obscurity, like those meteors of night gamboling over the misty surface of bogs, produced altogether the effect of a mysterious battle between the phantoms of the witches' sabbath and the stone monsters of the church. Imbued from infancy with the superstitions of the gypsy tribe, her first idea was that she had caught the strange beings peculiar to night in their unhallowed pranks. She then hurried back in affright to her cell, to bury her face in the bed-clothes, and to shut out if possible the terrific vision.

The first fumes of fear having gradually dispersed, she found, from the incessantly increasing din and divers other tokens of reality, that she was invested not by specters, but by creatures of flesh and blood. Her terror then, without being augmented, was changed in form. She had conceived a notion of the possibility of a popular sedition to tear her from her asylum. The prospect of still losing her life, her hopes, her Phœbus, which her imagination held forth to her, the absolute nothingness of her own strength, her forlorn situation, cut off from all support, all chance of flight—these and a thousand other thoughts overwhelmed her. She fell upon her knees, laying her head, covered with her clasped hands, upon the bed, filled with thrilling apprehensions; and, Egyptian, idolater and pagan as she was, she began with heavy sobs to implore mercy of the God of Christians, and to pray to our Lady, her protectress. For, be one's creed what it will, there are moments when one feels favorably disposed toward the religion of the temple near which one happens to be.

In this attitude she remained for a considerable time trembling indeed more than she prayed, her blood curdling at the indications of the nearer and nearer approach of that infuriated multitude, utterly at a loss to account for their proceedings, ignorant of what they were doing and what they meant to do, but anticipating some terrible catastrophe.

Amid this anguish she heard a footstep close to her. She looked up. Two men, one of whom carried a lantern, had just entered her cell. She gave a faint shriek.

"Fear nothing," said a voice which was not unknown to her: "it is I."

"And who are you?" she inquired.

"Pierre Gringoire."

The name gave her fresh courage. She lifted her eyes and saw that it actually was the poet. But at his side stood a black figure, muffled up from head to foot, which struck her mute.

"Ah!" resumed Gringoire, in a tone of reproach, "Djali knew me before you did!"

The little goat had, in fact, not waited for Gringoire to mention his name. No sooner did he enter than she fondly rubbed against his knees, covering the poet with endearments and white hair; for she was shedding her coat. Gringoire returned her caresses.

"Who is that with you?" said the Egyptian, in a low tone.

"Be easy," answered Gringoire. "'Tis one of my friends."

The philosopher, setting down the lantern, crouched upon the floor, clasped Djali in his arms, and cried with enthusiasm: "Oh! 'tis a darling creature, with its engaging ways, and withal shrewd, ingenious, and learned as a grammarian! Come, my Djali, let us see if thou hast not forgotten thy diverting tricks. How does Master Jacques Charmolue do——"

The man in black would not suffer him to finish. He stepped up to Gringoire, and roughly pushed him on the shoulder. Gringoire rose.

"Ah! true!" said he; "I had well-nigh forgotten that we are in haste. But yet, master, that is no reason for hurting people so. My dear girl, your life is in danger, and Djali's too. They mean to hang you again. We are your friends, and are come to save you. Follow us."

"Is it true?" cried she in extreme agitation.

"Quite true, I assure you. Come quick!"

"I will," stammered she. "But how is it that your friend does not speak?"

"Why," said Gringoire, "the fact is that his father and mother were fantastic people, and made him of a reserved disposition."

She was obliged to be satisfied with this explanation. Gringoire took her by the hand; his companion picked up the lantern and walked on before. The young creature was stupefied with fear. She suffered Gringoire to lead her away. The goat went forth with them, frisking about, and so overjoyed to see the poet again, that she thrust her head every moment against his legs with such force as to make him stagger. "Such is life," said the philosopher whenever he had well-nigh fallen; "it is often our best friends that throw us down!"

They rapidly descended the tower stairs, passed through the church, dark, solitary, but ringing with the uproar, which produced a fearful contrast, and went out by the Porte Rouge into the cloister court. The cloisters were deserted; the canons had fled to the bishop's palace, where they were praying together; the court was empty, with the exception of a few affrighted serving-men, squatting in the dark corners. Gringoire and his companions proceeded toward the postern leading out of that court to the Terrain. The man in black unlocked it with a key which he brought with him. The reader is aware that the Terrain was a slip of land inclosed with walls, belonging to the chapter of Notre Dame, forming the eastern extremity of the island, in the rear of the cathedral. They found this spot entirely deserted. At that distance already there was less tumult in the air. The various noises of the assault reached them more blended, more softened down. The breeze which followed the current of the river shook the leaves of the only tree standing on the point of the Terrain, the rustling of which was already audible: but they were yet at a very little distance from the danger. The buildings nearest to them were the bishop's palace and the cathedral. There was evidently a great bustle within the former. Its gloomy front was streaked with lights darting from window to window, as, when you have burned a sheet of paper, there remains a dun edifice of ashes upon which bright sparks play a thousand capricious gambols. Beside it, the enormous towers of Notre Dame, thus seen from behind, with the long nave from which they rise, standing out in black relief from the red glare which filled the Parvis, looked like the two gigantic andirons of a fire of the Cyclops.

So much of Paris as could be seen on all sides oscillated to the eye in one of those shadows mingled with light which we find in pictures of Rembrandt's.

The man with the lantern proceeded directly to the point of the Terrain. At that spot there was, at the water's edge, a decayed fence, composed of stakes crossed with laths, upon which a few sickly branches of a low vine were spread like fingers of an open hand. Behind, and in the shade cast by this trellis, lay a small skiff. The man made a sign to Gringoire and his companion to get in. The goat followed him. The man then stepped in himself, cut the rope which moored the skiff, pushed off from the shore with a long pole, seated himself in the fore part, and taking up two oars, began to row out toward the middle of the river. In this place the Seine is very rapid, so that he had some difficulty to work off from the point of the island.

The first thing Gringoire did, after getting into the boat, was to take his seat at the stern and to lift the goat upon his knees. Her mistress, in whom the stranger excited undefinable apprehensions, sat down by the poet, pressing close to his side.

When our philosopher felt the boat moving he clapped his hands and kissed Djali's forehead. "Oh!" he exclaimed, "we are all four saved!" With the look of a profound thinker, he added, "One is indebted sometimes to fortune, sometimes to stratagem, for the successful issue of great undertakings."

The skiff slowly pursued its way toward the right bank. The girl watched the mysterious unknown with secret terror. He had carefully masked the light of his dark-lantern; and he was faintly seen in the fore part of the skiff, like a specter. His cowl, still down, formed a sort of visor, and every time that, in rowing, he opened his arms, from which hung wide black sleeves, they looked like two prodigious bat's wings. He had not yet uttered a word or suffered a breath to escape him. He made no other noise in the boat than what proceeded from the working of the oars, which blended with the rush of the thousand ripples against the side of the vessel.

"Odds my life!" suddenly exclaimed Gringoire, "we are as merry as so many owls! Mute as Pythagoreans or fish! *Pasque Dieu,* my friends, I wish somebody would talk to me. The human voice is music to the human ear. By the bye, that saying belongs not to me, but to Didymus of Alexandria, and a most pertinent one it is. Certes, Didymus of Alexandria was no ordinary philosopher. One word, my sweet girl! speak to me, I beseech you. Do you know, my love, that the parliament has supreme jurisdiction over sanctuaries, and that you ran as great risk in your cell in Notre Dame as the little bird trochylus, which builds its nest in the jaws of the crocodile? The moon is breaking out again, master! 'Tis to be hoped we shall not be perceived. We are doing a praiseworthy action, to be sure, in saving the damoiselle, and yet we should be hanged in the king's name if they were to catch us. Alas! human actions have two handles to lay hold by. What is condemned in one is applauded in another. Many a man censures Catiline and admires Cæsar. Is it not so, master? What say you to that philosophy? For my part, I possess the philosophy of instinct, of nature *ut apes geometriam.* What, will nobody answer me? How dull ye both are! I am obliged to talk to myself. That is what we call in tragedy a soliloquy. *Pasque Dieu!* let me tell you I have just seen Louis XI., and have learned that oath from him. *Pasque Dieu!* then, what an uproar they are still making in the city! He is a mean old king, that Monsieur Louis. He has not yet paid me for my epithalamium, and it was a mere chance that he did not order me to be hanged to-night, which would have annoyed me exceedingly. He is stingy toward men of merit. He ought to read the four books by Salvianus of Cologne, 'Adversus avaritiam.' In good sooth, 'tis a close-fisted king in his dealings with men of letters, and commits very barbarous cruelties. He is a very sponge in sucking up the money drained from the people. His revenues are like the belly fattening by the leanness of all the other members. Complaints of the hardness of the times are therefore treated as murmurs against the prince. Under this mild, godly old gentleman the gibbets crack with the weight of the condemned, the blocks are clotted with putrefying gore, the prisons are bursting like cows in a clover-field. This king has a hand that takes and a hand that hangs. He is attorney general to Monseigneur Gibbet and my Lady Gabelle. The great are despoiled of their dignities, and the humble incessantly loaded with fresh burdens. 'Tis an exorbitant prince. I cannot love this monarch. What say you, master?"

The man in black did not interrupt the censures of the garrulous poet. He continued to struggle against the violence of the current which separates the prow of the city from the poop of the Isle of Notre Dame, which we now call the Isle of St. Louis.

"By the bye, master," Gringoire began again abruptly, "at the moment when we had passed through the enraged rabble and reached the Parvis, did you remark that unlucky little wight whose brains your hunchback was in a fair way to dash out against the balustrade of the gallery of the kings? I am too near-sighted to recognize him. Perchance you know who it was."

The unknown answered not a word; but he suddenly ceased rowing, his arms sunk as if broken, his head dropped upon his breast, and La Esmeralda heard him sigh convulsively. She had heard sighs of that kind before.

The skiff, left to itself, drifted for some moments at the will of the current. At length the man in black roused himself, and again began pulling against the stream. He doubled the point of the Isle of Notre Dame and rowed toward the landing place of the Port au Foin.

"Ah," said Gringoire, "yonder is the logis Barbeau. Only look, master, at that group of black roofs which form such singular angles —there, beneath that mass of low, streaky, dirty-looking clouds, in which the moon appears smashed and spread about like the yelk of a broken egg. 'Tis a goodly mansion that! It has a chapel with vaulted roof, beautified with excellent sculptures. You may see above it the belfry, with its rare and delicate tracery. There is also a pleasant garden, containing a fish-pond, an aviary, an echo, a mall, a maze, a house for wild beasts, and many shady alleys particularly agreeable to Venus. There is likewise a rogue of a tree called 'The Lovers' Tree,' because it served for the trysting-place of a famous princess and a gay and witty constable of France. Alas! we poor philosophers are to a constable what a bed of cabbages or turnips is to a grove of laurels. What signifies it after all! For the great, as for us, life is a medley of good and ill. Pain is ever by the side of pleasure, as the spondee by the dactyl. I must tell you the history of the logis Barbeau, master: it finished in a tragical way. It was in 1319, under Philip V., who reigned longer than any other king in France. The moral of the history is that the temptations of the flesh are hurtful and pernicious. Beware of looking too hard at the wife of your neighbor, much as your senses may be struck by her beauty. Zounds! what an uproar they are making yonder!"

The tumult around Notre Dame was in fact raging with increased vehemence. They listened. Shouts of victory were distinctly heard. All at once, a hundred torches, which made the helmets of the men at arms glisten, appeared on all parts of the church, on the towers, the galleries, the flying buttresses. These torches seemed to be employed in searching after something; and presently distant shouts of "The Egyptian!—the sorceress!—death to the Egyptian!" were plainly heard by the fugitives.

The unhappy girl dropped her head upon her hands, and the unknown began to row furiously toward the shore. Our philosopher was meanwhile musing. He hugged the goat in his arms, and sidled gently away from the Bohemian, who pressed closer and closer to him, as to the only asylum that was now left her.

It is certain that Gringoire was in a cruel dilemma. He considered that, as the law then stood, the goat would be hanged too if she were retaken; that it would be a great pity—poor dear Djali!—that two condemned ones thus clinging to him were more than he could manage; that, besides, his companion desired nothing better than to take charge of the Egyptian. A violent conflict ensued among his thoughts, in which, like Homer's Jupiter, he weighed by turns the Egyptian and the goat; and he looked first at one and then at the other, with eyes brimful of tears, muttering at the same time between his teeth: "And yet I cannot save you both!"

A shock apprised them that the skiff had reached the shore. The city still rang with the appalling uproar. The unknown rose, stepped up to the Egyptian, and offered her his arm to assist her to land. She refused it and clung to the sleeve of Gringoire, who, on his part, engaged with the goat, almost pushed her away. She then sprung without help out of the boat. She was so alarmed that she knew not what she was doing, or whither she was going. She stood stupefied for a moment, with her eyes fixed on the water. When she came to herself a little she was alone on the quay with the unknown. It appeared that Gringoire had taken advantage of the instant of landing to steal away with the goat among the cluster of houses composing the Rue Grenier sur l'Eau.

The poor Egyptian shuddered on finding herself alone with that man. She strove to speak, to cry out, to call Gringoire; but her tongue refused its office, and not a sound issued from her lips. All at once she felt the hand of the unknown upon hers. Her teeth chattered, and she turned paler than the moon's ray which fell upon her. The man spoke not a word. With hasty step he began to move toward the Place de Grève, drawing her along by the hand. At that moment she had a vague feeling that Fate is an irresistible power. She had lost all elasticity, and followed mechanically, running while he walked. The quay at this spot is rising ground; to her it seemed as if she were going downhill.

She looked around on all sides. Not a passenger was to be seen. The quay was absolutely deserted. She heard no sound, she perceived no movement of men but in the tumultuous and roaring city, from which she was parted only by an arm of the Seine, and whence her name, mingled with cries of death, was wafted to the ear. The rest of Paris lay scattered around her in vast masses of shade.

Meanwhile, the unknown continued to drag her along with the same silence and the same rapidity. She had no recollection of the places through which he took her. In passing a lighted window she suddenly made an effort to resist, and cried, "Help, help!"

The window opened; the inmate of the room appeared at it in his shirt and night-cap, with a lamp in his hand, looked out with drowsy eyes upon the quay, muttered a few words which she could not catch, and reclosed the window. She felt as though the last glimmer of hope was extinguished.

The man in black uttered not a syllable: he held her tightly, and began to quicken his pace. She ceased to resist, and followed him spiritless and helpless.

From time to time she mustered a little strength, and in a voice broken from the jolting of the rugged pavement, and from her being out of breath, owing to the rapid rate at which she was drawn along, she asked, "Who are you?—who are you?" He made no reply.

Proceeding thus along the quay, they arrived at a large open space. The moon shone faintly. It was the Grève. In the middle of it stood a sort of black cross—it was the gibbet. She now knew where she was.

The man stopped, turned toward her, and raised his cowl. "Oh!" stammered she, petrified with horror, "I knew that it must be he!"

It was in truth the priest. He looked like a ghost. Moonlight produces this effect. It seems as if by that light one beholds only the specters of objects.

"List to me," said he, and she shuddered at the sound of that fatal voice, which she had not heard for so long a time. He continued with frequent pauses and in broken sentences which betoken violent inward agitation. "List to me! Here we are. I would speak to thee. This is the Grève. We go no further. Fate delivers us up into the hands of each other. Thy life is at my disposal, my soul at thine. Here is a place and a night beyond which one sees nothing. List to me, then. I would tell thee . . . but not a word about thy Phœbus" —as he spoke he paced to and fro like a man who cannot remain quietly on one spot, and drew her after him—"talk not to me of him. If thou but utterest that name, I know not what I shall do; but it will be terrible."

Having proceeded thus far, like a body recovering its center of gravity, he stood still, but his words betrayed not the less perturbation. His voice became more and more faint.

"Turn not thy head from me thus. List to me. 'Tis a serious business. First, I would tell thee what has passed. It is not a thing to laugh at, I protest to thee. But what was I saying? Ah, yes! An order has been issued by the parliament which consigns thee again to the gallows. I have rescued thee from their hands. But yonder they are searching for thee. Look."

He pointed toward the city. It was evident, in fact, that the search was continued. The noise drew nearer. The tower of the lieutenant's house, facing the Grève, was full of bustle and lights; and soldiers might be seen running on the opposite quay with torches, shouting, "The Egyptian! Where is the Egyptian? Death! Death!"

"Thou seest that they are in pursuit of thee, and that I am not deceiving thee. Maiden, I love thee! Open not thy lips; answer me not, if it is to tell me that thou hatest me. I am determined not to hear that. I have aided thine escape. Let me complete the work. I can save thee. Everything is prepared. All depends on thy will. Whatever thou wilt shall be done."

He interrupted himself with vehemence—"No! that is not what I meant to say." Then running and drawing her along after him, for he still kept hold of her, he went straight to the foot of the gibbet, and, pointing to it, said coldly: "Choose between us."

She tore herself from his grip, and, throwing herself on the pavement, clasped the foot of the fatal machine; then, half turning her head, she looked over her shoulder at the priest. The priest stood motionless, his finger still raised toward the gibbet, like a statue.

"I feel less horror of that than of you," at length said the Egyptian.

He slowly dropped his arm and cast his eyes upon the pavement in deep dejection. "Yes," said he, "if these stones could speak, they would say—'There is the most miserable of men!'"

"I love you," he again began. The girl, kneeling before the gibbet, covered by her long flowing hair, allowed him to proceed without interruption. His accent was now soft and plaintive, wofully contrasting with the lofty sternness of his features.

"I love you. Nothing can be more true. No fire can be fiercer than that which consumes my heart. Ah! maiden, night and day—yes, night and day. Doth this claim no pity? 'Tis a love, a torture, night and day, I tell thee. Oh! my dear girl, 'tis an agony worthy of compassion, I assure thee. I would speak kindly to thee, thou seest. I would have thee not feel such horror of me. And then, if a man loves a woman it is not his fault. What! thou wilt never take compassion on me, then? Thou wilt hate me forever? 'Tis this that makes me cruel—ay, hateful to myself! Thou wilt not even deign to look at me. Thou art thinking perhaps, of something else, while I am talking to thee and trembling on the brink of the eternity of both. At any rate, talk not to me of thine officer! Were I to throw myself at thy knees; were I to kiss, not thy feet—thou wouldst not suffer me—but the ground beneath them; were I to sob like a child and to tear from my bosom, not words, but my heart and my entrails, to tell thee how I love thee, all would be in vain—all! And yet thou hast in thy soul naught but what is kind and tender. Thou art all goodness, all gentleness, all compassion, all charms. Alas! to me alone art thou unfeeling. Oh! what a fatality!"

He buried his face in his hands. La Esmeralda heard him weep; it was for the first time. His figure, thus upright and shaken by sobs, was more pitiable and more humble than if he had knelt. He continued to weep thus for some time.

"Alas!" he proceeded, this first paroxysm over, "I am at a loss for words. And yet I had well pondered what I should say to thee. Now I tremble and shudder; I shrink back at the decisive moment; I feel some superior power that overwhelms me and makes me stammer. Oh! I shall sink on the pavement unless thou take pity on me, on thyself. Condemn not both of us. Would that thou knowest how I love thee, and what a heart is mine. Oh! what an abandonment of all virtue, what a desperate desertion of myself! A doctor, I make a mock at science; a gentleman, I disgrace my name; a priest, I violate the most solemn vows and renounce my God!—and all for thy sake, enchantress; and thou rejectest the wretched one! Oh! I must tell thee all—still more, something even yet more horrible—most horrible!"

As he uttered the concluding words his look became quite wild. He kept silence for a moment, and then began again, as if speaking to himself, in a loud tone: "Cain, what hast thou done with thy brother?"

Again he paused, and then continued: "What have I done with him, Lord? I have taken him unto me, I have fed him, I have brought him up, I have loved him, I have idolized him, and—I have slain him! Yes, Lord, he it was whose head was but now dashed before mine eyes against the stones of Thy temple, and it was on my account, and on account of this female, on her account—"

His eye glared wildly; his voice became more and more faint: he repeated several times, and with pauses of some length, like a bell prolonging its last vibration: "On her account—on her account!" His lips continued to move, but his tongue ceased to articulate any audible sound. All at once he sunk down and remained motionless upon the ground, with his head bowed to his knees.

A slight movement made by the girl to draw her foot from under him brought him to himself. He passed his hand slowly over his hollow cheeks and looked vacantly for some moments at his fingers which were wet. "What!" he muttered; "have I wept?"

Turning abruptly toward the Egyptian, with irrepressible anguish, he said: "And hast thou coldly beheld me weep? Knowest thou, girl, that those tears are lava? Is it then true that thy sex are not moved by anything that can befall the man they hate? Wert thou to see me die, thou wouldst laugh. But I—I wish not thy death! One word! a single word of kindness! Tell me not that thou lovest me; say only that thou wishest me well: it shall suffice—I will save thee. Otherwise—Oh! the time passes. I implore thee by all that is sacred, wait not till I am again transformed into stone, like that gibbet which also claims thee! Consider that I hold both our fates in my hand, that I am mad—oh! it is terrible—that I may let all drop, and that there is beneath us a bottomless abyss, down which I shall follow thee in thy fall to all eternity! One kind word! one word! but a single word!"

She opened her lips to answer. He fell on his knees before her, to catch with adoration the words, perhaps of sympathy, which should drop from her mouth. "You are an assassin!" said she.

The priest clasped her furiously in his arms and burst forth into a terrific laugh. "Assassin though I be," cried he, "I will have thee. Thou wilt not have me for a slave; thou shalt have me for a master. Thou shalt be mine. I have a den to which I will drag thee. Thou shalt come, thou must come, with me, or I will deliver thee up! Thou must die, girl, or be mine—be the priest's, the apostate's, the assassin's! The choice rests with thyself—decide instantly; for I will not submit to further humiliations."

His eye sparkled with passion and rage. The damsel's neck was flushed beneath the touch of his burning lips.

"Loose me, monster!" cried she. "Oh! the hateful poisonous monk! Loose me, or I will tear out thy scurvy gray hair and dash it in thy face!"

He reddened, turned pale, released her from his grip, and eyed her with a gloomy look. She deemed herself victorious, and continued: "I tell thee I belong to my Phœbus, that 'tis Phœbus I love, that 'tis Phœbus who is handsome! As for thee, priest, thou art old, thou art ugly! Go thy way!"

He gave a violent shriek, like a wretch to whose flesh a redhot iron is applied. "Die, then!" said he, gnashing his teeth. She noticed the infernal malignity of his look, and would have fled. He caught her again, shook her, threw her down, and with rapid strides proceeded toward the angle of Roland's Tower, dragging her after him along the pavement by her beautiful arms.

On reaching that point he turned toward her.

"Once more," said he: "wilt thou be mine?"

She replied firmly, "No."

He then cried aloud: "Gudule! Sister Gudule! Here is the Egyptian! Revenge thyself on her!"

The damsel felt herself suddenly seized by the wrist. She looked: it was a skeleton arm thrust through a hole in the wall, which held her like a vise.

"Hold fast!" said the priest: "'tis the Egyptian who has run away. Let her not escape. I will fetch the sergeants; thou shalt see her hanged."

These inhuman words were answered by a guttural laugh from within the wall: "Ha! ha! ha!" The Egyptian saw the priest run off toward the bridge of Notre Dame. The tramp of horses was heard in that direction.

The girl presently recognized the malicious recluse. Panting with terror, she strove to release herself. She writhed, she made many a bound of agony and despair, but the recluse held her with supernatural force. The bony fingers meeting round her wrist clasped her as firmly as if that hand had been riveted to her arm, more efficient than a chain or ring of iron; it was a pair of living and intelligent pincers issuing from a wall.

Against that wall La Esmeralda sunk exhausted, and then the fear of death came over her. She thought of the pleasure of life, of youth, of the aspect of the sky, of the scenery of nature, of love, of Phœbus, of all that was past and all that was to come, the priest who was gone to denounce her, of the gibbet which stood there, and the hangman who would presently arrive. Then did she feel horror mounting to the very roots of her hair, and she heard the sinister laugh of the recluse, who said in low tone: "Thou art going to be hanged! ha! ha! ha!"

She turned, half dead, toward the aperture and saw the sallow face of the recluse between the bars. "What harm have I done to you?" said she in a faint voice.

The recluse made no reply but began to mutter, with a singing, irritating, and jeering intonation: "Gypsy girl! gypsy girl! gypsy girl!"

The wretched Esmeralda drooped her head, conceiving that it was not a human being with which she had to deal.

Suddenly the recluse exclaimed, as if the girl's question had taken all the intermediate time to reach her understanding: "What harm hast thou done me, dost thou ask? What harm hast thou done me, Egyptian! What, listen: I had a child, seest thou? a little child, an infant, I tell thee—a pretty little girl. My Agnes," she resumed, kissing something in the dark. "Well; they stole my child; they took my child away, they eat my child. That is the harm thou hast done me!"

The damsel replied, like the lamb in the fable: "Most probably I was not even born then."

"Oh, yes!" rejoined the recluse, "thou must have been born. Thou wert one of them. She would be about thy age. Just! 'Tis fifteen years that I have been here; fifteen years have I suffered; fifteen years have I prayed; fifteen years have I dashed my head against these four walls. I tell thee it was Egyptians who stole my babe, and eat her afterward. Hast thou a heart? then fancy to thyself what it is to have a child that sucks, that sleeps, that plays! 'Tis so innocent! Well, it was such an infant that they stole from me and killed, God wot. Now it is my turn; I will feast on the Egyptian. Oh, how I would bite thee if I could get my head between the bars! Only think—while the poor little thing was asleep! And if they had even wakened her when they took her up, her crying would have been to no purpose: I was not there. Ah, ye Egyptian mothers! ye eat my child! Come and see how I will serve yours."

She then began to laugh or to gnash her teeth—for both had nearly the same expression on that furious face. The day began to dawn. A gray light faintly illumined this scene, and the gibbet in the middle of the place became more and more distinct. On the other side, toward the bridge of Notre Dame, the poor condemned one imagined that she heard the tramp of horses approaching.

"Mistress!" cried she, clasping her hands and sinking on her knees, disheveled, overwhelmed, distracted with terror, "take pity on me. They are coming. I never harmed you. Would you have me die that horrid death before your face? You are compassionate, I am sure. 'Tis too frightful! Loose me—let me try to escape. Have mercy! I should not like to die thus!"

"Give me back my child," said the recluse.

"Mercy! mercy!"

"Give me my child."

"Let me go, for Heaven's sake!"

"Give me my child."

The poor girl sunk down, overcome, exhausted, with the glazed eye of one who is already in the grave. "Alas!" stammered she, "you seek your child, and I seek my parents!"

"Give me my little Agnes," continued Gudule. "Thou knowest not where she is?—then die! I tell thee, I had a child, a sweet little child; they took it away—those accursed Egyptians! 'Tis plain then thou must die. When thy Egyptian mother comes to ask for thee, I will say to her, 'Mother, look at that gibbet!' Oh, give me back my child! Knowest thou where she is, where my little daughter is? Stay, I will show thee. There is her shoe, all that is left me of her. Knowest thou where is its fellow? If thou dost, tell me, and if it is at the end of the world; I will fetch it, if I crawl thither on hands and knees."

As she thus spoke, putting her other hand out at the aperture, she showed the little embroidered shoe to the Egyptian. It was already light enough for her to distinguish its form and colors.

"Let me look at that shoe," said the girl, shuddering. "Gracious God!" At the same time, with the hand that was at liberty, she tore open the little bag adorned with green beads which she wore about her neck.

"Go to! go to!" muttered Gudule; "fumble away in thy infernal amulet!" Then stopping short, and trembling in every joint, she cried, with a voice issuing from her very bowels: "My child! My child!"

The Egyptian had taken out of the bag a little shoe that was quite the precise fellow to the other. To this little shoe was attached a piece of parchment, upon which was written this legend:

> "When the fellow thou shalt find,
> Thy mother is not far behind."

In the twinkling of an eye the recluse had compared the two shoes, read the inscription upon the parchment, and, thrusting her face, beaming with celestial joy, against the bars of the window, shouted: "My daughter! my daughter!"

"My mother! my mother!" responded the Egyptian.

Here we stop short in our delineation.

The wall and the iron bars were between them.

"Oh, this wall!" cried the recluse. "To see her, yet not be able to clasp her to my heart! Thy hand! give me thy hand!"

The girl put her hand through the window; the recluse seized it, fastened her lips to it, and stood absorbed in that kiss, giving no other sign of life but a sigh which from time to time heaved her bosom. Meanwhile, tears gushed from her eyes in silence and in the dusk like a shower at night. The poor mother poured forth upon that adored hand the dark, deep well-spring of tears which was within her, and from which her sorrows had been oozing drop by drop for fifteen years.

All at once she raised her head, threw back the long gray hair from her face, and, without saying a word, began to pull and thrust at the bars of her window more furiously than a lioness. The bars defied her utmost strength. She then went to a corner of her cell, fetched a large paving-stone which served her for a pillow, and dashed it against them with such violence as to shiver one of them into several pieces. A second blow drove out the old iron cross which barricaded the window. With both hands she then pulled out the rusty fragment of the bars. There are moments when the hands of a woman possess superhuman force.

The passage being cleared—and this was accomplished in less than a minute—she clasped her daughter in her arms and drew her into the cell. "Come!" murmured she; "let me drag thee from the abyss."

She let her down gently upon the floor, then caught her up again, and, carrying her in her arms, as if she had still been her infant Agnes, she paced her narrow cell, intoxicated, frantic with joy, shouting, singing, kissing the girl, talking to her, laughing, weeping, all at once and with vehemence.

"My child! my dear child!" cried she, "I have got my child! here she is! The gracious God has restored her to me. Come, all of you, and see that I have got my daughter again. Lord Jesus, how beautiful she is! The Almighty made me wait fifteen years, but it was to give her back to me in beauty. After all, then, the Egyptians did not eat thee. Who could have said so? My child, my dear little child, kiss me. Oh, those good Egyptians! How I love the Egyptians! And it is thou thyself. And this was the reason why my heart always leaped within me whenever thou wert passing. Fool that I was to take this for hatred! Forgive me, my Agnes, forgive me. Thou must have thought me very spiteful, didst thou not? Ah! how I love thee! And the pretty mark on thy neck!—hast thou it still? Let us see. Yes, there it is. Oh! how handsome thou art grown. It was from thy mother thou hadst those large bright eyes. Kiss me, darling. I do love thee. What care I whether other mothers have children? I can laugh at them now. Let them come. Here is mine. Here is—her neck, her eyes, her hair, her hand. Show me anything more charming than this. Yes, yes, she will have plenty of lovers; I will answer for it. I have sorrowed for fifteen years. All my beauty has left me and gone to her. Kiss me, love."

In this strain she ran on, uttering a thousand extravagant things, the accent of which constituted all their beauty—deranging the poor girl's dress so as to make her blush, stroking her silken hair with her hand, kissing her foot, her knee, her brow, her eyes, and extolling every feature. The damsel suffered her to do as she pleased, repeating at intervals, in a low and infinitely sweet tone: "My dear mother!"

"Ah, my darling," the recluse again began, interrupting herself at every word with kisses, "how I shall love thee! We will leave this place. How happy we shall be! I have some property at Reims, in our own country. Dost thou remember Reims? Ah, no! how shouldst thou! thou wert then quite an infant. If thou didst but know how pretty thou wert at four months old! Tiny feet which people came out of curiosity to see all the way from Epernay, which is fifteen miles off. We shall have a house, a field. Thou shalt sleep in my bed. My God! my God! who would have believed it? I have got my daughter again."

"Oh, mother!" said the girl, at length recovering power to speak amid her emotion, "the Egyptian woman told me this. There was a good woman of our tribe who died last year, and who always took care of me like a nurse. It was she who fastened this little bag about my neck. She always said: 'My dear, never part with this trinket. It is a treasure. It will enable thee to find thy mother again. Thou carriest thy mother about thy neck.' The Egyptian foretold it, you see."

The recluse again clasped her daughter in her arms. "Come, let me kiss thee! How sweetly thou saidst that! When we go into the country we will give those little shoes to an infant Jesus in the church. We certainly owe so much as that to the kind Holy Virgin. But, what a charming voice thou hast! When thou wert speaking to me just now, it was like music. Ah! I have found my child again. And yet who would believe the story? Surely nothing can kill one, since I have not died of joy."

She then began to clap her hands, laughing, and exclaiming: "How happy we shall be!"

At that moment the cell rang with the clank of arms and the tramp of horses, which seemed to be advancing from the bridge of Notre Dame along the quay. The Egyptian threw herself in unutterable anguish into the arms of the recluse.

"Save me!" she shrieked; "save me, mother! they are coming!"

The recluse turned pale. "Oh, heavens! what sayst thou? I had forgotten; they are searching for thee. What hast thou done, then?"

"I know not," answered the unfortunate girl; "but I am condemned to die."

"Die!" cried Gudule, reeling as if stricken by a thunder-bolt. "Die!" she slowly repeated, fixing her glazed eye upon her daughter.

"Yes, mother," replied the affrighted girl, "they mean to put me to death. They are coming to take me. That gibbet is for me. Save me! save me! They are coming! Save me!"

For some moments the recluse remained motionless as a statue; she then shook her head doubtingly, and suddenly burst into a loud laugh, her old terrific laugh: "No, no; thou must be dreaming! It cannot be. To lose her for fifteen years, and then to find her for a single minute. And they would take her from me again, now that she is grown up and handsome, and talks to me and loves me. They would now come to devour her before my face—mine, who am her mother. Oh, no! Such things are not possible. God Almighty would not permit such doings."

By this time the cavalcade had apparently halted. A distant voice was heard calling out: "This way, Messire Tristan. The priest says that we shall find her at the Trou aux Rats." The tramp of the horses began again.

The recluse started up with a shriek of despair. "Away! begone, my child! I now recollect it all. Thou art right. 'Tis for thy death. Curses on them! Away!"

She put her head out of the window and quickly drew it back again. "Stay!" said she, in a low, doleful voice, convulsively grasping the hand of the Egyptian, who was more dead than alive. "Stay! hold thy breath. The place is full of soldiers. Thou canst not get away. It is too light."

Her eyes were dry and inflamed. For a moment she remained silent; but with hurried step she paced up and down her cell, stopping now and then, and tearing out handfuls of her gray hair, which she dashed upon the floor.

"They are coming!" she exclaimed, all at once. "I will talk to them. Hide thyself in this corner. They will not see thee. I will tell them that I let thee go, that thou hast run away—that I will."

Catching up the girl in her arms, she carried her to a corner of the cell which could not be seen from without. Here she made her crouch down, taking care that neither foot nor hand should protrude beyond the dark shadow, loosed her black hair, which she spread over her white robe to conceal it, and placed before her the water-jug and paving-stone, the only movables that she possessed, fondly imagining that they would help to hide her. This done, she was more calm, knelt down, and prayed. Day had not yet so far broken but that dim obscurity still pervaded the Trou aux Rats.

At that moment the voice of the priest, that infernal voice, passed very close to the cell, crying: "This way, Captain Phœbus de Chateaupers."

At that name, at that voice, La Esmeralda made a slight movement. "Stir not!" said Gudule.

She had scarcely uttered the words when a tumult of horses and men was heard outside the cell. The mother hastily rose and posted herself before the window to intercept the view of the interior. She beheld a numerous body of armed men, foot and horse, drawn up in the Grève. Their commander alighted and advanced toward her. He was a man of truculent aspect. "Old woman," he said, "we are seeking a sorceress to hang her; we were told that thou hadst her."

The poor mother, assuming a look of as much indifference as she could, answered: "I know not what you mean."

"*Tête Dieu!*" cried the other, "what kind of a story did that crazed archdeacon tell us? Where is he?"

"Monseigneur," said one of the soldiers, "he has slipped away."

"Come, come, old crone," resumed the commandant, "let us have the truth. A sorceress was given to thee to hold. What hast thou done with her?"

The recluse, apprehensive lest by denying everything she might awaken suspicion, replied in a tone of affected sincerity and surliness: "If you mean a young girl that I was desired to hold just now, all I can tell you is that she bit me, and I let her go. Leave me alone, I pray you."

The countenance of the commandant betrayed a feeling of disappointment.

"Tell me no lies, old scarecrow," rejoined he. "I am Tristan the Hermit, the compere of the king. Tristan the Hermit, dost hear? 'Tis a name," he added, looking around at the Place de Grève, "which has an echo here."

"If you were Satan the Hermit," replied Gudule, regaining some hope, "I should have nothing else to tell you, neither should I be afraid of you."

"*Tête Dieu!*" cried Tristan, "there's a hag for you. So the young sorceress has escaped. And which way is she gone?"

"Down the Rue du Mouton, I believe," answered Gudule, in a careless tone.

Tristan turned his head and motioned to his troop to prepare to start. The recluse began to breathe again.

"Monseigneur," said one of the archers, all at once, "ask the old witch why the bars of her window are broken in this fashion."

That question once more overwhelmed the heart of the wretched mother with anguish. She nevertheless retained some presence of mind. "They were always so," stammered she.

"Pooh!" replied the archer, "they formed but yesterday a fair black cross, fit to remind a man of his prayers."

Tristan cast a sidelong glance at the recluse.

"By my fay!" said he, "the hag does begin to look confused."

The wretched woman felt that all depended on keeping up a bold face, and while her soul was racked with mortal anguish, she fell a-laughing. Mothers have this kind of force. "Pshaw!" said she, "that fellow is drunk. It is more than a year since the tail of a cart laden with stones was backed against my window, and broke the grating. How I did abuse the driver!"

"'Tis true enough," said another archer; "I was present."

Wherever you may be, you are sure to meet with people who have seen everything. This unexpected testimony somewhat revived the recluse, who felt, during this interrogatory, like one forced to cross an abyss on the edge of a knife; but she was doomed to a continual alternation of hope and alarm.

"If it was a cart that did this," replied the first soldier, "the stumps of the bars would be driven inward, whereas these are bent outward."

"Aha!" said Tristan to the archer, "thou hast a nose like an inquisitor to the Chatelet. What hast thou to say to that, woman?"

"Good God!" she exclaimed, driven to extremity, and in a voice, in spite of herself, akin to that of weeping; "I assure you, monseigneur, that it was a cart which broke those bars. That man saw it, you hear. Besides, what has this to do with your Egyptian?"

"Hum!" grumbled Tristan.

"The devil!" resumed the first soldier, flattered by the commendation of the provost; "the fractures of the iron are quite fresh."

Tristan shook his head. She turned pale. "How long is it, say you, since this affair of the cart?"

"A month—a fortnight, perhaps—monseigneur. I cannot recollect exactly."

"She said at first above a year," observed the soldier.

"That looks suspicious," said the provost.

"Monseigneur," she exclaimed, still standing close to the window and trembling lest they should think of putting in their heads and looking about the cell, "monseigneur, I swear to you that it was a cart which broke this iron-work. I swear it by the angels in paradise. If it was not a cart, may eternal perdition be my lot!"

"Thou art in good earnest in that oath," said Tristan, with a scrutinizing look.

The poor creature felt her assurance forsaking her by degrees. She was so confounded as to make awkward blunders, and she perceived with terror that she was not saying what she ought to have said.

A soldier now came up, crying, "Monseigneur, the old witch lies. The girl has not been in the Rue du Mouton. The chain has been up all night, and the keeper has not seen a creature pass."

Tristan, whose look became every moment more threatening, turned to the recluse: "What hast thou to say to this?"

"I know not, monseigneur," replied she, still striving to make head against this new incident. "I may be mistaken. In fact, I almost think she must have crossed the water."

"Why, that is the very contrary way," said the provost.

"Besides, 'tis not likely that she would have gone back to the city, where search was making for her. Thou liest, hag!"

"And then," added the first soldier, "there is no boat either on this side of the water or on the other."

"She must have swum over," replied the recluse, defending the ground inch by inch.

"Who ever heard of women swimming?" cried the soldier.

"*Tête Dieu!* old woman, thou liest! thou liest!" exclaimed Tristan, with vehemence. "I have a good mind to let the young sorceress go, and to take thee instead. A quarter of an hour's torture will bring the truth out of thy throat. Come, thou shalt go along with us."

"As you please, monseigneur," said she, eagerly catching at these words. "Go to, go to! The torture! I am ready. Take me. Let us be gone forthwith! Meanwhile," thought she, "my daughter will have opportunity to escape."

"'Sblood!" cried the provost, "what greediness of torture! The mad creature completely puzzles me."

An old gray-headed sergeant of the watch advanced from the ranks. "Mad, indeed, monseigneur," said he, addressing the provost. "If she has let loose the Egyptian, 'tis not her fault, for she is not fond of the Egyptians. For these fifteen years that I have belonged to the watch I have heard her every night cursing the Bohemian women with bitter and endless execrations. If the one we are seeking be, as I suppose, the dancing-girl with the goat, I know that she hates her above all."

Gudule made an effort and repeated, "Above all."

The unanimous testimony of the men belonging to the watch confirmed the representation of the old sergeant. Tristan the Hermit, despairing of being able to extract any information from the recluse, turned his back upon her, and with inexpressible anxiety she beheld him slowly proceeding toward his horse. "Come," muttered he, between his teeth. "Let us be off and pursue our search. I will not sleep till the Egyptian is hanged."

He nevertheless paused for some time before he mounted his horse. Gudule wavered between life and death, on seeing him cast around the place the restless look of a hound which is aware that the lair of the game is near at hand and is unwilling to leave the spot. At length he shook his head and vaulted into the saddle. The heart of Gudule, so cruelly oppressed, once more expanded, and casting an eye upon her daughter, at whom she had not dared to look while the soldiers were there, she ejaculated in a low tone, "Saved!"

The poor girl had remained all this time in her corner, without stirring, without breathing, and having the image of death before her eyes. She had not lost any incident of the scene between Gudule and Tristan, and she had shared all the agonies endured by her mother. She had heard the successive snappings of the threads by which she was suspended over the abyss; twenty times she expected to see them all break; and she at length began again to breathe and to feel herself upon solid ground. At this moment she heard a voice saying to the provost, "*Corbœuf!* Mr. Provost, 'tis no business of mine, who am a soldier, to hang witches. The beggarly crew are beneath me. I leave you to attend to it alone. You must permit me to go and rejoin my company, because it is without a captain." That voice was the voice of Phœbus de Chateaupers. What she then felt is not to be described. He was there, then, her friend, her protector, her refuge, her Phœbus! She sprung up, and before her mother could prevent her, darted to the window, crying, "Phœbus! my Phœbus! come hither."

Phœbus was gone; he had just turned at a gallop the corner of the Rue de la Coutellerie, but Tristan was there still.

The recluse rushed upon her daughter with the roar of a wild beast. Striking her nails into her neck, she drew her back with violence. A mother-tigress is not very particular. But it was too late. Tristan had seen her.

"Eigh! eigh!" cried he, with a grin, which discovered all his teeth, and made his face resemble the muzzle of a wolf, "two mice in the trap!"

"I suspected as much," said the soldier.

"Thou art an excellent cat!" replied Tristan, patting him on the shoulder. "Come," added he, "where is Henriet Cousin?"

A man who had neither the garb nor the look of a soldier stepped forth from the ranks. He wore a dress half gray and half brown, and leathern sleeves; had lank hair, and carried a coil of rope in his huge fist. This man always accompanied Tristan, who always accompanied Louis XI.

"My friend," said Tristan the Hermit, "I presume that yonder is the sorceress whom we are seeking. Thou wilt hang her forthwith. Hast thou thy ladder?"

"There is one under the shed of the Maison aux Piliers," replied the man. "Is it at this *justice* that we are to do the business?" continued he, pointing to the stone gibbet.

"Yes."

"Ho! ho! ho!" rejoined the man, with a more vulgar, more bestial grin than even that of the provost, "we sha'n't have far to go."

"Make haste," said Tristan, "and laugh afterward."

Ever since Tristan had espied the girl, and all hope was at an end, the recluse had not uttered a word. She had thrown the poor Egyptian, half dead, in the corner of the cell, and posted herself again at the window, with her two hands like claws resting upon the corner of the entablature. In this attitude, her eyes, which had again become wild and fierce were seen to wander fearlessly over the surrounding soldiers. At the moment when Henriet Cousin reached the cell, her look was so ferocious that he started back.

"Monseigneur," said he, returning to the provost, "which are we to take?"

"The young one."

"So much the better; for yon old hag looks like a Tartar."

"Poor dancing-girl with the goat!" sighed the veteran sergeant of the watch.

Once more Henriet Cousin approached the window. His eye quailed before that of the mother. "Madame——" he began, very timidly.

"What wouldst thou?" cried she, interrupting him, in a low but resolute tone.

"'Tis not you I want," said he; "'tis the other."

"What other?"

"The young one."

She shook her head, crying, "There is nobody, I tell thee—nobody! nobody!"

"There is," replied the executioner, "and well you know it. Let me take the girl. I will not harm you."

"Oh! thou wilt not harm me!" said she, with a strange sneer.

"Let me take the other, madame; 'tis by the order of Monsieur the Provost."

With a frantic air she repeated: "There is nobody! nobody!"

"I tell you there is," replied the executioner. "We all saw that there were two of you."

"Look, then!" said the recluse, grinning. "Put thy head in at the hole."

The hangman eyed her nails, and durst not venture.

"Make haste!" cried Tristan, who had drawn up his men in a semicircle round the Trou aux Rats, and posted himself on horseback near the gibbet.

Henriet returned once more to the provost, quite at a loss how to proceed. He had laid his rope upon the ground, and, with a clownish air, twirled his hat upon his hand. "Monseigneur," he asked, "how are we to get in?"

"By the door."

"There is none."

"By the window."

"It is too small."

"Enlarge it, then," said Tristan, angrily. "Hast thou not pick-axes?"

The mother watched them from her den, still leaning against the window-sill. She had ceased to hope; she knew not what she would have, but she would not have them take her daughter from her.

Henriet Cousin went to the shed of the Maison aux Piliers to fetch his tools. He also brought from the same place a ladder, which he immediately set up against the gibbet. Five or six of the provost's men armed themselves with mattocks and crowbars, and Tristan proceeded with them to the cell.

"Old woman," said the provost, in a stern voice, "yield up the girl to us quietly."

She gave him such a look as though she understood not what he said.

"*Tête Dieu!*" resumed Tristan; "what reason canst thou have for preventing this sorceress from being hanged, according to the king's pleasure?"

The wretched woman burst into one of her wild laughs. "What reason have I? 'Tis my *daughter!*" The accent with which she uttered that word made even Henriet Cousin himself shudder.

"I am sorry for it," replied the provost; "but it is the good pleasure of the king."

"What is thy king to me?" cried she, redoubling her terrible laugh. "I tell thee it is my daughter."

"Break down the wall," said Tristan.

Nothing more was required to make the opening sufficiently wide than to displace one massive stone under the window. When the mother heard the mattocks and the crowbars sapping her fortress, she gave a terrific scream, and then began to run round her cell with frightful swiftness—one of the habits of a wild beast which she had contracted from confinement. She said nothing, but her eyes flashed fire. The soldiers were thrilled to their hearts' core. All at once she caught up her paving-stone in both hands, laughed, and hurled it at the workmen. The stone, feebly thrown—for her hands trembled—missed them all and rolled to the feet of Tristan's horse. She gnashed her teeth.

Meanwhile, though the sun had not yet risen, it was broad daylight; the old decayed chimneys of the Maison aux Piliers were tinged with a beautiful roseate hue. It was the hour at which the earliest windows of the great city open cheerily upon the roofs. Certain of the inhabitants—sundry costermongers riding on their asses to the markets—began to cross the Grève. They paused for a moment before the party of soldiers collected around the Trou aux Rats, surveyed them with looks of astonishment, and pursued their way.

The recluse had sat down in front of her daughter, covering her with her body, listening with fixed eye to the poor girl, who stirred not, who spoke not, save that she murmured, in a low tone: "Phœbus! Phœbus!"

In proportion as the work of the besiegers seemed to advance, the mother mechanically drew back, and pressed the girl closer and closer against the wall. All at once she saw the stone shake—for she kept strict watch, and never took her eyes from it—and she heard the voice of Tristan encouraging the laborers. This roused her from the stupor into which she had sunk for some minutes, and she cried —the while her voice sometimes rent the air like a saw, sometimes stammered as if all the maledictions thronging forth at once were jostling one another upon her lips—"Ho! ho! ho! But this is horrible. Robbers, do ye really mean to take my daughter from me? I tell you it is my daughter. Oh! the cowards! Oh! the hangman's lackeys! Oh! the journeyman murderers! Help! help! fire! But will they rob me of my child in this manner? Can such a thing be suffered by the Almighty?"

Then turning to Tristan, with foaming lips, glaring eyes, on all fours like a panther, and bristling with rage: "Come a little nearer to rob me of my daughter! Dost thou not comprehend that I tell thee it is my daughter? Knowest thou what it is to be the mother of a child? And if thou hast young ones, when they howl, hast thou not within thee something that yearns at their cry?"

"Down with the stone!" said Tristan; "it is loosened."

The crowbars displaced the ponderous stone. It was, as we have said, the mother's last rampart. She threw herself upon it; she would have held it fast; she scratched it with her nails; but the massive block, set in motion by six men, slipped from her grasp, and glided gently to the ground along the iron levers.

The mother, seeing an entry made, threw herself athwart the aperture, barricading the breach with her body, waving her arms, striking her head against the top of the window, and shouting with a voice so husky with fatigue that it could scarcely be heard: "Help! fire! fire!"

"Now take the girl," said Tristan, cool as ever.

The mother scowled at the soldiers in so formidable a manner that they were much more disposed to fall back than to advance.

"On, there!" shouted the provost. "Henriet Cousin, on!"

Not a creature stirred a step.

The provost exclaimed: "What, men at arms afraid of a woman!"

"Monseigneur," said Henriet, "call you that a woman?"

"She has the mane of a lion," said another.

"Advance!" replied the provost; "the gap is large enough. Enter three abreast, as at the breach of Pontoise. Let us finish the business. By the death of Mahound! the first that recoils I will cut in two."

Placed between the provost and the mother, and threatened by both, the soldiers hesitated for a moment; then making their choice, they advanced towards the Trou aux Rats.

When the recluse saw this, she suddenly raised herself upon her knees, threw back her long hair from her face, and dropped her lank and lacerated hands upon her thighs. Big tears started from her eyes, trickling one by one down the wrinkles in her cheeks, like a torrent along the bed which it has wrought for itself. At the same time she began to speak, but in a voice so suppliant, so meek, so subdued, so cutting, that more than one old trooper who could have eaten human flesh had to wipe his eyes.

"Gentlemen and messieurs sergeants, one word. There is one thing that I must tell you. It is my daughter, look you—my dear little girl whom I had lost. Listen—'tis quite a history. I am no stranger to messieurs the sergeants. They were always very kind to me at the time when the boys in the streets pelted me with stones because I led a loose life. You will leave me my child when you know all. I was a poor unfortunate girl. The Bohemians stole my infant. Stay, here is her shoe, which I have kept for fifteen years. Her foot was no bigger than that. La Chantefleurie, Rue Folle Peine, at Reims—perhaps you know that name. Well, I was the person. You will take pity on me, will you not, gentlemen? The Egyptians stole her from me and hid her away for these fifteen years. I concluded she was dead. Only think, my good friends, I thought she was dead. I. have lived here these fifteen years, in this den, without fire in winter. 'Tis hard, is it not? The poor dear little shoe! I have prayed so earnestly that God Almighty has heard me. This very morning He has restored my daughter to me. 'Tis a miracle of His doing. She was not dead, you see. You will not take her from me, I am sure. If it were myself, I should not say a word—but as for her, a girl of sixteen, give her time to see the sun. What harm has she done to you? None whatever. Nor I either. Did you but know that I have none but her, that I am getting old, that she was a blessing bestowed on me by the Holy Virgin herself. And then you are all so kind-hearted. You knew not that it was my daughter till I told you. Oh! how I love her! Monsieur High Provost, I would rather have a hole through my bowels than a scratch upon her nail. You look like a good, kind gentleman. What I tell you explains everything—is it not so? Oh, monseigneur! if you ever had a mother. You are the captain; leave me my child. Consider that I am praying to you on my knees, as one prays to Jesus Christ. I ask nothing of any one. I am from Reims, gentlemen. I have a little spot left me by my uncle, Mahiet Pradon. I am not a beggar. I want nothing but my child. God Almighty, who is the Master of us all, gave her not to me for nothing. The king, you say! the king! How could it pleasure him were you to kill my daughter? And then the king is merciful. 'Tis my daughter—mine. I tell you, she is not the king's, she is not yours. I will be gone; we will both go. Who would stop two weak women, one of them the mother, the other the daughter? Let us pass, then; we are from Reims. Oh! you are very kind, messieurs sergeants; I love you all. You will not take my darling from me—'tis impossible. Is it not? quite impossible! My child! my own dear child!"

We shall not attempt to convey any idea of her gestures, of her tone, of the tears which she swallowed as she spoke, of her hands which she clasped and then wrung, of the cutting smiles, the moans, the sighs, the heart-rending shrieks which she blended with this wild, rambling, and incoherent harangue. When she had done, Tristan the Hermit knit his brow, but it was to conceal a tear which started into his tiger-like eye. Conquering this weakness, however, he said, in a dry tone: "The king wills it."

Then, bending to the ear of Henriet Cousin, he whispered: "Finish out of hand!" The redoubtable provost himself perhaps felt even his heart fail him.

The hangman and the sergeants entered the cell. The mother made no resistance; she merely crawled toward her daughter and threw herself headlong upon her. The Egyptian saw the soldiers approaching. The horror of death roused her. "Mother," cried she, in a tone of inexpressible anguish, "mother, they are coming; defend me!"

"Yes, my love, I will defend thee," replied the mother, in a faint voice; and clasping her closely in her arms, she covered her with kisses. Mother and daughter, as they thus lay on the ground, presented a sight that was truly pitiable.

Henriet Cousin laid hold of the girl round the body. When she felt the touch of his hand she shuddered, "Heugh!" and fainted. The hangman, from whose eyes big tears fell drop by drop upon her, attempted to lift her, but was prevented by the mother, who had intwined her arms round her daughter's waist, and clung so firmly to her child that it was impossible to part them. Henriet Cousin, therefore, dragged the girl out of the cell, and the mother after her—the latter, too, with her eyes shut, and apparently insensible.

The sun was just then rising, and a considerable number of people collected thus early in the place were striving to make out what it was that the hangman was thus dragging along the pavement toward the gibbet; for it was Tristan's way to prevent the near approach of spectators at executions.

There was not a creature at the windows. There were only to be seen on the top of that tower of Notre Dame which overlooks the Grève, two men standing out in dark relief from the clear morning sky, who appeared to be looking on.

Henriet Cousin stopped with what he was dragging at the foot of the fatal ladder, and scarcely breathing, so deeply was he affected, he slipped the cord about the lovely neck of the girl. The unfortunate creature felt the horrid touch of the rope. She opened her eyes and beheld the hideous arm of the stone gibbet extended over her head. Rousing herself, she cried, in a loud and heart-rending voice, "No, no! I will not." The mother, whose face was buried in her daughter's garments, uttered not a word; her whole body was seen to tremble, and she was heard to kiss her child with redoubled fervency. The hangman took advantage of this moment to wrench asunder her arms with which she had clung to the condemned girl. Either from exhaustion or despair, she made no resistance. He then lifted the damsel on his shoulder, from which the charming creature hung gracefully on either side, and began to ascend the ladder.

At that moment the mother, crouched on the pavement, opened her eyes. Without uttering any cry, she sprung up with a terrific look; then, like a beast of prey, she seized the hand of the hangman and bit him. It was like lightning. The executioner roared with pain. Some of the sergeants ran to him. With difficulty they extricated his bleeding hand from the teeth of the mother. She maintained profound silence. They thrust her back in a brutal manner, and it was remarked that her head fell heavily upon the pavement. They lifted her up, but again she sunk to the ground. She was dead!

The hangman, who had not set down the girl, continued to mount the ladder.

CHAPTER II

LA CREATURA BELLA BIANCA VESTITA [1]

WHEN QUASIMODO ascertained that the cell was vacant, that the Egyptian was not there, and that while he was defending her she had been taken away, he grasped his head with both hands, and stamped with rage and astonishment; he then began to run all over the church in quest of the Bohemian, setting up strange shouts at every corner, and strewing his red hair upon the pavement. It was the very moment when the king's archers entered the cathedral victorious, also seeking the Egyptian. Quasimodo assisted them, having no suspicion—poor, deaf creature!—of their fatal intentions; it was the vagabond crew whom he regarded as the enemies of the Egyptian. He himself conducted Tristan the Hermit to every possible place of concealment, opened for him all the secret doors, the double-bottomed altars, and the back sacristies. Had the unfortu-

1. The beautiful creature clad in white. (Dante)

nate girl been still there, he must inevitably have betrayed her. When Tristan was tired of the unsuccessful search—and on such occasions he was not soon tired—Quasimodo continued alone. He traversed the church twenty times, a hundred times, lengthwise and breadthwise, from top to bottom, mounting, descending, running, calling, crying, shouting, ferreting, rummaging, poking his head into every hole, thrusting a torch into every dark corner, distracted, mad. At length, when he was sure, quite sure, that she was no longer there, that she had been stolen away from him, he slowly ascended the tower stairs, those stairs which he had mounted with such transport and exultation on the day he saved her. He again passed that way with drooping head, voiceless, tearless, almost unbreathing. The church was once more clear, and silence again reigned within it. The archers had quitted the sacred edifice to track the sorceress in the city. Quasimodo, left alone in the vast cathedral, ringing but a few moments before with the clamors of the besiegers, returned toward the cell where the Egyptian had slept so many weeks under his guardianship. As he approached it he could not help fancying that he might perhaps find her there again. When, at the turn of the gallery which opens upon the roof of the aisles, he perceived the narrow cabin with its small window and its little door, clapped under a great flying buttress, like a bird's-nest under a bough, his heart failed him, poor fellow! and he leaned against a pillar, lest he should fall. He imagined that she might perhaps have returned thither; that a good genius had no doubt brought her back; that this little cell was too quiet, too safe, too charming for her not to be there; and he durst not take another step for fear of destroying the illusion. "Yes," said he to himself, "perhaps she is asleep, or praying. Let us not disturb her." At length he mustered courage, advanced on tiptoe, looked in, entered. Empty! the cell was still empty! The unhappy hunchback slowly paced round it, lifted up the bed and looked under it, as though she could have hidden between the mattress and the floor. He then shook his head and remained for awhile in a state of stupor. All at once he furiously trampled upon his torch, and without word or sigh he frantically dashed his head against the wall, and fell swooning on the pavement.

When his senses returned he threw himself upon the bed, he rolled upon it, he wildly kissed the spot where the damsel had lain; he remained thus for some minutes as motionless as if life had fled; he then rose, bathed in perspiration, panting, beside himself, and began to beat his head against the wall with the frightful regularity of a pendulum, and the resolution of one who is determined to dash out his brains. At length he fell a second time exhausted. Presently he crawled on his knees out of the cell, and crouched opposite to the door in an attitude of despair. In this state he continued for above an hour without stirring, his eye fixed on the vacant cell, more gloomy and more thoughtful than a mother seated between an empty cradle and a full coffin. He uttered not a word, only at long intervals a sob violently shook his whole body, but it was a sob without tears, like those summer lightnings which make no noise.

It appears that then, seeking in his doleful reverie to discover who could thus unexpectedly have carried off the Egyptian, he bethought himself of the archdeacon. He recollected that none but Dom Claude had a key to the staircase leading to the cell; he called to mind his nocturnal attempts upon the damsel, in the first of which he, Quasimodo, himself had assisted, and the second of which he had frustrated; he called to mind a thousand other circumstances, and soon felt not the least doubt that it was the archdeacon who had taken the girl from him. Such, however, was his respect for the priest, so deeply had gratitude, affection, love, for that man struck root in his heart, that even at this moment they withstood the tugs of jealousy and despair.

He considered that the archdeacon had done this, and instead of the mortal rancor with which the thought would have filled his heart for any other, the moment it fixed upon Claude Frollo, it only aggravated his grief. At this moment, when the dawn began to whiten the flying buttresses, he descried on a higher story of the cathedral, at the angle formed by the outer balustrade which runs round the apsis, a figure in motion. The face of this figure was turned toward him. He recognized the person. It was the archdeacon. Claude's step was grave and deliberate. He looked not before him as he walked toward the north tower; but his face was turned askance toward the right bank of the Seine, as if he were striving to see something over the intervening roofs. The owl frequently has this oblique attitude, flying in one direction and looking in another. The priest thus passed on above Quasimodo without perceiving him.

The hunchback, petrified by this sudden apparition, watched till he lost sight of him at the door of the staircase of the north tower. The reader knows that this is the tower which commands a view of the Hotel de Ville. Quasimodo rose and followed the archdeacon.

He went up the stairs to ascend the tower, for the purpose of ascertaining why the priest ascended it; if indeed the poor bellringer, who knew not what he did or what he wished, could be said to have any purpose. He was full of rage and full of apprehension. The archdeacon and the Egyptian clashed together in his heart.

When he reached the top of the tower, before he issued from the darkness of the staircase and stepped out upon the platform, he looked cautiously about to discover where the priest was. Claude had his back toward him. A balustrade of open-work surrounds the platform of the steeple. The priest, whose eyes were bent upon the town, was leaning with his breast against that corner of the balustrade which looks down upon the bridge of Notre Dame.

Quasimodo stole with wolf's step behind him, to see what he was thus looking at. The attention of the priest was so completely engrossed that he perceived not the approach of the hunchback.

Paris, viewed from the towers of Notre Dame in the cool dawn of a summer morning, is a charming and magnificent sight; and the Paris of that period must have been eminently so. It was then the month of July. The sky was perfectly serene. A few lingering stars were going out at different points, and there was still a very bright one in the east in the lightest part of the firmament. The sun was just rising. Paris began to be astir. A very white and a very pure light presented conspicuously to the eye the faces which its thousand houses turn toward the east. The giant shadows of the steeples extended from roof to roof, from one end of the great city to the other. There were quarters which already began to send forth various sounds. Here was heard the hammer of the smith, there that of the carpenter, and yonder the complicated creaking of a cart, as it passed along the street. A few columns of smoke issued from different points of this vast surface of roofs, as from the fissures of an immense solfatara. The river which dashes its waters against the piers of so many bridges, and the points of so many islands, was streaked with lines of silver. Around the city, beyond the ramparts, the sight was lost in a wide circle of fleecy vapors, through which might be faintly discerned the indefinite line of the plains and the graceful swelling of the hills. All sorts of sounds floated confusedly over this half-awakened city. Toward the east the morning breeze drove across the sky a few white flakes rent from the mantle of the mist that inwrapped the hills.

In the Parvis, certain stirring housewives, with milk-jugs in their hands, pointed out to one another with astonishment the shattered state of the great portal of Notre Dame, and the two streams of lead congealed in the interstices between the stones of the pavement. These were the only vestiges of the tumult of the past night. The fire kindled by Quasimodo between the towers was extinguished.

Tristan had already caused the place to be cleared, and the dead to be thrown into the Seine. Such kings as Louis XI. take care to have the pavement washed after a massacre.

Outside the balustrade of the tower, below the very point where the priest had stopped, there was one of those stone gutters fantastically carved, with which Gothic edifices are bristled, and in a crevice of this gutter were two fine wall-flowers in blossom, which waved, and, as if they were animated by the breeze, seemed to be sportively bowing to each other. Above the towers, aloft in the air, small birds were heard twittering and screaming.

But the priest neither heard nor saw any of these things. He was one of those who take no notice either of mornings or of birds or flowers. His contemplation was engrossed by one only point of that immense horizon which presented so many aspects around him.

Quasimodo burned with impatience to inquire what he had done with the Egyptian; but the archdeacon seemed at that moment to be out of the world. With him it was evidently one of those critical moments of life when a man would not feel the earth crumbling beneath his feet. He remained motionless and silent, with his eyes invariably fixed on a particular spot; and this silence and this motionless attitude had something so formidable that the savage bell-ringer himself shuddered before and durst not disturb it. All he could do, therefore, and this was one way of questioning the archdeacon, was to follow the direction of his eye; and thus guided, that of the unhappy hunchback fell upon the Place de Grève. He now perceived what the priest was looking at. The ladder was set up against the permanent gibbet. There were a few people in the place and a great number of soldiers. A man was dragging along the pavement something white to which something black was clinging. This man stopped at the foot of the gibbet. What then took place he could not clearly discern; not that the sight of his only eye was at all impaired, but a party of soldiers prevented his distinguishing what was going forward. Besides, at that moment the sun burst forth and poured such a flood of light above the horizon, that every point of Paris, steeples, chimneys, gables, seemed to be set on fire at one and the same moment.

Meanwhile, the man began to mount the ladder. Quasimodo now saw distinctly again. He carried across his shoulder a female, a young female dressed in white; this young female had a rope about her neck. Quasimodo knew her. It was the Egyptian!

The man reached the top of the ladder. There he arranged the rope. The priest, in order to see the better, now knelt down upon the balustrade.

The man suddenly kicked away the ladder, and Quasimodo, who had not breathed for some moments, saw the unfortunate girl, with the man crouched upon her shoulders, dangling at the end of the rope within two or three yards of the pavement. The rope made several revolutions, and Quasimodo saw the body of the victim writhe in frightful convulsions. The priest, on his part, with out-stretched neck and eyes starting from his head, contemplated the terrific group of the man and the young girl, the spider and the fly.

At this most awful moment, a demon laugh, a laugh such as one only who has ceased to be human is capable of, burst forth upon the livid face of the priest. Quasimodo heard not this laugh, but he saw it. The bell-ringer recoiled a few steps from the archdeacon, then suddenly rushing furiously upon him with his two huge hands into the abyss, over which he was leaning. "Damnation!" cried the priest, as he fell.

The gutter beneath caught him and broke the fall. He clung to it with eager hands, and was just opening his mouth to give a second cry, when he beheld the formidable and avenging face of Quasi-modo protruded over the balustrade above his head. He was then silent.

The abyss was beneath him—a fall of more than two hundred feet, and the pavement. In this terrible situation, the archdeacon uttered neither word nor groan. Suspended from the gutter, he wriggled, and made incredible efforts to raise himself upon it; but his hands had no hold of the granite, and his toes merely streaked the black-ened wall without finding the least support. All who have ever been up the towers of Notre Dame know that the stone bellies imme-diately under the balustrade. It was against the retreating slope that the wretched archdeacon exhausted himself in fruitless efforts. He had not to do with a perpendicular wall, but a wall that receded from him.

Quasimodo might have withdrawn him from the gulf by merely reaching him his hand, but he did not so much as look at him. He looked at the Grève. He looked at the Egyptian. He looked at the gibbet. The hunchback was leaning upon the balustrade, at the very spot which the archdeacon had just before occupied; and there, never turning his eye from the only object which existed for him at that moment, he was motionless and mute as one thunderstruck, while a stream flowed in silence from that eye which till then had not shed a single tear.

The archdeacon meanwhile began to pant. The perspiration trickled from his bald brow; the blood oozed from his fingers' ends; the skin was rubbed from his knees against the wall. He heard his cassock, which hung by the gutter, crack and rip at every movement that he made. To crown his misery, that gutter terminated in a leaden pipe which bent with his weight. The archdeacon felt it slowly giving way. The wretched man said to himself, that when his cassock should be rent, when the leaden pipe should yield, he must fall, and horror thrilled his entrails. At times he wildly eyed a sort of narrow ledge, formed about ten feet below him by the architectural embellishments of the church, and in his distress he prayed to Heaven in the recesses of his soul, to permit him to end his life on this space of two square feet, were it even to last a hundred years. Once he glanced at the abyss beneath him; when he raised his head his eyes were closed and his hair standing erect.

There was something frightful in the silence of these two persons. While the archdeacon, at the distance of a few feet, was experiencing the most horrible agonies, Quasimodo kept his eye fixed on the Grève and wept.

The archdeacon, perceiving that all his exertions served but to shake the only frail support that was left him, determined to stir no more. There he was, clasping the gutter, scarcely breathing, absolutely motionless save that mechanical convulsion of the abdomen which supervenes in sleep when you dream that you are falling. His fixed eyes glared in a wild and ghastly manner. Meanwhile, he began to lose his hold; his fingers slipped down the gutter; he felt his arms becoming weaker and weaker, and his body heavier and heavier. The leaden pipe which supported him bent more and more every moment toward the abyss. Beneath he beheld—horrid sight!—the roof of St. Jean le Rond, diminutive as a card bent in two. He eyed one after another the passionless sculptures of the tower, suspended like himself over the abyss, but without fear for themselves or pity for him. All about him was stone; before his eyes gaping monsters; under him, at the bottom of the gulf, the pavement; over his head Quasimodo weeping.

In the Parvis several groups of curious spectators were calmly puzzling their brains to divine who could be the maniac that was amusing himself in this strange manner. The priest heard them say, for their voices reached him, clear and sharp, "By'r Lady! he must break his neck."

Quasimodo wept.

At length the archdeacon, foaming with rage and terror, became sensible that all was useless. He nevertheless mustered all his remaining strength for a last effort. Setting both his knees against the wall, he hooked his hands into a cleft in the stones, and succeeded in raising himself about a foot; but this struggle caused the leaden beak which supported him to give way suddenly. His cassock was ripped up from the same cause. Feeling himself sinking, having only his stiffened crippled hands to hold by, the wretched man closed his eyes, and presently his fingers relaxed their grasp. Down he fell.

Quasimodo watched him falling.

A fall from such a height is rarely perpendicular. The archdeacon, launched into the abyss, fell at first head downward and with outstretched arms, and then whirled several times over and over, dropping upon a roof of a house, and breaking some of his bones. He was not dead when he reached it, for the bell-ringer saw him strive to grapple the ridge with his fingers; but the slope was too steep, and his strength utterly failed him. Sliding rapidly down the roof, like a tile that has got loose, down he went, and rebounded on the pavement. He never stirred more.

Quasimodo then raised his eye to the Egyptian, dangling from the gallows. At that distance he could see her quiver beneath her white robe in the last convulsive agonies of death; he then looked down at the archdeacon, stretched at the foot of the tower, with scarcely a vestige of the human form about him, and heaving a deep sigh, he cried, "There is all I ever loved!"

CHAPTER III

THE MARRIAGE OF CAPTAIN PHŒBUS

TOWARD THE EVENING of the same day, when the judicial officers of the bishop came to remove the mangled corpse of the archdeacon from the pavement of the Parvis, Quasimodo was not to be found in Notre Dame.

Many rumors were circulated respecting this affair. The general opinion was that the day had arrived when, according to agreement, Quasimodo or the devil was to carry away Claude Frollo, the sorcerer. It was presumed that he had smashed the body to get at the soul, just as monkeys crack the shell of a nut to get at the kernel. For this reason the archdeacon was not interred in consecrated ground.

Louis XI. died in the month of August in the following year, 1483.

As for Pierre Gringoire, he contrived to save the goat, and to gain applause as a tragic writer. It appears that, after dabbling in astrology, philosophy, architecture, alchemy, and all sorts of silly pursuits, he reverted to tragedy, which is the silliest of all. This he called "having come to a tragic end." In the accounts of the ordinary for 1483 may be found the following entry relative to his dramatic triumphs: "To Jehan Marchan and Pierre Gringoire, carpenter and composer, who made and composed the mystery enacted at the Chatelet of Paris at the entry of Monsieur the Legate, and arranged the characters, habited and equipped as by the said mystery was required; and also for having made the scaffolds which were necessary thereto, one hundred livres."

Phœbus de Chateaupers likewise "came to a tragic end"—he married.

CHAPTER IV

THE MARRIAGE OF QUASIMODO

WE HAVE just said that, on the day when the Egyptian and the archdeacon died, Quasimodo was not to be found in Notre Dame. He was never seen afterward, nor was it ever known what became of him.

In the night following the execution of La Esmeralda, the hangman and his assistants took down her body from the gibbet and conveyed it, according to custom, to the vault of Montfaucon.

Montfaucon, as we are told by Sauval, was "the most ancient and the most superb gallows in the kingdom." Between the faubourgs of the Temple and St. Martin, about one hundred and sixty fathoms from the walls of Paris, and a few cross-bow shots from La Courtille, was seen at the top of a gentle, imperceptible rise, yet sufficiently elevated to be seen for several leagues round, a building of strange form, nearly resembling a Celtic cromlech, and where also human victims were sacrificed.

Figure to yourself on the top of a mound of chalk a clumsy parallelopipedon of masonry, fifteen feet high, forty long, and thirty wide, with a door, an outer railing, and a platform; upon this platform sixteen massive pillars of unhewn stone, thirty feet high, ranged in form of a colonnade round three of the four sides of the masonry which support them, connected at top by strong beams, from which at certain distances hang chains, each having a skeleton dangling at the end of it; round about it in the plain a stone cross and two gibbets of secondary rank, which seem to spring up like shoots from the central stock; above all these in the atmosphere crows perpetually flying—and you will have a picture of Montfaucon.

At the conclusion of the fifteenth century, this formidable gibbet, which dated from 1328, was already very decrepit; the beams were rotten; the chains eaten up with rust; the pillars green with moss; there were wide interstices between the courses of the stone, and grass grew upon the untrodden platform. The profile of this edifice upon the sky was a horrible one, especially at night, when the faint moonlight fell upon those bleached skulls, or when the night breeze, shaking the chains and the skeletons, made them rattle in the dark. The presence of this gibbet was sufficient to induce a belief that all the environs were haunted.

The stone-work which served as a base to the odious edifice was hollow. Here had been formed a vast vault, closed by an old crazy iron gate, into which were thrown not only the human remains taken from the chains of Montfaucon, but the bodies of all the wretches executed at the other permanent gibbets of Paris. In this vast charnel-house, in which so many human carcasses and so many crimes have moldered together, many of the great of the world, and many innocent persons, have successively laid their bones, from Enguerraud de Marigni, who made a present of Montfaucon, and who was a good man, to Admiral de Coligni, with whom it was closed, and who was also a good man.

Respecting the mysterious disappearance of Quasimodo all that we have been able to discover is this:

About a year and a half or two years after the events with which this history concludes, when search was made in the vault of Montfaucon for the body of Olivier le Daim, who had been hung two days previously, and to whom Charles VIII. had granted the favor to be interred in better company at St. Laurent, among these hideous carcasses were found two skeletons in a singular posture. One of these skeletons, which was that of a female, had still upon it some fragments of a dress that had once been white; and about the neck was a necklace of the seeds of adrezarach, and a little silk bag braided with green beads, which was open and empty. These things were of so little value that the hangman no doubt had not thought it worth his while to take them. The other, by which this first was closely embraced, was the skeleton of a male. It was remarked that the spine was crooked, the head depressed between the shoulders, and one leg shorter than the other. There was, however, no rupture of the vertebræ of the neck, and it was evident that the person to whom it belonged had not been hanged. He must have come hither and died in the place. When those who found this skeleton attempted to disengage it from that which it held in its grasp, it crumbled to dust.

THE END